Diaphanous Paris

By Thomas Plazibat

Who would believe that so small a space could contain

the images of all the universe.   -Leonardo da Vinci

PART ONE: Diaphanous Paris

1: Moon River

For some reason, the song *Moon River* reminds me of Ohio. I have a vision, maybe a dream, or maybe a distant memory. The moonlight is glinting on the leaves of a tree swelling gently in the breeze, the leaves whispering and sighing, and nearby a river with moonlight reflecting on the rippling water.

Or maybe it had been the many interminable nighttime drives on the Ohio Turnpike during my childhood; I must have crossed more than a few rivers, and seen moonlight reflected on those rivers.

I remember the late-night stops at gleaming new toll plazas. In fact, the turnpike had recently been completed, bypassing the monotonous two-lane roads, and the small country towns of Ohio. Although, once we ventured further east, we left the turnpike behind and traveled entirely on the old two lane roads, winding their way through the Appalachian foothills as we continued our journey to a seemingly remote town in the southwestern corner of Pennsylvania. On those journeys, it was almost as if I was able to grasp the essence of the whole world just by traveling on this one segment of the globe between Detroit, and Pennsylvania.

One thing that seemed apparent to me was that as we progressed eastward, the buildings, and the people, all seemed to grow older. In fact, the whole world seemed to age as we headed in an easterly direction. The very earth itself, the hills and hollows, untouched by the glaciers that had scoured Michigan, were a legacy from ancient times, and the physical journey itself seemed to change something in me, allowing me to fall deeper into some hidden past.

I remember how the modern office buildings of Detroit, with its new concrete expressways and sprawling suburbs, gave way to quaint brick homes in pleasantly compact Ohio towns. And once we arrived in Pennsylvania, it seemed as if we had slipped into another century. I remember the novelty of porch swings, and small quiet towns nestled in deep wooded valleys.

On one of those early trips, we had stopped for a night in Cleveland to visit old friends of my parents. In a leafy suburb, there had been a gathering of people for a backyard party. Fireflies filled the air on that warm Ohio night, and there was a magic glow in the evening light. The adults were seated at tables beneath lanterns, and the kids ran among the lush grounds and played in hidden coves nestled among the trees.

At the height of the festivities, things went awry for me. I suddenly fell ill and was taken to an upstairs guest room well before the festivities had finished. I remember falling immediately asleep and into a delirious dream. In this dream, I was walking along a precipice, or across a narrow bridge, suspended above a bottomless abyss, and on my head, improbably, I was carrying the ball of the sun.

When I awoke, I was drenched in sweat, and overcome by a fever. The next few weeks I battled a grave illness, spending several nights in a hospital in nearby Canton. There was some hidden secret lurking back then during my stay in the hospital. Because of the illness, a sequence of events had been triggered on some unseen level, something essential had changed in my being, maybe even on a physical or molecular level, and my perception of the world was irrevocably altered.

Juxtaposed to this was another memory, a visit to Bermuda I knew of only from an old set of family snapshots. The pictures were tinted in the colors of an outmoded photographic process; there were brilliant magenta and purple flowers, and glimpses of the aquamarine, and turquoise of the sea. The oceanic setting seemed to evoke the promise of a fulfilled life, a feeling of expectation, and hopefulness. This sense of promise seemed to pervade my entire childhood; a feeling of something great about to happen, even something momentous.

All these memories were part of a larger preoccupation with the pictorial that had run throughout my childhood. There was a whole universe of pictorial memories from which I could draw upon; most of them I hadn't even experienced directly in my bodily form. The images all combined to create an inner visual compendium. A pictorial world parallel to the material world, that existed in my mind without ever having left the protected womb of mid-continental America.

So extensive and persistent was this body of images, that I can still call up an image of any place in the world: San Francisco or Sao Paulo; Sumatra or Scotland; Senegal or Siberia.

In these inner pictures the colors seem richer, more pure, as if the cones of my eyes had been more prolific back then, all painted in the rich hues of a bright summer day; even the rainy days were like the first days of spring, with its pure moist air, soft grey clouds, and rain drops collecting on cool green leaves.

Yet, at some unmarked moment, I seemed to have left this world behind. An entire continent was submerged. A wave had drawn away, receded, scattering an array of shells on a beach, leaving me high and dry. The course of our ship had been changed; a tipping point had been reached, a series of tipping points; then a cascade: a flood. There was some sort of proportional relationship that had been violated, between me and the world, even between humanity and the planet, and I was lost in this sea change. There had been a break in the fabric of the world, that I only recognized retrospectively.

The sense of expectation I had felt as a child now seemed like an illusion, a trick even. I now realized we had been shunted away from our intended path, and at some key juncture we entered a great switching station, and the original direction had been definitively altered.

We now lived in a world where a technological beast was running amok consuming the body of the earth; where a spider's web of satellites increasingly circled the planet, and where the masses had succumbed to an insidious addiction to digital technology.

In the wake of these forces, American life had been completely trivialized, a series of false narratives had been inserted into its cultural DNA; and with the dominance of social media; Facebook, Twitter, and such, the real world had been emptied out, sucked up by some alien force; all of our free psychic energy had been transferred over to a virtual realm like some kind of devious satanic trick of soul shifting.

America had become a bad algorithm; a place where everything seemed like it should be possible, but where none of it had any value anymore. It was like a viscous medium pressed down on my being, clouding my mind with misdirection, bending and distorting the felt experience of my life.

Only by escaping from America could I find any respite from its oppressive programming. In the transitory phases, in the in-between, shifting from one continent to another, I was able to muster enough velocity to escape, and cross the threshold into a different realm of possibility.

Of course, the present world doesn't correspond anymore with the pictorial world of my childhood, but sometimes though, in an unexpected moment, something just as simple as the afternoon light falling in a certain way, or merely the sight of a puffy cumulus cloud floating in the sky, will be enough to suggest or recall that half-forgotten reservoir of visual memories. And then, I suddenly rediscover that other world, again.

Paris is one of those places where the membrane still seems partially open. Perhaps that is why I keep returning here.

Moreover, I was meeting an old friend who was arriving from Basel on a business trip. Christy was originally from Ohio and now worked for a giant pharmaceutical firm. She had married a Swiss researcher, and left America some years ago.

I had first met her in the early days of my fine arts graduate program. She had been one of the few bright spots during a rather dreary stint in Columbus. Right from the start, on the first day we had met, I had a strange feeling we had known each other from long, long, ago. It was almost as if she had come out of the inner world of pictures that had crystalized during my childhood; one other remaining piece of that parallel world.

Back then, I hadn't quite realized who Christy really was for me. I had been unconscious on a certain level, preoccupied with a failed romance, and had been oblivious to Christy's true nature. Only now in retrospect did I realize her importance.

I had recently re-established an intermittent sort of contact through her Facebook page and had related to her some of my current artistic and intellectual preoccupations; one benefit of the so-called social media. We had agreed to rendezvous at a small cafe in the 7th arrondissement, on Rue de Babylone.

2: Rendezvous with Christy

I arrived early, lingering in front of an adjacent shop where a magazine displayed in the window caught my eye. It was a Le Monde publication with a picture of Rousseau on the cover. The title read: *Jean Jacques Rousseau, Le Subversif.* Intrigued, I went into the shop and purchased a copy and went back over to the cafe.

Sitting at one of the tables out front, I was engrossed in reading the magazine, trying to decipher a handful of French sentences when Christy's voice broke into my solitary reverie.

"Thomas!"

I recognized her southern Ohio accent right away. Both of us laughed as we embraced each other. She was dressed very stylishly, in restrained shades of dark grey and black, and carried a leather valise at her side.

I gazed at her face, re-familiarizing myself with the nuances of her features and manner and reflecting on all the years that had elapsed since we had last met.

I realized how good it was to meet an old friend, particularly here abroad, and a feeling of warmth and enthusiasm returned, canceling out my moody ruminations. Both of us were still laughing, perhaps at the absurdity of meeting again, when we fell into our usual banter.

"So, Tom, all those years you were in Ann Arbor, and you couldn't bring yourself to visit me in Columbus, and now you come halfway around the world to rendezvous here in Paris. What's going on?"

I laughed. I could tell Christy was gently teasing me, as she always used to do, taking delight in exposing my idiosyncrasies.

"Going to Columbus always seemed like I was going back in time, too musty, and old."

"And Paris isn't?" She swept her arm out gesturing to surrounding city.

"The earth is older in Columbus."

Christy laughed, and we started to walk down the sidewalk.

"So, what brings you to Europe, then?"

"I'm doing some research for an exhibit in San Francisco. They're calling it *Different Futures*. I've been invited to imagine a city where creativity and the quality of life are enhanced. The exhibition opens in October at the Yerba Buena Center."

"You finally did something with your degree."

I laughed to myself.

"That and some adjunct work," I acknowledged.

"Is this related to your research?" She looked down at the magazine I was carrying.

"Oh. I just picked this up."

Christy peered down at the cover.

"Trompe Le Monde."

It was one of her jokes. Christy had been an avid fan of the Pixies, and much of the music of that era, the so called New-Wave.

"I think I might have an affinity for Rousseau, actually," I proclaimed.

"Really?"

13

"Yeah, he was quite an itinerant. I was just struggling with this passage in French... the gist of it seems to be that the purpose of life is *"felicite"*.

"*Felicite?*" She raised her eyebrows.

"Well, yeah. I think it means something like ease or happiness, one of those words that don't translate into English well."

"I believe its best translated as bliss," she remarked.

"Bliss!" I laughed. "Well, we've certainly lost the art of that in America."

"And so, how is life in America?" Christy asked.

"Almost intolerable," I replied, perhaps exaggerating only slightly, and continued, "I should have left years ago, like you did."

"And why haven't you?"

"I don't know. Maybe lack of money, or some sort of inertia keeps me fixed in place, even though I feel like I'm not experiencing the full spectrum of life, even though I feel this sense of being bound by a host limitations. You almost forget that there are other possibilities, until you leave America."

"I know," she said. "You know, when I went back to Ohio several years ago, it was totally different. Strip malls had replaced the apple orchards around my old neighborhood, sprawling housing developments all around. All of it done in the most egregious manner."

"I keep trying to get away from all that blight, but the few remaining sanctuaries; even they aren't the same anymore."

"It's the same here on the continent, everything has become more systemized, even more so in the last ten years, with the adoption of the Euro."

"It's global, isn't it? It seems like there is a web, or a matrix, drawing tighter every year. More jets flying over, noise pollution, rampant development, everything is more regulated and more expensive," I complained.

It was an Armageddon created by banks and corporations, sucking the life force out of nature and pitting all the people of the world against each other in some insane competition for goods and services, I ruminated to myself darkly.

"Where can you escape to?" She asked.

"Well, one of my favorite places was Sleeping Bear Dunes."

"I went up there once when I was a kid," she said, smiling distantly.

"I used to go almost every year to the same spot, right on a bay near an old Coast Guard station. It looks north out to the Manitou Islands. There was a small grove of cottonwoods, and pines, right near the lake," I explained.

I thought back to one of those summer afternoons. The sound of the shore in the distance, a soft breeze moving through the dune grass, an orange butterfly fluttering across the meadow, the dappled light underneath the trees; the whispering of the wind through the pine boughs.

"I used lie under the trees in the afternoon after swimming and listen to the wind. And then in '07, I returned for my regular summer trip and they had cut down all the trees and plowed the entire area under."

"What! You're kidding me?"

"No. Apparently, their reasons were to eliminate invasive species. I was stunned, my special place, that I always expected to be there, was suddenly wiped out."

"It's the green meme," Christy added cryptically.

"What?" I asked.

"It's from this system called Spiral Dynamics."

"Spiral Dynamics?"

"That's what it's called. The green meme arrogates to itself the right to make what it deems as the morally right decisions for all concerned, regardless of the impact on various other groups."

"That reminds me of the structures of consciousness."

"Yes, you sent me the link," she nodded thoughtfully.

We paused a moment on the sidewalk while she retrieved her iPad.

"Here," she said, indicating for me to look.

On the tiny screen, I could see a colorful diagram comparing spiral dynamics to the structures of consciousness. The spiral ascended in stages from red, blue, orange, and green on up to yellow and turquoise at the top, corresponding to the integral structure.

"That's interesting," I remarked.

The two models explained the multi-dimensional nature of society and the competing world views that shaped culture and were particularly useful for unraveling the puzzle of the American political situation. There were probably at least four or five different Americas, or four or five different states of consciousness simultaneously opposing and intersecting each other in the American social sphere.

"The memes give us a way of understanding the different levels of consciousness," she declared, as we resumed walking.

"The notion of a deficient structure explains the seeming incapacity of the authorities to come to grips with our contemporary situation. There is a tremendous downward pressure economically on everyone, with more and more people being thrust into a dysfunctional situation."

"So, you're saying market capitalism is deficient?" She looked at me skeptically.

"Yeah, it's breaking down. It can't adequately address a whole host of problems."

"There was the financial crisis in 2008. But we're pretty much past that, now," Christy reflected.

"You think so?" I looked at Christy wondering; maybe she had more invested in the system than I had remembered from before.

"Our business has completely rebounded," she offered.

"They've just papered over the cracks. The whole system is definitively bankrupt," I responded a bit harshly.

"We're in a new age of connectivity, though," Christy asserted.

"Yeah, but you know I'm kind of skeptical about the benefits of technology."

"...that it leads to social fragmentation?" Christy intuited my thoughts.

"More than that even, it's like stripping the germ from the wheat, a processing of the social."

"No longer 'the whole grain', so to speak," she quipped.

"Exactly, and they keep people looking down at their digital devices instead of looking inward, as if there was really nothing left inside to develop."

"But wouldn't you say the technological developments are the culmination of the Western tradition?" Christy suggested.

"Well, a sort of attenuated version of it. I mean, it doesn't encourage deep thinking, nor is it looking out into the world and really seeing things, observing reality or nature. It's just a mode of low-grade distraction, merely connecting."

"Communication is increasing exponentially," Christy added.

"Yeah, but this is a huge experiment. New media is re-wiring the brain, altering thousands of years of development, all driven by commercial interests."

"It's probably accelerating human evolution, though. We have so much information at our fingertips now. How can you refuse that resource?" She insisted, holding her iPad up almost as if it was evidence.

"I don't know. Memory is hugely important. If memory atrophies, then artistic sensibilities diminish and even more. The city of the future needs one to one interaction, not self-absorbed people peering into their devices. Creativity needs the synergy of people interacting in physical proximity to each other. An integral city," I insisted excitedly.

"But maybe you and I wouldn't have reconnected if it wasn't for social media," Christy's voice sounded more serious now.

"Yeah, maybe not," I acknowledged somewhat reluctantly.

I had to admit that Christy was right about certain things. She always had a way of challenging me.

Still, I had an uneasy feeling about all the new technology. Something didn't seem right about the onslaught of social media, and how it was being shoved down our throats, as if we had no choice.

3: Salon de Tea

Once we crossed the Boulevard Raspail, we stopped at a salon de tea on a quiet side street. I didn't usually eat pastries in America. I could be sure in America they were usually made following some sort of corporate recipe, with a bunch of unnecessary ingredients, at an industrial scale. Here in France, they were made by artisan bakers, part of an over fifteen-hundred-year old tradition. Here were handcrafted delicacies *sans* corn syrup, *sans* growth hormones. Here, I could be sure I wasn't eating a tainted Monsanto product.

Inside, we gazed at the mouthwatering offerings. I was drawn to the *Croissant Ispahan*. The name itself intrigued me and hinted at something drawn from the *Thousand and One Nights*. The creation was glazed with tiny rose-colored crystals, and I was suddenly reminded of an old edition of the Arabian Nights I had read as a child. The illustrations had been done in an Art Nouveau style, with swirling lines, and arabesques, presenting to me a fantastic vision of these exotic tales. I had been fascinated by these visions of Arabia, and the memory of it evoked a distant feeling, laden with something indefinite, deeper, and richer, just beyond the threshold of my conscious recollection.

I also ordered a golden tea from Sri Lanka. Even the tea was different here in Paris. Christy chose the *tarte aux myrtilles*, and a *café au lait*. I broke my confection in two, revealing its raspberry and litchi filling inside. Christy couldn't resist sampling, so we ended up sharing the two delicacies between us. We had hardly sat down before we had completely finished off both the pastries.

Once we resumed our walk toward the Luxembourg Garden, we picked up the thread of the conversation.

"So, tell me more about your romance with Lutetia," Christy asked smiling at me.

I laughed, "It's interesting, isn't it, that the original name was so feminine?"

"Cities have genders, don't they? What about Chicago?"

"Yes, Chicago definitely has a masculine energy: the city of big shoulders."

"What about New York?"

"A dowager, with sadomasochistic tendencies," I said somewhat jokingly.

Christy laughed.

"So, how did Lutetia capture you in her orb?" She asked.

"It was a revelation, magical really. I always had this image of Paris. Of course, there was the art, and yet when I came here it was the experiential feel of the place that really caught me. I suddenly got it."

"When I think of my first memories of Paris, I always think of Ludwig Bemelmans *Madeline*," Christy mused, smiling to herself.

"Me too," I agreed.

Christy had this way of reminding me of my childhood.

For a moment, I thought back to another early image of Paris, an old pictorial encyclopedia I had as a child. The entry for Paris was illustrated with a map of the city. Various pictures placed around the edge of the map depicted the landmarks of Paris.

Even earlier, unconsciously, a certain sense for Paris had already entered my life. I remembered the soft feathery colors of two impressionist paintings, reproductions that hung on our living room wall; one was a Renoir, a portrait of a woman against a green diffuse background; the other, a Monet, a picture showing a child playing in front of a house on a sunny day, there was a garden, and in the background puffy white clouds floating in the sky. Even now, I can still see those images in my mind.

"There were some movies I saw as kid, like Peter Sellers, *A Shot in the Dark*," I recollected.

"Yeah," Christy laughed, "We all have our cinematic memories of Paris. There's Gene Kelly...Catherine Deneuve," She added.

"I saw Catherine Deneuve," I boasted.

"Where?" Christy asked excitedly.

"One night, I was walking through the Latin Quarter. There were people gathered around a café, I think there was a television crew, maybe it was an interview. I looked across the way, and there she was, seated by herself in front of the cafe. She looked beautiful."

I reflected on that evening, now almost twenty years ago. There had been an indefinable energy in the air, a certain frisson. I sensed something was going on that night.

Picking up the thread of my first visit, I continued.

"It was the last week of April, all the trees were green, and there was a soft, moist, aliveness in the air; it was more than that, though. When I came back to America, it was as if everything in the states seemed neutered and regimented."

"That's how they felt in Twenties too. Hemingway and Henry Miller, and all those expatriates," Tracy explained.

21

"Yeah, all those artists going to Paris like it was some sort of strange attractor," I mused.

"The City of Light," Tracy remarked.

"Yes, more an energy than a place of artifacts," I added.

"What about all the great art?" Christy inquired.

"Well, there is the Louvre, of course, but the Pompidou Centre really astonished me; like an Ark of modern art floating above the rooftops of Paris."

"What is the essence of Paris, the *Eau de Paris*, so to speak?"

"Maybe it's this juxtaposition of hyper-modern with the old."

"Like I.M. Pei's glass pyramid in the midst of the Louvre palace?"

"Yes. And at night it's all illuminated, like a scene from *2001*, as if they're displaying some strange alien intrusion in the heart of Paris."

"Staged, almost like theater. There is a sense of design that informs everything here," Christy reflected.

"Yeah, and when you go down into the Louvre Carousel, this opulent shopping mall with polished marble walls, you suddenly come across an area where they've excavated and exposed the original medieval foundations of the Louvre castle."

"The past is present in Paris; a city simultaneously ancient and modern," Christy declared.

"Exactly, the city is transparent." I thought about the Foundation Cartier, just up the Boulevard Raspail, nestled between the classic 19th century blocks, literally a transparent glass building.

"Paris offers you surprises, doesn't it?" she added.

22

4: Left Bank Ramble

By now we had reached the Luxembourg Garden, and by wandering down one of its gravel paths we found a bench in a quiet part of the park. Well shaded by various trees, this corner of the Luxembourg felt like a sanctuary of nature within the urban matrix of Paris. In silence, we listened to a light breeze rustling the foliage. We both fell into a reflective mood for a few moments.

"What are you thinking?" Christy looked over at me.

"The clouds," I almost whispered. "They're different. They aren't like they used to be."

"How can you tell?" She asked.

"I'm not sure."

I was being disingenuous. I thought it was because of the jet contrails crisscrossing the planet spewing out diffuse cotton candy clouds, but it seemed too weird to explain all that right now.

"You, the cloud watcher," she teased, and turned away.

Again, I studied the patchwork of clouds sailing through the sky, intermittently revealing openings of blue.

"The clouds move so fast here." I was thinking of the proximity of the ocean to Paris.

"Maybe the atmosphere is alive," she suggested.

"Yes, the whole earth is, but...I think Paris is alive too, like it's some living being, a living city, rather than a post-modern machine for consumption, like so many American cities."

"So, Columbus isn't the Paris of the Midwest?" She quipped. I laughed.

"No, and neither is Detroit."

Detroit had been a city of the future. It was there where my vision of the full scope and scale of a metropolis first crystalized. All the possibilities, all the elements had been present there. The vocabulary of a city was instantiated for me along the spokes of its wheel. There were mansions and slums, skyscrapers and museums, boulevards, banks and bridges, expressways and airports, factories, warehouses, department stores and colleges. There was Belle Isle, Cobo Hall, and across the river was Windsor in British Canada.

I remembered one nighttime drive down the Lodge Freeway, eagerly anticipating the first glimpse of the glittering skyscrapers of downtown Detroit; and in that moment, when our car turned a bend and the skyline appeared, it almost took my breath away.

Yet, everything had changed in almost a twinkling of an eye, a catastrophe had befallen Detroit, and that version of Detroit had been disrupted and altered, telling of some greater denouement in the world at large.

"What about London?" Christy interrupted my reverie.

"London's great, a special place. London and Paris are like twins. London is red, Paris is blue."

"A tale of two cities," she quipped.

"Yes. Paris is steeped in the domain of the visual. There's something in the Seine water that influenced artists. London is a city of sound, there is something musical in the air."

"Rain grey town known for its sounds."

"Exactly. Every city has an archetype, or a family of archetypes that govern the cultural expressions and creative

24

potential. The Beatles could never have happened in Paris, and Picasso would never have made it in London."

"What about the other European cities? Barcelona? Munich? Madrid? Vienna? Just to name a few. And didn't you once talk about moving to Barcelona?"

"I still want to. All those cities are great. They all have their charms, and they all have distinct energies, and flavors. And yet they all share certain common characteristics. There is a certain scale and proximity, a density of people and culture that seems to have a synergistic effect. Social networks operate at just the right scale, a confluence of personalities and ideas, allowing creative forms to be germinated, transformed, and developed."

"Your city of the future."

"Exactly, a creative wellspring; like when Picasso or Dali, would visit the Louvre, mining the paintings of the Old Masters for visual ideas."

"What about American cities?"

I thought of Detroit with its radial avenues, like the spokes on a wheel, and the concrete freeways that circulated throughout the metropolitan area like automotive cyclotrons. The energy of the city was perpetually flung outward to the periphery and beyond.

"The centrifugal forces are too great. Everything gets pulled apart, dispersed, social networks attenuate, splinter, and languish. And then technology provides a denatured surrogate in the form of social media. In Europe, the centripetal forces are structurally built in, and the cities are still organic. Again, it's a question of scale."

"The integral city."

"Yes, absolutely; there is a certain size and scale that is optimal, and once that scale is exceeded the energy isn't sustainable. Of course, it all depends on location and the social context. Manhattan works because of its history, its density and insular quality, whereas Los Angeles functions as a series of heterogeneous communities linked into the global entertainment industry. Each city has its own archetypal energy."

"So, you're saying the digital revolution disrupts this creative synergy?"

"It certainly presents a challenge. Technology distorts social forms. We get unexpected information cascades with social media altering the playing field and some cultural players are edited out; winner take all scenarios. Positive feedback loops where certain cultural memes proliferate, driving other memes into anonymity"

"Technology cuts both ways, though."

"Yeah, but if we let the human to human synergy die on the vine, or if the old social networks are eviscerated, and we're offered the new social media as some sort of digital substitute, then I think we lose," I replied excitedly.

"You mean when everyone is so busy in the screen world that they don't have time to connect in the real world."

"Exactly; and we also see it in the financial markets. Computer trading generates these wild gyrations, and distortions, enormous capital flows are manipulated; savvy financial players manipulating positive feedback loops to destroy their rivals or sabotage the entire economy."

"The black magicians of Atlantis," She remarked.

I chuckled. I wasn't sure if Christy was joking or serious. In truth, I could imagine a secret elite bent on controlling the world and disseminating a host of twisted memes to influence the masses in accordance with some unspecified social agenda.

"Yeah, well...it is quite nefarious, the effects are reprehensible, evil even, and global in scope, all driven by lust for power and greed by a small financial elite."

"Well, what does all this have to do with the structures of consciousness?" Christy was fumbling with her iPad, looking down. I couldn't tell if she was sincerely interested, or just being a good conversationalist.

"That about 500 years ago we entered the deficient phase, our so-called modern age. And now we're just starting to see signs of a new consciousness dawning, the integral structure."

"Deficient? What does that mean exactly?" She looked up from her iPad skeptically.

"There are two phases to the mental structure, one efficient, the second one a deficient period. The first phase was more qualitative and culminated with the invention of perspective. The deficient phase follows when the first was exhausted, and is marked by an impulse towards quantification, a measuring of everything."

"And so, the innovations in digital media are reflective of this as well?"

"Definitely, computers are an expression of the quantification of the mental structure. Think about how the digital media allows a more complete monetizing of social activity."

"You mean how our browsing habits are monitored and turned into data for corporations?"

"That's one example. Also, nowadays technology operates in an autonomous fashion. We seem to have no control over it. As a society we treat each new technology as a *fait accompli.*"

"Isn't technology offered as the solution to all our problems? We expect technology to rescue us from our modern dilemmas," Christy suggested.

"Yeah, but technology just amplifies all the problems."

"What about the integral structure?" She was looking down at her i-pad again, and then in a distracted way asked. "What are the hallmarks of the integral structure?"

"The two main ideas are the *achronon,* and the *diaphanon.*"

"*Di-ah-pha-non?*" Christy slowly enunciated the syllables.

"Yeah, making transparent all the hidden structures; like here in Paris with the architectural juxtapositions of different time periods. The origins of Paris are even present. Like how the very foundations of Louvre castle are visible, today. The juxtaposition of modern and ancient, like I said before, this is what the integral mutation is all about. We can even trace the irruption of time, back to the French Revolution, right here in Paris."

"So, Paris is *di-ah-pha-nous*?" She sounded out the syllables again.

"Exactly, the integral city. Take the Pompidou Centre; another perfect example, the transparency of the building, revealing the inside; the functional aspects of the building visible outside. The medium is the message."

***

We left the park, walking down the sidewalk toward the boulevard St. Germain, and crossed the busy thoroughfare right in front of the old church. I glanced down the street towards the Les deux Magot, and the nearby Café de Flore, this was where Apollinaire, and then Breton and Aragon hung out after the first war; this was where they conjured up the literary juxtapositions and dream imagery that gave form to Surrealism. Even later, in the thirties, the last wave of Surrealists would meet here before they decamped to New York. It was in New York that the narrative shifted, a new artistic order was established, more reductive, and more commercially oriented. New York had distorted the creative energy; something was lost in the translation across the Atlantic.

We crossed behind the church and then followed a narrow street that connected to Rue de Seine. The streets of the quarter were mostly lined with quaint restaurants, and boutiques. Still, there was a certain coziness I felt in this part of Paris, a grounded feeling. This had been the first part of Paris I had visited. It seemed there had been more art galleries back then, but now they appeared to be losing ground to the boutiques.

Some of the art I had seen on my first trip seemed to harken back to an older Paris, works still redolent of the first half of the twentieth century, giving me a lingering sense of the Paris of the Surrealists and the Existentialists. That was a key part of the energetic I had felt on my first trip, like I was receiving a transmission from the past. There had been a Roberto Matta exhibit here, with works that intimated something beyond the narrow parenthesis of mundane reality: openings to both inner worlds, and outer cosmic worlds.

Even now some of the galleries were still showing artists from the very end of the Surrealist period, those that had passed through the mesh of the Second World War and emerged in the Fifties, exponents of a new vision like Wilfredo Lam, or Hans Hartung. Some of the other galleries had a superficial edginess, decorative, or empty in some indefinable way. Here and there we came across an interesting place, and we paused in front of the windows looking at the objects of art displayed in their cramped spaces.

"What about the arts, and the structures of consciousness?" Christy asked.

"Artists are the first to really get the new structure. The whole history of consciousness can be read in the evolution of art."

"What about today?" Christy looked at me.

"I don't know. Sometimes, I feel like we've hit a dead end or something. The Post-Modern era. It's like we're waiting for the next transmission." I thought about the trivial nature of much contemporary art, how derivative it was of the earlier modern breakthroughs, how small minded it seemed in comparison.

"Maybe, the torch has passed to science and technology." She looked at me questioningly.

"I'm not sure." It was a possibility, I silently admitted. Could the artistic impulse have been played out, exhausted? I wondered.

Close to the river, we passed by a statue of Voltaire placed in the middle of a pocket size park. I remembered that Voltaire and Rousseau had been rivals of sorts.

We then exited the narrow streets of the quarter, and finally reached the banks of the Seine in front of the Institut de France. Here, the incessant traffic roaring down the Quai was jarring after the relatively quiet side streets.

We crossed the Seine at the Pont Des Arts, gazing to our right at the Île de la Cité, the prowl of the island appearing like a ship heading downstream. We lingered on the bridge for a few moments gazing into the river. I looked at the chalky brown waters of the Seine flowing below. Christy was intrigued by all the locks people had attached to the bridge. On both sides of the bridge the railings were packed with the ugly metal locks.

"It's kind of inane, really," I commented on the practice.

"You're not romantic."

"That's not true!" I protested, suddenly feeling hurt by her comment.

"They come here to celebrate their love."

"Yeah, but does it have to be in the form of a lock clasped to a bridge. What about a promise, and a kiss?"

"Well, they probably do that too; but this is a physical sign of their love for all the world to see."

I laughed, a little frustrated by Christy's conventional stance. We both leaned over the railing retreating into ourselves, silently watching the chalky flow of the river.

I guess my understanding of romance was different. I wanted to tell Christy that it was America that wasn't romantic; not me. A certain indefinable sense of drabness had crushed all the *joie de vivre* out of America. Maybe it was the marketplace, the business mentality and social media, or some combination of all those factors that had come to dominate every aspect of the culture and suffocate the flowers of the heart.

5: In the Louvre

We left the locks behind and stepped on to the Right Bank, crossing the busy Quai du Louvre, and then through a tunnel-like passage leading into the ancient heart of the Louvre. Here was the enclosed courtyard of the Cour Carrée, the oldest part of the Louvre; we moved on through another passage into the Cour Napoléon which opened out to the west with views of the Louvre Carrousel and beyond into the Tuileries.

In the center of the courtyard, I.M. Pei's glass pyramid stood like a giant crystal placed in the heart of Paris. Throngs of people were milling around the fountains that surrounded the pyramid and a long line of tourists stretched out from the entrance on the far side of the pyramid. I had purchased tickets in advance, and by showing the multi-day passes, we were able to enter the museum without waiting in the long line.

Deciding against reason to see the *Mona Lisa*, we worked our way toward the galleries devoted to Renaissance art. Moving out of the vast hall that was covered by the transparent glass of the pyramid we moved through a series of stone corridors where the crowds became increasingly dense and even louder. We came to a broad staircase that led up past the ancient *Winged Victory of Samothrace*. This was more than just a statue commemorating a naval victory; it was an exclamation mark heralding the crossing of some threshold in human consciousness. The true meaning of which was lost to the present literal mindset. A few clusters of people had paused on the landing to look at the statue, but many others moved onward barely taking notice. Next to me, in the flowing mass of people, a woman seemed completely oblivious to the triumphant statue soaring above; instead, she remained intently focused on her digital device.

We reached the top of the stairs and entered a long series of open galleries receding off into the distance. This was the *Grande Galérie*, where during the reign of the Sun King, Louis XIV, the royal collection had been displayed, the home of artisans and artists, and to the French Royal Academy of Painting, and where the first salons were held. Now it was named the Denon Wing, after the first director of the museum, and the principal savant on Napoleon's expedition to Egypt. It was Denon who had produced copious illustrations of the Egyptian monuments, the first comprehensive survey of that ancient land by any westerner. In this wing were some of the museum's greatest works. Here a giant Cimabue, there a Botticelli, here a Perugino. We slowed down to gaze at a large Mantegna, and then finally stopped in front of the Louvre's version of the *Madonna of the Rocks*.

Perhaps, this was Leonardo's greatest and most mysterious work. A veil of atmosphere enveloped the glowing figures arrayed at the stations of a triangle. My eye was drawn to the figure of the angel pointing to the left toward the infant John the Baptist. The eyes of angel were pregnant with some secret knowledge and looked out toward the viewer at a strange angle. The background was a brooding arrangement of stark monolithic forms modeled in chiaroscuro contrasts of light and dark, but my gaze was drawn further back into the recesses of a fantastic landscape of watery inlets and rocky forms all dissolved under the effect of Leonardo's *sfumato* technique.

33

We slowly walked over to another of Leonardo's works, a painting depicting John the Baptist.

"This was one of his last paintings," I whispered.

"What a weird smile."

"Yeah, it's amazing. There is something transformative about this painting. The first time I saw it I felt like I suddenly got some secret; the smile, and the eyes. There is this intimation of bliss waiting in the beyond."

"*Felicite*," Christy quipped.

"It's like he knows something, and he's pointing...beyond space and time."

"And each eye is quite different. Peculiar," Christy remarked.

"Yeah. There have been a lot of different interpretations of this painting, but for me it's Leonardo's intimation of the future mutation."

"The future mutation?" She whispered, looking at me with her eyebrows raised.

"Yes, perhaps, his intuition of the new structure of consciousness."

"Hmm. Like he could see around the corner, extrapolating the future"

"Yes. Leonardo kind of puts a seal on the mental structure, takes it to its limit. He must have seen the stylistic trends all around him, after his death we enter this long downward transition we're still in."

"Downward?" Christy said sharply, looked at me skeptically.

"Right. We entered the deficient phase of the mental structure."

"What about all the advances we've seen in just the last hundred years: Polio vaccine, antibiotics, jet airplanes, space travel, computers; the internet? Deficient?" Christy said more insistently.

"I don't know. Those advances are remarkable, but they also represent the quantification of society. Think about the boring assembly line jobs, dulled out workers in call centers. Drone warfare. There are negative aspects to all the innovations. And now the world faces unprecedented challenges."

"Still, we've made progress. Don't you think?" It was almost a question, but not quite. Christy looked at me with a strange expression. I left the thread of the conversation hanging, since I didn't have a good answer.

We turned a corner and entered the vast gallery where the *Mona Lisa* was cloistered. Scores of paintings hung on the walls, salon style, some of them immensely large. The scene was entirely different than my first visit in '95. The *Mona Lisa* was now encased in glass, and throngs of people were gathered around a curved dais separating them from the actual painting. Many of the people were holding aloft cell phones and digital cameras, and periodic flashes went off. The guards stood stoically to the side alertly watching the crowd. It was almost impossible to get close to the painting.

Instead of shoving our way through the crowd, we slipped off to the side. Christy pulled out her iPad and we viewed a reproduction on the Museum's website. The color was remarkably good, and we were able to get a better look at the picture on her iPad than we would have if we squeezed through crowd. Still, I was disappointed at the masses of the people. For many it just seemed to be a circus entertainment, or some sort of homage to a cult object. Just another tourist site checked off on their list, sealed with a flurry of cell phone images to be sent to friends and family as proof of their visitation. We drifted around the corner away from the mass of people and gazed for a few moments at the digital replica.

"Isn't this incredible, the image on my iPad is better than the painting," Christy remarked.

"You're right," I peered at the image.

35

"You can see details you never would have been able to see, and the lighting is perfect. You couldn't possibly see the painting this well in person."

"That's true. I haven't seen this digital version before." I continued staring at the picture, intrigued by the detailed representation.

"Designed in California; San Francisco; your city." Christy smiled at me, lifting the iPad up even closer to my face.

"I know. I know. It's not exactly my city, though."

"You keep on going back there. Always pulled west," she insisted.

"That's true. For some reason, I keep on being drawn back there."

"How many times have you lived there now?"

"I'm not sure. Four or five times, maybe." I laughed a little. It was a bit ridiculous, thinking back to the multiple stints I had done in the Bay area.

Christy was smiling.

Again, she had touched on something. Maybe I was a little embarrassed by her line of inquiry, even though it was quite insightful. Her comments seemed to point to some intrinsic instability in my life, a lack of roots that I presently didn't want to acknowledge.

"San Francisco, and now Paris. Two ends of a string. One is the tonic, the other the dominant," she said.

It was an interesting metaphor. Was the world a string of octaves? I had almost forgotten that Christy had been a musician.

"Paris is closer to the origin," I noted.

Again, she smiled at me in mysterious way.

6: An Integral Vision

We drifted away from the large gallery. Daunted by the crowds and the unceasing din, we tried to find the most efficacious way out of the more frequented galleries. Barely looking at the other paintings, we gradually moved out of the Denon wing and back down into the light filled courtyard beneath Pei's pyramid. It was probably much later than it seemed since the long afternoons of northern Europe confused my sense of time. Christy suggested getting something to eat, and we went up the polished marble staircase, outside, past the fountains and the crowds of tourists, and walked over to the Café Marly.

We were eventually seated outside facing the glass pyramid, and after ordering, Christy picked up her iPad again. She was busy for a few moments, checking on something, and then looked up pointing back to her iPad.

"It's brilliant. I can connect back with work, and we can look up paintings, all courtesy of Apple, and Steven Jobs."

"Right," I laughed at her continued emphasis on technology, and the allusion to the Apple founder.

"So why does all this new technology originate in California?" She asked.

"Silicon Valley, you mean?"

"Yeah, all the new developments are coming from the west, aren't they?"

"Well, it's not only technology," I replied.

"What do you mean?" She asked.

"Well, new ways of looking at the world. Historically, ideas like freedom, and the Enlightenment emerged in France and England. The cutting edge always seems to be the Western edge of Western civilization."

"And then it leapt across the Atlantic."

"Right; there is a westward movement of this impulse."

"And now it's on the west coast."

"Yeah, California has been in the vanguard going back to the 1960s, at least."

"Maybe next it will move on to China."

"I don't know about that," I objected.

It had been western capital that pumped up China's economy, billions of dollars invested in infrastructure and factories, outsourcing half the manufacturing jobs in America. Off shoring the pollution, too, the 8 billion tons of carbon China released to the world every year. There had been a massive transfer of capital to the east, unacknowledged by the media. Now, 30 years later the balance pans had shifted to the east. It was as if a secret pact had been signed to re-balance the world.

"Look at Shanghai, and Beijing; all the incredible construction."

"Yeah, but most of those buildings are designed by western architects, aren't they?"

"What about the Bird's Nest in Beijing?"

"That was designed by the Swiss firm Herzog and de Meuron. I think there is too much emphasis on China in the media. At least at this point, China still seems to be just an imitation of western forms; mostly a merging of Neo-Liberal ideas, with the old command and control economy. No, I think the next step will be more global."

It was true that China was historically one of the most advanced civilizations, but it seemed like America had voluntarily abdicated its position.

"Do you think we've made the shift to the integral structure?"

"We're in a transitionary phase, now. How it goes, depends on us, on all humanity, whether enough people can grasp the new iteration of consciousness."

"It's not just an autonomous process?"

"Not entirely. Though, I often think of it in terms of the different stages of growth latent in the child."

"That sounds pretty autonomous, like something encoded in our DNA."

"I don't know. That could be a good metaphor, but the driving impulse is outside of space and time. *The Origin* is driving events."

"Hmm," she looked thoughtful, and then added, "Is there the possibility humanity won't be up to it?"

"There is that possibility. It all depends on how we handle the intensity of the new consciousness. It may be too much for the rational mind, and the irruption of time will shatter the deficient structure."

Christy paused for a moment.

"The irruption of time?" She had a puzzled expression on her face.

"Yeah. Time breaking out, bursting into conscious awareness."

"Breaking out from where?"

"Space; Time confined in three-dimensionality; the whole partitioning of time." I attempted to explain.

"But time is time, isn't it?" She looked at me skeptically.

"Not exactly. It depends on how we perceive it."

"So, society's sense of time suddenly changes?" Christy asked.

"Yes. There are intimations of it earlier, like the French Revolution; but it really explodes into consciousness in the early twentieth century."

"Evolution isn't necessarily linear, then, there are discontinuities?"

"Definitely. Even as far back as the Renaissance some artists foreshadowed the integral mutation. Simultaneous with the deficient mental structure we see signs of the integral. You know, none of the old graphic models from the mental structure are adequate to describe the integral. Linear causality falls to the wayside."

"What about the overtone series?" Christy interjected; another one of Christy's musical ideas.

"I've often thought of radio frequencies in relation to consciousness, but I think the overtone series is actually a better metaphor," I responded.

"Play one C note on the piano and you'll actually here the octave, the dominant, the third, and so on, a series of harmonic overtones in the tone."

"That's brilliant."

"What about the irruption of time in painting? Where do we see that?" Christy asked.

"Well, that gets back to the thread of history. Around 1790, we have the invention of the steam engine in England and then the French Revolution, both signaling the breaking forth of time. The advent of the machine unleashes a host of autonomous forces, and the abdication of the individual follows in the wake of the revolution and its mob rule."

The waiter brought our meals: A risotto dish for Christy, and a steamed tomato with goat cheese for me. Christy nibbled at her dish for a while and then we resumed our conversation.

"You were talking about the French Revolution, what happens next?" Christy reminded me.

"Napoleon comes after the revolution, and then the Romantic Movement follows with poets like Shelley and Keats, and painters like Turner, and all the others who rail against the denaturation of humanity."

"Do you notice the irruption of time in Turner?" Christy had picked up her iPad again and called up several images of Turner's paintings.

"I do; definitely in his later work; his focus on the ground, as opposed to the figure, the atmospheric effect, a sort of incandescence of light and color. The horizon line dissolves. The entire notion of one-point perspective is replaced by a sense of infinite vanishing points. There is a sense of amorphousness, an inherent allusion to the dynamic quality of experience."

"I see," She said, looking at her iPad. "His *Rain, Steam, Speed,* seems like an explicit reference to the element of time."

"Right; time and motion breaking into awareness, particularly with the invention of the railroad people start to have this new sense of time."

"Travel becomes more common."

"Yeah: The democratization of travel."

"Doesn't the train act as a metaphor for Einstein's theories on relativity?" She remarked looking up from her iPad.

"That's true. He does use the motion of a railway carriage to illustrate his ideas on relativity. His theory collapses space into time. And now with the internet, the distortion of time and space is even more pronounced."

"So, without an invention like the railroad, perhaps Einstein wouldn't have been able to conceptualize his ideas."

"Maybe not; there is a strange correspondence between technical invention and conceptual breakthroughs."

"Maybe the internet will offer us new metaphors."

I laughed.

"Perhaps...global branching patterns, synaptic connections," I mused aloud. "Aren't these all abstractions drawn from the book of nature anyway?"

"What about the glass pyramid, is that drawn from nature?" Christy pointed out to the Pei's transparent architecture.

"I'm not sure."

"Do pyramids exist in the natural world?"

"There are some mountains that are sort of pyramidal; Mt. Kailash, for example."

"Are there straight lines in nature?"

"I don't think so."

"So, perfect geometric forms come solely from the human imagination?" Christy asked, looking at me.

"I guess, unless there are some perfect crystals."

Christy paused a bit, returning to the food, and consulting her iPad simultaneously, leaving me to stare at Pei's glass pyramid.

The glass pyramid was another transparent structure that pointed to the diaphanous nature of Paris. However, the pyramid was not really an integral form. The two-dimensional triangle was more representative of the mental structure, but here, the glass pyramid was three dimensional and transparent, and an explicit reference to the ancient pyramids of Giza. This implicitly revealed the previous structures of consciousness, a sort of structural simultaneity showing the evolution of forms over time.

"You mentioned earlier, this strange word, what was it again? *a-chro...?*" She inquired.

"The *a-chro-non*: time freedom."

Christy laughed a little, "Time freedom?" She looked at me skeptically.

"Yeah, maybe the best way to think about it is a breaking away from our usual experience of time as unfolding sequentially."

"You mean not watching the clock."

"That's part of it. Time is more than just clock time. It's tied in with breaking out of three-dimensional thinking and how time manifests as a fourth dimension. Somehow, it's related to the idea of a sphere, particularly a transparent sphere in motion, as being emblematic of the integral, as the perfect integral art form. I often think of..." I stopped, caught by a sudden thought. For a moment, the place holder of consciousness shifted.

... I could see the continent of Europe, the terrain laid out under a grid of longitude and latitude lines. I reflected on the differences in time between the American West Coast and Europe. I made an internal calculation, estimating the current time in California, and compared it to the present time in Europe. Simultaneously holding the 10 hours difference in mind, I also imagined the spatial displacement of thousands of miles across the earth's surface.

"What is it?" Christy was staring at me.

... The scope of my view expanded, and now I could see the entire half of the globe as if I was observing it from space. The longitudinal lines became more pronounced, and I saw the earth traveling, rotating, from left to right, from west to east through the stationary time zones. I had a sense of the zones being fixed in place, and we, travelers on the surface of the earth, rotating through them toward the approaching dawn, or departing from the daylight into dark side of the earth.

"That's strange. I just remembered a dream I had in Florence."

"What was it?"

"Well, it was a dream of a globe spinning through the time zones. It was actually an interlude between falling asleep and a dream, but now it reminds me of the four-dimensional sphere. That's weird." I was lost in my thoughts, for a moment.

It was an epiphany, really. Suddenly the theoretical notion of a four-dimensional sphere lined up with my own visions. In my mind's eye, in the strange twilight illumination of the dream world, I could see the spinning globe of the earth moving underneath the longitudinal time zone lines.

"Well, what about Teihard's *Noosphere*? Isn't that similar?" Christy broke into my reverie.

"Somewhat," I acknowledged.

"And wouldn't that mean with social media we're all engaged in weaving a planetary artwork," she suggested.

"That's a concept, isn't it?" I did think there was a corollary, but I had drifted off a bit trying to digest the import of my earlier vision and relating it to the idea of the transparent sphere.

We had wrapped up our meal. Christy paid the waiter and we exited the cafe and walked back into the central courtyard.

Weaving our way through the throngs of visitors, we moved toward the exit on the Rue de Rivoli side of the Louvre. I could sense now we were slipping into the extended twilight of early evening, and before long Christy would have to return to her hotel. We wouldn't have time to visit the Pompidou Centre, but I would walk past there later in the evening.

Once we had crossed the busy Rue de Rivoli we darted into a quieter side street and picked up the conversation. Perhaps I had grown tired; after all we had been walking and talking almost non-stop since mid-morning. Sightseeing in Paris could be an exhausting enterprise. I was feeling somewhat irritated, not with Christy, but with the general state of humanity I had seen on display in the museum, particularly the madness of the crowd in front of the Mona Lisa. The raised cell phones, clicking images, like they were recording a totem object, as if it was just another obligatory tourist site.

"Christy, here we are on the verge of the integral mutation, and the masses are completely in thrall to the baubles of technological media. No contact with the vital life forces of the earth. Those people snapping their digital images. How much time will they actually spend looking at those images?"

"They send them to friends and families."

"Yeah, but is there any feeling brought into looking at the picture? Do they spend time looking, and connecting themselves with the painting? Is there any emotional engagement? Sometimes it takes a while to really get into the art. Instead they're just skimming the surface," I insisted.

"I guess it's a way of connecting socially."

"It's not social, really."

"What do you mean?"

"Social media is an oxymoron. It's all an abstraction of the social, not truly social. And it's a diversion from what's really going on. It's like some opposing force wants us to be just satisfied with superficial stories, deliberately obscuring the real narrative: allowing technology to fix the mental structure in place, quantifying the social realm in zeros and ones." I was a little beside myself.

"Technology seems like the way forward, past the old model of isolated human beings. Now we have almost instantaneous interconnection."

"But the implicit assumption is that we've come to the end human evolution. That's so wrong. There is still so much we have yet to develop in our own inner worlds. We're just at the beginning, really. The future of the earth evolution is through us, in our inner being, at our soul level."

45

"And technology denies the soul's existence?"

"Yes. At least implicitly," I responded.

Why was Christy so insistent about the value of instantaneous communication? I thought about all those letter writers of the past, Like Rilke or Emily Dickinson, isolated by distance, having the time to foster an inner life, a space of introspection, a certain reflectivity that had become increasingly elusive, today. What was the intent of this impulse that incessantly pushed to decrease the gap? To what end, and was there a limit? And wasn't it the structure of the media, that actually shaped the nature of the exchange, producing a world of superficiality.

Coming to my senses, I dropped the thread of thoughts. I could sense we were approaching Christy's hotel, and regretted my almost single-minded focus on these obscure topics for the entire course of our day together.

"Oh, Christy, here I've gone and wasted our whole day ranting and raving about the integral mutation."

Christy laughed, and then added, "Perhaps, I incited you."

We were standing in front of the hotel. I could see she was also a bit weary from the day's activities, with our lengthy walking from Left Bank to Right Bank, and she was politely waiting on me to finish. The sun had just dropped behind the buildings of the street, and we were in the shadow, but above, the sky had cleared and was the pale blue of early evening.

"We haven't even talked about the really important stuff, like life." I remarked somewhat jokingly. However, there was something deeper I was trying to intimate in my own roundabout way.

Christy laughed at that, and we caught each other's eyes for a moment. Perhaps, I had wanted to confide in her the strange ennui that had overtaken me or found some answer to explain the terminus of inoperability that my social life had arrived at recently. Or even some explanation for the years that had slipped by since our last meeting.

Momentarily, Christy looked above me at the sky. Then she said, "You know Tom, we all make decisions, and incrementally, our lives form like a crystal around those choices."

I sighed, and Christy returned to gaze into my eyes. Somehow Christy had intuited the direction of my thoughts, and perhaps it had been better that we hadn't spoken of these matters.

Before I could respond further, she continued, smiling, "Next time, don't wait two decades to get in touch with me." We both laughed and then hugged. It had been a long day, we were both tired, and there was a lot to digest about life, this diaphanous life.

As she walked toward the entrance she turned and added, "I might be in San Francisco in October, so send me a letter, and let me know if you'll be able to arrange a rendezvous."

"I will." We waved goodbye and Christy entered the hotel. I turned away and started walking toward the Pompidou Centre.

7: Passage du Grand Cerf

In the moment we took our parting, I must have become disoriented since I turned in the wrong direction. Still deep within my ruminations about the integral mutation, and thinking about the things Christy had said, I walked for a while with my head down actually going more in the direction of Montmartre, than towards the Pompidou Centre. I had walked all the way down Rue Rousseau, and then crossed Étienne Marcel, and was proceeding up Rue Montmartre before I realized my misdirection.

Correcting my course was a little difficult since the Parisian street layout was strangely counter intuitive. I knew where west was, since that was where the sun went down, and the unseen towers of La Défense marked that horizon, but my backtracking would have to take a zigzagging course. Adding to my disequilibrium, this part of Paris was unfamiliar to me; and it didn't have the same comfortable energy that I felt around the Boulevard St.Germain.

It was while I worked my way back, walking down Rue Grenata, at the very moment I was expectantly looking down the street for the next right turn, my eye caught a glimpse of a woman dressed in a striking red jacket. She looked directly at me and our eyes briefly met. I was suddenly filled with an upwelling of excitement. She reminded me of Cassiopeia, a woman I had met almost seven years earlier on my first trip to Ibiza.

In fact, the likeness was remarkable. She looked away, and continued walking down the street, almost immediately slipping behind the corner of the building. I sped up my pace, trying not to be too conspicuous, but I was now squeezing past a few of the slower pedestrians, and to move faster, I started walking on the edge of the street. I had turned the corner, catching a glimpse of her red coat a little further down the street, maybe only 30 yards away, when she paused briefly, and then abruptly turned left into an old arcade.

I closed the distance in no more than ten seconds, and then stood in front of the Passage du Grand-Cerf, one of those magical arcades built in the early 19th century. The high ceiling let in a little of the fading afternoon light. Looking past the wrought iron work, down the arcade with its geometric floor pattern, I couldn't see any sign of the woman. I peered further down to the far end of the passage, vainly looking for the bright red of her jacket. Then I rushed into the passage. Perhaps she was visiting one of shops; that would be a likely scenario. One after the other, systematically, I looked left to right, and then right to left. One after another, yet I found no trace of her. Some people in the shops returned my gaze as I walked by, perhaps they knew her, and realized I was looking for her. I quickly realized that wasn't rational.

I worked my way almost to the end of the passage and came up just before the opposite entrance. Slightly winded, I paused, catching a glimpse of myself in the mirrored glass. I laughed at myself, almost surprised to recognize myself in the reflecting glass, suddenly realizing how ridiculous my momentary excitement was, and how idiotic I must have looked to any onlookers who may have observed my behavior.

Somehow, I had lost track of her. I felt a sense of disappointment welling up in my gut, mingled with embarrassment. I looked up from my reflection in the glass, staring up into the heights of the passage with its transparent skylight. I looked back behind me down the entire length of the arcade which I had quickly walked through, still vainly hoping to see her emerge from a shop.

I turned around, peering into a narrow cafe opposite of me. There was no sign of her anywhere. I paused a moment, then turned around, almost automatically walking back into the heart of the passage. This time I casually perused the different shop windows.

On one side, I found a display of tiny faience amulets, eyes of Horus and a scarab, all in shades of turquoise and aqua blue. On the other side, there was a shop advertising Asian massage, with bright magenta colored walls, and a diagram of the body indicating the chakras and various pressure points.

A little further into the arcade, I paused in front of a window display where a poster showed one a view as if looking down from a height on a group of people forming a circle on a beach.

The small shop was empty, a vase filled with pussy willows sat on the sill behind the glass, and a few small paintings decorated the otherwise bare white walls. The sign on the shop read: *"New Angles- Artistes createurs en mouvement."*

On the poster, in French, *"Pour change quelque chose construisez un nouveau modèle, qui rend l'existant obsolète. Buckminster Fuller."* I briefly struggled with the translation, 'For change' or rather 'to change something...construct a new model...that makes the existent one obsolete."

I briefly pondered this message, staring at the people on the beach, wondering if perhaps they were in California. How curious to find a quote from Buckminster Fuller, the creator of the geodesic dome, in of all places, this 19th century arcade.

I turned around, again walking toward the end of the arcade, and then back onto the street. Pausing in front by the entrance, lost in thought, I gazed though the glass at a floral display.

It had been only a brief interlude of passionate possession, yet I felt stimulated, even electrified by a distant memory. Reflecting back on the fleeting encounter some seven years previously, I passed into a momentary reverie. Simultaneously, my thoughts were agitated, pervaded by a sense of uncertainty.

Was it really Cassiopeia? Perhaps, I was confusing one woman for another; a case of mistaken identity; merely a seeming likeness, an illusion, a trick of my own mind triggering inside my body a rush of emotion and excitement.

Rationally reflecting, I realized many people have similar features. There could be hundreds of women in Europe who might bear a likeness to this woman. Even, I have been periodically mistaken for someone else, and people's appearances change over time. Could someone I saw seven years ago still actually look the same? Could someone still conform to the image in my memory? A mental image is maintained intact, more or less, I suppose, while the actual individual changes over time. Individuals even change from day to day, or week to week, not to mention over the course of several years. How absurd of me to think that a woman I had briefly met in Ibiza would look just like I remembered her, seven years hence. Was it possible, that my memory of her, the image of her face residing in my mind, had been a construction, an abstraction, one that over the intervening months had subtly altered, even deteriorated, becoming a false approximation of the real person? That notion frightened me a bit, calling into question the verity of any visual remembrances, raising the possibility that all memories are mere semblance.

Lost in thought for several moments, I realized I had been staring vacantly into the florist shop for a bit longer than would normally be appropriate. Glancing up, I couldn't jettison the lingering feeling that I might see Cassiopeia emerge from the arcade at any moment. After my ruminations, it also occurred to me that I might not recognize her, for example, if she had changed her coat, from red to blue, or altered her dress or style, in which case I might be left completely oblivious to the very same woman's appearance.

I now realized it was pointless to linger in front of the arcade any longer, and by now it was probably getting almost too late to visit the Pompidou Center.

8: The High Aerie

Jumping on the glass covered escalator, skipping every other step, I quickly arrived at the upper level terrace. Already the sky had cooled to a magical twilight blue. It was here more than anywhere else that I felt an extraordinary connection, even some revelation, about Paris.

Surveying the city from this vantage point it was as if I was riding on a futuristic ocean liner, floating, or perhaps temporarily moored, among the older structures of historic Paris. Appearing in the west above the towers of La Défense, the new moon hung low on the horizon in a gauzy mauve band, hardly a crescent- more a sliver with upturned prowls, shimmering like a boat; a glittering celestial emissary moored above the Île de France.

There was a most delicate breeze wafting through the air. A refreshing effervescence filled the atmosphere. I gazed over the sparkling lights of the city, surveying the urban expanse of Paris, my eyes reaching to the edge of the horizon where the distant buildings were outlined against the waning light of day.

I entered a most felicitous state of mind; one of those that arrives only with the proper alignment of circumstance. A door opened to me as I gazed into the sky and I fell into the evening blue, entering a deeper state of reverie. From this perspective,

I sensed the city was sitting on a great well issuing from the earth, with invisible flowing streams rising into the starry heavens.

Perhaps this was the secret of Paris. All those artists that had been attracted to the city over the years were drawn to the hidden well that I now fancifully discerned emerging from the bowl of the earth. Visually, I could confirm that the land seemed to dip in central Paris, and to the north and south the hills rose to frame the city: Montmartre and Montparnasse. However, this topographic correspondence was only coincidental with the deeper impressions I was receiving.

The city itself was a vehicle for initiatory experience. The constant barrage of sense stimuli, the overlaying of impression on top of impression, all requiring the engagement of will forces, leading to an intensification of consciousness, made Paris a place of accelerated development, and a valve that channeled new innovations out into the global periphery.

At the turn of the century the spirit of the avant-garde had been present in the air, a certain transformational energy had come together more prominently here in Paris than anywhere else. There had been an avalanche of styles, formal innovations reworking the DNA of western art, one after another in rapid sequence, compressed into a brief period of fifty years or so: Impressionism, Pointillism, Post-Impressionism, Symbolism, Art Nouveau, Fauvism, Cubism, and Orphism.

Then there was the rupture of the First World War; a discontinuity, followed by a new wave of transformational ideas, building on the previous wave. Dada and Surrealism picked up the thread, continuing the transformative process, altering the artistic DNA; cross-fertilizing cubist juxtapositions with psychoanalytic impulses, subverting the rational world view.

In my reverie, I could see these artistic evolutionary processes like some sort of biological metamorphosis, a double

54

helix of symbolic forms traveling on an invisible escalator into the sky. Not a fixed form, but an ever present becoming, an unfolding over time.

It then occurred to me that Paris was like a flower, opening its petals outward, issuing its perfume, attracting creative individualities like butterflies drawn to colorful spring blossoms. And as each flower has discernible phases in its life, so does a city or even a whole culture have clearly defined stages that build one after another in an organic fashion. For someone like myself, so geographically oriented, so place focused, it was difficult to make that shift to the undeniable sense of process I clearly saw taking shape in my awareness.

And so, the well that I initially discerned, was really a flower, and I could see this giant flower opening to the universe like an enormous satellite dish with an open bowl oriented to the heavens.

Looking up from the western horizon I saw two bright stars emerging from the evening blue. The first one of a much greater magnitude, shining brightly, lingering near the horizon just above the fast fading moon; the other higher, of a lesser magnitude: Venus and Saturn. The stars formed a triangular arrangement; two almost parallel lines rising up from the bright pentangle of Venus, a high attenuated form climbing upward, telescoping deep into space reaching an apex at the asterisk of a lesser magnitude.

I thought of the emptiness, the putative emptiness at least, of the vast legions of space. And in this quantum vacuum floats our planet, with its treasure chest of life, organic forms proliferating, surging seas, and lush forests, and its storehouse of artistic creation as well. Wouldn't visitors from the depths of space, from some stupendous cities at the galactic core, be drawn to this oasis of life and creativity in the forlorn reaches of the galactic arm, to this city as well, to even this building, a futuristic ark of modern art, a veritable museum of time, rising above the gabled rooftops of Paris?

A fluttering breeze wafted through my hair, dislodging me from my train of thought. Just then off to my left, near the escalator and the glass doors opening to the fifth-floor galleries, a pair of voices further disrupted my meditation. They appeared to be security personnel from the museum.

Disengaging from my reflections, I left the high aerie and quickly descended back down the escalator to street level.

9: The American Tourist

I crossed the river at Pont au Change, and once more over Pont St. Michel, and then paused in front of the fountain at Place St. Michel.

As usual there was crowd gathered around the fountain. The throngs of pedestrians flowing along the streets leading into the Latin Quarter further lent an energized quality to the atmosphere. I paused, leaning on a railing near the edge of the fountain, just observing the various people, soaking up the energy of this place. It was here in this part of Paris, the Left Bank, that I felt something special.

I noticed a man walking in my direction staring down at his digital device, oblivious to his course. Just as he was about to run into the railing, he pulled up right next to me, no more than a foot or so away, with a baffled expression on his face.

He was middle aged, but probably no more than 45, well over six feet tall, and somewhat heavy set, with short damp hair, and small backpack slung across one shoulder.

He looked up at me, and then bent over again peering at his digital device in a perplexed manner. Then in a rather stilted attempt at the French language he said, "*Monsieur, parlez vous...?*"

Inadvertently I chuckled. It was now obvious to me that he was an American. I replied, "Yes."

"What a relief. No one will speak to me here." Thrusting out his hand he introduced himself, "My name's Adam."

I extended my hand reflexively, and he proceeded to shake it with an excessive firmness, almost immediately looking back down into his digital device.

"What sort of problem are you having?" I inquired.

"My GPS is having a glitch. I'm trying to text my wife, and that's not working either. She'll be on my case if I'm not back at the hotel soon. I thought I'd slip away for a moment and check out the Pantheon."

"The Pantheon!" I laughed. "You're a bit off track. Do you have a map?"

"A map?" He looked blankly at me.

"Well, you're pretty much in the right neighborhood. You just need to walk up this street, the Boulevard St. Michel, until you come to the Luxembourg, the park, and then make a left. You can't miss it, but it's probably closed by now."

"Closed, oh...uh." Distracted in mid-sentence by some signal, he looked down at the digital device, momentarily fiddling with the texting features.

He smiled to himself then looked back up re-engaging with my presence, "Oh. Uh...I've got a few minutes. So, it's closed you say?"

"Yeah, definitely but you could walk by and check out the exterior though. That might be worthwhile."

"Are you from Portland?" He asked.

"No!" I was mystified by his comment.

"You look like you're from Portland," he responded.

"No. I'm from Michigan, but I left years ago."

"What brings you to Paris?" He asked, staring at me inquisitively.

I paused briefly since I was a little hesitant to articulate my work to someone who to all appearances would have little understanding of my many reasons for being in Europe.

"Well, I'm doing some research on architecture and cities," I explained, deciding honesty was the best approach.

"I get it; you're one of those artistic types."

"I suppose so," I admitted.

"Must be a nice lifestyle," he added.

"And what brings you to Paris?" I asked, trying to turn the tables on him.

"Just a short vacation: me and the wife, seeing the sites. In the morning we did the Louvre. After lunch we climbed the Eiffel Tower, and tomorrow we're headed to London, and then back to the states." He paused briefly and then added, "My wife loves it here, but I'll be glad to get back home."

"Really?"

"Yeah, well..." He paused again and then lowered his voice, "How can I say this? I guess I just don't get the French lifestyle."

"What do you mean?"

"I mean, don't get me wrong, this is a beautiful city, but I could never live here. It's like living in some kind of fantasy world; the whole city is a museum."

"Paris works, though, right?"

"What are you saying? They barely work 30 hours a week here!" He practically shouted the last statement.

"The Parisians are incredibly industrious," I countered, and then added. "You know, there are probably more entrepreneurs here in Paris alone, than in the entire United States."

"Here? Are you joking? This is a socialist country," he said, shaking his head in disbelief.

"A socialist country?" I always seemed to meet a certain type of American when I was abroad. In a strange way, I began to disconnect from actually looking at him, rather I was looking all around him. My attention was drawn to the cascading fountain, the bubbling waters surrounding the figure of St. Michel and the fallen demonic figure. I looked at the curves on Michael's sword, and his hand pointing upward much like the figure of St. John had in the painting by Leonardo.

"Isn't the free market just a theoretical construct?" I added somewhat obliquely, attempting to challenge some of his cherished beliefs.

"What do you mean?" He looked slightly baffled.

"I mean it's a fiction, really, just used in economic theory."

"I don't know about that," Adam responded tersely, almost as if I had hurt his feelings.

'Hasn't the free market been incredibly destructive to society, it's practically destroyed the middle class?" I continued.

"The market sorts out winners and losers: survival of the fittest."

"That sounds like the law of the jungle, as if we were no different than animals."

"It's just the market doing its work."

"Sure, but if we're so busy fighting to survive how can we really be free?"

"Capitalism produces more than any other economic model. It offers us more choices."

I paused a moment, thinking to myself. Is freedom really about more choices? Perhaps there was a problem with that definition of freedom.

"You don't mind that everything in society has been monetized?" I asked, pursuing another angle.

"Well, that's good for entrepreneurs. People can start businesses to capture a part of the marketplace."

Encased in his world view, he was impervious to the full scope of reality, denying anything outside of his preferred frame of reference. I turned my head toward the gushing waters of the fountain and looked back up at St. Michael triumphant with his foot on the devil's back. I felt, as I often did in these sorts of arguments, that I was drawing the lines of my response from some meta-space external to our physical position in front of the fountain. And also, I wasn't really engaging him directly as a person, since I regarded his ideas as not really his own, but rather some position he received through the conservative media.

"How was your flight over here?" I asked.

"Well, it sucked actually. We were crammed in like sardines."

"That's the Neo-Liberal model for you."

"Let the free market solve the problems, that's what I believe. People got to pull themselves up, by their bootstraps basically, and stop waiting for the welfare state to take care of them."

"What about people who of no fault of their own lose their jobs or even their homes?"

"I'm against income redistribution. That's social engineering. If you work hard, you should get rewarded. You make bad decisions, then you reap what you sow." He seemed to be possessed now, sounding increasingly irrational, and noticeably irritated.

"What about compassion or sympathy for those that fall on hard times?"

"Let them sort it out. America will be stronger for it. That's our heritage, going all the way back to the pioneer days. Stand on your own two feet." His face was now flushed red.

"If we help the disadvantaged, lift them up, it benefits society as a whole. Doesn't it?"

"That sounds like socialism. That may work here in France, but we're different in America."

"Hah," I laughed under my breath.

Looking again at St. Michel surrounded by the fountain, I realized I had come up against a wall, again. Adam was so emblematic of a certain strain of thinking in America, almost monolithic in its repetition of the same talking points, and half-truths. His free market social Darwinism was really some sort of group think pandering to inherent social insecurity, rather than an actual coherent body of ideas.

I looked back at Adam searching his face trying to disengage from the conversation in as neutral a manner as possible. I realized now that the entire tact of my conversation was ill suited to produce any meaningful results. Adam was probably just concerned about raising a family, and insuring his children had a good future.

Mustering as much compassion as I could towards him personally, if not for his woeful body of ideas, I said, "Listen...Adam, I'm starved, and I got to get something to eat before it gets too late. The Pantheon's down this street." I pointed up the boulevard away from the Seine. "Enjoy the rest of your trip."

"Well, thanks, uhh...What'd you say your name was?"

"Thomas."

"Well, good luck on your research, Thomas," he responded in a friendly manner, almost as if we hadn't voiced any conflicting viewpoints. After briefly shaking hands, his grip still excessively firm, I walked away without a specific direction in mind, except not up the Boulevard St. Michel, leaving him still staring at his digital device in front of the fountain.

Truthfully, I was starved. I left the Place St. Michel, and I took off somewhat aimlessly in the direction of St.-Germain-des-Pres.

10: Chez Sarasvati

I stopped at the corner of Rue Dauphin and looked down the street in the direction of the Seine. I suddenly recalled the card I had found at the hotel earlier in the day. Retrieving it now from my pocket, I briefly studied the orange colored card: *Chez Sarasvati, Rue Dauphine.*

It must be nearby.

I turned to the right proceeding down the narrow sidewalk glancing into the different shop windows as I passed by and within a few moments I was there, standing in front of the distinctive wooden exterior.

I gazed at the intricately carved wooden arabesques, evoking the *jali* of Mogul Indian. Up above, also carved from wood, the sign read: *Chez Sarasvati.* I paused to quickly look over the menu posted outside, and then decided to enter.

The interior was decorated with sensuous rose-colored carpet and upholstery. A sense of quiet softness pervaded the space. I was seated without much wait, and after reviewing the menu again I was able to order my dish without delay.

I had prepared myself for a relatively long wait, though. I usually carried a book with me just for these occasions. I didn't have the patience for deciphering the Le Monde issue instead I had an old paperback copy of Lewis Mumford's *Pentagon of Power*.

Mumford's tome was a classic that I had found in an old used bookshop in Ann Arbor. I hadn't been reading the book in any concerted fashion on this trip, just randomly opening to various passages as I happened to be waiting for a bus, train, or dinner. *The New Megamachine* was the chapter I turned to now.

The first passage my eye fell on read, *Changes that cannot be quantitatively measured... are outside the scope of the computer.*

It was a brilliant observation and written over fifty years ago. Digital systems don't have the subtle differentiation of the analog, and computers will never have the resolution of the human eye, or other human senses like touch. I looked up briefly as the waiter brought me some *papadum* along with a pitcher of water. I was famished, so I dug into the appetizer.

Returning to the book, I leafed ahead a few pages reading another sentence. It was another brilliant analysis, commenting on the myopic perspective of modern technological society.

Yes, our arrogance, even our autistic view of the world, was so obvious even back in the mid-Sixties. Of course, it's only worse now with the rampant technophilia. Everything is Facebook this, Twitter that, as if technology was the panacea for all our ills.

Even this book, if we're to believe the media propaganda, is obsolete. These interesting book covers with their old-fashioned illustrations and typesetting are so *passé* now. I should be texting or playing computer games on my i-phone. My mind turned to the old cabinets of the *bouquinistes* down by the banks of the Seine. I'll have to go down there tomorrow and look for some treasures, relics from the twentieth century before they're thrown into a landfill.

As I followed this train of thought I discerned the muffled sounds of other patrons in conversation nearby. The restaurant was constructed with several little alcoves, and since I was facing away from the entrance, I couldn't get a sense of the exact proximity of the voices I heard. I noticed, in a way almost unconsciously, only slightly unexpectedly, that a man was speaking English. The accent had a distinctly Indian flavor. Not surprising since this was an Indian restaurant, but I noticed a second voice, his partner, a woman whose accent seemed more Middle Eastern.

I returned to the book. It was a section commenting on the ephemeral nature of technological production, and the emphasis on constant change, with scant regard for anything else. Our disposable culture was like a forest fire burning through everything of the past, tradition, artistic styles all dispensed with. No time to pause and absorb anything.

The two voices behind me had a soft, even hypnotic quality, such that I couldn't help but track with their conversation as I continued to read Mumford. Moreover, the rest of the dining area seemed relatively quiet. So, in a kind of annoying, but compelling way, their conversation began to interweave itself into my reading even though I couldn't make out precisely what they were saying. Unobtrusively, I tried to turn around to maybe glimpse who they were, but I couldn't really make out exactly where they were located, and I didn't want to make it seem obvious they had attracted my attention.

I glanced back down at Mumford jumping across to the other page ...*technology has usurped authority over all other components...*

Yes, totally, we've ceded our autonomy to technology. I looked down again at the sentence just above it reading...*our own culture has fallen into a dangerous and unbalanced state.*

Just then the waiter came by placing a small bowl of lentil soup on the table. I paused a bit letting it cool before starting in on the soup. Continuing with Mumford another passage caught my eye...*it places the demand for constant technological change above any...*

Out of the suddenly more silent background, no longer even softly muffled, the lilting voice of the Indian gentleman rose slightly in decibels, crossing a discernible threshold, intruding into my reading so that I unmistakably heard him say.

"Of course, if people continue with a normal frame of consciousness they'll never get beyond a certain superficiality. Ordinary consciousness is insufficient."

Hmm, I perked up, putting Mumford down momentarily. How intriguing, I thought.

The woman's voice replied resonantly with a definite Middle Eastern inflection, "...Yes. Occasionally, one has glimpses or flashes of reality that break in upon the hypnotic normalcy."

Almost involuntarily I twisted myself around once again to try and get some sense of who this couple was and where they were seated in the restaurant. My location though was ill suited for ascertaining their whereabouts and the best I could do was look off to the side toward the kitchen door which abruptly opened and the waiter came out with a tray momentarily blocking out the conversation.

Turning back to my lentil soup, I dipped the spoon into the bowl and tasted the creamy orange contents. My taste buds received a fragrant burst of flavor.

Looking down at Mumford again, I turned the page and came upon another passage in mid-sentence ...*man's central historic task, more imperative today than ever- the task of becoming human.* I paused savoring that thought as well as another spoonful of the rich soup.

Incredible, Mumford has the boldness to assign meaning to the entire human endeavor, usually seen as a meaningless series of travails and transient pleasures. The passage continued...*failure to perform that task for a single generation might set the erring community back a whole geological epoch.*

Indeed, and here we are perhaps on the cusp of catastrophic global collapse. It's anyone's guess how the world will hold up in the next 80, or even 50 years.

Experiencing a kind of a synesthesia of taste sensations and intellectual sustenance, I took another spoon full of lentils and moved on to the next paragraph... *one set of discoveries and inventions these prophets of technology will not allow for are those internal human devices that would eventually bring technics under constant human evaluation..*

Exactly, no attention seems to be paid to developing the inner tools for enhancing or developing consciousness, as if we had reached the terminus of human evolution, and technology was the only way forward.

I began to realize there were some unusual acoustics incorporated into the restaurant's design for just then I heard the man's voice again softly but as clear as if he was seated next to me.

"...yes of course. Hypnogogic interludes, certain meditative states, crises, shocks, yes, altered states..." His voice trailed off. I looked up to the ceiling trying to ascertain how his voice may have carried over to be so clearly audible one moment and muffled at another instance.

Then his feminine interlocutor replied, "... it's like the shift in consciousness gives one a key- or one sees the key that was always there."

"Yes, knock and I shall answer..."

"One must know when to knock, though..."

Just then a waiter burst out of the kitchen door with a tray disrupting my surreptitious monitoring of the conversation. Walking over to my table he gracefully presented my dinner plate, and a bowl of rice.

"*Monsieur, bon appétit.*"

"Merci."

In the commotion, I lost the thread of the conversation. As well, the acoustic window of quiet seemed to be momentarily disrupted as a group of other diners entered the restaurant behind me engaged in an animated conversation.

I wanted to finish the soup before I started on the main dish. As I was still quite hungry, I eagerly dug into the half-finished bowl of lentils, allowing the main dish to cool off. I was partially grateful for the noise disruption so I could focus on my dinner without being distracted, though I was intrigued by the unusual conversation I was hearing.

The references to hypnogogic interludes and keys were tantalizing. I feel like in my own life I had been on the cusp of conversance with some of these ideas. However, since I couldn't make out the entirety of their conversation, I felt I was missing some key element. Some sort of context to unravel the main drift of their conversation or frame these ideas. Yet, maybe more significantly, who were these two people? And why hadn't I met people of this order previously?

Yes. Wasn't the dream of the earth and the time zones a hypnogogic interlude?

The images were still fresh in my mind. I could see the entire half of the globe as if I was observing it from space...the longitudinal lines became more pronounced, and I saw the earth traveling, rotating, from left to right, from west to east through the stationary time zones...the time zones were fixed in place, and we, travelers on the surface of the earth, were rotating through them toward the approaching dawn, or departing from the daylight into dark side of the earth.

Perhaps, I had experienced these interludes for decades, intermittently, yet with no control over their appearance. Not quite a dream, not a waking state, balanced, delicately, in the liminal state between waking and dreaming. I had experienced insights, and intricate visions, that seemed beyond the ken of any normal consciousness.

Abruptly interrupting my train of thought the waiter was at my side inquiring. "*Monsieur*, are you pleased with your dinner?"

"Oh yes. *Oui, Oui, Deliciuex. Merci,*" I exclaimed.

The soup was incredible, but I hadn't even touched the main dish.

I moved the soup aside, for it was largely finished off. I proceeded to spoon out a generous portion of rice, the aromatic cardamom pods scenting the dish with a mouthwatering pungency. I scooped up a larger spoon full of the main dish, a mixed vegetable curry prepared with carrots, potatoes, and zucchini, all immersed in a rich reddish colored sauce, and placed it on top of the mound of rice. The taste was an extraordinary explosion of flavor and spices. I closed my eyes savoring the perfection of the dish. Perhaps the best curry I had ever tasted.

As I closed my eyes, carried away by the flavors, the man's voice once again became audible.

"Time? Time is in part an illusion. Only by shifting our consciousness can we realize the illusory nature of our mind's relation to time and its apparent passage."

"Which is...?" inquired the woman's voice, echoing my own curiosity.

"Time doesn't move, say like the grains of an hourglass, but rather we are falling through time and space."

"A frightening notion; Perhaps, that is why we remain unconscious of it."

"Yes, indeed..." he responded further, but with a shift in the acoustic environment his voice was again muffled preventing me from making out the rest of the sentence.

I returned to eating the vegetable curry. Time, yes, perhaps I needed time just to digest these few ideas, as well as eat my dish. Time an illusion? Falling through space? Maybe I could relate to that. As one gets older time seems to proceed more and more quickly. A kind of acceleration takes effect, seasons fall by, one after another. One loses control over the course of time.

Alternately, I reflected on how interminably long childhood seemed. The horizon of life seemed limitless, undefined by any specific expectation. A summer seemed like an eternity, day after day of pleasant sunny days, playing in the woods, swimming at the lake. Free from any sense of obligation impinging on a limitless future, unformed, before the die had been cast, before the wave function had collapsed, to blend metaphoric schemas. Everything was still potential back then.

I thought of one of those endless sunny summer days way back in my childhood, a visual memory that somehow had survived the decades, and would return to me intermittently bringing with it a warm, hopeful, sustaining quality. A memory that seemed to harbor something integral to who I was as a being, holding some message for even who I might really be.

I could see the street we lived on in suburban Detroit, and the way a stand of tall trees framed the left side of my view. I was looking toward the north. The sky was blue, with a few puffy cumulus clouds drifting by. There seemed to be a soft stillness in the air, like the world hadn't been filled to the brim with hubbub, and billions of people. In the distance I could hear the drone of a propeller plane measuring out the distance. The ground was covered with unkempt dark green grass, a few flowers, randomly, untended, emerging from the grass; a field of weeds receding into the distance. A cluster of houses down the street, framed with abundant foliage, formed my horizon. What was in that moment that was trying to communicate with me now? Why did I come back to these disparate visual mementos of a time past?

Again, the voices of the couple returned to my ears. The man continued speaking unraveling the line of thought, "Yes, indeed. Unless there is the ability to shift the consciousness, intentionally, deliberately, one is as if spellbound unaware of our real predicament."

There was another momentary muffling of the conversation. Perhaps the woman had responded, however I didn't catch that. I took another bite of my curry, holding the food in my mouth without chewing. The man's voice continued, clearly audible.

"For example, in the plant world we have annual cycles, the rhythm of the natural world, whereby a plant goes through all the stages from sprout, to blossom, to seed, all in one season. Yet the human body matures over a much longer period, time slows for our bodies."

"Yes, the seven-year cycle from the loss of teeth to puberty."

"Of course, and this difference in relative time is what distinguishes us from nature. The relative slowness of our body," he continued.

"Seven times slower."

"We have fallen out of nature, expelled as it were."

"Yes. The Garden of Eden story," The woman remarked.

"Of course, all those myths tell stories about the human condition. The problem is the literal interpretation; taking it literally, as some sort of actual historical event that an archaeologist might find evidence for."

"Foolish, isn't it? The modern materialist tendency always to reify."

There was a muffling to their voices, but it almost sounded as if they were chuckling, laughing about the folly inherent in the modern human project. Humankind had lost the thread of the story, now grappling with fragments, pieces of the puzzle, and a strange collective amnesia concerning our past. Aside from fossil fragments and anthropological or paleontological speculation, we were lost, disconnected from our past.

Returning to my meal, redoubling my efforts to finish the curry dish, I realized it was getting late. Again, I was able to hear the man, he resumed, "Indeed, paradoxically, our thoughts move faster than nature."

"An intrinsic dissonance then"

"Indeed, for our thoughts, time moves too slow; for our body time moves too fast."

"Such a dilemma..." The woman's entire response faded out muffled. There was a rustling, as if they had finished dinner, and decided to leave the restaurant. I twisted around in my chair, pushing it back attempting to catch a view of the two people, but to no avail. I was almost finished with my dish, but I hadn't paid the bill yet. I could hear muffled voices, the waiter, and perhaps the man bidding the staff adieu. Then the entrance door opening and closing.

I returned to the remains of my dish. There was a lot to digest in their conversation. I slowly chewed the last few portions of the dish, by now definitively cooled. I looked down at Mumford again, opened the book and moved on a page or two from where I had left off reading. Finding another passage that again resonated with my own state of mind, I read ...*the system itself becomes more immobile and rigid. Man himself is thus losing hold on any personal life that can be called his own, he is now being turned into a thing destined to be processed and reconstructed...*

Totally, I could see this every day in America, even in Eurozone, with the systemization of corporate society: losing hold of any personal life; Social Media. Yes, the automatons, like that guy from Indiana, fixated on their mobile devices, Enthralled by technology. No time for smelling the roses, or watching the clouds move through the sky, like humans are chained up to machine time, *telepolitan* time, synchronized with the speed of the digital matrix, the wheels turning faster and faster, ever increasing acceleration. What did that man say about our thoughts running faster than nature? And now, the digital technology driving it all, incessantly, dragging all of us into some crazy future.

I was done. I requested my bill. Exhausted from the day's activities, even though I'd been sitting for the last hour or so, I left the restaurant and headed straight to my hotel.

11: Pompidou Centre

Lying in bed, not quite asleep, not quite awake, I had fallen into another reverie. Inside my mind, an inter-dimensional portal released its images one by one. Certain memories, places in my past, opened and presented themselves like I was almost still there.

Here was the softness of a distant summer evening, the twilight blue lingering in the western sky, lush summer foliage rustling in the night, and then a clear expanse of starry sky opening above. I was gliding through the night, in the back seat of the car, the windows rolled down, the breeze on my face, the coolness of the Michigan evening an antidote to a hot summer day.

It was a seemingly disconnected memory from my childhood. I had kept returning to this one passage. Something was pivotal there. Then again, why privilege one moment in time over another?

A place holder of attention is always fixed in the present moment, the Now. What is present, exactly?

In the present moment, I was riding the crest of the wave, approaching the edge of time: asymptotically? There are limits, yes, boundaries: a picture is framed, and a performance has its finale. But for now, I continue riding the wave, each moment presents itself as the fresh edge of time, a moving point in time. There was a paradox here.

I recalled the overheard conversation in the restaurant. What had the Indian man said about time; something about different rates of time; falling through time?

I thought back on the conversation with Christy: time-freedom, the integral structure. The words sounded in my mind. I struggled to confer some sort of meaning to them, and to my own experiences, outside of any conversation.

From the standpoint of the mental structure this dilemma between the present moment and the sea of memories seemed insoluble. Time freedom would seem to suggest that no memory had privilege over any other; all were to be integrated, but what of the present moment? Yes, but that slips away as well. Time freedom would indicate that our conscious presence was free from any point in time or space. This train of thoughts unraveled and slipped out of my control.

I sat up on the edge of the bed and looked at my reflection in a mirror propped against the wall. The edge of the mirror split my face in half. There was something baroque about my visage. The tumbling curls and waves of my hair matched up with the curvilinear embossed patterns on the wallpaper.

It was no accident I was in Paris. I wasn't really of America. I was born in America, but not really a part of it at all. I wasn't even really from this time. I knew that even as a child. I hadn't identified myself with America, I had always been intellectually suspended between America and Europe. Now, I was decoupling myself from any nation state. World citizen? I was an Earth citizen or Planetary citizen. There would still be nation states, and city states, fitting within a proper hierarchy: Paris to France, New York to America, San Francisco to California.

What did it mean to be a planetary citizen, then?

From the light on the building outside, I could sense it was already late into the afternoon. I reached for my phone to check the time. It read 11:24, still set on MST. I needed to add 8 hours to get the correct time. I made the mental calculation. Yes, it was now 7:24 pm. Another day had slipped away from me. Evening was quickly descending on Paris, but for the first time in days I felt somewhat refreshed.

****

I went down ancient Rue St. Jacques, the Roman axis that divided Paris into eastern and western sections. I passed Saint Severin, its weathered stone walls seeming almost geological in their antiquity, and then through crowds of people clustered near the river.

I traversed the Seine at Pont des Coeurs and stepped onto the Île de la Cité. This was the heart of the city, and the place of its origin; the sailing vessel that was emblazoned on the insignia of Paris pointed to this beginning. The island itself was like a boat. Here was Notre Dame to the east, and then Sainte Chapelle to the west, like the two pans of a scale, balancing out Paris, or perhaps they were the generators of the city's secret energy, with their repositories of hidden relics.

I crossed the river again and walked by Tour St. Jacques, its gothic façade illuminated against the purple twilight, and followed Rue St. Martin toward the Pompidou Center.

A large motley crowd gathered in the plaza in front of the museum. Inside, hordes of people milled around the lower levels, and a continuous stream of visitors headed up and down the escalators. I reached the upper levels and paused to take in the view of Paris at night. A feeling of festiveness filled the air this evening. A certain charge was in the atmosphere, tonight the museum would be open later than usual.

Looking out from the high deck over the city, my eye picked out the landmarks. To the west, the Eiffel Tower crowned with a rotating beacon, further west the towers of La Défense. To the north the domes of Sacré Cœur on Montmartre, and then to the south, the modern high rise, Tour Montparnasse, marked by a shimmering vertical band of blue light.

I turned away from the panorama and re-entered the museum. Walking up to the fifth floor, I started at the beginning of the twentieth century collection. The landing at the top of the stairs displayed two works by Picasso, a Braque, and a large work by Léger, these works acted as a prelude for the coming distortions of form.

From there, I entered the galleries, starting with the oldest works, a handful of smaller fauvist paintings. At first, I felt distracted and disengaged, still adjusting my mind to being in the museum as opposed to the streets, so that the initial works seemed uninteresting, even somewhat dull. Vlaminck, Derain, Matisse, these were works from a different era, still redolent of the 19th century.

Initially I felt insensitive to these paintings. I paused in front of one of the brightly colored works by Matisse. Trying to find the proper frame of mind after the physicality of walking through the streets, and through the hubbub of the plaza out front, required a shift in my sensibilities. Stopping my mind, I slowed myself down to read the forms and colors, trying to slip into the right frame of mind.

I moved on to the cubist galleries filled with the early explorations by Picasso, and Braque, and even a few works by the younger Spaniard, Juan Gris. These paintings captured my attention. Picasso was the perfect example of a formal innovator. He had the air of a perpetual outsider, a wandering harlequin, a shifter of shape transforming space. Arriving in

77

Paris, he crossed over some sort of hierarchical threshold, entering the more advanced symbolic order operating in the city. Here in Paris, he encountered other fellow travelers, agents of transformation, mutational individualities like Braque and Matisse. Roped together like mountaineers they transformed the symbolic order of Western culture, creating a new spatial and formal order perfectly suited for the dawning century.

I paused in front of a descriptive text, written in both French and English. Reading about the cubist artists...

"...borrowed from Cezanne... his geometrization of forms and finding in African sculpture a model for non-naturalistic expression...abjuring perspective their paintings first created volumes as cubic masses and then flattened and deconstructed them into facets."

A rapid series of realizations came to me. Here, at the beginning of the century, they were making a fundamental break with the entire 500 year tradition of rendering space; a complete metamorphosis of form- over just four or five years, a self-reflexive project within the discipline of painting, now a conceptual project, and a completely new representation of space.

I read on....*"Color and narrative disappeared. Still lives were suggested by fragmentary outlines, hinting at subjects. The edges of planes, half circles, arrows, all unified in muted grays and beiges. The rhythm of brushwork gives an energy to the composition that may be dense or translucent, forming and un-forming before the eyes."*

Incredible; energy, and dynamic patterns ascribed to painted facets, and inscribed lines. I thought about the revelations of quantum physics, breaking down reality into discrete elements, photons, particles of light. Was it possible that Picasso and Braque read about these scientific breakthroughs back in 1910? Did they know about Planck or Einstein? It hardly seemed likely.

I stopped in front of Picasso's *Guitarist* 1910, barely recognizable as a guitarist. The dissolution of form here was almost complete.

I read from the accompanying label. "...*a crystalline light characterized this phase of cubism...produced by a modulation of beige and silvery grays laid down in a thrum of brushstrokes. The figure of the guitarist seems to appear and disappear- to form and disintegrate...the same signs that construct the figure describe the non-perspectival space.*"

Yes. A sort of quantum effect, I reflected, an ongoing collapse of the wave function, a cycling back and forth; a field of particles in a state of perpetual collapse and re-constitution: A phantom guitarist.

I turned around surveying the room. The Picasso paintings were indistinguishable from the Braque paintings, like they were both channeling the same alternate reality.

I stood in front of one of the Braque's: *Woman with Guitar*, 1913. A face emerged from the planes of muted color, shoulders were framed by black forms. Just below the schematically represented guitar, Braque had painted "*LE REVEL*" with the "*L*" clipped in half by a white triangle. The woman caught between a dream and waking.

I moved on to an even more extreme abstraction. This was another Braque: *L'homme a la Guitar*, 1914. The figure was just barely recognizable, mostly a field of white and beige daubs of paint, and dark diagonal lines. The table simultaneously opaque and transparent. It was like they were pulling away the gauzy film of the macroworld revealing the underlying microworld with its swarm of particles, exposing the multiple planes of reality. Revealing reality as an ongoing metamorphosis.

Suddenly, I felt like I hooked into some train of realizations. Unexpectedly, I felt a chill running up my spine. It now seemed even clearer to me. This vision of how it was back then, some 100 years ago, how the various artists arrived in Paris, and were activated, energized by the preceding formal innovations.

I recollected the imagination from the other night, picturing Paris as a spring, the source of a series of artistic flowerings, one after another, as if there was some signal broadcasting from this place.

Walking away from the galleries, I headed over to the window, wanting to catch a glimpse of the skyline again. Yes, this particular narrative was strongest in Paris. This opening of new dimensions of seeing, triggered by cubism, and then followed by more consecutive flowerings, one after another.

I pressed my face close to the glass. Maybe I didn't want people to see me immersed in this realization, as I peered out at the city lights.

1914. Yes, it all came back to me now. It was June 28th 1914, the assassination of Franz Duke Ferdinand in Sarajevo, the trigger for the cataclysmic events that followed. Of course, nothing was ever the same afterward, an entire old world was left behind, or about to be, at least by the end of WWII.

Yet, weren't the wars symptomatic of some greater titanic upheaval rupturing the space time fabric, spilling the contents of the future into the world? There was an avalanche of technologies, and then the long train of social changes. Here in Paris, the artistic avant-garde glimpsed an image of the future, telegraphing their vision in the formal innovations of space and form. Now art was no longer limited to depicting narrative scenes; the forms were universal, a cosmic language of form. At the same time, the quantum scientists with their thought experiments and equations were sketching out an invisible reality.

I stepped back from the window a little, still looking out at the glittering lights of the city. Yes, with WWI a curtain was drawn on the old world, all that remained were intimations of a previous time, leaving the new generations to digest and integrate the onslaught of changes.

Perhaps, we're still sorting it out, the shock waves continue to reverberate transmitted through the global medium. I had an image of glass shattering, and the ever-expanding cracks branching out from some point of origin to the edges of a big picture window. What about the Arab spring? Tunisia, Libya, Syria, a series of dominoes tumbling eastward, even Ukraine. Were these just the latest fractures triggered by the events almost a hundred years ago?

I returned to the galleries, and the so-called synthetic cubist period. After Braque had left to the front, Picasso continued his ascent. Here were the paintings he made waiting out the war, adding collage, juxtaposing incongruous picture elements, foreshadowing so much to still come.

And then, after the war, it could never be the same. Something was lost, *Ma Jolie*, gone; Braque injured, Apollinaire, with a head wound, and later dead from the Spanish flu. But maybe it was more than those personal losses, he sensed something forever transformed, a world gone, changed in the great switching stations of life. For Picasso, his great perceptual vision of Cubism was dismissed by the grim events of war, and faded away, like a radio signal no longer within range, and cubism became just another stylistic technique in his artistic arsenal.

I moved on to the other galleries. Here were the early breakthroughs into total abstraction. Just on the threshold of the war, a host of artists simultaneously entered into a new pictorial dimension transforming the initial Cubist innovations into a dynamic array of colored form: Kandinsky in Munich, Mondrian in Holland, Kupka and the Delaunays' in Paris.

Sonia Delaunay's *Prism Electricity*, 1914. The world transformed into waves of vibrating color; blue and orange, green and red, bands of radiating color, matter as energy, and the infinite manifestation of light and color.

Nearby, I came to smaller painting, Futurist Giacomo Balla's: *The Planet Mercury Passing in Front of the Sun*, 1916. Suddenly an unexpected inter-planetary element was explicitly introduced, painted in cubist diagonals, and overlapping circles.

Out in the hall, there was a large square painting, Frantisek Kupka's *Autor d'un Point*, 1920. Here radiating circles of ultramarine and cerulean overlapped on a white ground. A blue solar disk enveloped by orbits, rings, auroras, composed of particles, and bands, decomposing, merging into one another. Inner space or outer space it was hard to determine, perhaps inner, turned inside out, a wormhole to the universe beyond. Micro space as the passage to macro space. The birth of cosmic citizenship, I mused.

Next to the Kupka, was a similar work, this one by Kandinsky, painted with a background of subtle pinks and delicate yellows, and circular forms, evocative of planetary bodies, intersecting transparent triangular forms of magenta, red, and orange, rayed out across a register of three parallel lines. Again, here was this theme of opening to a space beyond our usual earthly dimension, simultaneously an inner space, as well as an outer space.

Then Legér: *Element Mechanique* from 1929, a large painting with rigid geometric forms in grey and black, foreshadowing the mechanical world to come. Somehow it didn't feel consonant with the immediately preceding works, and I thought of Fritz Lang's dystopian vision, *Metropolis*.

Across the hall, I walked into a room devoted to the Surrealists. I was quite familiar with these artists. After the war, Dada, and then Surrealism rejected the bourgeois conventionalities, and the authoritarian establishment. Bypassing the rational mind, entering trance states, accessing the unconscious, playing with chance, automatic writing, and drawing, experiments like the *exquisite cadaver*, all in an effort to open up new creative frontiers. Of course, they were influenced by Freud's Interpretation of Dreams, but I couldn't help but think of the quantum notions of a random universe. Were the Surrealists acknowledging that?

I paused in front of a work by Picabia, an empty frame painted gold with wire strung across it, and pieces of cardboard with writing. *"Danse du St. Guy"*. A joke in a way. A similarly spare work by the Catalan Joan Miro followed. "Spanish Dancer". A framed white canvas, with a feather and a piece of cork pinned in the upper center. Miro was more clever, more evocative and poetic than Picabia. On the next wall, a Man Ray film was projected. Here abstract patterns in motion: dots, circles, overlapping, metamorphosing, and breaking down, particles disintegrating in time; psychedelia circa 1923.

Before I left the gallery, I paused in front of a medium size work by Yves Tanguy: *Jour le Lentour*, 1937. This painting seemed to picture an alien landscape, maybe the bottom of the sea, or a distant planet with biomorphic forms receding into the distance, the horizon line indistinct merging into the sky, thin diagonal lines drawn across the atmosphere connected points in space; Lines linking different dimensions?

Then moving on to a series of other galleries a shift seemed to occur. I didn't connect with these later paintings. Something was missing, some enlivening element was absent. I felt de-energized, even slightly depressed. These were works drawn from different European post-war movements that followed in the late-forties and fifties. Art Informel, Arte Povera, Art Brut.

There seemed to be an increasing emphasis on the materiality of the work, or the dominant conceptual aspect became so arid, and abstract, that these works no longer had a

83

living feeling. There was something cynical, world weary about them.

Something had changed. Certainly, speaking symbolically or spiritually, Europe had been eviscerated by the carnage of two wars. The last few galleries were almost totally sterile and mechanical works that seemed devoid of any living element. After the exhilaration I had felt following the visual transitions of the first four decades of the century, and my grasping of the rapid transformations in consciousness these visually represented, I suddenly felt let down. Was this the end of the transmission of new ideas?

I turned away from the last galleries without investigating the more recent works and walked back towards the staircase and went down to the second part of the collection. I sensed there was a break, a discontinuity, signaled by the descent to the fourth floor. This art was now from a different world, a definitively modern world that unfolded after WWII.

I paused gauging whether I should even proceed through the remaining half of the collection. I stood at the entrance of a gallery displaying works by the Color Field artists, a movement that rose to prominence in the post-war years. Inside, I could see a Kenneth Noland painting. White and blue colors; blue grey circles on a bone white canvas background.

Several other works flanked the entrance to the gallery. In front of me was a painting by Ugo Rondinone, a contemporary Swiss artist who was inspired by the original Color Field artists. Here were concentric circles of color vibrating at different frequencies: yellow, orange, red and blue; blurred edges, fluttering rings around a white center.

Next to the Rondinone was a similar work. Peter Sedgley: *Light Pulse*, 1968. A yellow ball of sun on a white field surrounded by a blue aura; blurred edges, vibrating and pulsing in and out on a dark background.

On the other side of the entrance was a work by Robert Irwin. *Sans Titre*, dated 1965. The painting consisted of a field of barely visible minuscule red dots that resolved into an immaterial halo.

Irwin was one of the California Light and Space artists, but this was light years beyond mere light and space, this was painting as hallucinogen. Only with the experience of psychedelics could one fully grasp the work of these artists. They had taken the formal elements isolated by the modern artists; light, color, shape, rhythm and re-assembled them to open some other dimension, or a path beyond to an art of the future.

Off to the side was a smaller room. I approached and read the signage first.

Nicholas Schöffer, Hungarian-French: *Prisms*, 1965.

Inside was a mesmerizing display of colors and light, almost like being inside a giant kaleidoscope, patterns receding into infinity, a hall of mirrors. But wasn't this only a model of the infinite? Aren't we already on the doorstep of the infinite?

The Earth's surrounding atmosphere acts as a sort of stopper, a *cordon sanitaire*, to protect our minds from the shock of the infinite, to prevent us from breaching to any point beyond. Images take us to the doorstep of the infinite. These were merely pointers, fingers pointing to the infinite. This art seemed disembodied, even non-human.

I pivoted out of the room and returned to the main hallway.

12: A Space Odyssey

Looking away from the main galleries that stretched further down the long hall, a nearby subsidiary gallery drew my attention. The signage read: *Stanley Kubrick: 2001: A Space Odyssey*. Intrigued, I entered the dim space.

The ambient light was quite low inside and it took a moment for my eyes to adjust. On the walls there was a display of still photography from Kubrick's film. The images were installed in some sort of backlit digital format. In the far corner there was another adjacent room where I could see the flickering light of a monitor, and I heard the faint sounds of the distinctive soundtrack. The darkness of the room seemed to reinforce the content of the pictures. While viewing the pictures I almost felt like I was floating in space.

I'd seen *Space Odyssey* years before, as a 12-year old in Grand Rapids. Even with my pre-exposure to science fiction, the movie had been beyond enigmatic, a threshold experience, that took me years to digest. The film had exposed me to a realm of experience beyond mere extra-planetary travel, something outside of all normal human conceptions, the cinematic equivalent of giving a child LSD.

But what did this film really represent? Why was Kubrick trying to drop into the normal consciousness of the day a parenthesis of total alienness? Who was Kubrick really? And what was he trying to do? I still had more questions than answers, even some 40 years on.

I looked at the image of the Pan Am spaceship soaring up to the space station. There was something beautiful, even serene about its flight; and the accompanying music, Strauss's *Blue Danube Waltz* added to this feeling. The interiors of the station were equally serene, advanced modern design, extrapolations from a point in the Sixties when it seemed, that the sky was the limit for western culture.

I drifted over to some of the final images. The space pod in the hotel room decorated in an antiquated style, the monolith at the foot of the bed. The ending was in some ways the most inexplicable part of the movie. Where in the solar system was this room? What about the strange sense of time elapsing in some uncanny segmented fashion?

Engrossed in my thoughts, I now realized that the other visitors had mostly left the gallery. There was only one other individual a picture or two to my side. I was still looking intently at the final image of the movie when a voice intruded into my reverie.

"It's astonishing isn't it? What a vision of the future."

I was briefly startled. I guess I had been more engrossed in my own ruminations than I expected.

"Yes, it is," I responded almost automatically.

"Yet at the same time a disappointment, like we as a society fell so far short of this incredible vision." The man swung around and gestured to the other images on the wall.

"I agree, totally," I responded somewhat tersely. It was still quite dim in the room, and I couldn't really make out the man's appearance. Moreover, I was still a bit absorbed in my own solitary train of thought. Oddly, at first it hadn't struck me as unusual that he spoke in English.

"Relegated now to our present mundane circumstances, as if we missed the next rung in the ladder of progress," he continued.

He did have a slight French accent, though he spoke English quite clearly. And as I shifted my position to face more directly towards him, I could now partially make out his features in the dim ambient light.

He appeared to be an older French man, somewhat taller than me, a long face, slightly balding with a long down turned mustache.

"No. Facebook and the internet aren't quite sufficient to make a future," I reflected aloud.

He laughed softly, and then continued, "We don't seem to have had anyone of such bold artistic vision of late; certainly not of the same caliber as Mr. Kubrick."

I thought a bit on the different art movements I had seen in the galleries below, and the faint sense of disappointment I experienced after walking through the galleries devoted to more contemporary art.

"Why do you suppose that's the case?" I asked.

"Nothing can be said definitively. There are many factors at play. Yet, look at this." He swung around gesturing toward one of the images with the monolith prominently displayed, illuminated on the surface of the moon. There was something strangely compelling about his manner and I was intrigued, enough, to hear his views about the film.

"The monolith, you mean?"

"It's a bit literal, isn't it?"

"You mean just using this slab of rock, some sort of cenotaph, or archetypal form, to represent an advanced alien consciousness?"

He shook his head. "I mean, I don't think we have to posit the physical intrusion of aliens onto the surface of the earth to account for our leap of intelligence. If you want to call it that, although even with all of our technological accoutrements it sometimes seems almost laughable."

"Like, we aren't really such a good example of intelligent life."

"Yes, it is disappointing, like I was saying. But that leap of intelligence is truly remarkable, even an inexplicable event. I mean, current evolutionary theory doesn't adequately explain this. So, there is this unaccountable leap..."

"A random genetic mutation," I interjected.

"Yes, but that's kind of placeholder explanation, doesn't it seem? And wherever you situate this event, and that is the other question. When?

"35,000 years ago? Or..."

"Or 90,000 years ago, or 140,000 years ago, or...And whenever we situate this event, we suddenly see the onset of this capacity for symbolic representation. All the artistic creations we see here at the Pompidou, or at the Louvre, are products of this random mutation, this breakthrough." He paused as if lost in thought and then continued in a softer voice, almost whispering.

"This ability to conceptualize is intricately related to abstraction, to have a picture stand in for some object or feature of the world, this leads to metaphoric thinking, yes? And this leads to pictograms and then to language."

"And of course, apes don't create art," I offered.

"Exactly, this is what distinguishes humans from the rest of the animal kingdom. We use our hands not just to draw something we perceive in the world, but rather something that has crystalized inside our mind, something we then make manifest. I mean we are talking about several incredible hurdles for the human animal, no?

"Yeah, most of the time people really don't take the time to reflect on this evolutionary leap, it's kind of glossed over."

"Exactly, it's a profound mystery."

"So, you're saying this idea of an alien intrusion, a monolith for example, that allowed the human race to ascend the ladder of evolution, somehow it doesn't sit right, seems a bit...ah"

"Contrived is the word I would use; exactly, a device really."

"Sort of a Hollywood trick?"

"Yes." he turned away from me a little as if he was surveying the room and then resumed in a lower voice, "Yes, actually a cinematic trope, an unusual one, but one that was imperative to use, because otherwise the story would have been even more incomprehensible, even more enigmatic for the average viewer."

"Kind of like Moses and the Ten Commandments, without a tablet."

"*Exactement*. And, what of the idea of an immaterial presence, an advanced intelligence coming not in a spaceship or in a flying saucer, but rather in the form of a mental intrusion? A long distance extraterrestrial telepathic communication?"

"Of course, that might not have made for the same sort of intense movie going experience."

"No, no. But Kubrick almost achieves this. All we see is the monolith, a placeholder, a cinematic device. Imagine, a being, or beings, so advanced they were able to insinuate themselves into the human mind stream and engender certain evolutionary breakthroughs."

"You mean that thoughts could change the brain matter?"

"Yes, exactly. Thoughts can change the structure of the brain. Imagine, ten thousand years of alien thought projections leading...perhaps, leading to the development of the neo-cortex or to symbolic capacities."

Although I had been enthralled by the drift of the conversation, I suddenly felt a sense of uneasiness, and this line of thought seemed a bit *outré*, even for my sensibilities. And by extension I also began to wonder, who was this man?

Stepping back a little, I surveyed the room briefly, and then added, "So, you're saying maybe Kubrick is trying to subtly jog the viewer's mind, open our minds."

"Yes, exactly, to point us in a certain direction, he is pointing, indicating."

"Of course, we can't take this literally. No monoliths, no excavations on the moon are necessary, really. The monolith is almost like a... joke," I ventured.

"Precisely. Yes, Kubrick realized he couldn't have a movie with nothing in it, but...thoughts. I mean we almost get there, to the moons of Jupiter and beyond without seeing an actual alien visage. And yes, he realized that would be too literal."

"You mean to have Bowman encounter bug eyed ETs, or grays, or some other stereotypic alien at the end?"

"Yes, that would have been kitsch. The movie would have escaped his control if he had staged that kind of scene."

"Yeah, I can see that would have been like a Lost in Space episode, or Star Wars; merely a cinematic cartoon."

We had inadvertently drifted over to the entrance of the smaller gallery where we could see a large screen monitor playing the film, the eerie soundtrack filling the space with dissonant sound. The last scenes were displayed on a wall size monitor; Bowman now an old man, eating a meal in the sterile but elegant rooms of his final destination.

"This is the strangest part of the film to me," I offered.

"Yes."

"Where are we exactly here? I could never figure that out. Moreover, after the plodding space trip to the moons of Jupiter, and then the trip to infinity, the whole sense of time seems to be distorted and altered in some unusual manner."

"Yes, exactly, after the fairly conventional sequence of events we find ourselves at some sort of terminal point where the laws of time are not as we know them."

"I mean, is he actually looking at his future self? And how is it that time seems to elapse in these discontinuous jumps? I asked.

"Precisely, and these aren't just cinematic devices."

"Right, the viewer of the film can see Bowman eating, and then he stoops down to the floor to pick up the broken glass, and we see both him, and his dying-self lying in the bed."

"Yes, glimpsing his future. No. This was intentional; the distortion of time at the ends of space."

In silence we watched the final scene.

He turned to me and said, "Imagine, then the possibility that the monolith actually comes from our future..."

I reflected on this for a moment; a transmission crossing the boundaries of time. I hadn't anticipated an interpretation from this direction.

The man resumed his explanation, "Imagine, as well, this intrusion, taking some form, perhaps a zoomorph, inside the theater of the human mind. A performance or play going on inside our minds for thousands of years, instructing, presenting, repeating, perhaps transforming our synapses, maybe even manipulating the DNA, or controlling how it is expressed. And that said, could these intrusions still be present within us? And what form might they seem to take now in the human mind?"

I had fallen into a train of visual images, thinking about the immensity of time, both future and past. So deeply was I thinking about the ancient past, reflecting on how history had unfolded over the millennia, that I almost glossed over his last statement. For some reason, I particularly lingered on certain images of ancient Egypt I had often seen.

"So, it's possible, you're saying that figures from ancient myths, say Thoth or Horus may have actually been a representation inserted into our minds?" I asked.

"Precisely. Consider this then, going back to the ancients, say ancient most Sumer or India- the beginnings of Vedic civilization, the ancients who guided the human race from time immemorial, even further back, shamans, medicine men; all communed with beings not of this material plane."

"Guides to humanity, going back to prehistoric time," I almost mumbled the sentence as I was picturing something, still inchoate, trying to digest the gist of the conversation. I felt a bit of unease just on the periphery of my thought process.

Disconnecting from the flow of our conversation, which I had been largely receptive to, an abstract voice in the back of my head wondered: How long had we been here in the gallery? And maybe I should be thinking about leaving?

As if intuiting my thoughts in some way, he touched my elbow and started to walk back towards the entrance of the gallery and resumed speaking, as if summarizing his interpretation in a more cheerful, even mundane manner.

"That's not to say Kubrick is not a genius. He is more than brilliant. He knew exactly what he was doing. Yes, absolutely. This was a very deliberate creation, for a specific time. It would not be possible today, nor would it be perceived in the way he intended it to be, if it was shown today. Yes, impossible."

"Really?" I replied, perhaps just as intrigued by this statement as any of the previous.

As we exited the gallery, I had the sense that things were wrapping up at the museum. In the light, I could now get a more accurate picture of who this man was. He was older, maybe late sixties or early seventies. His hair grey, somewhat curly, balding, his mustache elaborately coiled, his eyes congenial, and his face had a friendly mien.

He turned to face me and extended his hand, "My name is Jacques Ashmounian, so glad to have met you, and to have had such a stimulating conversation."

"It was great... a lot to digest." I shook his hand, momentarily forgetting to introduce myself, and then added, "My name is Thomas Moore."

"Well, good to meet you, Thomas. Are you from America?"

"Yes. Actually, I'm from Michigan."

"Michigan!" he exclaimed. "Where about?"

"Detroit, Ann Arbor."

"Remarkable! I taught at the University of Michigan for almost twenty years. I know Ann Arbor very well. I've only recently returned to France, to Paris, my home."

"Really, I spent many years in Ann Arbor; part of my childhood."

An announcement came over the public address system in French, and then in English indicating that the museum galleries would be closing in a few minutes.

Jacques turned to me and said, "You must join me upstairs, at the Restaurant Georges, I'm having dinner with some friends who have recently returned from the Middle East, and you would be most welcome in our company."

I hesitated a little thinking that I might rather just return to my hotel, since it was no doubt quite late already.

Deliberating for only a moment, I responded, "Sure. I would be honored."

'Excellent."

Riding up the escalator to the fifth floor, Jacques inquired, "You are an artist?"

"Of sorts. I'm currently working on a project looking at designs for the city of the future."

"Fantastic."

"And yourself, what did you teach at the University?" I asked.

"Cosmology."

"Really?"

It suddenly made sense to me. Only a cosmologist could conjure up such elaborate speculations on Kubrick's intentions, and the evolution of human consciousness.

"Your last name is Armenian, isn't it?" I probed perhaps somewhat intrusively, since I had a fascination with different ethnic origins, and I had had various friends in Detroit who were of Armenian descent.

"You know Armenia?"

"I'm knowledgeable about world geography, I know it's located in the Caucasus, and it's an ancient land, though, I've never been to Armenia."

"Well, you know more than most Americans. But yes, my father came from Armenia just after WWI, though I was born here in France."

13: Chez Georges

We arrived on the top floor and stood in front of the entrance to the restaurant. The outside dining area was packed with people and as we waited, I gazed out at the stunning view of the Parisian skyline. The hostess, a tall young woman wearing ankle boots, a sleek dress, and an elegant turban, exuded an air of refined insouciance. Jacques said something to her in French, and she waved us through.

I felt a rush of excitement as we crossed the floor of the restaurant. Surveying the crowd of patrons, trying in that moment to encompass both all the people and the spectacular setting, I ended up mostly looking beyond the crowd to the glittering lights of the city.

The interior was more like a surrealistic sculptural display than the interior of a restaurant. The space was filled by large modules with sharp angles and rounded openings; biomorphic forms drawn from the work of Arp or Tanguy. The hyper modern atmosphere was further accentuated with an array of austere geometric forms scattered across the floor; pink cubes that served as seating and sets of angular white chairs paired with tables. The biomorphic modules were placed strategically on the floor to create little coves of privacy that opened up to look out over the city.

We headed over to one module shaped like a skull, its curved interior skin painted gold. Here was a more intimate space, removed from the din of the surrounding space, opening out onto a high veranda with a shallow reflecting pool, and beyond to a view over the rooftops of Paris.

As we entered the module a woman's voice called out "Jacques!"

"Gemina!" Jacques responded warmly walking behind the table to greet an older woman.

Entering from the side, I didn't get a chance to see Jacques' friends until I was practically right in front of their table. The group sat close together facing out towards the city lights. I first noticed an older man who seemed to be of Indian descent, bearded, wearing a turban.

Gemina stood up and embraced Jacques. My eye was drawn to her silk head scarf with its bold red color and swirling arabesque pattern. Gemina was maybe in her sixties, but I couldn't tell for sure.

It was then that I noticed the younger woman. To my astonishment, she appeared to be the same woman I had seen walking into the Passage du Grand Cerf. I flashed back to that intense interlude from the previous day and wondered if she recognized me. I was for a moment dumbfounded as Jacques greeted his friends.

Then, Jacques looked towards me and said, "Let me introduce a new friend of mine, Thomas, an artist from America, formerly of Ann Arbor, Michigan, he is conducting research here in Paris."

There was a flurry of greetings from the group. By their response it seemed that some of his friends had been to Ann Arbor or knew about the place. Jacques carefully introduced everyone seated from left to right, and I shook their hands in order.

First there was Gemina; then Andreas, introduced as an artist from Switzerland, whose shaven head was counterbalanced by his robust beard; Monsieur Suhrawardi Sind, the Indian gentleman; and then finally sitting closer to the window, the young woman: Andromeda. Her dark wavy hair fell to her shoulders, and she wore a stylish burgundy colored dress with varied geometric patterns.

As I shook her hand, Andromeda seemed to betray no sense that she recognized me in any way. In fact, as I had a chance to take in her appearance, I was not entirely sure if she was the same woman, I had seen the day before. I laughed to myself, again reflecting on my foolish proclivity for mistaken identity in respect to certain women. She was atypically beautiful, with a slight trace of the Middle East in her appearance, her rounded cheeks framed her nose, and her brilliant eyes sparkled in the light.

Jacques turned toward me and explained, "Gemina, and Andromeda, have just returned from a lengthy stay in Beirut. And since Monsieur Sind is soon to depart for points even further east, we have arranged a meeting tonight here in this spectacular setting." In that moment, as I surveyed the group, I had a sense of some familial resemblance between Gemina, and Andromeda.

Gemina interjected warmly, "We're speaking English tonight since Monsieur Sind is with us, and Andreas, from Canton Uri, is fluent in English as well."

"Andreas and I have recently embarked on a collaborative project studying the nature of our solar orb in relation to the wider cosmos," Jacques explained looking towards Andreas.

"Yes, that is true," Andreas responded. His precise English betrayed just a faint Germanic accent. "My main focus for several years has been on light, and the influence of different electro-magnetic frequencies on consciousness; Jacques and I are now directing our attention further afield, so to speak."

In front of Andreas was a plate of stuffed grape leaves, with some hummus and chickpeas on the side. Andreas also had a glass of white wine, but the others were drinking only tea.

Gemina poured me a cup, and then volunteered generously, "Well, we were saying that it's only been in the last one hundred years that humanity has received a complete picture of the world."

"Yes, the human race had no idea of the true antiquity of its origin, nor of the nature of its biological genesis," Andreas articulated his words with an alpine crispness.

"A window was opened, revealing the secrets of the universe," Gemina added in a distant way, glancing out toward the night.

"Indeed," Jacques responded. "It wasn't until the early twentieth century that we could even confirm the existence of other galaxies beyond our own Milky Way. And now we know there is a universe filled with billions of galaxies."

I thought about those images of the void filled to the brim with stars and distant galaxies: The Hubble Deep Field. It was like some creator deity had squeezed out tubes of glitter paint to inseminate the cosmos. They were composite pictures though, compiled from hundreds of exposures and multiple orbits, nothing the human eye could actually see. Moreover, these galactic images were flat, devoid of any three-dimensionality. We couldn't really see the depth of space, its most salient feature; we could only read the surface.

I remembered an early road trip out West, one incredibly dark night on the side of a desolate highway deep in the Painted Desert, lying on the hood of a friend's car, and staring into that cosmic void. I don't know if it was just from the fatigue of a long days driving, but the guard of my mind was let down, and I suddenly had the sense of space having depth, the stars telescoping in and out; receding, floating, or standing out from the fathomless depth. All those thoughts came back to me in a mere moment, just like a million galaxies clustered in one small sector of space.

I took a sip of tea in part to be polite as the others conversed; unexpectedly, it had a refreshing sweet mint flavor.

"Yes, the scope of human knowledge has increased exponentially," Gemina added.

"First, we have Einstein's brilliant insight into the nature of the matter. Incredible forces bound up in very fabric of the universe. The existence of the universe itself contingent upon this perpetual release of energy," Jacques explained enthusiastically.

It was astonishing, I acknowledged to myself. The many scientific discoveries that had occurred hardly more than a hundred years ago, and even now still accelerating, even now so much information or knowledge we can barely process, anymore. All of it just uncoordinated facts, that don't answer the deep questions; that don't explain the human predicament of being placed into this cosmos, or the reasons for our presence on the earth.

"A primordial energy, even, persisting into this very moment," Andreas added.

"The work of Ptah," Gemina interjected.

In the middle of what seemed to be a scientific discussion, I was surprised to hear a reference to the Egyptian deity. I glanced briefly at Andromeda, who seemed to be contained within her own thoughts, her profile framed by the dark of the window as she gazed out toward the lights of Paris.

"Yes, the Memphite cosmogony." Jacques nodded his head thoughtfully.

"The fire of Ptah is the source of everything in the universe," Gemina explained.

"Indeed, our planet is enveloped in a radiant cocoon of solar energy, a vast electromagnetic field extending even beyond the farthest outer planets; the heliosphere," Jacques offered.

"This Earth is bound to the sun in many unseen ways," Gemina remarked.

"Yes, the sun is a dynamic entity," Andreas explained. "Consider the spectacular peak in solar activity in the late 1950s."

"Even now the sun is changing," Jacques added darkly.

"That's correct," Andreas responded. "The number of sunspots has decreased dramatically. We're approaching a pronounced solar minimum. The tide of cosmic rays is pressing in on the Earth from the galactic frontier. Even the thermosphere has contracted to an unprecedented extent. The sun is without question weakening. Our current research indicates that Solar Cycle 25 will be quite diminished, one of the weakest in centuries."

I looked out toward the night and the city lights glittering behind the windowpanes. The earth had changed in less than fifty years, something wasn't the same, I had felt this on some deep inner level of my being.

"There are many hidden orders that are coming to light." Gemina's voice broke into my reflections.

"To speak of global warming, or even climate change, is too reductive; the whole planet is being altered. The massive scale of the technological culture is literally destroying the natural world," Andreas added.

China's rise to power had altered the balance of the earth, it now seemed obvious. The enormous spewing forth of carbon emissions from its coal power plants; the lifting of a billion people out of poverty, all sucked into the maw of the Neo-Liberal economic system had definitively tipped the scales. I thought of the contrails again, crisscrossing the skies of the entire planet, spinning their gauzy webs. Wasn't there a correspondence between the dramatic increase in jet travel and the alteration in the climate?

"A moral choice confronts humanity. If the whole world embraces the western lifestyle, that will spell the end of the natural world as we know it," Gemina asserted.

"Yes, a grave threat faces humanity. Titanic forces, formerly bound within the earth; autonomous forces, beyond the control of any one individual, have been unleashed and are now shaping events." Andreas remarked.

Something had changed in the tone of their voices. A darker more serious mood now intervened into the conversation.

"We need to see who, or what is the real adversary," Gemina advised, and then continued.

"If we look clearly, isn't their ultimate goal to destroy the natural world? Their attack on the Earth proceeds from multiple fronts, not just the destruction of the natural world. The very ground of our existence is threatened, even what it means to be a human being is threatened. There are those who would cede control of the world to something less than human, a formula or an algorithmic code, ostensibly to improve our lives, but really it's a massive scheme to facilitate their profits; and even worse, there are the advocates of AI, who believe that consciousness can be duplicated, and who aim to integrate the machine intelligence into all facets of planetary life."

"Indeed, we approach a dangerous threshold in human affairs, a precipice." Jacques nodded somberly.

"Only a hundred years ago the Earth faced a similar turning point," Andreas added.

"The full import of which humanity failed to comprehend," Gemina interjected.

"Even with the loss of millions of lives, and a continent shattered," Jacques shook his head.

There was a pause for a few moments. The group seemed to be lost in some internal calculation. Again, I gazed out at the city lights visible behind the empty silhouettes of our reflections.

It was irresponsible to think that everyone on the planet should have access to the Western consumer lifestyle. The capitalist machine promoted this delusion. The symbiotic relationship between capitalism and human desire, coupled on a global scale, had released a terrible, even diabolical force upon the earth, the full extent of which was still unimaginable to the human mind.

The environmental crisis was often presented to the public as a mere byproduct of human progress that would be solved once enough people faced the scientific facts; but wasn't it really the fault of the elite capitalists who in their rush to maximize profit and market share, completely disregarded the scale of the industrial footprint in relation to the holding capacity of the planet? Was it even possible that those who controlled the levers of global development had succumbed to a destructive dystopian meme, and were bent on destroying the natural world?

"From the systems level we can see tremendous pressures are building up in the world, in all domains of human activity." Andreas broke into the silence. "Technology is accelerating all the trends, dangerously amplifying many negative tendencies. Fundamentally the technological system has become autonomous, outstripping the moral, the ethical realm...leaving the most intrinsic questions of the human condition hanging in the air, unanswered."

"Forces of fragmentation, and disintegration, rather than of integration," Jacques added.

"Exactly," Andreas affirmed. His voice shaped his words with a certain precision and sharpness, "The current economic regime drains meaning from the lived experience. For most of the world it is just a question of survival. For the rest, particularly here in the West, life becomes a superficial game of material acquisitions and diversions."

"Yes, yes," Jacques nodded. "The dominance of the consumer culture, subverting all other impulses, what's that expression...ah... bad money drives out good."

"Well, the truth is that a large proportion of the population are like automatons, controlled by media and marketing, lulled into a passive state of mind, barely cognizant of the new realm of understanding that has opened up, they are still embedded in an old paradigm, or even slipping into other more regressive and archaic tendencies." Andreas explained.

Gemina entered the conversation again, and as she talked, I now felt in some sense that her voice was familiar to me.

"The new consciousness is only partially operative at this stage."

She paused, seeming to look inward.

What new consciousness was she referring to? I wondered.

Strangely, in that moment, as if in answer to my own question, I had a vision of an extraterrestrial intelligence entering into our world, not by spacecraft, but rather by some invisible interstellar medium.

"...and there is a danger that the window will close before long," Gemina added, her eyes almost closed.

"The old models are no longer sufficient, no longer capable of handling the multidimensional nature of the current crisis," Jacques said.

Was Jacques cognizant of the structures of consciousness? I wondered. Had we referenced the structures during our conversation in the gallery? I couldn't remember for sure.

"Indeed, the challenges of this time are beyond the comprehension of the powers that be. The great nation states, like America, have become virtually ungovernable," Gemina said.

"Are you saying we've reached the limits of reason?" Andreas asked. He seemed to say it almost rhetorically. Perhaps they were expanding on all these topics mostly for my benefit, merely to bring me up to speed, I thought.

"I'm saying that we have reached the limits of a world where reason ruled," Gemina responded.

"Indeed," Jacques said. "And that was the situation just before the Great War, where supposedly reasonable men led Europe to a total catastrophe."

Suddenly, feeling like I could actually contribute something of relevance, and thinking about some of the art movements I had viewed downstairs, I added, "That's what the Dada and Surrealist artists thought; subvert rational thinking was their goal."

For the first time Andromeda looked towards me, and smiled briefly, nodding her head as if in agreement.

"*Exactement*. The Freudian unconscious flooded into the public consciousness, courtesy of André Breton and company," Jacques added excitedly.

Gemina continued, "In the Twentieth century we see this unprecedented infusion of new ideas, almost an overloading of the previous frame of reference. A cascade of technological innovations- air travel, radio, atomic energy, television, the collapse of the colonial empires, the doubling, then, tripling of global population, all pushing the world to this threshold, exploding the very framework of the old paradigm."

"The subtlety and complexity of the problems confronting the planet have outstripped humankind's ability to even represent or model them," Jacques declared.

Perhaps the conventional way of representing the environmental crisis was entirely wrong, even misguided. The problem seemed to be more ethical, maybe even aesthetic. How could we countenance living in a world where the integrity of nature was desecrated? The consequences of the path humanity is on were just plain ugly.

Gemina continued, "Only by shifting our perspective can we perceive the hidden orders." The tone of her voice had changed slightly, now lighter, even more hopeful.

"Like Petrarch on Mount Ventoux, except now it's not only one individual, it's the entire planet that needs to have a vision of the whole," Jacques added, seeming to smile underneath his mustache.

"In the Alps, we can sometimes see clouds materialize out of the empty sky, water vapor suddenly made visible," Andreas reflected in a calm, almost meditative manner gazing out the window.

An image came to my mind from a summer hiking trip in one of the sky islands of Southern Arizona. There the crisp blue air of the morning would miraculously give way to the billowing cumulus clouds building up higher and higher over the mountaintops to form the afternoon thunderstorms. The orographic effect, as water vapor condensed out of the air lifted over the mountains. The invisible water vapor flowing through the atmosphere, only made visible by the barrier of mountainous terrain.

"We can discern the hidden orders in many phenomena, climatic changes, in market fluctuations. And now, the universe is compelling us to recognize them in order to solve a puzzle, for the sake of humanity's future," Gemina stated.

"Or at least a desirable future," Andreas replied.

"Yes," Gemina remarked. "The consequences of not seeing these hidden orders would be catastrophic."

"I fear humanity would be relegated to some lower, material plane, a struggle for survival in a world of grossly diminishing expectations," Andreas added.

It was then that Monsieur Sind entered the conversation, "I'm not sure we can judge the future world in terms of our present frame of reference." His voice had a calming melodious quality, evincing a sense of composed certainty.

"It may be that future generations will be equipped to handle a degraded state of affairs. On some karmic level, they may still extract what they need from their physical incarnations. The planet will continue to act as a platform for realization."

"*Naturlich*," Andreas responded, "However we would be remiss if we fell into a stance of passivity."

"Of course, I'm not suggesting passivity. No, not at all." Sind sighed, and then continued, "Perhaps we've come to a boundary, beyond which we must travel by intuition, imagination, and inspiration."

"Not fantastic daydreams, mind you," Gemina added, as if entirely conversant with Sind's direction of thought.

Sind resumed, "It is true, I think we have to call to mind the needs of this time, as you have all intimated, moreover there is a call to recognize the transcendent dimension. Humanity has lost its pole star, its orienting guide. Imagine the great navigators crossing the oceans without reference to the true north. Yes, modern humanity is adrift. Our anthropocentrism has left us blind to the greater realities, even greater beings."

"The starry realms, as the ancients would say," Gemina interjected.

Perhaps triggered by hearing Sind's voice, and then hearing Gemina immediately afterward, I suddenly realized that I had heard both Gemina and Sind's voices the night before at the Indian restaurant on Rue Dauphin. A strange chill ran up my spine, almost an epiphany, as if the content of the conversation had been a response to my own inner questioning, a missing piece of my own personal puzzle.

"Yes, indeed," Sind responded. "I think in some ways modern humankind has entered an almost autistic mode of apperception, a refusal, in a sense, hard wired into the global technological culture, a refusal of the other side, the unseen world, even though these unseen dimensions are more than ever before acting directly on our world."

"Before long, the unseen dimension will collapse into the general awareness. An avalanche into the consciousness of an otherwise unconscious humanity," Andreas offered.

"I fear a catastrophe will be required before the planet will make the necessary shift," Gemina added distantly.

There was a pause during which Gemina looked out the window, and the others seemed lost in thought. Andreas took a bite of some of the food on the table, the first time that I noticed anyone eating.

Jacques picked up the thread, "So, why are we here?"

There was a sense of ambiguity in his question. I wasn't entirely sure of what context Jacques was referring to, if this was something for my benefit, or addressed to a larger question.

Andreas responded first, "As we said earlier, the consumer culture, and the preoccupation with basic survival has foregrounded material concerns. This combined with a sense of the accidental nature of life, and the pervasive belief in determinism, has without question drawn awareness away from the unseen realm."

"It is as if the global consciousness was deliberately drawn away from a view of the Starry Realms," Gemina reflected looking out to the city lights. "Yes, changes on the material level will only generate more disorder, only through the immaterial can effective change be made."

"It is through art that we can find a path beyond this predicament. A higher practice, drawn from the unseen realm, the wellspring of both art and science, reaching out to the mind stream of humanity," Andreas explained.

"Unquestionably," Jacques said firmly. "One cannot remain passive in the face of such an impending global avalanche. One must either get out of the way, or as they do in Switzerland, initiate preparations," He finished smiling, looking toward Andreas.

"In the dark of night, a lighthouse guides mariners on their journey," Sind added cryptically, with a sense of finality.

Something seemed decided, some unspoken consensus had been reached, but I couldn't put my finger definitively on anything concrete. There was a pause for a moment, and imperceptibly, a subtle shift in tone, and a warmer feeling suffused everyone gathered around the table.

Gemina looked directly at me, as if anticipating some sort of response from me regarding all these matters. "So, Monsieur Thomas, what sort of research are you undertaking here in Paris?"

Suddenly put on the spot, and still digesting the multitude of ideas presented at the table, I only partially composed my thoughts in order to respond.

"Well...I'm trying to find inspiration here in Europe for my own artistic work. I'm interested in the idea of the avant-garde, particular here in Paris, and how it moves on to New York during the war. And how these avant-garde movements and ideas stimulated a cultural revolution, and applying these ideas to designing the city of the future, I'll be contributing to an exhibit opening this October in San Francisco, called *Different Futures* that will hopefully promote innovative solutions to urban problems." I wasn't even sure if my response was coherent.

"Excellent!" Gemina exclaimed.

"Isn't this remarkable?" Gemina added looking briefly over at Jacques and then turned back to me, "Andromeda is an architect. She recommended meeting here at Georges tonight, with its astonishing futuristic interior." She gestured with her hand at the surroundings.

For the first time in the evening Andromeda spoke, "That's true. This is a perfect setting on many different levels."

Her soft, but self-assured voice captivated me as she continued, "I've been working with biomorphic design, drawing my inspiration from the hidden order found in nature, and bringing this order into the architectural process. A design more harmonious in its relation to the natural world, rather than the brutal intrusions we find in so much of the built environment."

"Yes, particularly those monstrosities found in much of the commercial architecture cluttering up the landscape these days," Jacques interjected.

"Well, Thomas, you may have some additional material for your research," Andreas added, seeming to smile beneath his beard.

"Yes. You might consider visiting Andromeda's studio," Gemina added.

As if prompted by an unseen signal, everyone in the group stood up, and the gathering was called to a close.

Slowly walking toward the exit, the conversation was focused on Sind's immanent departure for New Delhi and talk of some future meetings. Apparently, Jacques and Andreas were working on some sort of artistic project in a studio on the outskirts of Paris. We all went down the escalator together.

I was almost oblivious to the view of the city as we slowly descended from the upper floor. There was a kind of late-night excitement that permeated the atmosphere. All around us large crowds were exiting the Pompidou after a long and festive night. I was still caught up in the excitement of the conversation, and the remarkable turn of events that prompted me to meet such an unusual and stimulating group of people. And I was deeply intrigued, even enchanted, most of all by the presence of Andromeda.

I felt puzzled, even mystified by her appearance, tonight, still thinking, that there must be some connection to the woman I had seen the other evening. I played with the idea of asking her if she had been in Passage Grand Du Cerf. I decided it would be inappropriate, particularly after the elevated conversation, to raise such a mundane question.

When we reached the ground level, I shook hands with Gemina, and Monsieur Sind, and lastly with Andromeda. She expressed her warm regards, and best wishes for my research in Paris. The three of them left together. Jacques and Andreas lingered for a moment in the open plaza.

Jacques turned to me and inquired, "So, where are your accommodations?"

"Sorbonne Arts, just across the street from the Sorbonne."

"Excellent location."

Jacques reached into his coat and produced a card, handing it to me saying, "Thomas. You must visit us soon. Andreas and I are working on several projects, which I think you would find very intriguing."

With that they both walked off in the direction of Brancusi's studio.

14: Holy Planet

Weeks earlier, I had arranged to meet a British architect who was working on a project in Paris. And since I had overslept, I now found myself rushing to prepare for the meeting. The architect, Christopher Fields, had a temporary office on the Left Bank, and my goal was to discuss his work, and his vision of the future city. I had read an interview with him from a couple years back, and I liked his independent thinking. So, I sent him an email introducing myself and my interests, surprisingly he responded.

I also wanted to show him some of my own architectural ideas, a few drawings, rough sketches really, that captured some of my design strategies. By intimating that I might be interested in displaying some of his work in the upcoming exhibit in San Francisco, he had consented to a brief meeting. We had arranged to meet at a natural food shop called Holy Planet located on Rue Serpente just a few blocks off the Boulevard St. Michel.

The name of the shop reminded me of something I had wanted to say to Jacques and his friends. The mainstream's approach to global warming, or global climate change, was all wrong. The appeal to temperature increases and parts of carbon per million missed something more important about the whole situation. The planet was an oasis floating in galactic space. To contaminate it with plastics, or hydrocarbon discharges fouling the atmosphere, was more of a moral-aesthetic issue, an affront, really. This was an ethical, and artistic issue, more than a scientific or economic one. Until the dilemma was confronted on that level there would be no significant change.

The details would require huge sacrifices by the global population, many of them unacceptable to the current dominate global capitalist agenda, and dispiriting to the aspirations of the masses who groomed by global media aspired to all the appurtenances of the west.

To confirm our meeting, I logged onto the computer in my room, a sleek Apple product placed on a narrow table in the corner. The French keyboard baffled me at first, the letters on the keyboard were arranged differently, and it took me a while to get to the login page of my Outlook account. My expectations for a smooth entry into my account were further frustrated when Microsoft blocked my entry. I was logging in from a strange terminal in a foreign country and this was suspiciously unacceptable to Microsoft. I had no time to play around with Microsoft and their security questions.

I quickly jumped over to the bed, searching among my belongings for my phone. I could look at my email on my phone, I remembered. The battery was low though; I had yet to find a suitable recharging device and logging on to Outlook was often a pain on the device since it seemed to be dedicated to Facebook.

I turned on the device, and the annoying vibration surged through my hand. Just turning the device on and off was part of the control exercised upon the individual by the technological system.

"ANDROID", it read on the screen, apparently with no irony. This was certainly some sort of alien technology, perhaps from

Alpha Draconis, something wholly incompatible with human nature, even incomprehensible; the algorithms, and the data packets traveling through the ether, packets of zeros, and ones, transmitted over certain frequencies relayed from station to station finally reaching me and my device here in Paris.

Again, Outlook blocked my efforts. I was able to access my account. I could see an email from Christopher Fields: "Meeting at Holy Planet..." it read, incompletely. I tapped on the message. And, yet for some inexplicable reason Outlook wouldn't allow me to open the message. I tapped the screen several times trying to open the email message. Still, Outlook remained dead. I closed the program and tried to login again. This time the phone became sluggish. It wouldn't even allow me to reach the Outlook login screen. The battery power was now down to 19%. I dropped the phone back on the bed, frustrated.

***

Departing from my hotel, I walked through a small plaza decorated with gushing fountains, and then paused in front of the Librarie Philosophique, peering at the window display marveling at something that seemed improbable in America, the existence of a bookstore devoted exclusively to books on philosophy. I had seen so many bookstores here in the Left Bank, I jokingly thought to myself that there were probably more bookstores in Paris than in the entire United States. People here in Paris still read books, whereas in the States there was a veritable campaign to dismiss the book as if it was some antiquated medium superseded by the incessant demands of the technology age. No time for reading books when there were so many text messages to review. I turned down Rue Champollion, continuing my rumination.

The incessant emphasis on business, and utilitarianism, was a steady drone in the background of American society. One could be taken up by all the trivial demands on one's time. The whole structure of society seemed to siphon off one's personal energy; constantly driving to reach destinations in the sprawled metropolitan areas; the distractions of the media, internet; and endless bills to pay. Of course, everyone was designated as a consumer. Yet, what was really being consumed was one's own being, gradually eaten away, piece by piece. Everyone was yoked into, and regimented by the dictates of the corporate society, and just looking factually at the global situation, wasn't it the US that consumed the vast bulk of resources, and energy, as if America was some sort of global black hole sucking up all the available energy, inexorably dragging everything into its web.

Yes, America was a lunatic nation. It valued all the wrong things. All you had to do was look at the inane feed of trending searches on your digital device. That's what Americans seemed to value the most. More importantly America had a distorted notion of what freedom constituted, valuing the right of any given individual to do whatever they pleased, regardless of its impact on other people, or even on society as a whole.

Across the Boulevard St. Michel, I could see several more bookstores lining the street. I walked past the ruins of the ancient Roman baths, and finally reached the Boulevard St. Germain. Looking west, I was struck by the park like cityscape with its lush foliage, green against a dull grey sky. The trees softened the hard edge of the city and muffled the hubbub and commotion of traffic moving up and down the busy thoroughfare. I crossed the boulevards and then turned down Rue Serpente, a small quiet side street just beyond the intersection.

In America, I felt like I was held under the influence of a strange consensual hallucination, fixed into some predetermined configuration. Here, I was free of that strange constriction. Perhaps, by coming to Paris, I was somehow relieved of that drag on my energy, something was lifted, and I was temporarily liberated, discharged into an autonomous zone. There was an indefinable lightness I felt here in Paris, particularly on the Left Bank: A restoration of the full spectrum of possibilities inherent in life. Even more, there was an energy in the air here, one could maybe even call it a libidinal energy circulating about; a medium of Eros suffusing the city, an *engagement*, often signaled by the flirtatious eye.

In Europe, a vestige of the old social order remained acting as a buffer to the onslaught of American digital media. There were more chances or options for real social encounters in an organic city like Paris where people still walked the streets or traveled the Métro. In America, people set their lives up almost as if they wanted to avoid unscheduled social encounters. Here an unexpected encounter could happen multiple times each day; people were thrown together in public places. Cities like Paris and London were zones of accelerated social development.

I now approached Rue Danton, crossed over the diagonal of the side street, and paused for a moment to orient myself. I picked up Rue Serpente on the other side of the street and found the store just around the corner: Holy Planet.

The health food store was just a niche of a place. A brightly lit narrow space crammed with products, and up front, two small boldly painted tables by a large window affording a view of passing pedestrians.

I purchased a freshly squeezed *jus d'orange* and sat down by the window and awaited the architect's arrival. In my typical casual fashion, I had brought only a sheaf of hand rendered drawings. I stared out the window at the pedestrians, and above, at the undifferentiated grey sky hanging low over the city. I entered a reflective state, absent momentarily of my

116

usual ruminations. After a while, a well-dressed middle-aged man walked up to the storefront, paused for a moment, and then entered. I recognized him from the photos I had seen on his internet site.

Christopher Fields was probably in his early sixties, fairly young looking for his age, blue eyes, a ruddy complexion, dressed in a tailored suit, a cheerful cream-colored shirt worn casually with no tie. He had a rather congenial personality, and an easy disposition.

After cordial greetings, I once again mentioned my project envisioning the future of the city. He chuckled a little bit at my description, and then related that he had been working on a new project here in Paris for most of the year, while his main office was in London. Right away he started to talk about creativity and the contemporary global architectural climate.

"Well, I think these days it's difficult to be original, what with the internet affording everyone access to the same information. The same models are viewed by young architectural students everywhere, whether you're in Sydney or Sao Paulo, all the same things are popular."

"Really?" I replied, a little bit surprised at how quickly he launched into a polemic.

"Absolutely. The capitalist system homogenizes the center, and then defines creativity as whatever happens on the periphery." Such a statement would have probably labeled Christopher as a socialist in the States.

"The periphery of what?" I asked, fascinated by his line of thought.

"The homogenous mass; the zone of difference between the interiority and the outside." I pictured the anonymous suburban masses of America largely relegated to passive forms of entertainment.

"But there's a lot of innovative work, isn't there? Like some of the new designs for green architecture here in Paris, or in Spain."

"Yes, of course, there is great work. What I object to is the marketing mentality that has compelled architects to look at themselves as products, or even more absurdly, as a brand. Can you imagine Christopher Wren as a brand or Vitruvius?"

"The Vitruvian Brand," I laughed.

"It's appalling, really, the corrosive effect of marketing. We're in such an artificial environment now. It's more challenging than ever to be innovative, let alone get your work out there."

"Really?" I replied.

"Yes. We're developing into this global monoculture, where the vernacular and the idiosyncratic are buried under a tidal wave of redundancy. Everyone knows about Gehry, Foster, all the other big names. And then every city must have its own version of some star architect's exploding collapsing building. A replica culture, essentially."

"So, are you suggesting that some sort of sheltering can be fruitful for the creative process? Even by limiting knowledge, something more creative can open up?" It was a notion that went against the grain of the hyper connected contemporary ethos.

"Well, yes, if you put it that way. Limitations are the source of creativity, aren't they? If you already know every design permutation beforehand, if your visual sphere is already proliferated by all the possibilities, if your software can generate untold variations on a single idea, the wellspring of innovation is embarrassed into silence."

"That's a strange sort of paradox. Too many choices paralyze," I mused, part of me drifting off, thinking about the implication of this in fields outside architecture.

"Exactly, creativity has always flourished in situations that are contingent, even, adverse."

"And self-satisfaction isn't conducive to creativity?" I trailed off barely finishing my sentence. I was thinking again about the stultifying suburban environments in America, like those I grew up in, and had longed to escape, an environment that seemed to be the antithesis of any artistic creativity.

He paused a moment looking out the window as if marshaling his thoughts.

"An artist needs to differentiate themselves from the masses. In some way, a necessary distance must be created, and then a space opens up. A space in which to be creative."

"Would you say that social media disrupts creativity?" I posed the question rhetorically since I was totally agreeing with the direction of his thought.

"Social media destroys interiority. It disrupts the subjective experience. You could even say it foils a certain... brooding quality. It's during those brooding moments, maybe taking a walk in the country, going out into the unmediated environment. That's when one enters the most creative states."

"Of course, there is no subjectivity if someone is always back and forth texting, or busy sharing on Facebook," I said sarcastically.

"Social media is awash with narcissism. Isn't it? There is a certain facile quality to all those kinds of experiences, which is contrary to the interiority of the creative experience. All surface, all sameness of the corporate platform, even, a homogeneity that levels difference."

"On the other hand, do you think the history of form is important?"

"Yes, tremendously. A knowledge of a repertoire of historical forms is essential, in any genre. Paradoxically, there is a collective amnesia rampant in society, even to a certain extent in the architecture field. Of course, there is a balance to be found between infinite information flooding into the marketplace and the complete absence of knowledge."

"What about the market?" I asked rhetorically.

"The market amplifies certain memes, and these tend to dominate any given domain or discourse, the remainder are relegated to anonymity. Difference is increasingly diminished in the global market."

"Kind of like the popularity of vampire novels in America," I quipped.

"Vampire novels?" He laughed, and then continued smiling, "Yes, the market propagates mediocrity, and segments the populace, dictating tastes to different demographics."

"All top down instead of organic?"

"Exactly. Winners and losers are chosen by the dictates of capital, which only incidentally has any relation to the quality of life, to pleasure even, or any artistic sense."

"And we're stuck living in cities that are increasingly unsuited to human habitation; but they're great for capital investments."

"Sadly, that's true. And we architects are increasingly marginalized in the whole process." He laughed a little, and then paused looking out the window.

I thought about how great a distortion the market generated, probably even greater than we realized, immersed as we are in the medium of capital, impressing itself into our lived experience, even into our consciousness of self.

After a moment he continued, "Let me return to this idea of self-articulation. We see this throughout the universe, on every level. Every object, every being, expresses something intrinsically unique to itself, whether it's conscious or not."

"Even stars or planets?"

"Indeed. Nature is an incredible model of creativity, every star, and every human being has an inner capacity for self-articulation."

'What about nations, or peoples?"

"Of course, we see this historically, don't we?"

"I was thinking about the Arab spring, the impulse for freedom spreading like a chain reaction. And, in Spain, with an autonomous region like Catalonia," I mentioned, thinking of my plans for visiting Barcelona.

"Yes, exactly, an intrinsic identity manifesting itself, differentiating and then self-articulating."

"It's interesting to me that some places have been so conducive to artistic creativity." This was part of my central thesis.

"Places such as Paris, you mean?"

"Yes. It seems to exert a magnetic effect on artists. Like Picasso, and all the others being drawn here." I pointed out.

"There was something already going on here in Paris. There was a discourse present, a conversation in visual forms, a body of artistic practices. People were drawn here to enter into that conversation."

"The Café Guerbois." I remembered the famous café on the Avenue de Clichy.

"The Batignolles School," he acknowledged.

"They needed places to meet, and exchange ideas."

"Indeed, and they also had artistic predecessors on hand: Manet and Courbet, and a Delacroix to offer a theory of color, the old Masters in the Louvre to copy; all important elements for engendering their creative development."

"What were the conditions that allowed Picasso to make his breakthroughs, here? It seems almost unprecedented, the creation of Cubism, and then collage. Where did all these ideas come from?"

"Yes, it is amazing. All the elements came together here in Paris. He lives at the Le Bateau-Lavoir. The influence of Cezanne, the African masks, the Iberian sculpture, all contribute, maybe something more, though. His outsider status, gives him more perspective, more freedom to step back and see how things fit together."

"What about Florence in the Renaissance?" I asked.

"A fascinating case."

"I heard the city had only 60,000 people during the Quattrocento, and yet such an outpouring of creativity."

"It shows that quantity isn't the key."

"An optimal scale then is essential."

"That may be an important aspect. In any event, it's not a question of sheer numbers."

I had thought a lot about the idea of scale. Some cities in America seemed big enough but they lacked a certain creative inertia.

"There were the workshops, too. Ghirlandaio, Verrocchio, and others," I offered.

"Yes, a repository of artistic techniques, models and practices to follow. Even earlier, the examples of Brunelleschi and Ghiberti were important. Imagine Leonardo and Michelangelo walking through the streets and seeing all these incredible masterworks: The Duomo, The Gates of Paradise; inspiration for the aspiring artist."

"Wouldn't we be able to cultivate the proper creative environment, as some sort of design of the future?"

"If you could exercise such control on a large scale, hypothetically, yes."

Christopher stopped short of fully articulating this idea seeming to be temporarily lost in a more complex thought. He paused looking out the window for a moment. I started to become vaguely conscious of our conversation having exceeded its allotted time.

He looked back from the window, laughed almost to himself, as if recalling a private joke, and then started again, this time leading down a more metaphorical tangent.

"Let me extend the idea on creativity further, another inflection you might say, and utilize an insight from developmental biology that may pertain to what I was saying earlier. At a certain point in a child's life, a process called myelination occurs in the brain, a process of sheathing of neuronal pathways, and a cutting away of many of the earlier synaptic connections in the brain, a pruning, so to speak. And with that a certain quality we associate with childhood, the pliability is lost. Yet, this process sets the stage for a higher level of cognitive development."

"Less is more," I added.

"Yes, Mies van der Rohe; a poignant metaphor."

I thought of that wide-open quality of childhood, the sense of limitless possibilities. I wondered, was such a diminishment necessary to usher in the next stage of life? I felt something melancholy about this realization recalling the undifferentiated mélange of impressions from my childhood, more feelings associated with images than anything definite.

I asked Christopher about his project here in Paris.

He pulled an iPad from his suit pocket and called up some imagery from his latest work. The project was a multi-story structure located on the far edge of La Défense in the western suburbs. One entire face of the building was a sleek curved glass form. Peering closely at the image, I could see a slight undulation in the curved shape, giving the building an asymmetrical appearance.

"The southwestern face of the building is oriented towards the annual track of the sun, allowing maximum use of solar energy. Inside this glass facade we essentially have a greenhouse. Ten stories of hydroponic, and even more sophisticated aeroponic technologies are being installed."

"Urban agriculture."

"Yes. This is essentially a prototype. We propose to supply an on-site restaurant with produce on a fortnightly basis, as well as a public market located in a garden at the base of the structure. On the opposite side of the building we will have research facilities, labs for enhancing nutrient value."

"Christopher, before you leave, I'd like to show you some of my sketches," I interjected, starting to worry that we were running out of time.

"Well, I'd be glad to look them over," he responded warmly.

I pulled out my folder, feeling unprofessional in comparison to his sophisticated digital renderings.

I placed the drawings on the table and began a brief description.

"This first drawing is a project for a ferry terminal at San Francisco International airport."

The terminal was shaped like a giant seashell, narrowing at the entrance on the side of the airport, and then widening as it opened out onto the waters of the bay. The outer surface of the building was modulated with wavy bands much like a nautilus shell.

"Brilliant." He remarked smiling.

"This second drawing is an idea for affordable housing. 36 units, on a floating pod moored near an old port facility south of downtown." The building was a terraced six story structure based on a truncated hexagonal form.

I continued, "Essentially, these are loft spaces. Each unit has 1000 square feet, with a glass wall facing the bay. Windows can be opened, so a fresh breeze can enter the unit. There are two sections to each space, with a slightly elevated kitchen acting as a divider. The side facing away from the bay has a small balcony with views of the city."

"Interesting."

"And you can't see this detail, but the walls would be insulated sufficiently to deaden any noise coming from other units."

Christopher paused looking down at the sketches. "Intriguing ideas, do you have a client?"

"No."

"Hmm," he paused for a moment. "These are nice ideas, but I don't think any bank would ever give your project the go ahead."

"Why not?" Inadvertently, I sounded a bit defensive.

"There's no profit in this. It's not a high-end project. Most investors are looking for something that has a higher market value."

"But San Francisco needs this. Most of the existing housing stock are cramped, shared spaces, with astronomical rents. There's definitely a shortage of good space."

"Granted, that's all true. However, investors won't be interested in this kind of project; the market isn't interested. And honestly, the market will never solve the problems of affordable quality housing in San Francisco, or any other similarly afflicted urban center," he declared and then glanced down at his wristwatch.

"Oh...I am so sorry." He stood up abruptly. "It's a bit later than I expected."

I tried to maintain a cheerful facade even though I was a little disappointed at the harshness of his analysis.

"I appreciate you meeting me, here."

"Well, Thomas, it was good meeting with you." He smiled as we shook hands.

He paused a moment before leaving and seemed to be considering something.

"Listen, Thomas. I will be back in London this summer, and we have an internship available. If you are interested, contact me. There is only a small stipend available, but you would probably find the work stimulating. It would be good to have you onboard." He handed me his card and then briskly walked off.

15: Jardin du Luxembourg

I walked down the street, lost in thought. Crossing the boulevard near the Odeon metro, I continued along a smaller side street, Rue Monsieur de la Prince, steadily heading uphill.

I reflected how inextricably we were all defined by our times. How broad social events regulate the freedom of individuality, everyone carrying the burden of living within the web of historical circumstances. Nowadays, we have the burden of living in the era of free market, Neo-Liberal economics, the dominance of big capital, and big technology impressing into our lives, into our very being, imprinting the entire earth even.

But how to fight against these impersonal forces and find freedom. How to create an autonomous zone, my own private Catalonia of creativity? I was still thinking about the autonomous provinces of Spain, and perhaps mixing metaphors, trying to form some model for activating my own agency.

I felt a strange sense of time gone terribly awry. Even 30 years ago, America had been a more congenial society, possibilities seemed more open, the body social less hurried, less stressed, the structure of society more pliable, less hardened into some inflexible regime.

Perhaps this was a function of my own physical existence in time, the unfolding of my own life, the closing of certain pathways, all eerily consonant, even synchronous with greater world events. In a way, I felt I had lost touch with some intrinsic part of my personality in the avalanche of history, or the collision of my own life with historical events. The full spectrum of my being had been stifled, somehow, even now, it was mostly under wraps. The lost continent of pictures from my childhood, that I encountered intermittently, always signaled to me the distance between who I really was, and where I currently found myself in time. How was I to bridge this gap?

Certainly, there had been pivotal moments that marked the phase transitions into the present era: The Arab oil embargo of '73, and then the AIDS crisis of the 1980s, events definitively ending the expansiveness of the mid-century: and then the strange hardening of society since the turn of the century, the definitive corporatization, and even militarization of America since 2001.

Where does one find agency in the wake of these titanic historical forces? I thought back on what Christopher had said about creativity: break away from the masses and find your inner voice or something like that; self-articulation had been the word he used. Something of a deeper import seemed to be intimated by that idea, some thread that I couldn't quite get a handle on, something to do with freedom. Like, if there was freedom, or agency, and I did want to believe there was, though I couldn't really prove it, the truth of it may lie in this notion of self-articulation.

There was a funny sort of kinship I felt with Christopher, like we might have been destined to meet in some strange sort of way. A kindred soul, particularly when he mentioned the source of his creativity emerging from those subjective, brooding moments. Yes, a walk in the country, outside, in nature, away from the press of media, and away from the hubbub of the city, could be restorative, healing; even inspirational. I already knew that, of course. Those walks in nature had often allowed me to gain perspective on different issues, breaking away from the clutter and craze of daily life.

It was then, looking up the street, I realized that I was heading in the general direction of the nearest slice of nature in Paris, the Luxembourg garden. Slightly altering my course, I took the next right, and headed more directly toward the park.

I made my way behind the Odeon, and then crossed the street walking along the edge of the park, passing in front of the museum at the Petit Luxembourg. A sign out front announced the art exhibit "Pissarro à Eragnay. *La Nature Retrouvée*".

Pissarro was the key figure in the circle of the Impressionists. He saw the need for an alternative to the Salon, he was the glue that bound the group together. And then later, he influenced Gauguin, he spent time painting in the country with Cezanne, he showed Van Gogh how to work with light and color. Without him the artistic transmission might have foundered.

I came to the entrance of the park and entered through the large wrought iron gates of into its green space. The park itself was like an Impressionist painting. The lush cover of the trees, and shrubs also muted the din of the traffic. I felt like I was falling into some distinctly deeper space, one step removed from the city. The smell of fecundity, of earth, and plant matter softly touched my nostrils. If the Left Bank was the heart of Paris, then this garden was the green lungs for that heart.

Moving along the path, I instinctively headed for a spot I had visited once before. It was an opening along the western edge, more like a natural forest clearing, as opposed to the more groomed sections of much of the park. There were a series of openings, one could even call them rooms, formed by the arching trees, and different masses of shrubs acting as borders. I remembered previously finding an intimate space backed by flowering shrubs and a small bench in front of an old leaning catalpa tree.

I passed by a tall linden tree with green moss on its trunk, and then diverted from the path and walked onto the grass, over to a large copper beech. Its massive trunk was wider than my arms could encompass. I ran my hand along its smooth bark, inhaling the verdant scent of this woodland giant.

Pausing, I felt a certain rootedness, here, in this very place. There was a softening, a lightening of my being, an inner relaxing. I felt more relaxed than I had in a long time, a sudden casting away of accumulated concerns. The gentle waving of the tree branches and the leaves, a light caressing sound woven with higher pitched bird songs hidden off in the foliage, lulled me into an even deeper, almost meditative place. For some moments, closing my eyes, almost losing track of time, I just listened, following the rustling of the tree branches. I looked up towards the top of the tree gazing at the overlapping pattern of branches and leaf formations set against the uniform grey of the sky. Then, breaking into this spell of natural sounds, off on a more distant level, I heard the distinctive siren of the Parisian ambulance. I looked down again at the grass and moved away from the tree.

It was then, out of the corner of my eye I sensed someone sitting on the bench behind me, partially obscured by a flowering shrub. I hadn't noticed the figure before, and it was quite possible the person had silently seated themselves, as I stood by the base of the giant beech. Feeling a bit self-conscious, I walked behind the bush and back onto the path without really looking at the figure.

As I came back on to the path, I could see the man was wearing a turban perched low over his forehead, his eyes almost closed as if he were napping. I suddenly recognized the bearded profile from the night before. His garb had seemed incongruous in the modern interior of Georges, now it seemed to perfectly blend into the forested alcove of trees and greenery.

"Monsieur Sind," I said, almost reflexively, and then quickly wished I had been more discrete, since it seemed he was meditating.

There was just a moment's pause. Almost, without turning his head, he acknowledged my presence with just a subtle change in his posture.

A faint smile passed over his face.

"Ah. Monsieur Moore."

"I'm sorry to disturb you."

He now looked over at me, his dark eyes opening wider, seeming to fully take in my presence.

"Ahh...yes. Life is dissatisfying, isn't it?" He intoned mellifluously.

Whether he was referring to my intrusion, or maybe intuiting my own recent ruminations, I wasn't sure. I laughed a little, feeling a bit self-conscious, thinking he had probably noticed my pensive introspection at the base of the tree.

"It's peaceful here, a refuge from the hustle and bustle of the city," I offered as an explanation for my presence.

"Indeed. Here, one can feel the earth beings."

"Earth beings?" I had been so absorbed in my own introspections that I found his comment unexpected.

"Yes. Earth beings have resided here long before human habitation, before Paris was Paris, beings who were present at the origin of this place."

He looked about at the wooded clearing as if these beings were evidently visible to human sight. I wasn't entirely unfamiliar with the possibility of nature spirits. I had often wondered about my own connection with nature. On occasions, I felt I might have connected with some sort of natural energy particular to a given place. Yet Monsieur Sind spoke with a degree of certitude beyond my own vague notions.

"Maybe, I felt these beings when I was standing by the tree," I suggested, reassessing the surrounding foliage, blindly grasping for some more tangible sense of what Sind was talking about.

"It's possible you had some intimation of these beings. In the normal discursive consciousness, though, it would never be more than just a general feeling, a faint sense of something indefinable just beyond perception."

"Normal discursive consciousness?" My comment wasn't so much a question, as a pondering repetition of his phrase.

"Yes, our usual mode of thinking is a barrier to perceiving these beings. In fact, beyond the discursive intellect, is a greater part of yourself that is you that your conscious mind isn't even aware of. The waking consciousness is just a fragment of who we are, like a boat on an ocean. There is so much more that we are only dimly aware of."

"Like dreams, the subconscious, you mean?"

"It is true, in certain dreams we sometimes can get a glimpse of these other modes of consciousness. What I'm speaking of is beyond the sometime chaotic dream world, even."

He paused briefly looking about the clearing, as if checking to see if anyone else was in listening distance. Then looking towards me he resumed, "The normal human being is locked or fixed into a fairly restricted band of consciousness."

He paused, and looked back out into the clearing, laughed a little, almost to himself and then continued, "Yes, you might even compare it to a satellite or some Mars lander with only a limited bandwidth of visual perception, registering the extraterrestrial or interplanetary space only in the infrared or ultraviolet band of the spectrum."

The picture that formed in my mind was of an iceberg, with the greater part of its mass submerged below the surface.

"So, we need to increase our bandwidth, so to speak?"

"Well, yes, but it's not so easy. Especially, if you think you can just increase your normal analytical, linear way of thinking. That won't do," he paused a bit. "But, if you can recall the way children see the world that might..."

"The saying from the Bible, be like children, or something like that," I interrupted, recalling the well-known passage, but also thinking of my own childhood, and the continent of images that often seemed to beckon to me from that world. I was starting to feel a slight tingle of excitement, like I was on the verge of some answer.

"Indeed, there is the proverb from the New Testament. And that points to an important truth. Think back to how you were as a child. How you saw the world. Everything was fresh. No preconceived ideas, no baggage of memories or old emotional responses."

"Yeah." I almost had the feeling of being drawn into my childhood memories, back into that continent of visual images."

"Humans usually don't see things anymore. They just fall back into a semantic replica of the world, a facsimile, a simulacrum. Do we really see this tree?" He pointed to the Beech tree, "Do we feel its presence?"

"I'm not sure," I responded tentatively, looking upward at the branches and green foliage.

"Sometimes language gets in the way of direct experience."

"But that's all we have, to articulate our thoughts and feelings," I countered, maybe feeling a little unmoored.

"Exactly, that's the medium we live in, mostly, and it binds us, but trees don't speak English."

Sind stood up and walked toward the tree.

"Even our emphasis on precise 20/20 vision is sometimes an impediment to experiencing a different mode of consciousness. Take off your glasses," He added, looking toward the tree.

I was near sighted, and I usually wore my glasses in public, especially roaming around a city like Paris, trying to take in all the visual stimuli, but I removed my glasses and looked up at the tree. I could still see things, of course, but instead of well-defined branches and leaves rendered in precise detail, I just saw a blurry mass of color; after a moment though the outline of the tree resolved.

It was softer. The green foliage was almost like an impressionist painting with different daubs of green and grey-green, instead of the sharply defined details. I looked at the whole of the tree. The size of the tree somehow looked bigger. No longer confined to the frame of my glasses, it swelled out to fill my field of vision.

"Feel the tree's being," Monsieur Sind intoned before the tree.

I paused for a moment taking in the tree, moving closer to the trunk.

The two of us were gathered around the base of the tree staring upward. I slipped into a similar state of reflection as I had experienced earlier. This time lingering longer in that indefinite in-between state, trying to sense something, perhaps too self-consciously at first, but after a few moments, or minutes, my attention drifted, and I began to be conscious only of the scent of the bark, and another moist, leafy smell. The light seemed to become dimmer, as if the clouds were getting thicker, or the day light was diminishing. I closed my eyes.

In my mind I could see a tree of sorts, or rather, a branching pattern, leaves overlaying on leaves, green and brown, green and grey-green, roots reaching downward, an earthy fecundity tinged the edge of my thoughts.

The leaves rustled slightly. I felt a feeling inside me, a faint sense of joy welling up, mixed with a kind of nostalgia. I rested in that feeling.

"Yes," I exhaled. I felt slightly elated for seemingly no reason.

"The trees are dreaming," Sind said almost whispering.

"Dreaming?" I looked over at him.

"Yes, in a dreamtime, much slower than humans, closer to the source. Most of their being remains folded deep in another time."

"Another time?" I was puzzled by his mentioning of time and dreams in relation to the trees. Didn't we share the same time frame as trees? The same seasonal changes: Summer, Fall, Winter, Spring?

"Different rates of time define different states of being."

I had always felt myself more placed within a particular geophysical location, more moving through space, rather than journeying through time. The wind sifted through the leaves again and I thought I felt a drop of rain.

"Aren't we all meeting in the same time?" I wondered.

"Time is expansive enough, that it appears paradoxical to our typical viewpoint. In truth, we are falling through time," Sind remarked.

I had an image of human bodies, un-arrested, plunging into a great abyss.

"Yes, but what is time?"

"Time is the speed of love. The plural dimensionality of being means there are many different times. Part of you shares the same time as the tree, another part of you is captured by the sequential time of Western culture, another part of you is outside of space and time, and another aspect slips back and forth between these different temporal modes. Yet time appears to be an always present medium in which we find ourselves."

"The plurality of being," what an intriguing notion, I thought.

"Yes, one of the complications of being human; yet here in the West you wall yourself off into an intellectual bunker, exiled in tick-tock time."

"But why do we have this feeling that time eludes us, it slips away? Where does it go?"

I looked over at Sind, moving away from the trunk of the tree

"Where do we go?" He laughed quietly, as if he had told a joke.

Now, I felt a couple of rain drops in quick succession and heard a faint pitter patter on the leaves.

Sind continued, "The mystery of time is in the present moment. We are always with this moment, the eternal now, but our attention is too weak to hold it for more than a few moments. Think of how it can't be fixed, like quicksilver it eludes our grasp, yet we can't escape it. It is the true miracle of experience."

More raindrops were falling now, and the sky had taken on a darker shade, a light wind moved through the trees. I was caught in a deep thought, trying to register the import of Sind's remarks.

The present moment, I kept turning that phrase over in my mind like it was mantra. It had reminded me of something else, or the drift of Sind's remarks had triggered another constellation of thoughts. I dimly sensed a body of realization submerged in my consciousness slowly stirring to life. I was searching my mind for some connection and thought back to the previous night at Restaurant Georges, some question that had been raised by Jacques. I suddenly recalled that it had prompted me to wonder about the even broader question of our purpose here on earth.

"Why are we here?" I asked knowing almost immediately that it seemed naively open ended. I felt more rain drops coming down, now in earnest, the trees around the grove swaying together, sighed in a chorus of different leafy sounds.

Monsieur Sind looked towards me and seemed to smile slightly in the increasingly dim light.

"To consciously find our way back to the whole," he said, and then added, "And in the interim not to live in negative thought patterns, like anxiety, or fear. Free yourself from those burdens, that weight. Lighten yourself, be like a butterfly, floating, gliding. Less you free yourself from those burdens of negativity, nothing more need be known about our situation here as incarnated beings."

"I see."

I felt some sense of realization, though still many more questions lingered, inarticulate for the time being, in the back of my mind.

I intuited that Monsieur Sind had finished talking with me. Even though he was calmly standing, almost like a statue, seemingly unmoved by the rain starting to fall in earnest, I felt an impulse to leave the park before the rain increased in intensity.

Reading my thoughts, with hands folded, he bowed slightly towards me, turned around and started calmly walking away from me.

16: St.-Germain-des-Pres

I turned in the opposite direction, walking back towards the entrance on Rue Vaugirard. I hoped to find some shelter from the rain, perhaps under the sidewalk eaves or at a cafe down on the Boulevard St. Germain.

The rain had increased now to a steady drizzle. As usual I was unprepared, failing to have obtained an umbrella, even though they were offered at my hotel. Although the rain was falling steadily, it wasn't a cold rain. On some level, I was initially oblivious to the dampness, all the while still turning over in my mind some of the things Monsieur Sind had mentioned.

To get back to the whole, he had said, as if we were only broken fragments of being marooned on this planet in some sort of flawed condition. Then he had mentioned the eternal present moment, as if there was only this one present, one that we somehow couldn't take in, in its entirety.

In that case most of humanity also seemed doomed to a sort of terminal incompleteness. And then there was that phrase, bodies falling through time; another strange metaphor. I tried to get my mind around this notion. If this was so, then even the few minutes since our encounter, I had fallen past that particular moment in time, hurtling who knows where.

137

Apparently, everyone else was also falling through time, so their movement wouldn't be apparent either. Hadn't Einstein had a similar visualization, something about jumping off a roof, and falling momentarily into a weightless condition where gravity and acceleration canceled each other out? Perhaps our experience of time was analogous to this. For a moment I felt like I wasn't walking but rather falling down the sidewalk towards the Boulevard St. Germain. Was I falling towards something? A threshold? I wondered.

I tried to remember some of the conversation I had overheard at the Indian restaurant, or even the night before at the Pompidou Center, but my mind seemed frozen.

Perhaps, merely the physical activity of negotiating my way through the wet sidewalks of the Left Bank was preventing me from remembering those moments.

Yet, that was strange. How could I access a memory one moment, and then in another it would seem to be withheld? Like someone hunting through a warehouse for a stack of memories as if they were stationary goods. Another visual metaphor.

Perhaps, I needed something like Ariadne's thread to find my way through the labyrinth of the mind. It was a funny metaphor to come to me here on the rainy streets of Paris, the city as a labyrinth, Paris as labyrinth, the city as mind, with different structures representing internal functions or congealed memories. It was a funny chain of thoughts, visual images, that seemed to unravel in less than a moment.

Almost simultaneously, I thought about the sunny isle of Crete, and the ruins of Knossos, another trip, years ago. That was all like a dream, now, really; the verdant Mediterranean landscape surrounding the ruins, the mountainous backdrop, a sculpture of the bull horns framing the mountains, the double axe, the Minotaur, and the cave of Zeus somewhere up there in the mountains, another chain of images unwinding in less than a moment. Where is thought, anyway? Perhaps I should have asked Sind that question.

As I approached the boulevard the rain started to come down even harder. The noise of the traffic, tires driving on wet pavement combined with the sound of the rain pouring down. Across the street I could see the Metro entrance, and the old church, Saint-Germain-des-Prés. Hadn't I come this way before with Christy? The other day we had caught a glimpse of the church, I was sure, perhaps from a different angle. Even that seemed like a distant memory, a different slice of time. Maybe I could take the subway somewhere to kill time until the rain ceased.

I crossed the street toward the church. Inexplicably pausing for a moment, I stood in the rain in front of a kiosk that was promoting a music festival. Visually taking in the bulk of the ancient church veiled by the rain, aside from the tower, the structure seemed to resemble a boat, an ark even. Changing my mind, instead of taking the Metro, I decided to enter the church. Looking through a small garden, I noticed a partially open side door, the nearest entrance that I could see and quickly walked towards it.

Upon entering the church, what struck me first was the smell of incense. I was aware of the sound of the rain outside, but all was quiet inside. The contrast between the din of the streets and the interior was marked.

Once my eyes adjusted to the dimness, I realized the ancient church lacked the more elaborate decor of the typical gothic cathedrals like Chartres or Notre Dame. There was an almost unfinished, even rundown quality to the interior, like it was under repair. I looked to my right up toward the altar, and then walked toward the front gazing to my side at a succession of alcoves, and above at a procession of stain glass windows that brought a soft grayish blue light into the interior.

I stopped in front of one of the windows with an intriguing geometric design of repeated cubes tessellated over the entire surface of two arched panes. The pattern ambiguously flipped back and forth. At once seeming to recede into space and then conversely to project outwards. Within a circular upper window, a smaller circle framed a design of a solar radiance surrounding a gold pyramid containing strange lettering. I gazed for a moment at the symbolic image, trying to recall where I might have previously seen anything similar. While contemplating the imagery, the feeling came over me of being removed from the elements, sheltered from the chaos of the world, both human and natural, in an almost timeless medium. There was a persistence over time, something even more ancient than the Roman Catholic Church, came over me.

The muffled sound of thunder reverberated outside.

I turned away from the window.

After having stared at the illuminated windows, my eyes needed to readjust to the dim interior. Gradually, I surveyed the many rows of chairs arrayed in the center of the church. There seemed to be no one else in the church except one lone figure several rows back from the front, hunched over, probably in prayer. Approaching closer to the altar, I gradually discerned more of the figure. The person was bent over, almost entirely wrapped in a drab brown garment.

Not wishing to intrude, I held back, and sat down a couple rows further back at the very edge of the aisle. Looking toward the altar I surveyed another array of stained-glass windows, seemingly from a different workshop or era, depicting the various saints or apostles perhaps.

Suddenly my silent contemplation was disrupted. The person in the front broke out in a spasm of physical contortions, knocking the chairs aside, all the while loudly moaning, the sound echoing through the hollow chamber of the nave. The figure fell to the floor writhing and moaning.

Reflexively, I rushed toward the trembling person splayed out on the floor. I could see now that she was a young woman, a nun. All but her face and hands covered in the coarse brown garment of some monastic order. She looked to be barely twenty, with dark eyes, and a soft, unblemished, childlike face.

Bending down over her, I was speechless. A distant memory from my childhood came back to me, a time during a Sunday mass, a young boy sitting next to me had suddenly, and startlingly, fallen into an epileptic fit, breaking the stiff decorum of the church service.

Leaning closer, I gingerly touched her arm, and looked into her face. Her eyes were dilated pools of black, filled with tears streaming down her cheeks. Saliva was running out of her mouth, and she seemed to have trouble breathing, a labored inhalation, gasping for breath. Her legs were splayed, kicking away at the neighboring chairs, with one hand on her lower abdomen, the other one clutching at her hips.

The moans came in between almost whispered words that I couldn't make out.

The cries came increasingly louder in pitch, resounding loudly through the hollow chamber of the church. There was the sound of footsteps rushing up from the back of the church. I turned to see two other similarly garbed nuns running down the aisle.

She continued crying out. It sounded like she was speaking Latin, or maybe Spanish. She was lifting her hips off the ground, shuddering, vacantly starring at the ceiling. Impulsively, I firmly grabbed her torso with both arms trying to pull her body down.

"It's Ok," I said uselessly.

Two nuns rushed up toward us, and I moved aside as they knelt on either side of the afflicted woman, one holding her right arm down, the other with a small plastic bottle pouring water on her forehead, wiping it with a white cloth.

"*Tranquilo. Tranquilo,*" one of them loudly whispered. Large and more robust, she was now holding the younger nun down with both arms.

The other nun was rapidly chanting a prayer, "*...gratia plenum, Dominus tecum. Benedicta tu in mulieribus et benedictus frutus ventris tui...*"

It had been decades since I had been in any church service, but the Latin intonations came back to me now like an ancient memory. Just then in the background, I heard the sound of more footsteps, and more remotely, the sound of a walkie-talkie or some communication device punctuated the sacred space with the sound of static. Someone must have called emergency personnel. Another older nun, and a man, a priest or monk of some sort, ran up and knelt at the side of the woman.

The young woman's fits seemed to be subsiding. Her body was calmer now, but her breath was still heavy, and a vacant, dreamy expression remained on her face. I stepped back a little bit, disconnecting myself from the group. I was quite startled, and suddenly realized how much this young woman's state had touched me as well. I realized my heart was pounding, and my own eyes were watering, as if, just by proximity, I had been affected by her condition.

It was then, in the back of my mind, some disconnected part of me began to consider that someone might think I may have triggered this young nun's epileptic fit. I stepped back a little further as the group seemed to be totally focused on the girl's condition.

I heard another group of people coming down the aisle, with heavier footfalls. The sound of choppy static, intermixed with some garbled words in French from a communication device, announced the arrival of the emergency personnel. This group seemed to include the church caretaker who cleared the chairs away from the prostrate nun and picked up other chairs from the floor moving them to the side. The emergency crew bearing a stretcher knelt by the woman's side.

Even more people arrived. Tourists, or other visitors, gradually flooded into the center of the church where the young woman lay. Their intrusion had the effect of breaking the spell of my subjective experience. Turning around I was ready to slip away when I momentarily hesitated. Wanting to get one more glimpse of the young woman, I approached the crowd huddled over her, and saw her head now lying on a pillow of some sort.

Someone had removed the brown hood from her head, and I could see her soft dark hair pushed back from her forehead. Though she wasn't conventionally beautiful there was something attractive, even compelling, about her youthful features. There was a certain freshness to her face, and still flushed from the strange interlude, it now seemed to me she barely looked over 16; such a young age to join a convent, and forgo any of the regular pleasures of life. She seemed to be talking softly, conversing with either the medical personnel, or one of the other sisters, now that she seemed to have returned to a relatively calmer state. I leaned closer trying to catch a strand of the conversation.

"...*una luz verde*," I heard her say. It was Spanish. I wasn't precisely sure what it meant. 'luz', like from the English word 'lucid', meant clear, and also there was the name of the province, Andalusia, the land of light.

Not trying to be too conspicuous, I edged slightly closer. "...*una luz brillante verde, a mi alrededor..*," She continued.

I was unsure of my understanding of the language, but it seemed she was saying something about light' and then...' *alrededor'*. The last phrase was beyond my abilities to translate. '*al-re-de-dor*' I played with the rhythmic repetition of the syllables.

I moved away tentatively. Part of me was reluctant to break away from the group. Or perhaps it was really the young woman I didn't want to leave behind. Although, I was tempted to ask one of the other nuns what the young woman had been saying, I restrained myself from engaging them, feeling perhaps it would be too intrusive, even an embarrassment for them.

Also, I felt some personal connection, even something intimate, about my encounter with the young woman. And a conversation, and further questions, might dispel the feeling I had, a feeling I wanted to nurture on my own, perhaps in private contemplation. There was something I couldn't put my finger on, beyond words even. Even something beyond my rational mind, some other part of my being had been touched.

I pulled away and walked down the aisle towards the main entrance. The door was open, and I could see the emergency vehicle outside. It was strange, I hadn't heard the distinctive Parisian siren. It was still raining, but now only a light drizzle. I walked out on the sidewalk briefly pausing in front of the church before turning the corner and heading down the street towards the boulevard Saint Michel.

As I walked in the light drizzle, I sensed that a certain energy had been released, freed, in me, but also all around me. There was that indefinable electricity of the Left Bank flowing along the thoroughfare, and all about, in the air even. It was early evening by now and the crowds and traffic had a lighter, even festive air.

When I reached the hotel, the concierge handed me a message. It was from Jacques, a brief note. It indicated I should visit his studio space in Belleville the following night at sunset. His address and some directions were included.

17: A Cosmic Perspective

Late in the afternoon I crossed over the Seine, walking to Châtelet where I took the Métro to Belleville. I recited the names of the stations like they were mantras: Hôtel de Ville, Rambuteau, Arts et Métiers, République, Goncourt, Belleville. Each name conjured up an undifferentiated mélange of colors and associations.

From the Belleville station I went by foot. The streets led me increasingly upward, through the park, and up a steep series of steps climbing ever higher. At this rate Jacques must live on the highest point of Belleville. I paused at the top of the steps taking in the view of the city spread out below me, lights twinkling against the faint fading glow of the sunset.

It had turned out to be a beautiful spring day, and I had spent most of the afternoon leisurely walking along the Seine. The rainy weather system that had lingered over Paris for the last few days had shifted further to the east as it raked across the continent, replaced by atypically cool and dry air. The sky had completely cleared out, and as I ascended the steps, a soft breeze followed me, and I marveled at the deep blue of the early evening sky. The earth was just perceptibly turning, rotating into the night.

As twilight descended on Paris, I noticed that none of the lights were on along the street. I stopped for a moment in the middle of the narrow street, partly to get my bearings, but also just to savor the atmosphere. It seemed atypically silent, with no vehicles going by or any other pedestrians in sight. I felt something remarkable inside, a feeling of delight flowing through my limbs. I listened to the sound of the breeze coming up the sloped street.

Yes, there was something in this present moment, a feeling almost like waking up. Something had clicked. I was more myself than before, maybe than ever before, like part of my being, an immaterial part, slipped more completely into my physical body. It was also true, that for the first time since my arrival in Europe, I felt I was finally adjusting to the time zone.

I continued climbing the steep incline of the street, and shortly came to a small passage off to the right that Jacques had indicated.

There was an iron gate, a small garden, and behind it I could see a staircase climbing along the outside of the building. Before I could even press the doorbell, Jacques called out from the garden waving at me with a flashlight.

"Thomas, welcome, so glad you could make it, just in time."

He opened the gate and ushered me into the garden.

"Yes, just in time. Follow me up the stairs. Something quite amazing has occurred, even remarkable. There's been an explosion at a sub-station in Pontoise, the electricity has been cut off for almost the entire city."

Jacques quickly sprang up the stairs, illuminating the path with his flashlight, and I followed him up the narrow metal steps. I was surprised at his agility as he climbed up the stairs. The staircase was almost like a fire escape, zigzagging up the side of the building for several flights.

146

We finally arrived at a high balcony on the roof of the building. The view encompassed the entire southern half of Paris, and beyond.

"Wow! What an amazing view," I exclaimed trying to take in the entire scope of the city, identifying the various prominent landmarks from the Eiffel Tower, far off on the right, to the Tour Montparnasse, just from their darkened silhouettes against the velvet blue of the twilight sky, and on the fringes of the city I could make out a scattering of tiny lights.

"I thought you might be impressed by the view. There is more though. Come over this way." Jacques directed me further along the balcony where a rather large telescope was placed on the edge.

"We don't often get such exceptional viewing opportunities here in Paris, anymore."

"I've noticed."

"Remarkably clear. Yes, a remarkable evening." Jacques seemed palpably excited. He started to adjust some of the controls on the telescope, looking through an eyepiece and punching in some numbers on a small tablet attached to the scope.

I looked up from the city and scanned the night sky. It was an incredibly clear evening, and I could now see a host of different stars emerging out of the deep indigo of the sky.

"Thomas, do you know your constellations?" Jacques inquired still looking through the eyepiece.

"Yes, at least some of the major ones," I replied.

I looked up trying to make sense of the different star pattern. Several years before, I had started to think about the sky in terms of the zodiac, and the plane of the ecliptic, yet some of my knowledge was spotty, and I was momentarily at a loss to make sense of the stars.

"That's Leo, up there." I pointed toward the constellation sailing above the southwestern corner of the sky. Between Leo and the horizon, the crescent moon floated above the buildings of La Defense, their darker forms silhouetted against the dying edge of the twilight. The moon had increased in size since the first night I had glimpsed its delicate sliver on the terrace of the Pompidou Center, and it was moving further eastward with each night.

"Yes, Leo is certainly the most prominent constellation this time of year."

"A harbinger of summer. I remember seeing it in Michigan." I mentioned.

"Ah, yes. Indeed. Michigan has wonderful skies. Especially up North. Very dark along the Great Lakes."

He was still adjusting the scope. And I looked left across the sky trying to visualize the order of the zodiac. It always took me a moment to get the proper sequence in my mind. Confusingly the zodiacal procession in the sky was kind of backward, or more accurately, from right to left, rather than our customary left to right direction for reading words on a page.

"What's that bright star, over there, east of Leo?" I asked.

"That's Saturn, my friend, and that's exactly what I'm attempting to locate here."

I then noticed that the scope was pointing directly towards the bright pinpoint of light.

"Take a look." Jacques stepped away from the scope and directed me towards the apparatus.

I leaned over and looked into the eyepiece.

At first, I wasn't sure if I was looking at the right thing. Within a moment though, my eyes focused on the distant object. A small, surprisingly so, image of the planet was revealed to me. There was a slight tilt to the axis, and I could see the rings crossing over the surface and extending to the sides. A faint trace of color on the surface just barely defined the planet's horizontal bands. The longer I gazed at the image, the more remarkable it seemed to me. This tiny image in the eyepiece was actually the planet Saturn. In that instant I had a faint intimation of the immensity of space and the scale of astronomical distances. There was the feeling of taking in something that I only partly comprehended. The image seemed to be gradually moving to the edge of the lens, and then in a moment it slipped out of view.

"That's amazing."

I looked up to locate the planet in the greater field of stars, and added, "It was smaller than I expected."

"Isn't that incredible? Even with larger telescopes, Saturn is still a diminutive object. Keep in mind the enormous distance, it actually takes the light from Saturn an hour and a half to reach us."

"An hour and a half!" It took me a moment to digest that. I knew that light traveled immense distances, and that even at its tremendous speed, it still took years for the light of distant stars to reach the planet earth.

"Yes, Saturn is quite distant, but only comparatively speaking. The light from Regulus takes 77 years to reach the earth."

A light breeze wafted over the deck. I looked back towards the brightest star in the constellation Leo, a blue giant, and attempted to make a mental calculation of sorts, comparing its distance with the remoteness of Saturn. My mind balked at any sort of comparative scale. The light from Regulus would take a lifetime to reach the Earth.

"Moreover," Jacques continued pointing to the eastern horizon, "If we could see the center of the Milky Way; it lies between Scorpius and Sagittarius, the light would take 26,000 years to reach us here on planet Earth."

"The distances are mind boggling."

"Yes, it's truly beyond human comprehension. The truth is, starlight is traveling from the distant past, entering our field of vision."

"Like fossils of light."

"Indeed. What is astonishing is that humanity didn't have a grasp of this until a hundred years ago. The knowledge, an understanding of these immense distances wasn't even remotely understood at least until Einstein's breakthroughs, and even then there was only the dawning realization that there were other galaxies, many, many, times further out than even the center of the Milky Way. And even more astonishing discoveries followed."

"It's incredible," I remarked.

"And then, in the 1920's, Hubble, and other astronomers, made the determination that the universe was expanding. No longer was the known universe a static, limited domain, it suddenly was much, much, larger, and a dynamic quality entered our understanding of the cosmos. The universe was actually some sort of unfolding event in time."

"I see," I muttered quietly, lost in deep thought. I had read some of this before. Yet now, gazing at the night sky, and listening to Jacques' account, it took on a more intense quality for me. I could almost visualize the unfolding of the universe over time, like some sort of cosmic flower.

"Yes, it is astonishing. We are embedded in a stupendous event of cosmic genesis. And this knowledge was only revealed to us in the last one hundred years. We've truly arrived at some sort of threshold in human history, where the gates of knowledge have been thrown wide open, in all domains, it's like an initiation."

A breeze swept over the high terrace. I was still looking into the sky, not at any star in particular, but it was as if I was reading some sort of starry script, for I was visualizing a train of images that I couldn't rationally make sense of. I

150

momentarily had the feeling I was on a ship again, like on the flying deck of the Pompidou Center, a ship traveling through the universe. The eerie feeling I had felt briefly the night I first met Jacques in the galleries of the museum returned to me, and I felt a slight shivering though my body. Perhaps this transmission of knowledge was overwhelming my current capacities.

Trying to distract myself from the sudden chill, I asked, "What sort of initiation do you mean?"

In the dim light it seemed Jacques paused, as if deliberating before he spoke. "I believe it is humanity's initiation into a kind of galactic citizenship."

"Really?" Part of me seemed to intuitively grasp the idea, but another part of me was strangely resistant, even skeptical. 'Galactic citizenship', I repeated it to myself.

Yes, I wanted to believe that this was the situation in which the present-day Earth was sleepily groping toward, a dawning incipient awareness, probably beyond the reach of the masses of humanity. Yet, it seemed totally outside the domain of consensus thinking. I again thought back to the night at the Pompidou Center, and wondered again, just slightly, who was Jacques really? Perhaps, my skepticism was a reflex, a dismissal that allowed me to control the strange chills that had overtaken my body under the crisp evening stars.

As if intuiting my doubts, Jacques chuckled slightly, and then leaned back over the scope and re-calibrated the settings.

"Take another look at the planet and observe closely just to the sides, and you might get a glimpse of some of the moons of Saturn."

I leaned over and again examined the image in the eyepiece. Moving my gaze to the side of the planet, I could see two small white dots to the right of the planet and another to the left.

"I see them."

"Three small dots of light, these are just the most prominent of the moons. Saturn has over 30 moons."

"Incredible."

"The most intriguing one is the closest to Saturn. Enceladus."

"I've heard of Enceladus. A frozen surface, with liquid water believed to be below the ice, even the possibility of life."

"Exactly. Yes, a very intriguing place. In addition to liquid water, Enceladus also is seismically active. The push and pull between Saturn and the other moons create a dynamic instability."

"Isn't there some volcanic activity, as well?"

A picture of Enceladus formed in my mind. Following a train of thoughts, I suddenly had an image of a research station located beneath the ice, in the depths of the cold lunar ocean, a floating sphere inhabited by scientific explorers.

"Cryovolcanic activity to be precise: geysers of frozen ice spouting off into space. Yes, an incredible place. I have detailed images downstairs in my studio, taken with a more powerful scope, and in darker skies than here in urban Paris."

Jacques was adjusting something on the telescope and then added, "There's a bit of chill in the air now, isn't there? Perhaps, we should go down in the studio."

Even though I was fascinated by our stargazing, I was glad to break away from the exposed terrace. A steady breeze had started to pick up, and maybe that was the source of my chill. I took one last gaze encompassing the expanse of the night sky, and the distant stars.

We walked back down the metal stairs one flight to a narrow terrace and came to the entrance of Jacques' studio. In the foyer, Jacques paused in front of a panel on the wall, flicking on a couple of switches, and the lights came on.

"I have a back-up power supply. Sometimes, these disruptions happen; unions protesting against government reforms." He chuckled to himself.

As I looked around, my attention was drawn to a large colored glass partition. The beautiful illuminated colors of blue, violet, and orange-red depicted an angel of sorts, holding a sword. The figure reminded me of the Saint Michael from the fountain on the Left Bank.

"Saint Michael?" I said, not entirely sure if I recognized the iconography of the angelic figure.

"Ah. You recognize Michael? Very good," Jacques replied heartily.

"I was at the Place Saint Michel the other evening, and remember the figure standing over some sort of demonic being."

"So, you know the story?"

'Something about commemorating the Franco-Prussian war in 1879?"

Jacques laughed, "There is that historical event, yes, but I mean the story of the archangel Michael, casting the fallen angels out of heaven."

"No."

"Well, the sculpture is quite symbolic, and still important for our own time..."

Before he could explain more, Jacques had opened the door and we entered his studio.

The interior was rather spacious with high ceilings and three large floor to ceiling windows, each opening onto the long narrow balcony. All about were stacks of books and papers on the floor and heaped on the top of a low black marble table in front of a sofa upholstered in lavender velour. There were numerous pictures stacked along the walls, and against the back wall was a large geode, with a pocket of dark violet crystals.

Another higher table between the windows held a large globe, and off to the side of these windows was a large abstract spherical sculpture placed in the corner next to the fireplace. There was a Tibetan thangka hanging above the fireplace mantel, and a set of sculptural reliefs carved out of rough limestone lay on the floor. Taking in the whole expanse, I finally noticed the ceiling corners were molded, so they were not sharp angled, but rounded, the walls were colored with just the lightest tint of violet.

"Pardon the disarray. I've been working on so many projects, I haven't had time to organize the place properly," Jacques said.

"No need to apologize. What an amazing space."

"Well, make yourself comfortable, sit down. I'll be back momentarily."

I walked over to the windows and gazed out at the dark forms of the city while Jacques went into the kitchen. I paused in front of the large globe that was placed almost at eye level. It showed the physical features of the Earth without national boundaries. The globe was turned to reveal the great landmass of the Asian continent. For some reason, my eye fell on the area just north of Tibet, a vast desert depression bordered on all sides by soaring mountain ranges.

Jacques returned with two glasses.

"So, what part of the world has captured your imagination?" He inquired handing me the glass.

"The *Takla Makan* Desert" I touched the surface of the globe.

"Ah, The *Takla Makan*, a mysterious place, indeed," He responded as if he had first-hand knowledge of the place.

I thought about some pictures I had looked at as a child. Black and white photographs of rolling dunes, an expedition to some remote location in the depths of the Gobi Desert, or further into Central Asia. Pictures of Bactrian camels crossing the desert waste, headed towards Samarkand or somewhere else, travelers on the Silk Road.

"I see an antelope shape in the forms of the mountains. The way the Hindu Kush and the Himalayas meet, forms the head; the horns are the Tien Shin." I traced the outline of the figure on the globe.

"Really!" Jacques exclaimed, leaning over to peer at the Asian landmass. "What more do you see?"

I looked over the globe tracing a path with my eye from East to West, simultaneously slowly turning the globe from West to East.

"I was always intrigued by the desert expanses, the names were almost magical *Kyzyl Kum, Kara Kum, Rub al Khali*." The names evoked pictures in my mind; indeterminate images, a taste as much as an image, or a sound of wind whispering through sands.

"Yes, like words of an enchantment, or some magic spell."

I turned the globe onward and then paused looking at the European peninsula.

"When I see the mountain chains of Europe, starting in the Balkans, the arch of the Carpathians, the Alps, the Italian peninsula, and then the Pyrenees heading further west, I think of some sort of mythical beast, maybe a dragon, guarding its horde."

Jacques laughed, "You're a natural geomancer."

"Where does the West begin?" I asked.

"You're the geographer, where do you think?"

I paused a moment moving my hand lightly over the globe.

"Traditionally, the Urals marked Europe from Asia." I offered.

"Ah, but that's a contrived division, driven by political geographers." He then added, "Further west, I would say."

I looked again. I remembered the German terms of Abendland and Morgenland; Germany would then be like the pivot between the East and the West. That all makes sense particularly in light of the events of the Twentieth century.

"OK, the middle of Europe seems more likely. Maybe if you drew a line from Berlin to Vienna down to Venice, that marks the division between west and east. Venice looks to the east."

"Good, that would place Egypt definitively in the East."

My eyes continued tracing a path westward, toward the Western hemisphere, up over the northern Atlantic, Iceland, and then Greenland. Greenland was depicted on this globe without its ice cap, and the massive island was shown with a great inland lake, almost a sea folded into its interior and opening to the west below the Thule Peninsula. My eye continued down over the far north. It always surprised me the way the Great Lakes emerged inconspicuously out of the North American landmass.

"The Great Lakes, such a unique feature on the planet," I remarked.

"Indeed, an enormous quantity of fresh water."

"Yes, that too, but the way they're buffered from the Atlantic by the Appalachians, and framed to the West by the Rockies, hidden in the heart of the continent, like a secret jewel," I reflected.

"On the threshold between the north and the south."

"I know. Sleeping Bear Dunes, 45 degrees north latitude, one of my favorite places, a refuge from the increasingly mad world."

It had been years since I had been back. I remembered the afternoons lying down in the shade of the pines, listening to the waves and the wind blowing through the needles or watching the dune grass blowing in the wind, or a butterfly floating by in the air. In my mind's eye, I could see the expanse of the lake, look out to the band of deep blue, gaze out toward the Manitou islands, and the remote lighthouse visible in the distance.

I continued turning the globe drifting into another reverie. I recalled the dream I had in Florence. The time zones fixed, the surface of the earth rotating through time. Like time was actually space unfolding.

"I had a strange dream last week. I was still recovering from the flight over here to Europe. In the dream I could see the Earth rotating through the different time zones."

"What do you think it meant?"

I had to think for a moment.

"It changes the way we think of time. Conventionally we think the sun rises in the east and crosses the sky moving west, and then drops below the horizon. The dream presented a more active, dynamic way of thinking of the earth and time. The world turns into night, and the day ebbs away from us leaving the orange red of the horizon as its fading edge."

"Yes, a beautiful vision."

I finally took a sip of the drink. A delicious mix of lime and lemon flavors tingled my taste buds.

"*Nimbu pani*?" I inquired.

"Yes. My favorite," Jacques smiled.

"What are these paintings over here?" I asked turning toward the back of the room.

There were several large paintings propped against the wall. One of them was painted in luminous aqua blue and orange colors. At first, I thought it was a butterfly rendered in some abstract fashion. Moving closer, I could see the painting depicted a multi-colored spiral diagonally stretching across a backdrop of stars.

"Andreas has been assisting me with some of my projects, working on visualizing different astronomical and cosmological phenomena. This is a painting of the heliosphere."

"The heliosphere, is that..."

"The sheath of charged particles surrounding our solar system, generated by the sun, it acts as a buffer, maybe even a sheath encapsulating our planetary system. From the latest data we now believe it to be a dynamic spiral transforming over time in some unexpected manner."

"I've heard of it. Wasn't the Voyager spacecraft just approaching the edge of the heliopause?"

"Yes. So, you are a follower of the space program." Jacques smiled, and then added enthusiastically, "Let me show you something else we've been working on, very exciting."

I followed him out of the main studio into a second room, not as large, and even more cluttered. There was an assortment of film equipment, light projectors, old cameras, and a computer monitor on table. Jacques chuckled quietly as he walked over to a console mounted on the wall and made some adjustments to the lights until all was dark in the room.

Off to one side a lozenge of illumination stretching across the entire surface of the wall gradually emerged from the darkness.

"Voila," Jacques said with a touch of theatricality.

The wall appeared to be hollowed out into an elongated oval, like some space age aquarium. I recognized it as a diorama of sorts, something I might have seen in a museum when I was a child. There appeared what seemed like hundreds of glimmering dots of light. At first, I couldn't make out what I was looking at, but as I gazed into the space a form came into focus.

"The Milky Way!" I exclaimed.

"*Exactement.*"

I walked up closer to the wall, and peered into the glass, gazing at the intricate model of the spiral galaxy.

"Where would the earth be?" I asked.

Jacques made some adjustments on the console and the galaxy slowly rotated until one of the spiral arms came into view. I could see a pulsing yellow pinpoint of light located about two thirds of the way out from the galactic core.

"There. And you should be able to see a red star, quite near our sun, at least in this model."

I did see a small red point of light pulsing slowly, not too far removed from the location of our sun, yet slightly closer toward the core.

"Yes, I see it."

"That's Antares, the red giant in Scorpius. To maintain the proper scale of this model, in relative terms it's quite close to our sun.; in reality, it's located some 550 light years from the Earth. Keep in mind both the earth, and Antares, are still over 25,000 light years from the galactic core."

"And how far did you say Regulus was from the Earth?"

"Only 77 light years, a neighbor, relatively speaking," Jacques chuckled.

The scales were astonishing, and my mind again faltered in any attempt to comprehend the distances. I had often looked at the constellation Scorpio, and its principle star, the distant red Antares.

"So, Scorpius is more of a summer constellation, isn't it?"

"That's true, and during early autumn as well. Antares is one of the guardians, marking the gateway to the center of the Milky Way."

"I remember now. In the summer, the Milky Way intersects the southern horizon just between Scorpio and Sagittarius."

I could see in my mind's eye a dark night sky one summer evening on the dunes. The glittering arc of the Milky Way tumbled down to the southern horizon, and the curved tail of the scorpion raked low across sky.

I was mesmerized by the diorama's slowly turning spiral arms and the luminous color of the stars set against the dark velvet background.

"Let me show you something else, quite intriguing."

What could be next? I wondered.

Jacques dialed down the controls on the console, and I followed him back into the main room.

He sat down on the sofa and picked up what seemed to be flat milky colored box from the table. It was maybe no larger than a hard cover book but had a shiny lustrous surface.

"Andreas made this." Jacques rubbed the top of the box and an inky darkness gradually spread across the surface of the box.

"Here..." He pointed to the surface of the box, as an aureole of light started to emerge from the inky blackness. Strangely, the dark background had a seemingly impossible sense of spatial depth, as if I was actually looking into a piece of the cosmic void.

"A window opens from another universe, there is a titanic dilation of the space time continuum; maybe an anti-universe, whose membrane impinges on our universe; in truth the alternate universe is always here just below the surface, or just behind our level of reality, always incrementally releasing quantum particles. It's just that at some point, something much more powerful happens, a quantum portal at the beginning of time seething with incipient energies..." Jacques paused.

The dark void seemed to exert an uncanny physical pull on my body, I wasn't sure if it was my imagination, but it seemed to pull the upper part of my body towards the box.

"...and from this other universe spills a profusion of energetic particles, a matrix of undifferentiated energy, at incredibly hot temperatures, way hotter than the sun by an exponential degree."

The strange gravitational pull of the void had subsided for some reason, and I leaned back on the couch.

"Perhaps a hundred million times hotter than the core of the sun. We can't be precise since at this moment, during the first moments, even seconds, of the universe our knowledge is very limited, of course. But at this early moment the temperature is so hot that nothing has mass. It's all energy. There are no elements, no atoms, no particles; everything is just an undifferentiated seething ball of energy."

Jacques paused a moment, as if for dramatic effect, and then continued.

"Then something breaks the perfect symmetry. The electromagnetism, gravity, and the nuclear forces separate out, there is a great differentiation. Following this, in some mysterious way that we don't really understand, the entire universe enters an intense inflationary phase."

The image on the box exploded with a flash of light, and the entire screen filled with swelling orange and white colors.

"Inflating into what?" I was a bit puzzled.

I wondered, what could the exploding energy expand into? Where would it go?

"The actual fabric of space expands. There is nothing it expands into. Rather, it's more constructive to imagine an expanding of the inside, outward. For example, if the walls of this room suddenly moved further and further out."

"Hmm," I mused, trying to imagine the cosmic acorn exploding outward in some incredibly momentous expansion of energy.

Jacques laughed. "This is one of the hurdles we have with our conventional way of thinking. To imagine this, we need to picture a different sort of reality. Moreover, what's even more astonishing is this expansion happens in an instant, covering millions and millions, probably billions of light years in a mere moment of time, the entire universe expands at a supra-luminal speed."

"Supra-luminal?"

"Yes, faster than light."

"But how could anything be faster than light?"

Jacques chuckled. "Yes, I know these ideas play havoc with our conventional thinking. Light is limited to a certain speed, yes, that's true. Yet, the fabric of the universe has no such prohibition."

I had to ponder this idea. How could the invisible fabric of space travel faster than light? It seemed incomprehensible. I thought light was the fastest thing in the universe. What was space, then?

Returning my gaze to the image, I could see the bright yellows and whites had shifted down the spectrum to a cooler orange color, and some of the pulsing energy waves were coalescing into particle like dots, islands in the cosmic sea.

Jacques continued, "Then, after the first 500,000 years or so, a gradual cooling of the cosmic matrix occurs. Electrons and protons start to bond, and we see the birth of atoms, like hydrogen, helium, and the universe becomes transparent."

I continued watching the swirling colors. It was only a few seconds before the particles came together into a swirl of nebulae, and the first stars emerged twinkling in the depths of space. The hypothetical observer's point of view pulled back, and the stars and nebulae coalesced into galactic spirals and elliptical discs. The clarity of the image was extraordinary. Finally, the picture resolved into a sea of galaxies similar to the images I had seen from the Hubble Space Telescope. After a moment, the image dissolved further, and the box returned to its original milky white color. Jacques seemed absorbed in thought.

"What came before the big bang?" I broke the silence.

"That's beyond the scope of present-day science. The beginning, the origin, can't be situated in time or space." He paused, and then added, "Truthfully, there is something deeply unsatisfying about the entire big bang theory. In this conception of the universe humanity is locked into a parenthesis in time and space. We can't see beyond this fictive placeholder."

"So, going back to the beginning; the universe was one at the origin?" I asked.

"You could describe it that way. In the unified field theory, all the forces, electromagnetic, weak, and strong nuclear, are unified in the initial moments of the cosmos. Then there is a slight cooling, a condensation so to speak, and the different forces unfold themselves out of the unitary matrix of energy. This points to some sort of primal asymmetry."

"That reminds me of the ancient Egyptian origin story. Atum floating in the cosmic sea: Nun. At some point, the original unity splits into two and this leads to creation of the world as we know it."

"Yes, the scission of the primordial void."

"There often seems to be a grain of truth in the ancient stories," I suggested.

"There is. You should speak with Gemina, she's involved in the mysteries of ancient Egypt. I gave her your number at the Sorbonne Arts."

"I remember she mentioned Ptah."

"Yes, she lived in Egypt, for many years, in the south." Jacques seemed to gaze off into the distance as if recalling an event in the remote past.

"Interesting."

"Yes, Gemina is a remarkable woman. They should be in Paris another week or so."

My blasé responses camouflaged my intense fascination with both Gemina and Andromeda. It seemed, Gemina was more mysterious than I realized, and I wondered at Jacques' relationship with the two women. How long had he known them? And what had brought them together? I wasn't ready to ask more probing questions about their personal lives, so I feigned disinterest, and shifted the conversation back to cosmology.

"Didn't you say earlier that the universe is still expanding?"

"Indeed, creation is constant, even in this present moment."

"Aside from galactic nebula thousands of light years away, where else is this creation taking place?"

"All around," Jacques laughed, "in the oceans, in the heart of the sun, but moreover inside of you."

"Me?" I was surprised by the direction of his thought.

"Yes, in you, and every human being. Every moment the universe unfolds in your being. Of course, the onlooker consciousness of the western world has forgotten this truth."

"The onlooker consciousness?" Again, it was an unfamiliar term.

"Yes, yes, the point of view that would place us in some abstract position as outside observers; conventional science, for the most part."

"But there are others, aren't there, who still maintain a connection to the ancient wisdom?"

"Of course, but we're entering a new period. Intimations of it came in the early part of the 20th century, a dynamic new perspective dawning into human consciousness, throughout the world. Global conditions compelling people to see our actual situation. Yes, it's a dawning awareness of a dynamic, self-organizing, even living cosmos."

"Living cosmos? So, the universe isn't propelled by random, chance events?"

"There is an intentionality in the universe. But then, what is chance? This is a concept that is particular to our modern sensibility. What we call chance, is maybe necessity to the universe. All of these ideas, like chance, chaos, and even the infinite, betray our limitations as embodied beings."

"Earlier, you mentioned something about a global initiation?"

"Yes, our planet's initiation into a galactic citizenship, so to speak, although most of the Earth isn't quite ready to see it as such. Yes. We're on the threshold of incredible realizations, and challenges, all of us here on Planet Earth." He gazed off into the distance briefly.

I had felt some doubts earlier when he had mentioned this idea, and now perhaps because I was becoming a bit fatigued from the events of the day and from the intensity of so many unfamiliar ideas, my skeptical side emerged again.

"I don't know. Something seems like it has gone wrong. I mean in America...well, there are certain aspects of the culture, memes that seem to trigger a sociopathic reaction. It's almost institutionalized, from big Wall Street firms, to the military, down to aberrant individuals." I was thinking of a long list of incidents from the nepotism of the financial sector down to the random acts of violence that seemed to erupt regularly in the states.

Jacques demeanor changed, taking on a serious concerned expression.

"This is the work of the adversary. Remember Saint Michael cast the adversary out of the heavens and onto the earth. This has significance for our time."

"But haven't there always been crises, and social disturbances?"

Sometimes history seemed to me like a long train of disasters, and perhaps there was even some intrinsic flaw in human nature.

"Yes, of course, but nothing on the scale we're facing now."

"Isn't it cyclical, though?"

I thought, wasn't time cyclical? Weren't we making the same mistakes, time and time again?

"Yes, the adversary wants us to think that it's all been done before."

"Really?" I was confused by what Jacques was saying. His talk of the adversary was kind of eerie, although, I had always railed at those friends of mine who had dismissed the idea of original creative effort as impossible, or redundant.

"That's a dangerous illusion. The world is definitively different now. Different even than it was a mere 100 years ago. Never have we had seven billion people on the planet, never have we had this encircling ring of technology."

"That's true," I acknowledged.

"Just think, it wasn't until 1968, with the Apollo mission, that we actually saw that most remarkable image of the earth, the blue planet floating in space, an oasis in the vast cosmic expanse; evidence of our true situation."

"That was unprecedented."

I had to admit that was a definitive event. Never could we look at the Earth in the same way.

"And now, many of your compatriots don't recognize this, but the actual composition of the atmosphere is changing, something as fundamental as the physical and chemical makeup of the air isn't the same as it was even 30 years ago."

"The increase in CO_2, you mean?" Admittedly, that was a profound alteration of our environment. Nature had changed, I felt that. I had experienced a strange pre-sentiment of this all years ago, and now Jacques was confirming this intuition.

"Yes, just think, how over the course of thousands of years, Natura unfolded her treasures, and now in a short span of time, humanity is gobbling them up, like some all-consuming...dragon."

He hesitated before saying "dragon" and had used the term "Natura" like it was a person, a being.

"But what is it with America?" I asked, sobered in the face of this presentation of the facts.

"Ah, yes. It is troubling. Like inside the head of the beast swallowing the world. Everything is amplified and accelerated there. All the extremes are juxtaposed and folded together."

Perhaps, I had been too skeptical. Jacques had reminded me of many things I had already accepted as known facts, evidence of our changed situation on the planet. It was irrefutable. I did agree, but now in the wake of digesting these truths, I felt a sense of weariness come over me as if the weight of the issues had drained me. I was too tired to discuss things further.

Jacques also appeared to be fatigued.

"We have to be careful; the adversary brings confusion and doubt. There is more to say on all these matters but..." Jacques twisted around on the sofa to look outside. The wind seemed to pick up and rattle the windows lightly. He paused for a few moments, even closing his eyes.

"I think it's getting a bit late. You're welcome to spend the night here. There is a spare room upstairs, the meditation room."

Something had shifted in the energy of our conversation. Even though Jacques was visibly tired, he now seemed to have returned to a lighter disposition.

In my state of low energy, I wasn't eager to walk down to the nearest Metro and make the journey all the way back to the Left Bank.

Jacques continued.

"Yes, Thomas, there is a much to consider about our present situation on our planet, but we don't want to exhaust the entire subject matter, yet." he chuckled. "In fact, you must first visit Andreas. He has a workshop in an old hanger out in Le Bourget."

"Le Bourget? Out in the suburbs?" I thought I had seen the stop on my way in from Charles De Gaulle.

"Yes, the site of the old aerodrome. Andreas is working on some intriguing new creations that you must see."

Jacques led me upstairs to the meditation room and bid me good night.

18: An Inner World

The room was relatively spare in its décor, a daybed in front of the window, a Persian carpet on the floor, lit only by an old Moroccan lamp of wrought iron, casting alternating zones of colored light on to a table and over the floor and walls. An old clock ticked away on a mantle by the bed.

Outside, the view looked away from central Paris. A monotonous perspective, and in the darkness, I could make out only the shadow shapes of the buildings.

I sat down on the edge of the bed. Although I was fatigued, my mind was still churning. I was trying to make sense of the different strands of thought, the entire range of ideas that Jacques had introduced this evening: Supra-luminal, the fabric of the universe, the constellations; Leo, Regulus, 77 light years away; Andreas, and his light projections; a studio in Le Bourget; galactic citizenship, and the adversary. For some reason my mind hung on that notion; the adversary who Saint Michael with his raised sword had defeated, and then cast to the Earth. What was the date? 1879? The fountain at Place St. Michel; what did it commemorate, actually?

It wasn't that I ruled out the possibility of evil in the world. It seemed hard to deny the evidence, particularly based on my own critique of the situation in America; the agents of discord, battling for control. What had Christy said? "The Black Magicians of Atlantis"? That had seemed a bit over the top. I hadn't wanted to accept that notion. Jacques was right though, and why had I resisted his position? I couldn't say for sure, but the world had changed in some fundamental way just in my own lifetime. I could see it. Could it be that our time was faced simultaneously with the best and the worst of possibilities?

I looked outside, and saw an image of my shadowed self, silhouetted against the interior, and outside, darker forms, some buildings, and a few trees.

I turned off the light and leaned back on to the bed.

The wind rustled outside, and the windowpanes shuddered. A light from outside cast a shadow of a tree branch on the upper section of the wall and onto the ceiling. I watched the shadow as it swayed back and forth in the wind. I could hear the wind sighing through the trees. In the background, or welling up from somewhere inside, I heard a drumbeat, then the faint sound of music. I dimly realized it was Beethoven's Ninth symphony, the second movement. Gradually the music seemed to increase in volume and tempo, and with it the branch started to sway more dramatically. The silhouette of the branch seemed to twist and bend into a swirling arabesque, and the music became more insistent, while the rolling boom of the bass drum beat louder and louder. There was the sound of thunder. I looked out the window, suddenly alarmed, and saw a great ball of white light. Almost like a supernova, I felt it was drawing me towards it, lifting me out of the bed, sucking me out of the room. I was going to go through window. I was filled with dread, and panic. I couldn't let myself go. I shook myself violently, resisting the pull of the unearthly force. I shook myself again, and again, trying to halt the force.

I felt like I was coming up through layers and layers of sleep. I jumped upright and leaned over the side of the bed. My heart was beating wildly.

I looked around. All was silent. There was no wind outside, or at least nothing audible. Some shadows on the wall, but they were still. I looked outside. Nothing but rooftops, not even the moon. In the background, I heard the steady ticking of the clock. Turning over to the table, I grabbed the clock and looked at the face. It was barely a quarter to two. I laid back down.

My heart was starting to calm down, but I was left with an eerie sense of uncertainty. Had Jacques played the music I had heard welling up from below?

I didn't feel insecure in the room. Rather there was something else, inside of me, or maybe something outside of me. Maybe a disembodied being was able to access my inner being. I looked around the room. Or perhaps, the stimulating conversation had invoked some deeply buried memories. I wasn't sure.

I turned the images over in my mind: the light, the ball of light, the music, and the swirling shapes. I listened carefully for any errant noises. All was quiet, in the distance, outside, only the drone of the city at night. I started searching my memory for any similar dreams. I cast my mind back to my childhood, and a train of images from the distant past followed. Before I knew it, I fell into a dreamless sleep.

I woke to soft gauzy sunlight spilling into the room. In the morning light, the walls of the room were revealed to have the slightest tint of pink, like the inner petals of a rose, or the inside of a conch shell. Outside, it was windy, and I could hear the breeze blowing through the nearby trees.

I walked downstairs. Jacques was nowhere to be seen. I looked in the kitchen and found a note on the table.

"Tomas,
Unexpectedly, I've been called away this morning.
Please help yourself to breakfast.
Will be in touch soon, Jacques
P.S. The door locks automatically."

I looked around the kitchen. There was teapot on the stove. On the counter there was a glass jar with various tea bags and a plate of different pastries and breads, including some rustic dark bread, and even a few sesame bars. From the glass jar I removed a bag of chai tea. I set the water to boil and chose one of the sesame bars.

Despite the intensity of the dream, the rest of the night had been quiet, and I had managed to get a sound sleep, perhaps for the first time during my trip. There was a calm quality to Jacques' place that seemed to engender in me a thoughtful introspection. Natural light poured into the kitchen from the windows. The kitchen decor was clean and sparse, and aside from some colored accents of the most delicate shade of violet, it was predominately white. While I waited for the water to boil, I walked over to a set of pictures hung on the wall.

They were old engravings, maybe from the 17th century. One was set in a typical European cityscape of the period. Though that was the only normative aspect, for the picture was dominated by a strange box with a cut away portion revealing a bearded man, lying partially upright, naked except for a crown on his head. Looking closer, I could see that underneath the box, a fire had been set, and smoke issued forth from both sides.

Just then the teapot started to boil, and I walked back to the counter to fill a cup.

171

Waiting for my tea to cool, I returned to the pictures. The second one was even stranger than the first. Placed on a dark background with dense cross-hatching were an array of paired figures, many of them seemed to be drawn from the signs of the zodiac and set amidst swirling clouds, flames of fire, all partitioned off by dark boulders. One pair consisted of a scorpion and a bull facing off against each other in combat. Another pair showed a man hurling a jar of water towards a charging lion. It appeared that all the figures were joined in some sort of clash of opposites.

I had expected to see astronomical or scientific imagery in Jacques place, not surreal pictures conjured from the baroque imagination. Somehow it didn't fit with the image of an astronomical scientist, or a cosmologist. Even as I had vaguely intuited the night at the Pompidou Center, there was something mysterious about Jacques, a hidden aspect that I wasn't able to fathom.

Again, his reference to the adversary had been unexpected, as were his remarks about galactic initiation. And just what did that mean? Some sort of indoctrination into a galaxy wide network? It then occurred to me he had said something similar in the gallery at the Pompidou, with its images from *Space Odyssey*. As well, there had been subtle intimations of a similar sort at Georges, though I couldn't recall the specifics.

These pictures on the kitchen walls were merely visual representations; the dream had been something more real, a super reality, an intensification of consciousness within a dream. An internal void had opened-up, an inner abyss, and a frightening acceleration towards a supernova of light, as if some unspecified dark energy had been sucking me towards a final terminus.

I sipped the tea and mused. Now, some of the details of that night at the Pompidou were coming back to me. It had been such a blizzard of unexpected incidents and ideas. And since I

172

had been still recovering from the disjunction of travel, much of this material I hadn't processed yet.

I remembered that even before meeting Jacques, I had had multiple insights at the Pompidou Center. There was the procession of modern artistic styles, breaking through to different levels of creativity, but also entering into different levels of conceptual imagination, all of them opening up the view of the world, all an expansion revealing the broader context of the planet Earth, the greater galactic context. I thought back to the Apollo image of the earth hanging in space: Spaceship Earth.

And then, I recalled, seemingly buried like a dream, my first evening at the Pompidou Center, the night after I met Christy. I had had an unusual vision that now seemed strangely congruent with all of that followed: A picture of Paris as some sort of creative way station in the immensity of inter-galactic space. The events of the last three or four days suddenly didn't seem as wildly incongruous, now. As if by entering a heightened state of consciousness on the deck of the Pompidou Center, I reached a higher frequency, unlocked the door to a different level, and linked myself into a higher order.

I laughed to myself a little. Wasn't this more wild fantasy?

I sipped the tea again, and then walked out into the other room to look at the view of Paris. Yes, Paris was a magnet, a creative zone, some sort of autonomous zone for engendering creative expression, maybe nothing more than that. Looking toward La Defense I could see clouds ushering in from the west; another front moving into the area. The weather systems moved quickly here; I often forgot that the Atlantic was not that far away from the city.

***

By the time I arrived back at the hotel it was almost noon. The clouds had moved in completely, and it was threatening to rain. The concierge had taken a message from Gemina. It was brief, in the third person, and read.

Tomas: Gemina and Andromeda are meeting you at Musée Cernuschi. Parc Monceau. Métro Monceau. Today - 1 :30 pm.

I barely had time to return to my room and change clothes before rushing back down to the Metro station at St. Michel.

It seemed now like the metro carriages were like neurotransmitters shuttling down synaptic pathways of the city brain. Below the Seine, I traveled along the corpus callosum of Paris, bridging Left Bank and Right Bank: St Germain to Châtelet, under the Île de la Cité, and the jeweled crystal of Sainte-Chapelle.

I always felt a certain heightened energy traveling on the Metro, now even more so. There were all the attendant decisions to make about what route to take across the city, the switching to different lines; all the people crammed together; the multitude of faces. It was like some sort of initiation into the science of life. There was also some unspoken significance in the sequence of stations; and each change of lines, like the rotation of a combination lock, could open one up to a higher level of consciousness.

I looked around at my fellow passengers. Nearby two men speaking Urdu, one with a wide-eyed child; across the aisle an African man wearing a leather jacket, maybe speaking Sango or Swahili to his neighbor; further ahead of me an older Scandinavian couple, or maybe they were visiting from Brittany.

Wasn't all humanity coming together here in this metropolis? Wasn't Paris a model for the city of the future? Not the model proffered by HSBC and other global financial and

174

corporate entities; not predicated on some commercial vision, but more artistic and spiritual; not a consumer mono-culture designed by corporate marketing departments, but more of an Aquarian unity with different levels of technological, and industrial development possible within multiple currents of peoples and cultures, all organically coming together, even intersecting here in the City of Light. And didn't I understand the value of this confluence from studying the transmission of artistic forms, coming from Africa, coming from Japan, and all the artists from the four corners of the world, all meeting here in Paris? And since they were operating within the higher symbolic order of Paris, their activities were imbued with a greater significance.

I changed lines at Strasbourg-St.Denis. Each station had a different chromatic theme, as if the different colors were the key to my progress across the city: Sentier, Bourse, Quatre Septembre, Opera, Havre-Caumartin, St. Lazare, Europe, and then changing again at Villiers, spelled out the final combination to open the lock. I arrived at Monceau.

19: Parc de Monceau

The *Musée Cernuschi* was a relic from the *ancien régime*, its ornate white stone cladding framed by lush foliage. Above the entrance two circular portraits in profile were placed facing each other, one of Leonardo, the other of Aristotle. Below, a sign in Art Nouveau lettering announced an exhibit: *Rêves de Lacquer*.

I recognized Andromeda immediately, standing near the front. Something about her seemed more expansive, freer, than her somewhat restrained elegance the night at Restaurant Georges. She seemed like a flower whose petals had opened. Her hair was luxuriant, and her eyes were accented with a subtle touch of violet color. She wore an emerald green raincoat still glistening with rain drops from the recent showers, underneath, a yellow turtleneck, blue jeans, and belted leather boots.

After we exchanged greetings, I asked. "Where's your mother?"

"Something came up at the last moment." Her English was clear, with only the faintest hint of an accent, indefinable, neither British, nor French.

"She's moving to London at the end of the month," she announced.

"London," I exclaimed. I was concerned that both Andromeda and Gemina would leave Paris before I had a chance to properly know them.

"Yes, she used to prefer Paris, now she prefers London," Andromeda remarked somewhat flippantly. "Something in the energy has changed," she added.

"Well, London does have a different feeling, more commercial," I volunteered.

"Yes, there is the Anglo-Saxon predilection toward commerce. One step removed from the continent physically and otherwise."

"I often think London and Paris are like twins, Paris on the Seine, London on the Thames."

"There is an inverse commutability of sorts."

The Thames flows to the east, and the Seine flows west," I noted.

Andromeda laughed lightly, and then added, "Yes, more significantly, though, there is the English language, a different frame of consciousness. That's actually quite important for my mother."

It was the first time I heard Andromeda acknowledge Gemina as her mother.

"What part of London is she moving to?"

"In the north, a place called Belsize Park."

"Will you go as well?" I asked.

"Oh, no," she laughed quietly, looking away. "I have a project abroad and a studio here as well."

A flurry of questions arose concerning her architectural practice, but impulsively I asked a more adventurous question, "Andromeda. Where did you grow up?"

"Most of my childhood we were either in Lebanon, or in Egypt, and at one point we tried to go back to Beirut, but it was too chaotic." She paused for a moment looking distant.

"We went for a while to Spain. Then I went to study at ETH Zurich."

Again, another host of questions simultaneously came to mind. There was too much to know, and I didn't want to seem overly enthusiastic or impolite.

"Egypt, really?" I blurted out.

"Yes, in the south, near Syene. Or as they call it now: Aswan. My mother was doing archaeological research. Jacques was there as well."

"What was it like growing up there?"

"Every day was an adventure, but at times, I was lonely. I would draw pictures of Egyptian deities while my mother worked on the site."

"Which one was your favorite?"

"Ma'at"

"Ma'at?" I couldn't remember the specifics of the deity.

"She's the one with the feather in her headband," she offered.

It seemed like a whole continent was just emerging into view. I felt like I was putting together the pieces of a puzzle. Moreover, I had no idea what the final picture looked like. I mentioned my meeting with Jacques the previous evening. She said that he was one the main reasons they had come to Paris.

It was then that Andromeda suggested we enter the museum. She was particularly interested in the special exhibit showcasing the work of Shibata Zeshin, a Japanese artist acclaimed for his extraordinary lacquer ware.

Once inside, an atmosphere of serenity and calm pervaded the galleries. Andromeda was intrigued with the delicate skill of the artist's work and looked closely at the details of each work.

The highlight of the exhibit were many small lacquer boxes, all decorated with intricate miniature designs drawn from the natural world. The forms appeared to float on the glossy wood like autumn leaves on the surface of a still dark pool.

There was a beautiful writing box with a finch perched on a cherry tree; gold and silver figures on black, blossoms arrayed across the surface. There was a rounded incense box with yellow and gold flowers floating on a dark ground. Particularly remarkable was a tobacco container with a silvery egret illuminated on the black ground as if the artist had drawn the figure with moonlight. Another box depicted the crescent moon emerging from swirling clouds on a gold background.

On the walls were an array of silk paintings, all executed with equally brilliant skill. Like the lacquer ware, all the designs were composed with a simple elegance, negative space perfectly balancing out the positive natural forms.

It was a relatively small exhibit, and within an hour we had finished viewing the works. Returning outside, we leisurely walked into the park. Andromeda began expressing her admiration for the artistry of the Shibata Zeshin, and the traditions of Asian art in general.

"There is a Japanese word: *shibui*, referring to an aesthetic of subtle beauty. The artist is able to convey, in the most perceptive manner, with a great economy of means, the essence of the subject. A harmony between nature and art, something you don't find in most contemporary art."

"Yes, I felt a stillness in there; even a tranquility," I volunteered.

"Exactly. The art short circuits your rational intellectual mind and addresses a greater part of your being."

"The work reminded me of the Tao, or a haiku."

"Precisely. Likewise, in those forms we see a certain balance, a simplicity, yet at the same time a complexity, a contradiction, a synthesis of opposites."

"Empty, yet full."

"Yes. Nature and art in harmony: a healing impulse. The East sees nature and art, as a complete whole, mirroring each other. Historically, though, the West made a break with nature, a misperception, based on a fragmentary view of the world that leads to a split, a divergence."

"Was it Descartes?" I ventured.

"Earlier, much earlier."

"The council of Nicaea?"

"You know of that?"

"Yes, isn't it where the spirit is dropped from the trinity?"

"That's right, a dissonance enters into Christianity. But the split is even earlier."

"Aristotle?"

"Perhaps in the reception of Aristotle, certainly, with the institution of Christianity, this tendency becomes manifest. I'm afraid the split with nature goes quite far back, all the way back to the Old Testament."

"Which part of the Old Testament?"

"Well, you can start with the expulsion from paradise. A false pattern is implanted in Western humanity."

"A false pattern," I mused. "It's interesting though, the West seems to have the mind or intellect of ancient Greece, and the soul of Christianity," I suggested.

"A split personality. Yes."

"And we have to wrestle with these different energies, and resolve them within ourselves, in our own being," I said.

"That's the challenge of our time. More so, though, there is the task of working against the alienation from nature. Particularly since this tendency has proliferated exponentially."

"The so-called free market doesn't help."

"Exactly. The Neo-Liberal mechanism has unleashed a viral attack on our world," She spoke with a sharpness I hadn't noticed earlier.

180

"An attack on nature, obviously," I replied.

She continued more intensely, even insistently, "We've been led down the wrong track. The Neo-Liberal mechanism, the regressive tendency, aims to fix us in time. Lock us into a fixed economic regime, maintain their status quo financially, and energy wise. Even provide ready-made identity controlled by the media, instead of constantly forging one's identity in the present moment."

My perception of Andromeda was expanding in the instant. I agreed with everything she said but was momentarily speechless. She seemed older, now, more definite, more resolute.

"Are you on the same level?" She turned toward me.

"Definitely, yes," I said, looking away at the trees of the park, thinking back on my experiences in America.

"Do people in America, get this?"

"Some people scattered on the fringes, maybe; outliers in between."

I thought of some of my friends across America, some was the operative word, though, who in varying modes and manners struggled against the inertia of the corporate culture.

"But people are hesitating, holding onto a fixed frame of reference? They're actually in denial, even, sleepwalkers, aren't they?" She asked pointedly, looking for confirmation.

"Mostly, that's true. The masses are lulled into complacency, locked into habitual patterns," I averred.

"Remaining in a fixed state inevitably leads to deterioration. Unless the system is open, regression invariably sets in," she said calmly.

"Yes. I agree." I felt a sober sense of realization, a confirmation of my own speculations.

Yet, I was caught oddly inexpressive, even mute. Perhaps, it had been the years of being trapped in America, in a situation where these truths were barely acknowledged. I realized, in comparison to Andromeda, I had been strangely passive for the greater part of my life.

For decades, ever since my teenage years, I had sensed a drag on experience. All around, I saw a society caught in some sort of viscous medium. No different than flies in amber. Almost everyone else seemed oblivious to it, even dismissive when I would try to articulate my feelings. Now, I had met someone who seemed to understand, in a much more militant and determined fashion than me.

Perhaps, growing up like she did, almost like a gypsy: Egypt, Beirut, Spain, Zurich, Andromeda had seen this more clearly. Was it the constant changes of location that afforded a more definitive glimpse into the way we were bound? I didn't know. Based on this afternoon's conversation, there was much more to Andromeda than I had realized, a whole continent waiting to be discovered.

We had wandered deeper into the park, almost oblivious to the lush landscaping, and had arrived at a bridge, a white stone structure, in a faux Venetian style crossing over a small water way. We paused in the middle, leaning over, gazing at the reflections in the dirty water.

Andromeda continued "The Earth we grew up with is over. The air isn't even the same. The changes cannot be managed by humanity." She was lucid in her expression, neither depressed, nor dour in manner, despite the gravity of her words.

"You mean the CO_2 levels?"

"That's part of it, more though. How can this planet sustain 10 billion people? Even, the entire idea of sustainability is misdirected. The future of the biosphere is completely out of our hands."

"You're not suggesting complacency?"

"No. I mean that sustainability as currently envisaged by the media is an erroneous, even dubious notion. Yes, riding a bike to work is good, if you feel more relaxed for doing it, and if enough people embrace this in your community; it is locally beneficial. But it's not going to save the planet, particularly if 100 million Americans still drive big cars, or if billions of other people in Asia, and Africa, are running to embrace the Western lifestyle."

"Seven billion experiences bound into the Neo-Liberal apparatus," I mused.

"Can we let that happen? Even if the being of the planet will sacrifice herself for her children," she said insistently.

"The die seems cast," I shook my head, part of me hated to sound so fatalistic.

"They want the world to think that. You see, Tomas, the corporate and scientific elite aim to maintain the current economic structure, no matter its effect on the planet, even, despite the time having arrived for a new more evolved humanity."

"What do you mean by a new more evolved humanity?"

"Ever since the Renaissance, man has placed himself outside of nature, in some imaginary perspective, and used that to control and dominate the world. Now, that mode of thought has exhausted itself. Yet, most still cling to the outmoded system, all along the impulse of a new consciousness calls to us. The earth demands it, even."

I suddenly broke out of my mental paralysis.

"Even in this compromised situation, we still have agency, we can change things?"

She abruptly turned toward me and touched my arm.

"Absolutely. We have creative agency, and we always will if we choose to exercise it. That's the key. To use our creative agency to break the spell of the controlling elite who have fixed the terms of the contract. And, unless we become consciously aware of the entire scope of our being, the opposing forces will manipulate those hidden levels of our being for their own benefit."

"Even as they do now with advertising and marketing."

"Exactly, Tomas. The corporate elite claim they have our best interests in mind, and imply their way is the only solution to the problems of the world. And they'll employ deceit, sleight of hand, and all their other tricks to maintain their deficient regime."

I had never heard anyone put it so directly.

"How can we fight the corporate elite? Look what happened to the anti-Wall Street movement," I countered.

"Working with nature instead of against it; that's why I see myself as a biomorphic artist, in league with the earth."

"But you don't think of your work as sustainable?"

"No, we're past the point of the merely sustainable. Art for the new planet being born, now, must have a certain resonance, even a dialogue with natural energies."

"You mentioned a project you were working on abroad."

"Yes, in the Islands."

"The Islands?"

"A small island with a coral reef, and the water, so beautiful, a brilliant turquoise blue," Her eyes lit up as she spoke, "We're designing an oceanic voyager, and an accompanying research facility."

"An oceanic voyager?" I hadn't considered that architects would design ships.

"Yes, a vessel to fathom the mysteries of the sea."

"The ocean, so much of our planet, but we just live at its edge and skim its surface," I pondered thoughtfully.

"Precisely. Now, with the coming earth changes, the sea will be even more important for the world than ever before. We could even call this the century of the ocean."

"What about here, in your studio in Paris?"

"Here? Mainly, I've been working on a smaller structure, a building fitted with a photosynthetic skin, turning opaque or transparent by the time of day, welcoming the sun's vital energy into the architecture, a receptacle between the earth and the sun. Not a machine for living, but a living architecture."

"A relationship, then: The Earth receiving the sun."

She smiled. "You could say that, yes. People typically think of the sun as being out there," she pointed up into the sky, "but when viewed from space, we're really within the sun's sphere."

"The heliosphere." I pondered how our earth and sun would look from a planet in a distant star system?

"Exactly, I could even call it *Heliospheric* architecture."

Despite our talk of the sun, the sky had grown increasingly grey. Leaning over the bridge, I looked down at the still water. In the liquid mirror, I saw our faces had merged into one form. I was intrigued by the abstract rippled image, and how the liquid parts of her flowed in with the liquid parts of me. In that moment of pondering, a droplet of rain fell on the reflection. Concentric circles radiated outward like the orbits of planetary bodies.

Then a breath of wind dismissed the reflection, and the trees sighed in response. A spray of raindrops fell across the water. I turned back to Andromeda who was already pulling a compact umbrella from her coat pocket. The rain started falling in earnest.

20: On the Métro

Huddling under her umbrella we walked swiftly to the nearest Métro. Once we arrived inside the underground station, Andromeda suggested we visit her studio in the 6th Arrondissement.

We stood in front of a wall map of Paris trying to figure out the best route through the labyrinth of Metro lines. All the choices required at least three changes, and we were entering one of the busiest times of day. The best route seemed to be the green line to Charles De Gaulle, then changing to the red line going to Châtelet, and finally the plum line to St.-Germain-des-Prés.

We boarded the metro and the train lurched forward. The train was so packed we had to stand up, crammed in with the mass of commuters we didn't have time to converse. As the stations passed by, I noted their names, silently repeating the sounds.

Courcelles, Ternes.

After only two stations, we arrived at Charles De Gaulle Étoile. We had to push our way through the crowd to disembark in time. This platform was packed with commuters rushing to catch their trains. I followed Andromeda as she walked quickly down the corridors to reach the connecting train.

Despite the rush hour crowds we found a seat together on the next train. Andromeda sat by the window. I was on the aisle. I looked above at the Métro route map, searching for our line, and silently reading off the station names one by one.

George V, Franklin Roosevelt, Champs Élysée-Clemenceau, Concorde, Tuileries, Louvre-Palais Royal, Louvre-Rivoli. Châtelet.

The train lurched forward, and we entered the dark of the tunnel.

At first, we didn't converse, but when the train halted at the Roosevelt Métro Andromeda looked out the window. Plastered all across the walls of the Métro station, were an array of large posters advertising an American action film.

"The cultural products of America," Andromeda said looking at the posters.

"Even here in Paris there is no escape," I replied.

"The whole world has changed tremendously, more so since the turn of the millennium. More fragmented, more polarized, more commercialized," I noticed Andromeda's voice had changed slightly. I noticed her accent more, now sounding more like her mother's voice.

"That's true even in America," I responded.

"There is a certain, duplicitous quality to the American message. The stated message is freedom, but..."

"Freedom to be entertained," I interjected.

"A whole society in thralldom to its gadgets."

"24/7."

"Yes, even that expression, spells it all out. No escape, no silence, never ending media, binding humanity in a world of redundant communications and trivial games, thwarting the awareness of the hidden dimension of human nature, drawing the masses down to a sub-human level of engagement."

"Tethered to their drag'n click dungeons," I quipped.

"That is where the *doppelgänger* enters into the social," she remarked.

"What?"

"The *doppelgänger*."

"A double? Like someone who looks just like, say, Catherine Deneuve?"

"Yes, that's an example. More than that, though. On one hand, social media creates this sense that we are not distinct, unique individuals. You find out there are hundreds of people engaged in the same activities, pursuing the same interests as you are. We're diminished in some way by that realization."

"Just another American artist visiting Paris," I said thinking of Sam Francis, Ellsworth Kelly, and many others who came before me. Was this my karma, to be just another anonymous American artist, one among the many who had visited Paris?

In the pre-networked world, the horizons of one's consciousness seemed unlimited.

In the networked world, consciousness was sized down, reduced, so billions of souls could fit on the one-dimensional substrate of the digital realm. What was the ultimate purpose of it all?

"Exactly, the effect is to weaken your sense of self. To dilute or erode your distinct individuality."

There were the anonymous masses, those that you didn't know, or would never personally know, who you were now enabled to encounter, to peruse their lives in virtual form, mostly through pictures, and inane written posts. This led to the dawning realization that there were thousands of people who liked the same color of blue, or other thousands, who liked the same color green. The effect was dismaying, and I was left with the feeling that we were all just puppets of some unseen impulses.

"Since the internet, I found out there are hundreds of people named Thomas Moore."

"More than you thought," she laughed.

"Maybe I should change my name."

"The *doppelgänger* is actually something different, though." She countered, "The actual effect is more insidious, more serious than all that. It happens in the space between your digital communication and your real person, a force, a being even, enters; a distortion, in the reception of your true persona."

"The misreading or misunderstandings that arise in communication?"

"That's a large part of it. That's why there is such a crisis in communication today," she remarked.

"The incivility of discourse on social media."

"The *doppelgänger* contributes to that. It arises as a false image, a projection that obscures the true self."

"A digital simulacra."

"Yes. All this emanates from America, particularly out of America, a technological hubris that saturates American society. It's like a faith, a new creed. To technology we pledge. Technology is our future. I see it when I read the New York Times, in the advertisements, throughout all the media."

Champs Élysees-Clemenceau: *Azulejo Geométric*.

"The New York Times often adopts a derisive tone toward France," I remarked.

"Yes, they do. Anything that contradicts their New York centered narrative of the world is dismissed."

"So, when the financial meltdown spread to Europe it conformed to the idea of Europe as being the old continent, out of step, behind the curve, vulnerable."

"More than that even. The Neo-Liberal elite placed a Trojan horse filled with credit default swaps and bad loans into the European system to diminish the prosperity of the social democracies. A new Europe that was forging a distinct path away from the American style free market approach," Andromeda explained.

"A deliberate gambit to torpedo an alternative approach."

"That's right. And we have an entire nation: Greece, as a sacrificial lamb to the Neo-Liberal gods, and even in America, whole generations sloughed off as redundant, addicted to opiates, or burdened with astronomical debt."

"I know. I've seen examples of this in my own life." I paused a moment, looking around the subway car. I noticed that the other passengers were not all well dressed, and even some of them appeared worn down, depleted.

Concorde: *Décollage*.

And then I added in a quieter voice, "At times, actually, most of the time, I feel like a stranger in my own country, a disconnected witness, cut adrift."

"We all do, particularly those of us from Lebanon. It was no longer feasible for our family to live there the way we had for generations. And with my mother's Sufi-Egyptian blend of spirituality, the situation became intractable." A certain hardness was in her voice now.

"Too polarized?" I asked.

"That's right. It was hard to find a peaceful middle ground, and finally..." She paused turning away and looking out at the darkness of the subway tunnel. "And finally, our old family home was destroyed. It was the last straw, and we moved back to Egypt." There was a bitterness in her expression I hadn't recognized before.

The train snaked accordion like around a curve. Just then another train appeared around the corner, a flash of lights, and almost like an amusement ride the trains jerked away from each other at the last moment.

Though, my own circumstances seemed trivial compared to Andromeda's life, how could I express the feeling of being in a

190

country, like America, but somehow being disconnected? Moreover, I didn't think I could explain to Andromeda the subtle ways in which I had seen my own home and connection to place dissolve due to the destructive energy implicit in the American way of life. How rampant commercialization had transformed my country into a place I barely recognized as my own.

Tuileries: 1920, *Josephine Baker, Chanel No°5, The Spirit of St. Louis.*

Josephine Baker's tits plastered on the wall. The free sensuality of Paris was conveyed in just a pair of images on the subway wall.

Turning back towards me Andromeda continued, "Nationality and patriotism, all those virtues are obsolete now. They belong to another century."

"Not even the Twentieth," I said, thinking back to the events that precipitated WWI.

"That's true. Importantly, though, it is in those moments, when one feels placed in the role of the stranger, alienated from your social identity, that we have the possibility of recognizing a higher level of our self. Then we can cultivate, or rather, awaken to the multi-dimensionality of our being."

"So, opening up to these dimensions expands what it means to be human?"

"Precisely, it's our birthright. But from the perspective of the corporate and financial elite being in touch with the higher aspects of one's nature is not amenable to consumerism."

"And neither is a world of people who own their creative agency."

"No. That would be inconveniently free."

I was thinking back to how the idea of creativity and freedom were becoming linked in my mind. Maybe it had been something Christopher Fields had said, or something I had read in Pico.

Palais Royal-Musée du Louvre : *Grand Theft Auto V*.

But I came back to the circumstances of my own life; my childhood and the strange disjunction I felt when I compared those days to my present life. The game had been changed; the rules were switched. What had been promised had been stolen, replaced with a simulacrum, a fake and false devalued future. It was some great theft. A master deception with the lives of billions of people irrevocably altered.

"Was it a gift, then?" I asked.

"What do you mean?"

"Well, this disjunction I feel. The world I knew as a child seemed to be washed away. There was an intermediate period, that also dissolved, and at some point, I was left with the sense of being like an island broken away from my home continent."

She smiled knowingly.

It was this other part of me, sometimes not discontinuous, but sometimes a discontinuity, or a fragment, in the present; better if it was part of a continuum where one wasn't sacrificed to the other.

"I still feel hope for life. Sunsets are beautiful, flowers, clouds. But the social world, everything has changed. It seems so undeniable. The evidence is so complete, you almost have to pretend it's not so, just to proceed with life," I explained.

"People don't remember anymore."

Louvre-Rivoli: *Sekhmet, Venus de Milo, Minerva*.

"They have no historic consciousness," I offered looking out the window at the statuary.

"Yes. Memory is so important. It defines who we are."

"To remember one's self," I pondered.

"Yes. Maybe it is *our* karma to be different," she suggested.

"What *is* our karma?"

She smiled. "One of the mysteries, even the Buddhist monks can't always answer those questions, but it might have been a path you arrived at, a choice for you....and for me, too." She looked at the window again.

"A choice?"

"Yes. Many are called but few are chosen."

We had arrived at Châtelet, and there joining the mass of people exiting the train we again made our way through a series of long corridors. As we rushed through the crowds Andromeda grabbed my hand and quickly led me through the maze of hallways.

From Châtelet to St. Germain-des-Prés, crossing the corpus callosum of Paris, we came under the Seine and back to the Left Bank. The compartment of the train was so crowded we had to stand. I held onto a metal pole and Andromeda, leaned against my side. Here in the confined public space of the subway car, I was physically closer to Andromeda than I had ever been. Her body pressed against mine when the car gently swayed around the corners. Her body seemed simultaneously taut and soft. I stared impassively straight ahead trying to remain composed, her breath on my neck; the scent of her perfume enveloping me.

21: A Sanctuary

We arrived at St.-Germain-des-Prés and disembarked. The clatter of the crowd echoed down the hallways as we walked briskly through the brightly lit corridors and back up to the street.

Emerging from the underground, the rain was pouring down the staircase, and Andromeda retrieved her umbrella as we climbed the steps. It was apparent that this was no ordinary rain shower, the wind was gusting, and sheets of rain were blowing sideways. Despite the shield of the umbrella the rain was drenching both of us. A violent gust of wind collapsed the umbrella and Andromeda and I hurried around the corner to the entrance of the old church, St.-Germain-des-Prés.

The door was open a notch and we entered the ancient interior. I briefly recollected my visit a few days earlier. Again, the first thing I sensed was the smell of incense. The light inside seemed dimmer than before, and it took me a moment to see the surroundings. I followed Andromeda into the nave, and we walked slowly along the side aisle past the votive candles with their flickering light. Far ahead the altar was dimly lit.

The sound of the rain continued battering the outside of the structure, and the wind buffeted the windows. Here inside there was a deep stillness and quiet. We seemed to be the only people in the church. I felt the same feeling of protection from the elements, both natural and man-made, as I had felt on my earlier visit. This was a shelter, a sanctuary. But, now the feeling felt more intense, much more intense, like I had fallen into some deep well, a buried crypt removed from the churning of the world. I felt a palpable vibration, or maybe I was just shivering.

For some reason I thought of one of Christy's comments about the tonic and the dominant. Here in the church the silence of the interior generated or revealed a fundamental vibration, a harmonic juxtaposed against the dissonance of the outside world. In the solitude of the church, I also suddenly became more conscious of Andromeda's body, her physical presence, of her being physically close to me, and the both of us momentarily separated off from the mass of humanity.

Each niche on the side of the church was different. One contained a haphazard collection of objects: A large box-like wooden structure, statuary, a pulpit. In another niche, I recognized a confessional placed against the wall. The next niche contained paintings and ornamental figures. We stopped at the end of the aisle and looked up at the stain glass window. The glass was decorated with a field of geometric shapes, cubes stacked endlessly one on top of another. I gazed upward, and at the top, the symbol I had recognized from my previous visit: a radiant sun with a golden pyramid, and in the middle the strange lettering. I craned my neck back to look up at the mysterious symbol.

"The *Tetragrammaton*," Andromeda whispered.

I looked down at Andromeda. She had loosened her jacket and pulled it aside. Her turtleneck was soaked from the rain, and for the first time I noticed the gentle swelling of her breasts beneath the damp fabric. For the entire afternoon, our conversation had been strictly intellectual, and now in this sacred space, I felt the sudden warmth of sexual attraction, even an unanticipated excitement.

"*Tetragrammaton?*"

"Yes, the four letters representing the deity, revealed to Moses in the burning bush." She was still looking up, neck arched back.

"Why the pyramid, and the sun?" I was looking up again trying to discern the shape of the letters against the gold background.

"This was designed by Freemasons, after the revolution. The pyramid represents the supreme being."

She looked down, and for a moment our gazes met in the dim setting. Briefly, I caught the glint of blue green in her eyes, almost like faience. There was a pause, just for a second; I felt a deepness to the moment that touched a spot inside of me, a feeling of serene comfort and delight.

"The Freemasons?" I wondered aloud.

"Yes. You can find this symbol on the great seal of the United States, as well."

"The dollar bill, right." I had heard at some point about the Freemasons being involved in the American Revolution but had dismissed much of what I had heard as merely wild and weird speculations. Now, seeing this symbol inside the church I linked the two threads together, and felt some sort of strange confirmation.

I turned around to look at the rest of the church. On the opposite window was another gold pyramid, although, this one was pointing down. I thought of I.M. Pei's glass pyramid at the Louvre. Wasn't there another pyramid that pointed down, the one in the Louvre Carousel?

Looking over the assembly of chairs in the middle of the nave, I thought back on my earlier visit. Somehow with the intense rainstorm, our sudden unexpected diversion into the church, and Andromeda's presence next to me, I had forgotten the strange incident the other evening.

We walked back down the side aisle towards the flickering lights of the votive candles, all the while gazing up at the other stained-glass windows. The sound of the rain lashing the windows seemed to have diminished. We paused in front of the tray with the candles. There were tall white candles, and a combination of smaller candles placed in blue, red, and white glass cups arrayed on a step like tray. Andromeda picked up a red colored candle and searched around for a matchstick.

"Here," I said.

I had picked up one of the already lit white cups. She held the red glass at an angle, and I lit the candle. She placed it on the stand, and for a while we stood there just staring at the flickering lights and listening to the rain on the windows.

After lingering there a few moments, we walked back towards the entrance. Just inside from the exit, we noticed a door to our left propped open. Inside, a cavernous room opened up to the side. The walls were composed of a different material than the main body of the church. The whitish colored masonry glowed with a warm amber color in the light of the flickering candles.

"This is the oldest part of the church," Andromeda whispered. The interior seemed bare, and austere. The material seemed to confer a different feel to the space. Muffled, and more closed in, and even more quiet than the main body of the church, the air dense and still, like being inside a cave.

"St.-Germain-des-Prés is the oldest church in Paris. This was once the site of temple to Isis in the Roman times."

"Isis?"

"Yes, this would have been on the edge of the ancient city. The kernel of the city was founded on the Île de la Cité, and what's now the Latin Quarter."

"A two-thousand-year-old city," I thought aloud.

"Older."

Looking around the hallowed space, I thought back once again to my previous visit. What had it been that the young nun had shouted out?

"You know, I was here a couple days ago, and..."

"*Mademes, L'eglise est fermi*," a voice spoke loudly and with a severe tone.

We turned around startled by the sudden intrusion into our space. At the door was a short elderly man with large glasses. He was holding a large flashlight in one hand and ring of keys in the other.

"The church is closed," he said firmly in English, emphasizing the last word.

We walked back to the door.

"We're sorry," I said.

The man glared at me as we walked by. Once we exited the church, he closed the door with a loud thud.

22: Andromeda's Studio

It was still raining, although much lighter than before, and though the wind was blowing, it alternated between a light wafting breeze and occasional stronger gusts. The temperature had plummeted. We walked out to the edge of the street. Looking south, wreathed in scattered grey violet clouds, the Tour Montparnasse was partially visible, with its band of blue lights glittering like a sentinel over the city.

Andromeda's studio was only a few blocks away. Walking along the sidewalk in the blustery weather, I resumed telling Andromeda the story of my previous visit to the church. Andromeda listened quietly as I gave her an account of the incident involving the epileptic nun, and the exclamations she made in the throes of the seizure.

"That's very strange," Andromeda reflected.

"I believe she was speaking Spanish," I offered.

"Did you understand any of it?" Andromeda looked over at me

"I just remember a few words, something like *ver-des luz, ver-des luz*." My knowledge of Spanish was rudimentary at best, and I probably destroyed the pronunciation.

Andromeda stopped suddenly and looked off down the street.

"What is it?" I asked shivering as the coolness of the evening air penetrated my clothes.

"That's intriguing. *Verdes luz*," she repeated the phrase with a distant expression on her face.

"What could it mean?" I asked.

"This woman had some sort of visitation. Perhaps, she saw an angel surrounded by green light. It's very unusual, even remarkable. Something about this reminds me of..." She stopped and looked over at me.

"Are you shivering?" She asked.

"No." I lied. My clothes were soaked, and perhaps it was a combination of the cool night air, and the strange excitement I had felt inside the church, all conspiring to affect my body with an almost uncontrollable shuddering.

"We're almost to my studio." She then added, "Your account reminds me of something my mother mentioned once. You'll have talk to her about this, soon."

Andromeda's studio was a long narrow white space with a high ceiling and tall mullioned windows looking down on to a courtyard. Everything was neatly arranged on a series of long tables along one wall or placed on a row of bookshelves covering most of the other wall. Near the window there was a small kitchenette, and a round silvery table. Around the side, behind the door was what seemed like a large walk-in closet with a Japanese style screen placed in front of it, as soon as she closed the door, she excused herself, and went behind the screen.

Returning in a few moments she had changed her clothes, and now wore a bulky violet colored sweater with a funny wispy texture almost like cotton candy. Now changed into more casual clothes, and having removed the coloring from under her eyes, she looked somehow different, younger maybe, and in the setting of her studio more like an architectural graduate student.

"You are shivering! You need to dress like the Parisians. Here," she said, grabbing another heavy sweater and a long scarf which she handed to me.

I changed out of my damp shirt and put on the heavy sweater, wrapping the scarf around my neck, crossings the long ends over my chest, where the trembling seemed to be emanating from.

Andromeda went over to the window and prepared something on the stove. I walked over slowly, gazing at some of the books, and other items on the tables while she was busy.

She had a large collection of architectural journals. I noticed several decades' worth of *Domus*, *Abitare*, and other more obscure design publications. On a separate shelf there was a collection of seashells carefully displayed with many different colors and sizes, each shell was labeled with a location and species name.

On the other side, the table was neatly stacked with sheets of paper and Mylar, drawing implements, and a large map partially rolled up amidst the different drawings. A shelf above the table held models of various shapes and materials. In the middle was a keyboard and monitor. At the end of the table, a series of lower open shelves tilted at a slight angle, held an assortment of materials of different textures.

Soon, I smelled the odor of mint wafting through the air. Andromeda signaled for me to sit down at the table, and she placed an ornate Arabic tea dispenser on the table, and a pair of glasses.

"I mixed a few additional herbs in with the mint," she said, pouring the tea into our glasses with a slight flourish holding the tea pot aloft and allowing the liquid to stream through the air.

She also brought over a pair of sandwiches placed on a ceramic plate covered with a bright pattern of green and yellow arabesque designs. The sandwiches were made with thick slices of bread, and filled with mint leaves, tomatoes, and some sort of soft cheese.

"*Man'ouche*, a Lebanese specialty, with *Halloumi*," she informed me.

"*Halloumi?*"

"Goat's milk cheese," Andromeda remarked as she took a sip from her tea.

The tea was a potent mixture of fresh mint, with just the slightest hint of some other flavors, the unidentified herbs. After a few moments of sipping the tea, I noticed the shivering inside my chest subside, and I started feel more relaxed and returned to a normal state of mind.

I took a bite of the sandwich, suddenly realizing how hungry I was. The bread was rustic and whole grain, with the flavor of thyme.

"Where did you get this bread? It's delicious," I remarked.

"A Lebanese bakery on the right bank, if we have time, I'll take you there."

"How much time do we have?" I asked.

"We'll be leaving Paris on Thursday."

I quickly realized it was Sunday.

"So soon?"

"Yes. The project is nearing completion. Here, let me show you."

She walked over to the table and unfurled the rolled-up map. At first it looked like a nautical map, since most of the surface was covered with different shades of blue, and numbers scattered across the map indicating water depth. Here and there I noticed small islands, sand bars, and two larger islands.

"The research vessel will be based here."

She pointed to the largest island, a long thin crescent of land, and on its far right, a small protected harbor sheltered by a promontory to the west and the east. A reef bordered the shore along the northern side protecting most of the curved bay.

"What a location!" I studied the map trying to find some indication of where the island fit into the context of the greater Atlantic Ocean.

"It's called Splendent Cay. It's about 1000 miles west of Dakhla."

"What's this?" I pointed to a small rectangle on the promontory to the west of the bay.

"The ruins of an old Portuguese castle, a waystation on the route to Brazil."

I was a bit overwhelmed by the remoteness of the location; I couldn't seem to orient it with any known tourist destination.

"What about the research vessel?" I asked.

"We're calling it the Ocean Explorer."

She opened a file on the desktop, and a series of elevations and plans appeared on the screen. The Ocean Explorer was a multi-leveled vessel that resembled a streamlined version of a conch shell. A star like armature wrapped around the top deck mimicking the pointed projections of the shell.

"We could travel from Splendent Cay all the way to Seine, and dock on the Left Bank here in Paris; the entire trip made without refueling. It's a self-sustaining vehicle, equipped with a greenhouse, a desalinization facility, solar and wind power; all non-motorized facilities."

"Non-motorized?"

"Yes, there are too many motors in the world. We want to promote a vessel that not only has the capacity to use sails, wind power, but all the infrastructure, or mechanicals, on board are made with a new technology employing valves and resonators instead of motors."

She pulled out a large diagram covered with long curved lines connecting colored ovals and cylinders next to large blocks of writing and numbers.

"I agree. There are too many motors. Not just the global use of fuel, but the insufferable noise created by all the motors," I interjected as she centered the large diagram on the table.

I was thinking of the madness of an ancient town like Florence with its swarm of motor bikes; all those personal motors roaring down narrow streets or the incessant noise of cars and trucks throughout the United States. But I also thought of the sound of motors inside apartments or houses, air conditioners, generators, refrigerator motors, all powering the conveniences of life.

"Exactly. This is one of our aims at the Atlantis Station, not just to discover the marvels of the ocean but to build a prototype for a new future, again, looking to nature as the teacher. The entire cooling system of Atlantis Station is built using this new technology," Andromeda explained.

She paused a moment and turned toward me, "Just think, how does nature keep human bodies at a steady temperature? Or rather where do we see changes in temperature in nature, all without motors?"

I was being quizzed. I tried to think of where natural temperature changes occur.

"Well, going from the mid-latitudes to the north, to the Arctic," I mused aloud.

"Yes, keep going."

"The Arctic receives less sunlight, or rather the sun is at an angle," I continued pondering.

"Keep going, you're getting warm."

I was getting warmer, literally, since Andromeda's demonstration had stimulated my senses, I had removed the scarf, and no longer felt the chill that had overcome me earlier

"Arctic air masses, colliding with warm humid air from the gulf." I suddenly thought again of the strange hypnogogic interlude I had experienced. Different weather systems like different atmospheric beings, each with different temperaments. Some cold, some hot. I pictured North America in my mind and saw the conflicting extremes of north and south; the different beings that contested the continent from the Gulf of Mexico to the Great Lakes.

"Yes. More."

"Air masses rising, hot air rising, expanding..."

"Exactly, hot air rises and then expands, particularly at higher elevations."

"I see. Like the mountain tops are cool, while the desert valley is hot, right?" I thought of Death Valley, with the hot air compressed at an elevation below sea level or the Sky Islands in the Southwest with their cool pine forested summits.

"Precisely, they call it orographic lift; the air is cooled adiabatically, and the moisture in the air condenses to form clouds; the expansion of air molecules induces a cooling effect. On the other hand, compression of air increases heat. This is the same principle behind air conditioning. Standard air conditioners use compressor motors, and fan motors, and Freon, of course."

She pointed to the cylinder on the diagram, "In the research station, and on the Ocean Explorer, we use thermo-acoustic technology to expand and compress air molecules."

"Thermo-acoustic?"

"Yes. Sound creates oscillations in pressure and temperature. No Freon, no moving parts, no motors, just the resonator, and a diaphragm inside this tube, and a low voltage solar cell."

"Amazing." I stared at the flow chart like diagram, trying to make sense of the details. The image was quite simple, showing the air flow through the cylinder, then expanded or compressed by the sound waves, and afterwards circulating through the vessel.

"How come this isn't being used more often?"

"The Neo-Liberal machine is controlling the expression of all new innovations, of all new ideas, even."

"Yeah," I knew that was true.

The Neo-Liberal system worked to eliminate any competing narratives. And wasn't the dominant system at the root of many of the impoverishments of the present global society, the breakdown of so many structures, the rampant insecurity of most of its citizens, the shredding of the social compact? Could it be that even the strange disjunction in my own life was due to the horrendous distortions, the hollowing out of the social world, pushed by the Neo-Liberal project?

"Certain players don't want to see this get too big. It's acceptable if a few people, researchers and such, employ this, but not the masses," Andromeda added.

"Control the competition, control society," I said.

"Yes, exactly."

Shuffling through the papers on the desk, she then picked up a small color snapshot.

"Here's a picture of the island," She handed me the photograph.

The picture showed a shaded patio with a wood table and a few woven cane chairs, all sheltered by luxuriant tropical vegetation, and in the background a swath of turquoise blue, the sea.

"Beautiful," I remarked. I hadn't been to the tropics in years, but fondly remembered swimming in the warm ocean waters, the breezes, and the incessant rustling of the palm leaves.

"You must visit us on Splendent Cay."

She leaned closer to me, offering me another similar snapshot.

"I'd like to. That would be amazing." I was momentarily overwhelmed by the offer.

Still staring at the snapshot, I suddenly remembered that following my week in Paris, I had planned on spending two weeks in Spain looking at various architectural sites in Barcelona, and Andalusia; I had never visited the Alhambra.

"We should be in the islands for about three weeks."

"I'm not sure if I can fit it in my schedule." I was trying to think of alternatives. The invitation was so unexpected that I barely had time to consider the possibilities. Maybe I could fly from Spain to the island.

On one hand, I was excited, even thrilled at the idea of spending time with Andromeda on a tropical island. On the other, it seemed almost too adventurous, too radical a deviation from my intended plans. And since I didn't really have the extra money, there would have to be some creative financing with different credit cards.

"We could help you make arrangements."

"I'll think it over. I'd have to make some changes to my flight plans."

"Let me know, in the next few days. I'm leaving out of London, and my mother and Andreas are leaving earlier."

I was intrigued at the mention of the others and wondered about the full extent of the Ocean Explorer project and Atlantis Station. And for the first time, since the night at Georges on top of the Pompidou Center, I felt a strange sense of uncertainty about the relationship between Andromeda and the others.

I had been so taken by my initial attraction to Andromeda, that I hadn't paused to consider who she really was, whatever that may involve. And, with the exception of her mother, I wondered what was her relationship to the others, Jacques, Andreas, and even Monsieur Sind? Moreover, what was the basis for their association?

207

As if intuiting my questions, Andromeda walked back towards the window, and seemed to search for something.

"Andreas initiated the idea of building Atlantis Station. He had an office in Zurich, and a couple of years ago he enlisted my architectural services though ETH."

"I remember he was from Switzerland."

Among the group I had met that night at Georges, aside from Monsieur Sind, Andreas had seemed the most mysterious. He projected the rustic aura of someone who had delved deeply into nature, a woodsman even, or a natural doctor. Based on what Jacques had shown me, and now from what Andromeda was telling me, he appeared to possess advanced engineering skills, displaying an incredible level of technical expertise.

"Yes. I was a graduate student, still. One day I noticed a small bulletin announcing a call for architects to work on a maritime project. It might have gone unnoticed for months, there in landlocked Switzerland. Apparently, I was the only one who responded."

"Jacques showed me some of his work; amazing stuff."

"Yes, his work is quite advanced. Eventually Andreas met Jacques, and my mother, and they started to collaborate." She paused, looking for something on the shelf.

She continued, "He's been working on some important new material technologies for the Ocean Explorer, here's a sample."

She handed me a smooth flexible disc that appeared to be made of a sort of milky plastic material. It was no more than an inch thick, initially only a sheen of color appeared, a chatoyance of reflected light. From one angle, I could see through it to my hand, tilting it the other way, against the light, it seemed to go opaque. I noticed that from the side it was composed of several different thin layers.

"What is it?" I asked looking closely at the material.

"It's an outer sheathing for the structures. When it receives direct sunlight, it becomes opaque. It's also semi-permeable, so the material breathes, like the pores of the skin, and there are capillaries, to allow the circulation of minute amounts of liquid to cool the surface."

"Incredible."

"Yes, his work is futuristic."

"He's more than just an artist," I remarked.

"Yes, much more, although he does create works of art. When I first visited his studio in Zurich, I was astonished."

"Jacques talked about showing me his studio here in Paris. Le Bourget."

"You should definitely go. First, though, you must leave some room on your schedule tomorrow evening to visit my mother's place." Andromeda paused a bit to sip the remainder of her tea, "And that reminds me, I have to be going to bed soon. It's quite late."

"Will you be there?" I asked.

"Definitely, I'm helping her pack her belongings, and also my cat is over there with her."

Andromeda quickly drew up a map to assist me in finding Gemina's place just off the Boulevard Raspail.

Letting me keep the sweater until the next day, she thanked me for joining her for the day's adventures. At the door she politely offered her hand, and we said good night.

23: Gemina's Place

The evening star sparkled against the velvet blue of the twilight sky. Transfixed by the luminous color, I was seated in Gemina's apartment looking through her balcony window over the rooftops of Paris toward the brilliant star in west.

Andromeda was preparing mint tea in the kitchen, and I was seated with Gemina around a heavy wooden table. On the table was placed an antiquarian book of Arabic origin, the binding was covered with swirling silver script. Underneath was a drawing that Gemina had started.

There seemed to be three separate threads of conversations simultaneously. One was related to the nature of Venus, the planet's movement through the zodiac over the course of the years. The second involved my possible venture to Atlantis Station, and the third was connected with the unusual incident I had witnessed in St-Germain-des-Prés, and maybe a fourth was starting to emerge, some permutation of the first and third threads.

"We'd love to have you come," Gemina remarked, as she peered into the ancient book.

On the walls of her apartment were a series of paintings, all nocturnes, almost abstract, but recognizable in their shades of dark, and silver, as portraits of the moon. One, was a picture of the crescent, emerging from a wreath of clouds.

Behind Gemina, leading to the small kitchen was a large bookcase built into the wall. Packing crates were randomly scattered about the floor. In the doorway to the bedroom, Andromeda's cat, an orange striped tabby, Attabiya, stood sentinel like, staring at me.

Something about Gemina's presence put me at ease, a sense of comfort and even familiarity. Sitting in her living room almost gave me a feeling of being at home. She was dressed almost the same as the evening at Georges, except her hair, loose strands of silver and black, was partially restrained by a bandanna.

"You could probably find a good price with a discounter in London," Andromeda offered from the kitchen.

"It might be relevant for your research," Gemina added.

It was partially true. The innovative design of Atlantis Station might be valuable to my research. In truth, I didn't have a clear program of research anyway. Instead of spending money on two weeks traveling through Spain, I could visit a remote island somewhere in the Atlantic Ocean. It was a tempting option.

"It would be amazing, no doubt," I remarked, breaking my gaze from the luminous blue green of the sky, "I would have to pay some cancelation fees, though."

"Your expenses would be virtually nil on the islands," Andromeda added.

"Excellent food on the island, too; incredible fresh juices, conch soup, and creole cuisine," Gemina remarked.

"Yes, complements of our chef, Mattheus," Andromeda added.

"Tomorrow, I'll have to look into the flights," I responded. I felt hesitant about changing my plans.

211

Gemina seemed excited as she came to a passage in the old volume.

"Yes, here it is. A remarkable correspondence. Let me read this to you. It's from Najm al-din Kobra's *Risalat*."

Tilting the heavy volume up at an angle to see it more closely, she read aloud from the book. The pages seemed brittle, and so thin, that I could see the shadow of her hand through the paper.

"Therefore when you have risen up through the seven wells in the different categories of existence, lo and behold, the Heaven of the sovereign condition and its power are revealed to you. Its atmosphere is a green light." She paused.

"A green light," I pondered the import of the passage for a moment, thinking back on the young nun lying on the floor of the church.

"Yes, in this particular transmission, at least; sometimes there are references to other colored lights."

"What are the seven wells?" I asked.

"These are the stages of the subtle physiology. In Arabic we call them *Latifa*. Spiritual organs which through meditation or devotion are opened, made transparent. Normally, they would be dark, or working below the level of conscious awareness."

Gemina continued reading from the ancient tome, *"This green color is so intense that human spirits are not strong enough to bear it though it does not prevent them from falling into mystical love with it."*

"Incredible." Again, I flashed back to the strange evening at the church.

"Yes. A certain degree of intensity, of spiritual yearning and then there is a breakthrough. Perhaps even something specifically about the church, St.-Germain-des -Prés, prompted this. The young woman you saw encountered a powerful angelic presence. The green light signaled her entrance into a certain station, into the domain of a specific angelic intelligence." She paused, "I might suggest, based on your description, it was, even an erotic encounter, with her spiritual guide."

"An erotic encounter?" I thought back to that evening. For some reason, I wanted to outwardly deny the feelings I had felt watching the young nun lying on the floor, my own sense of momentary sexual arousal.

"Absolutely, you're familiar with St. Theresa of Avilla?"

"Yes, a little bit."

"Even though Najm al-Din Kobra was a Sufi mystic from Central Asia, there is a universality to spiritual experience that transcends any cultural boundaries; something modern anthropology explains in a strictly determinist manner. Let me show you another related passage." Gemina jumped up and went over to the bookshelf and pulled down another thick volume.

"Here, from the New Testament. Revelation, Chapter 4." She paused a moment as if taking in the gravity of the passage. *"At once the spirit took control of me. There in heaven was a throne, with someone sitting on it. His face gleamed like such precious stones as jasper and carnelian. All around the throne there was a rainbow the color of emerald."*

I felt a sudden shock of realization dawning. Inside, it was almost, as if a door opened, and a current of air slowly turned the wheels of my mind. A silence had fallen over the room, and I looked outside again at the twilight sky, now the blue was tinged with chartreuse near the horizon. Venus still lingered just above the rooftops. A bird sang off in the distance.

"That's amazing," I said almost whispering.

"Yes, another remarkable correspondence. Your presence in the church on that evening, these passages from holy books, are all evidence of a hidden dimension breaking into human awareness; beings in the unseen dimensions, calling. Christianity, Islam, the Hebrews, they all believed in a hierarchy of angels, archangels and seraphim, communicating to and through human beings; even right now." She paused and looked around the room, "Even now there are angelic beings just beyond our conscious awareness."

"I see." I was looking outside again, and for a moment I almost felt something palpable.

"Yes, for so many centuries this possibility has been ignored, particularly here in the West. We sacrificed our contact with these other dimensions, in order to develop a different facet of our being," Gemina added.

"And look what disasters have ensued," Andromeda remarked. She walked in from the kitchen with the pot of tea, and another plate of the same rustic bread I had savored the evening before. Attabiya followed her, stopping just behind Gemina's chair.

"Yes," continued Gemina, "Ever since the Renaissance there has been a drive toward a more materialistic view of the world. The focus on faith so dominant in The Middle Ages diminished, and reductive thinking came to the forefront; rational thinking."

"Of course, the Enlightenment was an advance in human evolution," Andromeda added.

The room had grown dim, and Andromeda lit the lantern on the table.

I thought of Rousseau again. I then added, "Right. I'm familiar with the evolution of consciousness, and how after the Renaissance, humankind entered what is sometime called a deficient phase of the mental structure."

"Precisely, the possibilities of the old structure have been exhausted. The door to the other dimension has opened, again." She seemed to point outside with her gaze, "like the sky at twilight, revealing the starry worlds." I looked through the window again. Our place on the earth had turned into the night.

Gemina continued, "Yes, we humans are in the anteroom, so to speak. Will we open the door? That is the question." She paused again looking out the window, "The universe evolves through humanity. We are now called to participate in a different way than before, working along with beings from the unseen dimensions."

"Yet, most people are still hypnotized by the baubles of modern commercial society," I offered.

"Exactly, did Andromeda relate this to you?"

"In part."

"There are forces that would desire to keep humanity captivated by the materialistic aspects of society, to divert the energy of human experience away from our self-development," Gemina explained.

"For obvious financial reasons," Andromeda added. She was pouring the tea into our cups and the aroma of the mint filled the air.

"The Black Magicians of Atlantis," I remarked sarcastically.

Gemina laughed.

"I don't know if we need to go back to Atlantis," she said.

"The Black Magicians of Capitalism," Andromeda interjected.

"Well, yes. If manipulating the masses for some ulterior motive, some grand scheme to control, and channel humanity without its knowledge. Then, yes, that would be a black magic," Gemina declared.

"Using the new digital technology, they, the captains of capitalism, seem to be tightening control over all facets of the economy, over the social world, even. What was once a looser more open arrangement, forty or fifty years ago, now seems to be all-encompassing in its scope and ability to monitor. Now the market sucks everything into itself," I said ruefully.

"Indeed, so true. It's all about controlling the narrative, not brooking any alternatives," Gemina said.

215

"That technology is our future. Better accept it or get left behind. That's the main narrative in America," I said ruefully.

"There are many narratives. Some of them linked together. One narrative might also be that life is accidental, that there is no meaning to our lived experience; that there is no greater narrative. That's an insidious narrative, an anti-narrative narrative," Gemina said.

"Some people want to protect certain narratives," Andromeda added.

"There are often careers at stake, even entire professions," Gemina said.

"The problems of society can often be attributed to being locked into one narrative framework. A paradigm that comes to rigidly configure an entire culture," Andromeda explained

"And there are blocks that react against all the modern narratives, reactionaries. Look at the Middle East. Hezbollah, The Muslim Brotherhood. Fundamentalist strains, pulling us back to The Middle Ages," Gemina explained.

"As if the Enlightenment never happened," Andromeda said.

"But we can't go back. That's not the way forward." She paused a moment looking out the window and sipping her tea.

"We left the Middle East, in part to escape that reactionary trend. Always West, the way opens up, dilates. Even back in the ancient times the Phoenicians sailed west. Yes, we all yearned to go west. California was the magnet for my generation: the coast, the Golden West. It symbolized freedom for us. Jacques and I were drawn to California in the Sixties. We drove up the coast many times to capture that spirit," Gemina spoke glowingly.

"You lived in California?" I said eager for her to tell me more.

"Yes. We moved to Los Angeles in 1961. Of course, there is a certain resonance with Lebanon, both are sunset coasts. Both places have changed so much, haven't they?"

Gemina finished with a touch of wistfulness. In my mind I could see a road running along the coast above some cliffs. I could hear the sound of the waves and looking up I saw a city glowing in the golden hues of late afternoon light climbing up the foothills against a backdrop of mountains.

"Yeah," I answered.

I remembered my own burning urge to get to California, and the image in my mind of what California used to be, still lingered there. On my first trip there had been a certain quality of light as I approached the coast, the mountains emerged, range after range, from the haze as I came closer to Los Angeles. There was the golden light of the sunset hour, and the sudden coolness, after the unrelenting heat of the desert.

I returned to the present.

"When you're already West: Where do you go? New Zealand?" I asked.

Gemina laughed a little, "You come to Paris, of course."

"I was trying to explain to Andromeda the disjunction I feel in America, a kind of field of distortion that has warped my experience of life; I feel more free here in Paris."

She smiled, "I can see." She paused a moment looking again outside, as if gathering a thought from out of the sky, and then continued, "Once you start to write your own narrative, a narrative separate from the dominant paradigm, a dissonance results, you are no longer satisfied, you can't go back, any longer."

I hadn't considered the idea, before. Yet, her final remark left me with a strange feeling of nostalgia and reminiscence. I recalled the train of thought from several days ago, the repository of visual memories from my childhood. For some reason I thought of an old book I had as a child. I almost thought I could smell it. It was a feeling more than an idea even. It was so intangible. There was something bittersweet to my recollection. But I stopped following that line of thought and returned to the present experience, my presence in Paris.

"I think by leaving America, I get some breathing room. I'm able to imagine a new narrative, perhaps."

She took a sip of tea, and then continued.

"Of course, America is ground zero for laissez-faire capitalism. So, I wouldn't be surprised you feel that drag on your spirit."

She sipped her tea, again. "But all times have their difficulties. The earth is a difficult place. Sometimes things move slowly here. This is the realm of gravity, after all. There are openings, though, at certain junctures. Ways out of the sluggish atmosphere. Ways of breaking out. That's why we came to Paris, too."

She paused again, looking out the window. The sky was now the color of indigo blue, the long twilight of the northern latitudes. Venus was gone from sight.

Turning to me, Gemina continued, "Yes, this is an interlude of exceptional possibility; if we can awaken to the present situation; if we adopt the right presence of mind, the right keynote, is so important for making the transition to another level."

"The right keynote?"

"Yes. Just the color of the evening sky can alter our mood. The old lamp here on the table, certain paintings, a passage from a holy book, the aroma of mint, a sunset. We can control certain things. Impressions that allow us to slip into the right state of mind."

Her listing of these qualities evoked another train of images in my mind. I savored each one like some delicate perfume or pastry. I saw something, then, or rather tasted the flavor of oranges and cinnamon, and another flavor like roses.

Wait, I thought, and looked over at Gemina. I laughed to myself, it seemed impossible that I could have such a memory.

"Gemina!" I said just under my breath.

She smiled, and then continued, "The usual state of mind, the work world, media, television, all those banalities are not suited to really moving ahead. The way of the controlling powers of this world is through diversion, diverting our attention, our energy. If you can break their mechanism, you can gain freedom."

The last words lingered, suspended in my mind.

I couldn't be sure what had happened to me in the preceding moments. I realized that Gemina's talk had lulled me into a receptive state of mind. The guard of my personality had dropped down, and the running commentary about life in America, my usual internal monologue, had faded away, and something else entered. For a while we stared out into the twilight sky.

I broke the silence, "Earlier, you were talking about the path of Venus through the sky."

"Yes, I was saying that Venus won't be visible much longer."

"You mean, tonight. It's slipped below the horizon."

"No. I mean Venus is approaching an inferior conjunction in a matter of a few weeks. And the evening star will no longer be visible at all until next year."

"Really?"

"Yes. Venus goes through a series of conjunctions with the sun, and disappears from view, switching from Evening star to Morning star, alternately, between going behind the sun, and moving in front: The superior and the inferior conjunctions."

She pulled out the diagram from underneath the book. Andromeda lit another lamp, and we leaned over the paper while Gemina resumed drawing.

'Here, we have the zodiac," Gemina added the symbols to the perimeter of the circle, starting with Gemini on the left, at nine o'clock. Then she added a dot in the center and two smaller concentric circles within the larger circle. "Venus is approaching a conjunction with the Sun in Gemini." On the line of the smallest circle she made a large dot at nine o'clock.

"Then in late March next year, Venus makes a superior conjunction with the Sun in Aries." She drew a thin line sweeping across the zodiac counterclockwise from Gemini and landed on the outer concentric circle in the sign of Aries.

"And in January of the following year there is another inferior conjunction, this time in Capricorn." Gemina drew another thin line swirling around the zodiac counterclockwise and placed a dot on the inner circle opposite from Gemini.

"Then in late October of that same year there is another superior conjunction with the Sun in Scorpio."

Again, she drew a spiraling line counterclockwise from the inner circle through the zodiac and landed on the outer circle in the sign of Scorpio.

Gemina continued drawing sketching out another inferior conjunction, this time in Leo, followed by another superior conjunction in Gemini. Then she quickly added two more inferior conjunctions in Aries, and then Scorpio.

"The conjunctions are rotating backwards through the zodiac," I remarked.

"Exactly, we now have five inferior conjunction points. So, if I draw a line connecting these points." She paused, and taking a green colored pencil, drew a diagonal line connecting Gemini to Capricorn, then another line linking Capricorn to Leo, Leo and Aries, Aries to Scorpio, and then Scorpio back to Gemini.

"A five-pointed star!" I exclaimed.

"It's beautiful isn't it? A symbol of Venus. It takes eight years for Venus to cycle through the pentagram, from Gemini to Gemini, but the place of return always rotates backward through the Zodiac, very slowly. In fact, it takes almost 1200 years to make this passage completely around the zodiac."

"The sign where the evening star re-appears keeps shifting backward," Andromeda explained.

"Hmm, I see." I studied the diagram, and added almost thinking aloud, "1200 years, then each sign of the Zodiac would be associated with a specific hundred-year period, right?"

"That's true, there's more, though," Gemina responded.

"What was going on 1200 years ago?" I asked.

"In the Middle East we find the court of Haroun al Raschid, a golden age in Baghdad. Intimations of it are found in the stories of the Arabian Nights." As Gemina explained her eyes seemed to focus on a point outside of the room.

"Here in France, the year 800 was the time of Charlemagne. The Holy Roman Empire," Andromeda added.

"The movement of Venus through the zodiac signals the beginning of distinct cultural moments," Gemina explained.

"It's like a multi-dimensional star clock," Andromeda offered.

"Precisely. There are many different cycles represented, namely, the eight year, the one hundred year, and then the 1200 year." She paused a moment and then picking up the colored pencil again continued, "And moreover, if on top of the inferior conjunctions we draw in the superior conjunctions, we actually have a ten-pointed star."

She drew in the dots of the remaining superior conjunctions and with emphasis boldly outlined the second pentagram. She then took another colored pencil of a slightly different color, more of blue-green, and drew in a series of elliptical loops around each of the points of the star for the inferior conjunctions, and then another series of loops around the superior conjunctions, the result were two flowers, one smaller than the other, nested inside the larger one.

Gemina continued, "The points of the star can also be imagined as petals of a flower, and so we end up with a ten-petal flower." She paused and looked up toward me, "Now, you remember earlier when we read about the seven wells that Najm al din Kobra mentioned, the *Latifa*, or stations of subtle physiology. This ten-petal flower is a representation of one of the stations."

"Ah!" I exclaimed just under my breath, surprised to come back to the passage from the old Sufi book.

"The chakras, or lotus flowers we often see in Buddhist art," Andromeda added.

I suddenly remembered the window display at the Asian massage store in Passage du Grand Cerf. On its magenta colored walls there had been a diagram of the human body illustrating the chakras. For some reason, the magenta color had remained in my mind more than the details of the diagram.

I looked at Andromeda again, also remembering the strange encounter I had had that evening. There was still something mysterious about the incident. Was it possible that it had been Andromeda, after all? She had the same flowing hair as the woman I saw, and the shape of her face was also consonant with that memory, and with another undefinable form residing somewhere inside of me that I hadn't remembered before. A consonance was triggered, something beyond my mental purview. Another feeling was emerging, but I temporarily dropped the line of thought, returning to the question of the chakras.

"What would cause these stations to be activated?" I asked, thinking back again to the ecstatic experience of the young Spanish nun.

"Devotion, and surrender; love, in a word," Andromeda offered. "This has been the traditional path for centuries."

"Yes. All the traditions speak of those qualities as the way of true spiritual development. In Islam there is an emphasis on the aspect of surrender, or submission," Gemina explained

"Love is a messenger from the hidden universe," Andromeda said.

What was it exactly that I felt about Andromeda? I had been so caught up with just being with her the previous day that I hadn't reflected on what to call my attraction. The excitement of being in Paris with this beautiful woman, the energy of her ideas and the unexpected activities of the group, had momentarily muted a certain ordering or labeling faculty in my mind. Was love governed by a conscious decision? Or was it some unseen movement that grew in the twilight of the unconscious?

"That's right. Love is like a medium that allows us to communicate with the angelic realm, opening the lotus flowers, allowing us to receive messages, opening up a path to the angelic hierarchies. Each one of us was born with one half of the lotus flower already developed, an endowment from ancient times, and the other half waiting, sleeping inside of us. Yet, for those living outside of a monastic setting, it may be more difficult to activate the latent petals," Gemina elaborated.

"What about the other stations?" I asked.

"In the Egyptian system these correspond with the other heavenly bodies, Moon, Mercury, the Sun, Mars, Jupiter and Saturn. The Moon at the base of the spine, and Saturn is placed at the top, at the crown of the head, for example. Each lotus flower has a different configuration of petals," Gemina explained.

"In the East they call Saturn the thousand petal lotus, known for its scintillating violet light," Andromeda remarked.

I had a vision of a brilliant wheel of sparkling light.

"Yes, Saturn is one of the most important of flowers, a doorway to the Universe, a part of us already in the spiritual world. Through Saturn we can communicate with the angelic beings, and through Saturn cosmic influences and interventions come to the earth," Gemina added.

"Interventions of what sort?" I asked.

"Miracles, inspirations, and unexpected events; interventions that break the rigid order of earthly events, that circumvent the mechanical law of this realm of gravity, transmissions from the Universe beyond the limited range of human experience."

"What about the other planets beyond Saturn: Like Neptune and Uranus, or Pluto?" I asked

"Ah, the invisible planets. We call them trans-personal planets. They signal great social changes. Uranus, the herald of revolutions, like the French Revolution, and the Sixties." Gemina's voice had deepened now to a certain resonant quality, and I started to suspect that it was much later than I thought.

"Are they relevant on the individual level?" I asked.

"In their aspects."

"Do you read people's charts?" I immediately realized how self-centered this question seemed, and I felt a little embarrassed.

"I can read your chart. Of course, you must realize that the arrangement of planets and their aspects are not predictive, but merely reflective of the starry realm at the time of your birth, in the sense that an individual is a part of the whole universe. The chart gives a picture of how you are placed within the greater cosmic events."

For a moment I had a picture of the entire galaxy. Perhaps it was a memory from the diorama I had seen the other night. I briefly saw myself as transcending the bounds of the earth, moving toward some fabulous city on another planet. It was an ephemeral fantasy, with a brief impression of colors and light encompassing some vast scale, all this in a compressed moment.

"It's sort of a selfish request, I know."

Gemina laughed a little, and then added.

"Write down your birth data."

She handed me a pencil, and the paper with the Venus diagram on it.

Andromeda picked up the tea pot, and the plate, and walked back into the kitchen, turning on the electric light as she entered the small alcove like space. I noticed for the first time a stack of boxes placed against the wall of the kitchen, and more in a hallway leading to the back room.

"Perhaps, on the island I could look at your chart." Gemina smiled, placing the Venus diagram into the old book.

She then continued, "And we'd have more time, of course, a week, in the leisurely atmosphere of the Islands."

Andromeda laughed, as if her mother had made a joke.

"In the meantime, just a beginning, though, to start with picturing the movement of Venus through the different constellations over time might be a good exercise," Gemina offered.

There seemed to have been an unseen signal that the evening was drawing to a close.

Gemina now seemed older than I had perceived her earlier. Andromeda came back from the kitchen, and Gemina stood up.

I could now clearly see the familial resemblance. In a way, Gemina could have been an older sister to Andromeda, their resemblance was that close. Gemina's hair was shorter, but similar in texture, but she also seemed thinner. Then, in a moment, I realized that Andromeda seemed less Middle Eastern than her mother, there was something softer more rounded in her features, more Western European. A stronger French influence perhaps in her face.

"We look forward to seeing you on the island, Tomas," Gemina said as we walked to the door.

"Yes Tomas, please let me know by Wednesday at the latest. Send me an email message, as soon as possible," Andromeda emphasized, and handed me her card.

"I'll see what I can do tomorrow."

As I said this, our eyes briefly met, and it was like I fell into the deep well, again. It was a moment suspended in time.

Then Gemina interjected, handing me a business card.

"An Egyptian friend of mine in London can offer you some good flights. Let us know your decision."

"Yes, London to Cape Verde, from there we can make arrangements for you," Andromeda added.

Gemina hugged me, and then Andromeda did as well. We all warmly bid good night.

24: Drive to Le Bourget

The clouds had returned and hung low over the bowl of Paris. This far north it seemed like the sky dropped down closer to the earth. Around noon Jacques picked me up in front of the Sorbonne in an old Peugeot station wagon. He turned down the radio as I entered the car and seemed to be in the middle of a stream of thought which he started to articulate as soon as I settled into the car.

This was the first time I had traveled through Paris in an automobile, and I marveled at the different perspective on Paris. We drove down Boulevard St. Michel and shortly turned on to a road that ran along the left bank of the Seine. Across the river I could see the Louvre and the gardens of the Tuileries.

"It's completely impossible to keep up with all the information available to us today. The world is flooded with data. Data and words, humanity is completely incapable of digesting this tidal wave of information," Jacques said excitedly.

"You mean the internet?"

"Yes, since that is our greatest source, though, more than that. Even reading all the newspapers and journals available to us, or the latest technical literature, one is overwhelmed."

"The reign of quantity"

"Exactly," Jacques smiled. "The problem is that in the media all information is treated as equal. There is a certain leveling effect."

"I've heard they have these data mining algorithms for sorting out relevant information."

Jacques laughed.

"Yes, they have those, but until we can get a sense of the big picture, and where we ourselves fit in it, this abundance of information is more of problem than a solution. We need to move from data points, bits of information, to a more complete picture. The information age is touted as the great new advance, but unless we change something inside, internal to us, something in our being, something essential, this information will not advance the human condition."

I now realized Jacques was not just relating some personal frustration with information, there was something more directed in his conversation.

"Internal to us?"

"Exactly. The great supposition of the internet age is that we don't need to change our being, that we only need more information. Information will set us free, so they say." He laughed again. "Unless we change our being all the information in the world will be virtually useless."

He paused a moment, negotiating a traffic change as we crossed the Seine, and circled around the Place de la Concorde. In the center was the ancient obelisk brought by the French from Luxor. After completing the turn onto the Champs Elysees, he continued.

"Think of the brilliant minds from ancient times, Archimedes, Pythagoras, the Egyptians, how did they solve the great problems? They saw the world without the aid of a flood of information."

"The pool of the mind was still clear; undisturbed."

"*Exactement*, less noise. Knowledge was proportional to the situation."

"Knowledge as opposed to information."

"Excellent. In Buddhism, for example, one develops the capacity for discriminating wisdom, there is a sifting process, looking for the gold of life. Of course, there are differences in levels of being, and then there are also differences in levels of information. On the lowest level, there are the mundane signals usually geared for facilitating survival, or the flood of trivial data from the media. Then there is a second level of information, maybe we could even call it knowledge. Certain concepts, art works, or even scientific discoveries that embody more advanced ideas. Not all ideas are equal. Some ideas are more powerful; impulses that expand our notion of self and the universe."

"Like Kubrick's monolith?"

Jacques laughed. "Yes, ideas from a higher mind, metaphorically speaking, of course. Not necessarily extra-terrestrial, but beyond the normal circuit of human possibilities."

"How can we change our being?"

"Experience changes being, of course. Over time, life changes us. However, if we wish to pursue this path," he emphasized the last two words, "It becomes necessary to intentionally transform one's self. Seeing yourself in the world from a different perspective is one way, remembering yourself," he paused and then continued, "Realizing more acutely our true predicament here on the planet earth. In large part, this requires extensive self-observation; realizing who you really are in the present moment."

"Who are we?" I asked, somewhat distantly, since the conversation had suddenly opened up a stack of memories, some of it only partially conscious.

My thoughts returned to the previous evening at Gemina's, and to the even earlier reflections on my childhood, the continent of pictures that called to me from the past. Yes, this was the question I had been grappling with for some time. Wasn't that former part of me still valid, or was it just washed away by the ongoing stream of present events? Was it possible for both the past and present to exist simultaneously? I felt stuck on this paradox.

"Yes, that is the main question." Jacques smiled looking over at me.

Then his voice shifted in tone, and he continued more seriously.

"Do we know what our capacities are?" He asked.

"I don't know for sure. Surely, we're only tapping into a fraction of our consciousness. I've read about the memory theaters from medieval times. Those accounts show our minds to be more powerful than we generally think. We no longer rely on memory as much, though, that's for sure. It's atrophied."

"Yes, precisely. People are relying on external memory, the internet, their digital devices. More troubling than that even, most people aren't fully present in each moment. The Buddhists talk about pure awareness. How can you experience pure awareness when you're constantly distracted by trivial events? I don't mean just those texting messages, but the constant news events that color our daily world, or even the regular emotions that sweep through our lives. One moment the wind blows one direction, and people bend one way, and the next the wind blows another direction and they bend the other way. Like a flag on a flagpole."

"People aren't in control of themselves, even."

"Exactly; trapped in a prison of circumstances, you could say. Many people live their lives as virtual automatons, shaped by accidental events and informed by a fragmentary picture of the world."

"Doesn't the current economic system control our situation? Global capital?"

Jacques nodded, "Yes, in part that's true. However, the Neo-liberal system is merely an instrument of a certain level of consciousness. It's a reaping machine set on automatic, harvesting the wheat from the chafe, so to speak, and unconsciously wreaking havoc on the world, destroying old social structures and nature. In that system human life is an incidental element. However, there are factors even more intrinsic to our situation," he paused and then quietly emphasized, "As we're presently configured, we don't have true freedom. Something limiting is deeply embedded in our nature, and in nature itself, that fixes us into place."

"Don't we have agency?" He had said several things that caught my attention, but I could only grasp one thing at a time.

Jacques smiled, "Not unless we develop it. Otherwise, it lies dormant, a sleeping gift."

"What about Pico della Mirandolla, and his declaration of human freedom?" I exclaimed.

"Yes, the Platonic Academy of Florence. What a period! Ficino, and Mirandolla, such brilliant minds." Jacques smiled, and seemed to drift off into a brief reverie, ignoring my question for the time being.

"They were on a higher level, perhaps," I interrupted the silence.

"Yes," He nodded, returning to the moment, "They were a vehicle for more advanced ideas, certainly. The fire of realization burned more brightly in their consciousness than it does for most of us. And the time had come for those ideas to enter the world, at least in germinal form. Yes, freedom, agency, these were held out as potentialities for our development."

I thought back again to my life, to my childhood memories. Perhaps the fire of experience had burned brighter then also, like my impression that the sun or the colors of the world had been richer, more intense. And lastly like a drop at the end of a stream of water, a thought fell into place, the idea of a subtle fire, inside of me, moving through time.

We had passed the Arc de Triomphe, and I had barely noticed, and now with the towers of La Défense on the horizon, we turned on to the Périphérique.

"What would cause such a flowering of creativity in Florence at that time? I've heard there were barely 60,000 people living there."

"Yes. It's astonishing, isn't it? A time of amazing individualities grasping a world of ideas: Brunelleschi, Ghiberti, Leonardo, incredible minds. Something must have been in the water, you think?" He laughed again, and continued expansively, "Creativity is latent all the time, though, in our being. It's just a question of the circumstances allowing it to flourish. Our time is controlled and regimented. Sometimes, only by resistance can creativity escape from the confines of conventionality."

"Fight the Power."

"Ah. That's what we used to say." Jacques smiled broadly. "Fight the limitations. We were fighting against everything that cramped our spirit. Even friends and family can discourage one's creative expressions. Of course, creativity doesn't happen in a vacuum. You need a fertile milieu, the right *terroir*, the right sun, moisture. The right friends, even."

"A fertile milieu, like here in Paris or in Florence," I was starting to think that my contribution to the exhibition on the future of cities, the stated reason for my visit to Europe, really needed to be about creativity and the city, for wasn't that the real future?

"*Exactement*, Paris a workshop of creativity, different streams converging at the turn of the century. Picasso, and Braque, formal innovators par excellence."

"What about the Surrealists in the twenties?"

"Yes, absolutely, they unfolded many new creative techniques, and called attention to perception, opening up new levels of awareness; a fertile confluence, all those artists of the Twentieth century. The ideas are still generative today."

I thought about some of the more recent work I had seen at the Pompidou Center, some of it that seemed sterile, and left me with cold feelings, art machines of the late modern, and also there was the new media technology, so pneumatic and clean.

"What about today? I mean..." I paused a bit, because it almost seemed absurd to think of it in the same breath as the great artistic innovations of the modern era, "What about Facebook is that creative?"

Jacques chuckled, "Only if we change the definition of creativity." He looked over at me smiling.

"In America, they're constantly promoting digital media as representing the new creative technology," I offered.

"A typical misperception."

"Maybe Facebook is a massive interactive performance art project," I said, somewhat unconvinced even myself of this possibility.

"Yes, you might look at it that way." Jacques laughed again. "Of course, there are degrees of creativity, all across a continuum. Mostly, new media simply re-contextualizes older media formats. Popularity is not proof of creativity, an example of confusion between mass appeal and creativity. It's not that it couldn't be a creative outlet on some level, but for most, it falls far short of true creativity."

"People can post their photographs on Facebook. In a way, they become curators of a collection of images," I suggested. Some part of me was thinking of my own flagging efforts to tend a Facebook profile.

233

Jacques looked slightly amused. I wasn't sure if he was humoring me now, or whether he thought I was playing the devil's advocate.

"If someone did approach it from a more creative standpoint they would still be limited by the Facebook format. Better that people create their own forms than coasting on some pre-existing template. The question is how mechanical or repetitious is it? The more repetitious the activity, the further it is removed from individual agency," he explained.

He paused a moment and then continued more definitively, "Most of modern media aims to disengage one's agency. They provide a facsimile version of creativity, giving one the illusion of being creative. In truth, people are just mechanically responding to marketing cues. The goal of the system is all about subverting and channeling our energy for their ulterior motives, framing our world in their own vision."

"So, they provide a false view."

"In essence they provide a substitute picture, a very powerful, and seductive one that is difficult to counteract. Most people aren't able to construct or create an alternative world view. And since that is a difficult creative act, this substitute view dominates."

Was I capable of forming an alternative world view? What would it take to complete such a creative act? We entered a long tunnel. I marked the distance by watching the array of lights mounted on each side of the curved ceiling. The lights streaming by reminded me of the scene from *Space Odyssey* when Bowman is hurtling through the Stargate.

Exiting the tunnel, we slipped beyond the confines of Paris. Aside from the signage in French, traveling along the Périphérique was reminiscent of the trenched freeways of Detroit. And now, moving into the drab urban fringe of Paris, with its areas of green foliage and displays of graffiti unfurling on concrete walls, all beneath a grey sky that seemed to suck the color out of the landscape, I felt this strange consonance with Detroit again.

I tried to pick up the thread of our conversation, assembling the different ideas in my mind.

"Digital media seems to make me forget my physicality," I said, after we emerged from the tunnel.

"That's true. These devices divert our attention away from our physical nature. In the Vajrayana practice the human body is the transformative vehicle. Without our physical body, we wouldn't have a subtle body, and the channels and drops that offer us the possibility of realization. Even in the Egyptian tradition, the body is essential since the entire cosmos is embodied in the human being. The digital technologies are profoundly limited compared to the multi-dimensionality of life. Just think of the intricate structure of the human eye, and the entire perceptual apparatus. What a marvel."

"Vajrayana?" I knew the word, but I wanted Jacques to elaborate more on the subject.

"The lightning path, the quickest way to reach enlightenment; where desire and pleasure are transformed."

I was surprised by the mention of desire and pleasure. Could this explain the strange constriction I always felt in America, my inability to transform the desire energy within, even the sense that my desire was irrelevant, neutralized, in the face of all the other social and utilitarian issues.

"In the Vajrayana, the body is considered a precious gift, and not just in the ordinary ways of thinking. Unless we take into account the multiple levels of our being, we abdicate our full potential as human beings. Contemporary society systematically channels our energy away from these important realizations," Jacques added.

"This issue always feels more acute when I'm in America," I offered.

Jacques nodded, "Yes, everything there is more exposed to the new. The economic system operates unencumbered, harnessing desire for commercial interests, manipulating base human drives and insecurities. However, these trends are moving throughout the world, and it would be a mistake to think of this as strictly an American experience. There is a global quality to our current predicament."

"But I feel my desire isn't recognized in America," I blurted out, as if I was freeing something that had been harbored silently inside.

"I see," Jacques nodded thoughtfully, "It's important that you recover the full scope of your desire body, deepen into your complete presence as a human being, and once you do, realize that it is yours, and not something that is external to you."

"It's only here in Paris, that I feel the recognition of this part of me, my desire," I admitted, thinking not the least of my time with Andromeda the previous two days.

How was this feeling of desire engendered in me? I wondered. When I had seen Andromeda for the first time, what was triggered inside me? Wasn't it some internal sensibility? Some inner knowing, something I knew inside, some connecting, like two notes forming a harmonic resonance.

"Yes, yes, of course Paris is different than America. After all, America was founded by puritans."

"Right." It started to make sense to me in a way that seemed more real than before, more than just my private ruminations and brooding thoughts. Jacques' broaching of the subject seemed to validate an aspect of myself that had previously been merely internal, arguably imaginary.

I continued, "After my childhood, almost my entire adult life, I felt something was missing, something that other people seemed to receive with ease. And then there was something else. I know it seems almost contradictory, but something others didn't seem to notice, something compensatory, like I

236

was somehow being set aside." Perhaps I was revealing too much of my self, too many inchoate feelings, but now I felt the need to express the truth of my inner experience however farfetched or strange it might seem.

"Hmm, I see." Jacques nodded thoughtfully, "The world is a battleground for the individuality, a battleground of opposed tendencies that struggle within our souls. Yes, particularly in our lifetime, it's become more critical. It is, as if Pandora's box was unleashed again. Manifold possibilities, all of them felt to be our right to have or experience. All around the world, people feel this entitlement insistently, the right to experience, to have, to possess. Media amplifies this, of course. It was so different in ancient times," He finished sounding more reflective, as if he wasn't saying this just for my benefit.

"You mean society was more structured?" I wasn't sure where Jacques was going now. Everything he said today seemed to be a departure from what I had expected to hear, yet it all felt strangely resonant with some suspicion I felt inside.

"In part, at least socially, more differentiated, more contained. The law of the mass rules now. On the periphery there remains another path, a hidden door, if you will, where a different law applies. Therein is the conflict." He paused.

I wanted to ask a host of questions, many that I could hardly put into words. I noticed that we were turning off the motor way. The exit ramp crossed back over the highway, and we dropped down into Le Bourget.

Jacques continued, "Yes, that you found yourself to this level indicates something significant. For whatever reason, your upbringing, chance circumstances, perhaps certain decisions you made, something coalesced inside of you, and you seem to have formed a personal station apart from the masses that affords an alternative perspective."

"An alternative worldview?" I asked reflexively, almost joking. I was trying to process the picture Jacques had painted of my life. In my mind, I saw a castle on the edge of some remote barren desert. I wondered about my childhood, reviewing the different memories that floated on the surface of my recollection. What had it been in my upbringing that had allowed this, so called, station to coalesce?

Jacques chuckled a little bit and looked over at me smiling. "Perhaps, the beginnings at least, otherwise, you probably wouldn't have run into me in the galleries of the Pompidou Center, a magnetic attraction, if you would."

I laughed, responding to the light-hearted turn in his demeanor. Yet, I couldn't help wonder about everything he had said, returning again to the strangeness of our initial encounter that evening. How improbable it seemed, at least from the perspective of an American traveler so used to the staged and predictable routines of life America.

25: The Nature of Light

We now approached the airport, entering an area of aviation facilities. In between the buildings I glimpsed the airfield, and an assortment of large private aircraft parked on the tarmac. Jacques made a turn and pulled up in front of a large nondescript white hanger.

The Interior initially had the appearance of an art gallery. We walked down a long hallway with white walls and high ceilings perfectly lit to showcase the works displayed.

There were large framed digital photographs of Saturn. Some of the images were abstract visions showing the rings and the planet in intensely saturated colors, oranges and violet reds. Other images were not recognizable to me as any known planets. The planetary bodies were rendered in exquisite detail, colored land masses, some with continents floating in oceans, or partially shrouded in clouds; others were barren desiccated orbs with burnt violet terrain, others, gas giants with feathered bands.

Were these strictly conjured from Andreas' imagination, Photoshop creations, or did he have some high-powered telescope that allowed him to view these distant orbs?

"Galactic worlds," Jacques said dryly as we walked by.

Once through the gallery, we entered a more cavernous warehouse space with polished concrete floors. Large wooden crates were stacked all around and hidden behind a row of them was a sleek curved desk with several Apple monitors. While I stared at the planetary images on the screens, Jacques momentarily disappeared.

Again, the rings of Saturn were displayed. On the table were two books, an old hand bound volume, and another with writing on the side "Optical Thesaurus". As I peered at the monitors, Andreas appeared from behind me.

"Thomas, good to make your acquaintance again, I hear you'll be joining us on Splendent Cay." He spoke with just the slightest hint of a German accent, and warmly shook my hand.

"Yes, I got a flight out of London, Saturday evening."

During the drive out to Le Bourget, I had completely forgotten about the reservation. Improbably, at this late date, I had found an affordable ticket. Gemina's contact, the Egyptian travel agent, had located an available seat on BA for far less than I had expected.

"Excellent," Andreas responded looking at me intently.

Jacques reappeared, "You see we're preparing for our journey".

He gestured with his arm at the numerous crates staged next to the hanger doors.

I was intrigued by the extensive preparations for the trip to the islands, and surveyed the contents of the room again, this time noticing a large metal structure looming in the shadows behind some of the stacked crates. I looked down again at the images of Saturn displayed on the monitors.

"These are incredible images of Saturn," I remarked

"Yes, Saturn is the true gateway to the beyond."

"What caused the rings to form?" I asked.

"Perhaps a large moon, through some perturbations in our region of the galaxy, veered too close to the planet, and was destroyed in a massive cataclysm."

I nodded trying to imagine such an event, while Andreas continued.

"The rings are a work of cosmic art; a sublime abstract composition; an astonishing natural wonder on such an enormous scale it would dwarf the earth itself. Imagine viewing the rings from the proximity of one of the moons."

I hadn't thought of the rings as art before. However, after walking through the gallery, and seeing the display of images on the screens, it seemed so obvious. A natural work of art created by some titanic disturbance in our solar system.

"How long would it take to reach Saturn?"

Andreas chuckled.

"By current propulsion systems it would take years," Jacques interjected.

"They could use hibernation," I offered, thinking about the journey of the Discovery in *Space Odyssey*.

"Science fantasy," Andreas responded, "A harrowing journey in any event, if survivable." He paused a moment and then continued.

"Yes, there are those who would want to decouple us from the Earth, even separate us from our physical bodies. Some even envision traveling through the vast inter-stellar void by engineering the transferal of human consciousness onto a digital array, placing our minds into some sort of abstract medium; a cloud, in the current vernacular."

"The singularity," I added.

Jacques chuckled, and looked knowingly at Andreas as if they shared a joke.

"Ah yes, another fantastic notion, troubling in the vision of the future it promotes. And more troubling in how accepted this notion has become in popular culture," Jacques added.

Andreas paused a moment.

"Yes, physically traveling through space would be quite harsh, a primitive experience, and in the end would cause us to lose part of our humanity. One doesn't need to travel in space, since the earth already moves through space, and all the alien environments of the galaxy are replicated here on the earth in a more accessible form." Leaning over the table he touched the keyboard, and a new series of images flickered into view.

On the screens appeared the strangely striated, and pock marked surface of an icy moon.

"Enceladus," Jacques said.

All three screens filled with images of the moon. Some closer-up than I had ever seen before. In one image I noticed the slow-motion eruption of geysers ejecting fluid material into space.

"Yes, Enceladus, is a most intriguing place," Andreas remarked, "beneath the frozen surface, a saltwater ocean, and perhaps, life." Andreas seemed captivated by the images.

"Geothermally active, this could be one of the most important worlds in our system, aside from earth of course," Jacques added enthusiastically.

"Saturn holds many mysteries. Here," Andreas touched the keyboard, and a close-up view of the rings of Saturn appeared.

"Saturn's moons induce density waves within the rings. We see density waves in the rings of Saturn, and also in the presence of spiral arms of our galaxy."

Andreas shifted his attention to one of the other monitors and called up an animation of the Milky Way. I could see the spiral arms slowly rotating through the galaxy.

"The earth itself is profoundly influenced by these density waves. In fact, the entire solar system may have been constellated by the passage of these waves, maybe even life itself."

"Yes, even more. The evolution of humankind is predicated on these resonances traveling through the galaxy. The earth itself is now traveling through new parts of the galaxy. All is not the same," Jacques remarked.

"It's easy to forget that in each moment the creation of the universe is still unfolding," Andreas added.

Each moment is fresh, I thought.

He touched the keyboard again, and another image of the rings appeared on one of the screens.

"Here, look closely just below the rings," he implored.

The vast bulk of Saturn was eclipsed in darkness, the rings were illuminated, and below them floated a small dot of light. He touched the keyboard and we zoomed in tighter. Now I could see the image of a bluish white orb, partially in shadow. He zoomed in even closer.

"The Earth!"

"Yes, most remarkable, isn't it?"

"Incredible."

We stared for some moments at the image on the screen.

Jacques broke the silence.

"This helps one focus on our situation."

"You mean that we're just floating in the endless space?" I asked.

"Yes, in part. More intrinsically, though, the circumstances on the surface of the planet have become increasingly problematic."

"The Earth is under a great threat at this time," Andreas added.

"You mean the increasing global population." I was thinking about the scales tipping demographically, almost certainly causing further degradation for the planet.

"That is a serious problem. However, I mean something more fundamental, something more integral to the situation. On one hand there are forces that would divorce us from our bodies, fabricating a simulacrum, an alternative space, living in virtual worlds, computer games and such," Andreas explained

"In essence the networked space as opposed to the physical space," Jacques added.

"On the other hand, there are those who would have humanity believe the material world is the only dimension of experience. That we have no extension into the unseen worlds, a philosophy of strict materialism, where everything is predicated on physical and sense perceptible causes, excluding the hidden dimension of the spiritual. Both of these alternatives threaten our existence on the planet Earth. If the present path of materialism is pursued to its logical conclusions, humanity will descend into a state of sub-humanism," Andreas concluded direly.

"And there are signs we've already crossed that particular threshold," Jacques added.

"Could the internet be a way of assisting humanity, perhaps changing the consciousness? After all, they used to call it the World Wide Web. Maybe it's a training structure for a more global consciousness," I asked.

Jacques chuckled, looking at me with a wry expression.

"It is a model, perhaps; simulacrum is a better word. The danger is that we confuse the materially networked web, with its Facebook pages and corporate sites, with a global consciousness on a more subtle level," Andreas responded.

I wasn't playing devil's advocate exactly, but maybe trying to find an optimistic side to what seemed to be the most significant social and technological development of the time.

"The shortcomings of the networked space are its intrinsic fragmentation, and its lack of transparency. It doesn't provide us with an image of the whole. Of course, the digital structure itself points to a breaking down of reality, into zeros and ones, to the point of a virtual disintegration of space," Andreas continued.

"These developments were not unexpected. In fact, they've acted as a catalyst. The problem is that certain powers would like to fix the earth at a specific stage of development, retarding and blocking the new impulses coming from a higher level," Jacques remarked.

"Sometimes, I feel like we're already stuck at a certain level," I offered.

"We're in a great eddy, recycling upon itself, particularly in the commercial entertainment industry. The internet exacerbates this retrospection, and the corporate world reaps profits from exploiting these tendencies. Even the art of Post-Modernism points to this stagnation," Andreas explained.

"Culturally we're in an incoherent era," Jacques declared firmly.

"Suspended in this viscous medium humanity runs the risk of not advancing any further," Andreas added.

"By global consciousness, do you mean the *Noosphere*?" I asked.

Jacques chuckled.

"There is that expression." He smiled, and then looked towards Andreas.

"The planetary mind of Teilhard de Chardin," Andreas said thoughtfully.

"I don't think Teilhard envisioned a world where everything was internet enabled," Jacques quipped.

"No, his vision was more spiritual, certainly," Andreas mused.

"I'm troubled by the totalitarian nature of this vision," Jacques added.

"More problematic would be a totally materialistic version of Teilhard's vision, one where there was no cosmic heart drawing human consciousness upward," Andreas remarked thoughtfully.

"Unfortunately, this false materialistic vision of the future appears to be the dominate vision," Jacques said firmly, and then continued, "It's an extrapolation. The global technological culture is a physical metaphor for something that has always existed on the subtle level. In those who are receptive, we can discover that our consciousness seems to have access to a greater sphere of ideas and forms."

"Yes. This has been referred to by all the ancient traditions. In the East they speak of the *Akashic* record, a repository, so to speak, a continuum of ideas and thoughts, immaterially woven into a counter space," Andreas explained.

"In truth, we hold a picture or model of the entire universe within our being." Jacques looked out the window for a moment, and then continued looking toward me, "Consider that we have two types of mind. One, an intelligence of the heart that can access this picture of the universe in its entirety."

"The other, a more cerebral intelligence, that breaks things apart, analyzes and rationally attempts to figure things out," Andreas finished the idea.

"Yes, the problem is the dominance of the cerebral intelligence, and the current imbalance between these two modes," Jacques explained.

"What about the East? In their rush to modernize they seem to have forgotten the ancient wisdom. Their increasing industrialization and mass consumption threaten the earth," I declared.

"Those physical dangers are real. Unfortunately, any change of course can no longer be affected on the physical level," Jacques responded

Andreas signaled to all the crates positioned around the room, "Our aim here, aside from these modest material preparations, would be to neutralize the adversary on another level."

"What do you mean?" My mind flashed back to the evening at Jacques place. The adversary had come up then, and I had felt a strange energy come over our conversation. Again, I felt the same eerie feeling come over me.

"Within the current global system all possible interventions are potentially corruptible. The adversary controls the parameters of action on the material plane. Our only recourse is actions on a subtle level," Andreas explained.

Jacques joined in excitedly, "A resistance, for example, like an Occupy sort of group, could not be effective unless they assumed vows of voluntary simplicity on a mass scale, rejecting all modern conveniences provided by the marketplace, casting off all their worldly possessions. Imagine millions walking through the streets in bare feet, each adopting the manner of modern-day Franciscans. Anything short of this could not succeed in derailing the rapacious machine of capital. And all that, is highly unlikely, unless there is a change on the subtle level." He paused a moment lost in thought.

"A shift in being is necessary. This is a difficult path, yet not an impossibility," Andreas said calmly.

"To change the inner world is the key," Jacques remarked.

"Through dreams?" I offered, thinking of my own vivid dream experiences.

"Yes, that is one way," Jacques replied nodding his head thoughtfully

"Gemina, would be able teach you much about traveling in the dream world," Andreas remarked.

"She can." Jacques smiled, and then looked out the window again. An aircraft was now taxiing up to the front of the warehouse.

"However, attending to one's inner state while awake is the most important way to counteract the adversary. Conscious actions are essential in order to make progress," Jacques added.

"It is through our creativity that we can access the origin, outside of space and time, circumventing the forces that control the material plane," Andreas affirmed.

"We're on the cusp of something tremendous. The whole world is, potentially," Jacques said.

"The path that we've adopted here," Andreas turned around slightly, gesturing with his arms to the objects gathered in the warehouse space, "...is the harmonization of art and science, trying to heal the rupture that has defined the Western culture."

"Yes, Andreas has brought together the severed parts, constructing a figurative corpus callosum, bridging right brain with left brain." Jacques chuckled.

They both smiled briefly as if they had shared a joke. Jacques looked past Andreas into the rear of the warehouse.

"Let me show you an example of our research," Andreas said motioning me to follow him.

Andreas led the way through a phalanx of stacked crates into a dark recess of the warehouse where a large structure, the size of a shipping container, loomed. As we approached, I realized it seemed to be made of a smooth dark glass like material that glinted here and there with reflected light. I noticed the corners were perfectly rounded. We stopped in front of the device and Andreas pressed his hand against the surface, and the outlines of a door appeared.

"This is a prototype, essentially an experimental model. The finished version is now on display at the Palais de Tokyo. Most of the instrumentation has been removed from this prototype and is in place at the exhibit."

He opened the door, revealing what appeared to be a large room. Everything was black inside, except an array of green running lights that partially illuminated the floor, and I had no idea of the real extent of the interior space. I hesitated, feeling a bit tentative as I stood on the threshold of the door.

"Where's Jacques?" I asked looking around suddenly realizing Jacques wasn't with us anymore.

It wasn't that I distrusted Andreas, there was just something uncanny about the whole situation. Here I was no more than a week in Paris, and I had the feeling I was now stepping into some completely unexplored realm of experience, a realm that might change something intrinsic to my being. Did I want it? The question unexpectedly reared up into my awareness, crowding out any other thought. Why would that question even enter my mind now? I wasn't even sure what 'it' was. I was momentarily stuck, as if there were two parts of me vying for control. Maybe the feeling of eeriness was causing a paralyzing air of uncertainty.

Andreas flipped on another light allowing me to see more of the interior.

I stepped up into the module.

A pure white light illuminated the interior revealing three parallel walls facing each other in the center of the room. Set off to one side was a low-slung couch, almost like a row of seats from some futuristic airliner.

"Essentially, this is just a modified camera obscura," Andreas remarked pointing towards the wall.

On the nearest wall the light emanated from a cluster of circular forms shaped in a triangular configuration. There were four circles on the base of the triangle, three on the second tier, two on the third tier and one on top.

"The sacred *tetractys*," Andreas explained.

I looked towards Andreas, still confused.

"The *tetractys*: the decade of four. All the possibilities of the universe are contained in this mystical triangle; revered by the Pythagoreans and revealed in the Egyptian mysteries."

"Egypt?" I hadn't expected a reference to the ancient land inside this space age module. My curiosity intensified. I remembered Gemina's immersion in the teaching of Egypt.

"The source of all the Pythagorean knowledge: the Heliopolitan mysteries. In that transmission we have the creation of the Ennead, the nine principles, born out of the primordial waters: Nun, the source of all: The one."

Looking more closely, I counted nine separate lights, surrounding a slightly larger central one.

"I see."

"The nine angels surrounding the hidden God," He walked over to an elevated platform just visible in the shadows of the room.

The feeling of eeriness I felt earlier was accentuated in a strange way, such that now, I felt a chill of excitement, even wonder come over me.

"I've modified the camera obscura for more intricate demonstrations on the properties of light. Perceptual experiments with light and color."

"The optical thesaurus," I said thinking back to the book on the desk in the main room.

"*Ausgezeichnet*. You know Ibn-Al Hazen. I've taken his teachings to a higher octave; an intensification, so to speak." He seemed to smile to himself, though I couldn't tell for sure since his beard and the shadowy light obscured any attempts to read his face.

"Yes, the module at the Palais Tokyo is the culmination of this line of research. Using light and color, the aim of the device is to filter out the psychic smog of contemporary life, re-tune the perceptual apparatus, and subvert the operation of the rational mind, revealing the hidden aspect of one's being." He flicked a switch on the console, and I heard a low murmur.

A small hole opened in the center of the middle wall. The pure light from the *tetractys* streamed through a tiny aperture and rayed out across the room.

On the opposing wall the light formed another triangle, this one with the apex pointing downward.

"It's upside down, just like our eye perceives things," I remarked. I was somewhat familiar with the operation of the camera obscura, but still intrigued to see its actual demonstration.

"Exactly, this crossing over is significant, and occurs once again inside out brain. Our perceptual apparatus is a remarkable example of how the order of the universe is inscribed in the human being. The light enters the eye passing through the vitreous humor and strikes the retina. Signals from the retina in each eye travel through the optical nerve. Inside the brain, at the site of the optical chiasma, the optical nerve from the right-side crosses over the one from the left side and the impulses travel to the visual cortex on opposite sides."

He walked over to the aperture and standing just to its side switched the opening to a square shape.

"The image is not determined by the shape of the aperture. The bulbs emit the light into the room, and some of it passes through the hole. The darkness surrounding the light also belongs to the image, and wherever we position the aperture, the image of the *tetractys* is captured."

He manually slid the middle wall back on some sort of track mechanism, and continued.

"There are no isolated rays of light. That's an abstraction. Each position in space carries an image of the whole. The aperture merely fixes the image at a particular place and time."

"So..." I paused a moment, taking in the concept. "It's like the collapse of the wave function and..." I stopped. Something about this realization called up a constellation of feelings and memories. Hadn't my own life irrevocably crystalized into some form? Wasn't this at the heart of my ennui, my sense that something had gone massively wrong, that at some undefined moment the wave function of my life had collapsed into a specific place and time, fixing me into one particularity?

Of course, there were the events of conception and birth, but I was thinking of afterwards, how the events of life unfolded after birth. To my mind there seemed to be a series of ever more infrequent crystalizing thresholds in my life, until I was defined, stuck at this seeming terminus of inoperability. Only now, since I'd arrived in Paris, and encountered Jacques, and the group, did I feel a sense of re-entering the flux of possibility.

"It's almost holographic, isn't it?" I came back to the present, reminded of something from the earlier conversation. Hadn't Jacques said that the whole universe was contained within our consciousness? The universe folded into each human being, giving us access to the entire gamut of experience. Yes, and therein the entire body of knowledge was accessible.

"Yes, that is a valid metaphor."

Andreas walked back to the console.

"Here; another aspect of light."

He turned off the lights, and for a moment it was entirely dark. I heard another switch, and the light came on again. I was temporarily disoriented, since the entire configuration of the room seemed altered, as if a whole new dimension of the chamber was opened up in a perpendicular direction.

The illumination now emanated from a single bulb, and in the middle of the room I could see a rectangular glass container, almost like an aquarium, mounted on a platform. Andreas redirected the light, so it now shown through the entire vertical length of the glass box. At first, I could see nothing inside the glass box, just darkness. He then made some adjustments on the console.

Gradually, I now could see slowly turning curls of vapor illuminated by the light, languidly coiling inside the glass.

"By itself, light is invisible," he said distantly.

Is light diaphanous? I asked myself, thinking back to the conversation with Christy.

252

"Only when light encounters an object or some suspended matter does it become visible. Think of the colored orb of the earth floating in the purported emptiness of space. It is only when light strikes the earth that we see evidence of its presence."

It was a strange notion. For a moment I glimpsed something greater, something indefinable. I thought of the entire vastness of space, as a medium, teeming with different wavelengths of electromagnetic energy cloaked by darkness.

"Fiat Lux." Jacques suddenly appeared next to me. How he was able to silently enter the module without calling attention to himself, I could not tell.

"Ah, yes. The marvels of light," Jacques added.

"Our universe is revealed through light," Andreas responded seeming to smile beneath his beard.

The demonstration was finished, and we exited the experimental device. Through the windows I noticed an aircraft sitting in front of the hanger. I realized that Jacques must have attended to some of the issues associated with their impending flight to the islands. There was the matter of all the crates assembled in the warehouse.

Jacques turned to me, "A major weather system is coming off the Atlantic later this evening, and we're going to depart a little earlier than scheduled. Here you can see our incredible Grumman Albatross." Jacques gestured out to the plane waiting on the tarmac.

"We'll be taking a longer route, first south to Morocco and then south by southwest over the Atlantic, a remarkable flight."

The aircraft was an older propeller plane, equipped for amphibious take offs and landings, its two engines mounted above a wing that stretched over the top of the fuselage. Though I couldn't see it clearly, the insignia on the side of the plane appeared to be the same *tetractys* Andreas had shown me inside the camera obscura. Several men wearing blue overhauls were standing next to a ramp that had dropped down from the back of the plane. I was intrigued by the aircraft, but also a bit startled at their sudden immanent departure.

Before I could ask them about their preparations, Andreas cordially bid me farewell, indicating that if all went according to plans, he would see me on Splendent Cay.

With my visit concluded, Jacques drove me to the train station in the town. During the short drive he talked enthusiastically about the sojourn to the islands. He also informed me that by the time I arrived, he would be temporarily occupied by various responsibilities, and that I wouldn't see him for almost a week. I wanted to ask Jacques more questions, particularly about the holographic nature of the universe, but I couldn't seem to formulate the right way to approach the subject. He warmly bid me adieu in front of the station, and I was left feeling a combination of excitement associated with his eminent departure, and my own sense of suddenly being alone in Paris.

26: Altered State

I took the RER back into Paris and returned to my hotel. Later in the evening, I decided to visit the Palais de Tokyo, since the museum was open till midnight.

When I exited the Metro, a misting rain was falling. The ambient urban light illuminated the underside of the cloud cover that shrouded Paris. I walked up a slight incline and near a pocket of greenery I was afforded a view of the magnificently lit Eiffel tower. A searchlight beacon rotated around the top. For a moment, it reminded me of some sort of alien artifact plopped down among the stately structures of the 19th century city. I thought about Jacques and Andreas flying somewhere south, southwest, of the Ile de France escaping just ahead of the inclement weather.

Apart from a few people lingering at the entrance, the Palais Tokyo seemed virtually empty, only a few scattered voices echoed within the vast marble and concrete interior. The wind buffeted the trees outside. Silhouetted against an amber streetlight, the branches restlessly moved against the window. The rain was coming down harder now. The attendant sold me a ticket, nonchalantly handing me the program. I paused in front of the large bookstore near the entrance. Innumerable books and magazines were displayed many of them stacked or laid out flat on tables. Automatically, I placed my fingers on a few of the titles as if through touch alone I could absorb the contents. Inside, the clerk, self-absorbed, was poring over some text.

Unobtrusively, hanging on the wall near the entrance, was a picture of the presiding spirit of the place: Pierre Restany, a fellow traveler from the cosmic utopia of art, a rebel against the contagion of consumerism.

I entered the dimly lit vast galleries. Andreas had his work installed on the main floor, and I plunged deeper into the interior.

I walked past an exhibit of abstract paintings, large paintings with fields of color poured across swaths of bare canvas, past a few installations that seemed to be mostly a cataloging of disparate objects, or curios: a rock collection, illustrated magazines from the 1920s, old maps of Africa and South America.

Wandering deeper into the heart of the building, I came across the module sitting alone in a cavernous hall. The object was similarly shaped, though more compact, than the one in the hanger at Le Bourget. In appearance it reminded me of some sort of space technology. It was constructed out of a milky glass like material.

Close up it seemed to consist of many different colors, sparkling like some sort of translucent marble. I paused a moment to look closely at the surface. There appeared a thousand tiny stars suspended in the glassy medium. Various tubes and wires wrapped in foil and banded together, descended from the ceiling and entered into a shiny rectangular black housing on top of the module. I walked around counterclockwise, and found the entrance, a swiveled door that softly sealed shut behind me.

The interior seemed to be made of the same material as the outside, but here it was opaque, and entirely white in color. The

256

floor seamlessly merged with the walls, and the ceiling. In the center was a modular seating arrangement. The textured upholstery was colored royal blue, two seats back to back reclining back slightly tilted toward the ceiling. Like the device in the hangar, the design of the interior reminded me of some sort of futuristic airline.

I sat down into the soft chair. The interior seemed to sense my presence for the lighting dimmed slightly. The whiteness appeared to be lit from behind, in such a way that I couldn't determine the shape or the depth of the space that surrounded me. I relaxed for a moment and stared ahead into the white.

For the first time in days, I felt like I could gather my thoughts and survey the events of the last week. I was finished with Paris. I thought back to the first days of my visit. There was the meeting with Christy on the first day, and the visit to the Louvre. I tried to reconstruct the series of chance events that had led me to the meeting with Jacques and the rest of the group. I traced the beginning of the encounter back to my visits to the Pompidou Center. There was the first evening standing on the high balcony. In my mind's eye, I could still see myself looking out over the city. Within that memory, I felt a certain lightness letting my gaze glide above the lights of Paris. I thought how, from that perspective high up in the Pompidou Center, I would have looked down to where I was now situated somewhere within that constellation of glittering lights that was Paris.

Then, there was the second night at the Pompidou Center. It was while I walked through the exhibits that evening that I had experienced another realization, even an epiphany, having to do with the development of art in the Twentieth century, the unfolding of formal innovations, and the rupturing of the space time fabric.

The memory of Andromeda returned to me, then. I could see her face, her blue-green eyes accented by her makeup. I felt a rush of excitement, and a sudden feeling of warmth. I recalled the chance encounter near the Passage du Grand-Cerf. Another wave of excitement washed over me. Could it have been her there, as well? I compared the two different visual memories. Even now, only one week later that earlier memory seemed remote, as if cut from a different cloth, from an entirely different era, like there had been a juncture or fissure that had opened up in my life.

I reached back to the other memories and tried to distill a sense of everything that had happened during my visit to Paris. I couldn't encompass the entirety of it all, only fragments, now, like a deconstructed abstract painting.

I came back to myself. Hadn't I been diverted from my original intentions? I wondered.

In my innermost feelings, the artistic project had been a pretense for something else that I was unconsciously searching for. What had been troubling me for all these years? Wasn't it something buried in the lost continent of childhood memories, a sense of incompleteness, the sense of expectation? I couldn't tell for sure anymore.

I remembered some of the ideas Jacques had mentioned in the course of the day. There was the holographic nature of the universe, the intelligence of the heart, and the two types of mind. The entire universe folded into our consciousness, into our souls.

The entire universe caught in one glance of affinity.

What then, were the stars and nebulae? What was infinite space? Internal? External?

More thoughts passed through my mind: invisible light, a time free present, an irrational origin. Was our perception of time regulated by some apparatus in our brain?

I touched each of these for a moment. They were almost like labels, flat impressions that I sifted through one after another. I couldn't seem to get inside these notions, I tried to turn them over, or open them up. It was just then that I must have nodded off.

I opened my eyes. Nothing seemed to have changed within the interior of the module: Opaque white. I almost stood up, but a feeling of inertness overcame me. I closed my eyes again. Or, I thought I did. Or, did it actually become darker inside the module?

Out of the darkness color started to emerge. First on the borders, one side blue, and the other yellow, then the entire band of spectrum colors, separated into brilliant discrete hues, some dilating some contracting. Then a merging into one luminous shade of red, like a burning tropical sunset. A coral red, hot like some incandescence smeared across the sky. The color continued to change. Now, my entire field of vision was filled with a deep magenta red, gradually intensifying, into an ethereal shade, a most delicate, cooling shade of violet red. I fell into a profoundly relaxed state. It was as if all the concerns of worldly life slipped away, sloughed off me. I dropped deep down into a well of rejuvenation.

I opened my eyes again. The room was white. I felt different, somehow. A steady feeling of joy came welling up inside of me. With this change in feeling, there was a subtle but commensurate alteration in the quality of the white light. It became more radiant. Then suddenly there was a simultaneous dilation and contraction in the field of white.

It was if the floor dropped out from under me. Like one of those dreams where you feel like you're falling. I laughed to myself at the feeling of exhilaration. It felt like I was levitating. In the next moment, I was suspended above the Palais de Tokyo, floating over the bend of the Seine, looking down on the glittering night lights of Paris. I looked up, toward a small opening in the clouds where I could see the glinting of stars.

Suddenly, I shot upward through the hole in the clouds, and in some infinitesimally, compressed moment, I took in an expanse of the earth with the clouds illuminated by a spectral nocturnal light, then, the entire earth, the moon, the sun, and even further, beyond.

I saw myself traveling on a light beam, or rather, in an instant, I was the light beam encompassing the entire galaxy, and even to the edge of what was the universe. I was part of a continuum of light stretching in all directions simultaneously. In that moment, the dimensions of space and time seemed to collapse into one. In some indescribable way I, or some extension of myself, was, or reached, the origin, that was not behind, or before, but still now. Within that brief moment of awareness, I slowly collapsed back down through a panorama of possibilities into the Earth itself, into Paris, into the module, all folded within the universe.

It was a strangely delayed collapse, since I felt like I didn't completely descend into my body at once; some component of my being still remained in transit, like the carriages of a train coming into a station. Only gradually did my complete being inhabit my bodily form: That small narrow space, that vital parenthesis of life that is our earthly body. Yet, from the cockpit of the module, I could see a flotilla of spaceships moored above Paris. The vessels were of many different colors: Crimson red, amethyst, jade green, and lemon yellow.

Momentarily, I came down another level descending more completely back to the module. My eyes focused, and I realized the spaceships appeared to be part of a painting on the wall. Several paintings were hanging on the side of the module wall. Softly, a door slid closed to cover up the paintings.

The interior of the module was now completely opaque white. It took me several moments, or maybe it was a few minutes to recognize where I was.

Wait, I thought, when I came to myself. I wasn't entirely sure what had actually happened. Was the module some sophisticated visualization machine, or had I just imagined this

260

incredible vision? A train of thoughts rushed through my mind. The lasting image I had was of the light beam, and the galaxy, and the connection beyond space and time of everything in this world to the moment of origin. As if the planet, with all its lush forests, rivers and oceans, the multitude of beings, and teeming cities, were all implicit in the universal origin right from the very beginning.

Into this reverie, I heard some knocking on the side of the module. Voices were speaking in French. The door opened and a security person from the museum peered in.

"Monsieur..."

Though I didn't comprehend the precise words, it appeared that the museum was now closed, and I was required to depart.

As I walked out of the museum into the damp night air, I smiled to myself. I thought I could see things clearer than ever before. I felt strangely liberated from the ennui that had lingered in the corners my mind. The constellation of ideas I had experienced in the module, seemed to fade away, but I wasn't concerned, for I felt something substantive had been reawakened in my mind, a definitive threshold had been crossed, and all these ideas, even the entire universe, would never be far from me.

PART TWO: Sea Station Atlantis

1: Splendent Cay

I passed through a couple time zones on the long flight southwest over the ocean, my eyes almost constantly peering out the window at the changing scene. Multifarious shades of white and blue, clouds and water. The varying patterns etched in the water thousands of feet below, the traces of wind on water, the sunlight glinting, sparkling, the light increasingly reflective, finally the dazzling late afternoon light shimmering to the west. Towards sunset some islands appeared, intermittently below, shards of sand or rock emerging from the eternal ocean.

Later in the evening I made the connecting flight to a more remote island.

After disembarking, I entered the arrivals lounge, and among a small cluster of people I was met by a Rastafarian figure with long dreadlocks and a beard, holding a sign "Splendent Cay". It was Mattheus. He led me back out on to the tarmac and the two of us climbed aboard the waiting Grumman Albatross. Exhausted, I fell asleep in the passenger cabin, and several hours later, well into the night we finally arrived at Splendent Cay.

***

Even before I opened my eyes, I could hear the ocean in my ears. Listening to the unceasing rhythm of the waves, I could almost feel the vibration of the waves pounding against the shore.

The sun light streamed into the white interior. A pure, over saturated light infused all the room like a soft liquid. After the weak sun of Paris, the effect was overwhelming.

Walking onto the balcony, I was enveloped by the warm humid air, and the sound of the breeze rustling the palms.

The room was perched above the beach, providing a slightly elevated perspective. A slash of dark blue marked the edge of the horizon, and an ever-changing fringe of foamy white marked the site of the reef. The waters closer to the shore were variable shades of lighter, brighter blue, aquamarine and turquoise.

The curve of the bay was larger than I had expected. I followed the shore far to my left and recognized the ruins of the old Portuguese castle on a terrace of elevated land, and beyond, on the distant horizon an armada of puffy clouds floated above the island. To my right a promontory jutted out into the sea.

Looking out at the boundless blue my mind tried to imagine in what direction was Paris, or where the continent of Africa would be. Unlike Paris, I could gauge the time of day. The sun was not overhead yet, it was positioned somewhere between early morning and midday. I thought back on the dream I had in Florence, the meridian lines that longitudinally marked the earth, zones of time that the earth passed through on its course through day and night. I tried to imagine the turning of the globe, ever eastward.

I looked out into the center of the ocean, again, trying to fathom the immensity of the ocean, the world ocean, the source of life. Something, almost primal came over me as I pondered the idea of the depths, and the unceasing waves.

Looking again toward the promontory, I noticed a small domed structure rising partially above the vegetation. Pennants were blowing in the breeze from a mast on its top.

Taking in the whole scene, I felt an inexpressible sense of delight, and joy well up inside. I almost felt like a kid again. I had the urge to run down to the beach immediately and jump in the water.

I went back inside and changed. I took a moment to study the interior of the room, unmistakably Moorish in its style. The metal interlacing of the lanterns, the sumptuous upholstery in rich hues of red and purple added to the effect. Intricate geometric patterns were faintly etched into the stucco walls. The only thing that didn't seem entirely Moorish was a large framed mirror, with a sculptural relief of an open shell form placed at the top.

The exterior of the Hotel Splendent continued the same Moorish theme. My room was situated at the top of a slight hillock, and walking downward, I passed no more than ten other units. Each unit had a white dome, and a separate entrance framed by an arch. The grounds were lushly landscaped. The tropical green rustled lightly in the breeze matching the incessant sound of the palms in the background. Many flowers, the bright yellow of the mimosa, some deep purple flowers, and the fiery reds of the hibiscus filled the garden.

Stopping for a moment, I gazed into the heart of a hibiscus. The brilliant red took on an even deeper hue inside the petals, a deep red that bordered on violet. Here was revealed the source of the stamen and pistil. I studied the pollen with its tiny yellow clusters, and the intense red of stigma. I marveled at the way the light and shadow crisply delineated each form, each crinkle in the petals. The light of the sun captured in the heart of the flower. Everything seemed so vivid here, especially after the dull grey light of Paris.

Arriving at the bottom of the path, the main building of the complex was little more than an open-air restaurant. The wooden structure, painted white was of a completely different style than the Moorish style accommodations. It had the feel of an old mid-twentieth century resort. The veranda shaded a dining area perched on the edge of the beach.

I headed down a plank path to the edge of the beach, dropping my stuff underneath the shade of an umbrella, and ran down to the water. The light was so intense I could barely look at the expanse of aquamarine water. The sound of the waves resounded in my ears, and the smell of the sea filled my nostrils. The surf moved with a gentle swelling motion, and after wading in only a few feet, I dived into the warm salt water. I swam for almost twenty minutes, swimming way out toward the reef, until the water must have been more than thirty feet deep. Eventually, I returned to the shore. Pausing at edge of the water, I looked down the beach and watched the incoming waves lap the sand. Finished with my swim, I walked back up to the restaurant, feeling refreshed and exhilarated.

Gemina was seated at a table on the edge of the dining area, facing away from the beach. Aside from the staff, she was the only person there.

"Thomas, you've arrived." She was wearing all white, with her hair wrapped in a colorful bandanna that mimed the colors of the tropical vegetation.

I smiled, still a bit dazed at the spectacular ocean setting.

On the table was a plate of tropical fruit, avocados, papaya, and mango, sliced in crescent shapes, and a tea service. She directed me to sit down and join her for breakfast.

"So, how did you sleep in these splendid accommodations?" She asked, gesturing with her arm to the surroundings.

"I had a remarkably restful sleep, maybe the best in years." I gazed out to the azure blue horizon, resting my eye for a moment at the point where the white waves encountered the reef. "Maybe, I should live here by the sea."

Gemina laughed, "Ah, the healing ocean. We all feel it." She seemed to take a deep breath.

"You look different, better," she added.

"I feel better than I've felt, maybe, in years." It was funny sort of admission for me to make since I usually wouldn't have been so expressive of my feelings.

"You burned away some of your shadow," she remarked.

"What shadow?" I asked, smiling, but a bit confused.

Gemina smiled, "The shadow that blocks your angel of light. The Germans call it a doppelganger. Once your being becomes transparent, you are free to experience a pure angelic consciousness."

"Maybe something happened in Paris," I admitted, slightly amused at her perceptive analysis. The entire week must have altered my constitution on some level, I thought.

"Your dissatisfactions, all that you were struggling with, trying to articulate, were a sign that your angel was trying to wake you up."

"Perhaps, that's true," I acknowledged.

"Sometimes we confuse the shadow with ourselves. We get so bound to our negative emotions, thinking that they are part of ourselves."

"But weren't they real?"

"What is real? The negative emotions that we generate are merely phantoms,"

"It's hard to be aware in those moments, one seems swept away by the intensity of the emotional reaction," I complained.

"Yes, Emotions are faster than our thoughts. One must employ a powerful positive antidote to counteract their effect."

"What do you mean?"

"Think of the scales, the sign of Libra, become conscious of yourself as the axis, the agent of discriminating wisdom, empty the negative emotions from the pan of your lower soul, place more weight on the side of the heart, the spiritual heart. Then your true being will become clear, more transparent."

"I see," I said, a little embarrassed with my ignorance.

"Negative emotions are a lower expression, almost like a wild beast inside that you must tame, and control. Otherwise you become a captive of their ferocious energies. The controlling powers want to keep us entrained to our negative emotions."

"The adversary?" Evoking this possibly fictive entity in the splendid seashore atmosphere seemed doubly incongruous to me.

Gemina laughed.

"The adversary, yes, but not just the adversary, even Nature." She seemed to gesture out to the sparkling sunlight reflected on the ocean, "There are certain limitations placed into our being."

"What sort of limitations?"

"We have our place in the order of the world. From the womb of nature each living being unfolds as a perfectly differentiated creation." She gestured outward, pausing to look into the sky, "Nature prefers we remain within certain parameters. Only individually can we move beyond this framework, and even then, there are barriers, challenges that must be surmounted. On a mass scale it would be catastrophic for the planet, therefore nature sets limits."

She looked aside, and a darker mood seemed to come into her face. "This is a problem, in fact. Humanity has already decoupled from nature. The predicament of the present world

268

is a result of humanity moving beyond its proper relationship with the natural order. There has been a violation."

"I agree," I responded energetically, "The over population of the world, the global nature of pollution." I was concerned that she might think I was ignorant to these developments.

"Look all around. Events are rapidly accelerating. Realizations, that should have been limited and internal, have been expressed, externalized, and implemented on a massive scale. The world has already crossed multiple thresholds. The Earth is in danger," She explained.

Gemina swung around in her seat and partially faced the ocean, talking in a more insistent tone, "The Earth feels this disharmony, all the beings of the Earth feel it. The institution of science approaches the world from the outside, so called, objective knowledge of molecules and atoms. Yet what do we really know? Do we know the being of the ocean? Do we know the inner being of the ocean, the matrix of all life?"

"The world ocean," I remarked thoughtfully, looking out on the horizon, trying to visualize an inner dimension to the ocean.

Gemina turned around only part way, seeming to close her eyes.

"Do we even know our own being? Do we know all the possibilities within ourselves? Trillions of neurons and synapsis is the picture science presents to us. Do we really understand ourselves?" She spoke almost to herself.

"I don't think so. It's like we live on an interface, between the outside world, the impression of our senses, and the inner function of our physical body," I said.

"Yes, Exactly," she turned, completely facing me, opening her eyes again.

"I feel like the language of science is incompatible with my inner experience. Sometimes I think of the metaphor of a television set. We receive the program, yet we don't understand the nature of the transmission or the electronics of the monitor," I offered.

"Yes, that's perceptive. There is more to our being than we realize. The human being is a magnificent creation. We embody all the functions of nature in one form, the culmination of natural evolution. Indeed, we are a living image of the universe."

"But we don't seem to be aware of all the different functions inside of us. Do I know the action of my pituitary gland?"

"Yes. Nature has set up a barrier, a screen, to keep us from entering the workings of our being. In ancient times there was still an intuitive awareness of our body, for example, in the description of the different temperaments. Even today we have a vestige of this old wisdom, in words like bilious, pointing to the action of the bile."

"Then, our conscious experience seems to exist in a different domain than the physical organs or glands," I offered.

Gemina was slow to respond, looking into the sky, then she continued, "Of course, we are more than just a sum of our physical parts. It is necessary, particularly in this time, if we are not to become totally enthralled to technology, to develop an awareness of the complete scope of our being. Otherwise humanity will face a future of bondage to mechanical forces beyond their control."

Just then one of the staff, a young woman, walked over to our table and handed Gemina a note. She read the note slowly, and then looked back up to me.

"A message from Andromeda, she's wants us to join her at the Sea Station."

2: The Observatory

We left the shaded porch, and I followed Gemina through the garden leading away from the beach. The sound of the surf diminished into the background, replaced by the rustling of the palm fronds. We passed under a vine covered arch, and into a sandy lot where an old jeep was parked.

I hadn't considered the possibility that Gemina would drive, but she was completely at ease with the jeep's manual transmission. She quickly turned the vehicle around, and we drove out beyond the lush grounds of the hotel, on to a rough track leading through the barren landscape.

The intensity of the light was overwhelming. I could gaze into the sky only for a few moments at a time. The bright white clouds, billowing upward reflected the full spectrum of light, seeming to burn my eyes. Intermittently, we drove into the shadows they cast, and then back out into the bright sunlight. I had forgotten how intensely hot the sun was at this latitude, and without the cooling sea breeze, or the shade of tropical vegetation, the temperature and humidity were overpowering.

The track followed a long roundabout route. At first, we curved away from the Sea Station, only to approach it from the other side of the island. I studied the landscape for any signs of human habitation, but the island seemed empty. From this side of the island, the domed profile of the Sea Station was practically invisible, camouflaged by palm trees, and a few erratic boulders that surrounded a prominent hill.

The dirt road swelled upward as we gained elevation. By the time we reached a parking area at the foot of the Sea Station we must have gained almost a hundred feet. Gemina parked the jeep, and I looked out across the island to the sea in the west.

The clouds and sky interspersed creating a pattern of light and shadow on the water. Off in the distance, I glimpsed the raised profile of another island faintly emerging from the sea mist. From this prominence I could see how the green vegetated area clung only to a small band along the bay where the lodge was located; the rest of island seemed completely barren. The wind whipped around us, and the temperature was more manageable up here.

We climbed up a winding staircase of stone steps wedged into a narrow space between the boulders. The breeze rustled the palm fronds, and I looked up at the gathering clouds wondering about the possibility of rain. We climbed around to the front of the structure, where the top of the hill was level with the first tier of the station.

Although the front of the structure faced out to the ocean and was designed like a boat with a deck and a forecabin, the center had the domed shape of an astronomical observatory. We entered the station, and Gemina closed the door leaving the tropical air behind.

I felt a sense of relief at returning to an air-conditioned environment. Walking through a short narrow passage, we entered what seemed to be a library, minimally illuminated, mostly by a pair of computer screens. Inside, Andromeda was seated at the end of a table looking intently at a satellite image of the earth, clouds flowing eastward, left to right, across the screen.

"Tomas," Andromeda stood up from the table smiling, "Welcome to Splendent Cay." She reached over one of the chairs to embrace me. In that moment, I smelled an indefinable freshness in her hair, a flowery fragrance mixed with the scent of the ocean. She was dressed as if she had just come from the beach, wearing a white macramé top, only partially concealing a red and green colored two-piece bathing suit underneath.

Gemina sat down in front of the other monitor, and intently focused on the satellite animation. Looking down at the image, I could make out cloud patterns moving over the Atlantic. The currents of air slowly flowed across the screen in spiral shapes, undulating and unfolding across the ocean. On top, they traveled from west to east. On the bottom, they moved from east to west, seeming to form a great circle turning in a clockwise direction.

As my eyes adjusted to the dim light, I was able to take in more of the interior of the room. Indeed, it was a library of sorts, with shelves on either side filled with books and document binders. More books piled up on the table, and another monitor displaying an image of the solar disc. It was a dark sun. A negative image surrounded by an orange corona.

Above in the ceiling was a semi-circular opening with slanted windows that let in light from the front and sides of the station. Through the windows, I could still see the palm fronds silently waving outside.

"This is what I wanted to show you," Andromeda said to her mother, reaching over to click on the monitor displaying the solar image. Instead of the sun there now appeared row after row of numbers.

"Jacques has been monitoring the solar activity for years, studying the solar magnetic field. Initially, this was the reason for building the observatory here," Andromeda explained.

Gemina leaned over the monitor and intently scrolled through rows of numerical data.

Andromeda pointed to something on her monitor, and the perspective changed. The entire planet was now displayed in a global format from the western Pacific on the left, to the eastern extremity of the Asian landmass on the right.

I could clearly see how the weather patterns of the North Atlantic fit into a larger global picture. One prominent curve undulated across the northern hemisphere, dipping south here, rising north there, splitting, and then rejoining, eventually circumnavigating the entire globe. She touched the keyboard and another level of data dropped into the image, a colored overlay of various shades of blue moved slowly beneath the clouds.

"Look at this." Andromeda pressed the keyboard. The screen changed again, and I could see the outline of the continents and undulating blue bands flowing across the Northern hemisphere.

Andromeda looked up at me, and explained, "The speed of the jet stream is slowing over North America. Also, we have the stagnant high-pressure systems over California and Europe. The North Atlantic jet is shifting further north, here." She pointed to the screen, and then added, "We started to see significant changes to the jet stream starting in the 1960s; something is altering the climate."

I looked up at the windows, suddenly remembering that our position on the island was part of this global image. A few raindrops were now falling against the windows.

"Yes," Gemina broke her silence, "this is troubling." She was still staring intently at the numbers on the screen.

Andromeda looked up to me again.

"We're on a threshold of a pronounced solar minimum, all the data points to an exceptionally low upcoming solar cycle."

"What does it all mean?" I asked.

"It signals changes for the Earth."

"The weather, you mean?"

"Not just the weather, more. The ebb and flow of the solar cycles effect the entire unfolding of planetary civilization. We see evidence of this throughout history. We reached a tremendous peak of solar activity in the late 1950s. Now, it's declining quite dramatically. It does affect the climate, but there are deeper implications. There's an inverse relation between solar activity and cosmic rays penetrating into the earth's atmosphere. The sun protects us within a cocoon of friendly radiation. And without the suns radiation we become more and more vulnerable to the cosmic radiation."

"The heliosphere, right," I replied.

Gemina turned to me and smiled.

"Yes, Thomas. The changes in the sun have a profound effect on humanity, even influencing our biological expression. Indeed, each of us is marked by the solar cycle of our birth."

Then looking toward Andromeda she added, "I'll need to stay here for the rest of the day, you and Thomas will have to walk back to the hotel."

3: Walk on the Beach

Andromeda exited the library, and I followed her into the front cabin. We paused a moment silently looking out at the ocean, the water reflecting many different shades of blue, and grey green. The rain had already finished, and in between the clouds shafts of light fell intermittently across the sea. I looked down the long curve of the shoreline toward the hotel.

"We'll take the scenic way back," Andromeda said, touching my arm.

The rain had cooled the air, and a light breeze lent a fresh dynamic feeling to the atmosphere. Down a narrow stone staircase, underneath a canopy of wet foliage, we descended toward the beach. To our side a cascade of water emerged from a crack in the rock and tumbled down toward the beach.

We walked along the edge of the beach where the receding surf left the sand wet and firm, Andromeda seemingly lost in thought, walked ahead of me. I gazed up at the interplay of light and shadow in the sky, now clearing more, opening patches of deep blue juxtaposed against the bright white of the clouds.

We stopped for a moment in a little scallop of a cove. An old stone pier jutting into the water partially arrested the waves and formed a sheltered basin. We both waded into the swaying water.

I was captivated by the play of the breeze and the energetic flow of the waves, trying to maintain my balance as each new wave rolled in. Andromeda peered into the water, seemingly searching for something, rocking back and forth with the incoming waves.

Working against the flow of the waves, I waded over to be closer to her. In the soft afternoon light, I noticed the texture of her bare skin, her hair tousled by the breeze. I paused in the water next to her.

"The sea: the source of all life." I looked out to the aquamarine horizon, trying to fathom the essence of the ocean.

"Yes," Andromeda sighed. "And the mystery of how it came about is hidden somewhere in these depths." She gestured out to the waves.

"How did it happen?" I asked, "And is it still happening, somewhere, out there?"

She looked thoughtfully out to the horizon, not answering my question.

"I mean, the leap or jump from the inanimate to the animate," I asked, looking wistfully out to deep blue."

"No one is entirely sure." She looked pensively out to the waves, then continued, "Life is immanent in the universe, only on a planet like this are the conditions right. The earth, the sea, the atmosphere, are all always in a state of flux. The sea currents, the breezes, are never still, always dynamic, a condition of non-equilibrium, and only in such a place, could anything as complex as life ever come about."

I waded in deeper, reaching down into the foaming surf, trying to cup a handful of water, almost losing my balance as the waves swelled around my legs lifting me up.

"The sea," I said, holding my hands up as the water slipped between my fingers, "there's something almost viscous about it."

"Can you feel the life?" Andromeda responded, laughing lightly, and dipping her hands into the water and touching it to her lips.

"It's so different from the Great Lakes. Freshwater seems almost sterile compared to the salt water."

"Yes, there is more complexity to the salt water," Andromeda smiled at me.

"Perhaps salt is the key. Without salt there could be no life?"

"That's probably true. Once the primal oceans become saline the first transition is reached. Something in the structure of the salts, perhaps an organizing property or a chemical clock of sorts, responds to environmental conditions, leading to increased complexity. Salt fixes life." she paused looking into the water. "There are still so many questions. There had to be a catalyst for life to appear." The incoming waves rocked her slightly back and forth.

I stared down into the water, studying the changing ripples. Watching the patterns, I suddenly recognized my reflection in the water, the light of the sun silhouetted my figure with a circle of light. An image of the whole captured on the surface of the water.

"The sun," I almost said to myself. "Maybe a solar storm bombarded the earth with high energy particles, triggering the shift from inanimate molecules to animate."

Andromeda smiled at me, "It's a possibility. Some pivotal event, like that was necessary."

Moving closer to shore, she reached down into the water and pulled up a handful of shells and held it out toward me. Looking down into her cupped hands each tiny colored form glistened in the sunlight. Some were pointed spiral shapes others were more open fragments, pearly pink, glistening bright reflecting the sun.

"These are all organic. The calcium carbonate shell is extruded by a living creature."

"Really?" I hadn't actually realized how shells were formed. The foaming surf washed up around our legs.

"Yes, invertebrates. Here," she held out to me a larger spiral shaped shell. "A conch shell."

I held it in my hand examining the shell, with its star like pattern, turning it in the light, the sun glistening on its wet surface. Inside the pocket like opening, a smaller spiral shell was lodged along with some grains of sand.

Andromeda offered me another shell. This one was smaller, with a fan like pattern.

"The Shell Oil sign," I said.

Andromeda laughed, "It's a scallop shell. The symbol is used by pilgrims on the Road to Santiago de Compostella."

I recognized it also as the same shell as the one at the top of the mirror in my room.

She held up another fragment; it glistened golden pink in the sun.

"Beautiful," I remarked, peering closely at the shiny shell in her hand.

She turned it in the light, the colors shifting like a tiny rainbow.

"The mother of pearl," she said.

I kept the two shells and we walked back up on to the sand. The sun had started to break out even more from the clouds, and we moved up to the bluff, and a stand of palm trees that provided some shade. The rustling of the fronds drowned out the sound of the surf. Here we sat down on a fallen tree and turned to face the ocean. Looking out from our shaded perspective, the color blue was blended from turquoise to ultramarine, and further out a deep shade of indigo appeared beyond the line of the reef, here and there, foaming bits of white marked waves hitting the reef.

I strained my eyes looking out to the edge of the horizon, looking for any other islands or maybe a passing ship. There was nothing visible except for clouds and the expanse of blue.

"In what direction is Africa?" I asked, almost as if I could see the Atlas Mountains, or maybe Atlantis.

"Out there." She pointed much further to the right of where I had been looking, almost parallel with the shoreline, just beyond the Sea Station. I had been almost completely disoriented.

"What about Paris then?"

"Maybe, out there, to the north 30 degrees." She pointed a little bit further out to sea.

"Then north is almost directly out there." I pointed to the center of our field of vision.

"Yes. The curve of the bay opens to the north, over to the west would be North America."

I looked over to the left, taking into my mind the motion of the sun going down over the bulk of the American continent. I tried to visualize the expanse of the continental landmass, surely covering the entire western horizon, and how it might curve around the surface of the earth. Somewhere far over the horizon, was Florida; further to the north, the Great Lakes, and much further west, the Rocky Mountains.

"When was the last time you were in America?"

"It's been years since I've been there. It's become such a toxic culture; the market dominates every aspect of society."

"Yeah, and the media saturation is almost total," I responded.

"Everything is driven by what the marketplace wants, and not what's appropriate for the human individual."

"It's intolerable," I added.

"It's not much better in Europe, or the rest of the world. The whole world has succumbed to the Western model; the power of capital to exert its control over the entire planet. A Faustian bargain."

She paused, looking off into the sea wistfully. Like the day we spent in Paris, I felt I intuited something in her thinking, something that related to my own experience.

"Everything's changed, in less than a lifetime. The felt experience of life seems altered."

I was grasping at words trying to articulate the strange disjunction I had felt for years, returning to that sense of ennui that seemed to evaporate on my last evening in Paris, and all that seemed distant now that I was on the island, and near Andromeda.

"The scale of technological implementation is turning the earth into an inhumane place," she said.

"If we could only reserve natural areas, zones of zero or minimal technological development, even in proximity to the great cities," I offered, thinking of one of my designs for the city of the future.

"The will of capital is to fill in all areas, every inch of the earth, even the sky and seas. Everything must be available for total technological exploitation, even our bodies. There are no limits to capital, no sense of natural proportions."

"The more capital is allowed free reign, the less free we are as humans," I offered.

"So true," Andromeda nodded.

I thought of the jet aircraft crisscrossing almost every sector of the globe, the satellites circling the planet, drone aircraft monitoring the skies, ever increasing noise pollution masking the silence of nature, all the accoutrements of technology asserting themselves into our lives, pressing in on life itself. A prosthetic layer of technological debris, plastic bags, back up beepers, car horns, advertising, news reports, codes, passwords, all polluting my psyche. There seemed to me no escape except for an island like this.

"Technology seems to interfere with the real experiences of life," I suggested.

"Yes. It obscures something more important. It's not just the machines of technology, the apparatus of technology, although that is a problem. It's rather the way it shapes our view of the world. How it subtly alters and manipulates our consciousness and diverts our attention away from the essence of our being, from the real purpose of life."

I momentarily lost myself in contemplation. There was something hypnotic about this place; the sea spread out below us, the ever-present breeze. I looked up to the palms, the sun light glittering on each swaying frond. An image of the sun captured in each facet of green, like a mirror.

"It's a sleight of hand," I said, almost to myself, "except the whole world is the mark."

Andromeda seemed to smile ever so slightly.

"Something integral to our being is blocked by the message of the technical system. Science claims there is no freedom, no choice, that we're determined beings, and we're turned aside from our most important faculty, allowing the technical system to enter into our psyche, substituting its algorithmic patterns for the organic."

Here on this island we could be safe, thousands of miles from the technical apparatus, and escape, at least temporarily, the way it insinuated itself into our minds, like some sort of alien virus.

"Freedom? You don't mean the freedom to eat ice cream any time you want?"

"No." She laughed, "That's a base level sort of response, and the marketing apparatus plays on and manipulates this kind of desire. Capital would have us believe that was freedom. There's a confusion of meaning, substituting in our minds actual freedom with something that is really just a desire, an urge. There are many erroneous ideas about freedom."

"This idea of freedom, isn't it a new element? I mean relatively speaking it almost seems like a recent introduction to the human story." I was thinking of Pico, and then the revolutions of the late 1700s.

Andromeda smiled again.

"Yes, there is a story to the unfolding of human capacities, the evolution of consciousness over time."

"It seems that, while freedom is introduced into the human experience, like during the Renaissance, there is another element that increasingly comes into play at the same time. Something related to technology that begins making inroads, dominating our lives, and limiting our freedom, when we should actually be more free," I argued.

Andromeda looked at me, her eyes seeming to look deeper into me than before.

"That's true. Simultaneous with the development of freedom, there is another force acting on human consciousness. With technology come the forces of death. There is a challenge, so to speak, to humanity that is even now reaching an extreme point, a climax perhaps. This is why it's so important to exercise the faculty of freedom we have, and not merely surrender to the autonomous forces of technology."

"The adversary," I said almost to myself, even though I wasn't even sure I even believed in such a personification.

"Yes, we could call it that. And yet it's more complicated. Humanity is being called on to develop something deeper, new faculties, part of a greater movement, or we run the risk of being subjected to these contrary powers."

It was almost too beautiful of a setting to speak of such matters. I stared into the expanse of ocean. I could direct my attention to the blue of the sea, or to the wind; my attention was free, at least, if I could remember I possessed such an object. I soaked up the pure blueness with my eyes, and listened to the sound of the palm leaves, the healing blue of the sky; the soothing wind. The pure elements of the world; water, wind, these would purify me.

Andromeda touched me on the shoulder, as I looked out to the blue.

"Yes, perhaps we shouldn't speak of these matters in such a beautiful place," she said, as if reading my thoughts. I thought for an instant about the evening in Paris where for a moment I thought I was looking into Gemina's mind.

"We should be getting back to the hotel, it's late and we should rest before dinner."

She stood up, "You must be tired, as well, after your long flight," she added.

"Yeah, I am, actually." I hadn't quite noticed it until we had sat down on the fallen palm trunk. Looking off into the distant blue had an almost soporific effect on me, and now I felt a bit weary as I stood up.

We walked away from the beach, and Andromeda found a path amidst the palmetto scrub that led us back to the hotel. The late afternoon light was golden, and all the colors of the landscape were glowing. We approached the hotel from the east, I realized, with the sun hanging over the hotel on the western horizon. The sun light glinted on the swaying palm leaves, sparkling like starlight.

A wall surrounded the edge of the hotel, and here a cascade of flowers tumbled down to the ground. There were many tiny white flowers, like millions of stars: jasmine, redolent with a sweet aroma. We laughed at ourselves as we each buried our faces in the flowers, lingering for a moment breathing in the intoxicating fragrance.

4: Evening at Chez Splendid

We parted for a while, each of us going back to our rooms. Andromeda seemed tired, as well, and once back in my room I laid on the bed and fell into a heavy slumber. I woke up later, it was dark. What time it was precisely, I couldn't say, since there was no clock in the room. Andromeda hadn't specified a particular time to rendezvous, so I felt a bit anxious about not seeing her for dinner. I quickly changed into some fresh clothes and went down to the restaurant.

The restaurant was empty except for some of the staff. The only person I recognized was Mattheus who was standing behind the bar.

"Monsieur Tomas, welcome," Mattheus greeted me with a warm smile, stretching out his hand.

"What time is it?" I asked somewhat abruptly, "I think, I overslept," I added.

"Oh, it's around nine, perhaps." He looked out towards the ocean. "Yes. The sun goes down quickly here."

"I had forgotten that. It's been awhile since I've been in this part of the world." I relaxed, still feeling a little foolish. I laughed to myself, realizing all my anxiousness had been unnecessary.

"Yes, the tropical night comes quickly. No, don't worry about time. You're free, here. You're not used to the island life. Yes, America, is such a crazy place, so artificial. Here on the islands we're blessed. We live such a pure life: fish from the sea, the bounty of the earth. Living out in the open, and then there is the work at the Sea Station."

I wasn't sure how much to ask Mattheus about the work. The previous evening, we had flown in together, but I had been too exhausted to ask him any more than the most perfunctory questions about the flight duration, and the weather conditions.

"What have you been working on here?" I asked, remembering from the night before that he had mentioned he was an engineer.

"We're building a new solar observatory for Monsieur Ashmounian."

"Really?"

"Yes, on the other side of the island. A more advanced facility to monitor the solar minimum. We're measuring the flux of the heliosphere." He paused a moment and then continued, "The cosmic radiation will impact the earth much more than people realize. It will affect the mass consciousness, even the life force. We can already see this, in the breakdown of civility, in the increasing political polarization, global tensions; stormy weather ahead, indeed."

"The cosmic radiation is worse, than the solar?"

"Oh, yes; much worse for our human bodies. It's like a battle between different beings, like a Greek myth, but on a cosmic scale. The sun is our benefactor, when it weakens, the cosmic beings sweep in with a different regime."

"Why here, on this island?" I asked

"A magnetic anomaly. Going back to the time of the Portuguese explorers, this was a way station on the way to

Brazil. They noted the magnetic anomaly hundreds of years ago."

"Where are Jacques and Andreas?"

"They're out on the Explorer, investigating the marvels of the sea. They should be back in a couple of days." He explained looking out to the ocean.

"Yes, and before I forget, Andromeda has prepared this for you." He smiled handing me a dinner tray with a slight flourish.

"For Monsieur Tomas, our American guest. No. We don't get many Americans, that's for sure, you may be the first."

I felt a funny mixture of embarrassment and camaraderie at his gentle teasing. The dinner plate looked inviting consisting of a Moroccan carrot salad with raisins, a side of yogurt, and some stuffed grape leaves; I realized I was famished.

Mattheus excused himself, and I took my dinner over to a table on the edge of the veranda looking out over the ocean. The breeze was refreshing, and the moon broke out from behind a veil of clouds and cast a pearly light on the water.

I paused, while I was eating just to listen to the wind in the palms, and sound of the surf. It seemed like I was almost in a dream. I could barely register my presence on the island. The events of the day, and now the beautiful evening atmosphere seemed like a fantasy. I tried to give my attention up to the wind, almost as if I was riding the wind. However, the ceaseless movement of the waves conspired against a meditative state of mind.

"Tomas," Andromeda suddenly broke into my reverie.

She was unrolling what appeared to be a nautical chart on the table next to mine and had placed a pair of flickering lamps down on the corners to anchor it down. I had mostly finished my dinner and was glad that she had finally arrived.

"You must look at this." The tone of her voice seemed concerned, even troubled.

She was dressed in a tropical fashion, with white slacks, and a fiery orange-red blouse. She leaned over the table studying the chart, and another piece of paper.

"What is it?" I asked, coming over to the table.

The chart was a map of the ocean in the vicinity of Splendent Cay. Several of the outlying islands were visible. There was a line of broken reefs, and shallow sand bars, and areas of deeper water swirling around, all surrounded by the dark blue waters of the open ocean.

"This is criminal." She seemed unusually agitated, "I just printed this data from a line of floating sensors on the edge of the archipelago." The expression on her face was strained as she looked at the map.

"What's going on?" I asked again

"Micro-plastics!" She pointed to a long thin island on the outer fringe of the archipelago.

"Micro-plastics?"

"Yes, tiny plastic nodules. Thousands and thousands of them, no bigger than a sesame seed. Here, where the current swings past the headland. The sensors have registered a three-mile long body of them dispersed in the current."

"Is it industrial waste?"

"It's hard to determine the point of origin. It's the effluent from global consumer culture, carried from thousands of miles away." She moved her fingers repeatedly over the map as if she were drawing or measuring something.

"The dogs of capitalism are destroying the natural world. They want to make this sort of degradation normative, as if pollution is a natural event." She stood up, rubbing her eyes and forehead.

"It's only a matter of time before it spreads further into these islands."

"It's spreading everywhere, then?" I asked.

"I'm afraid that's true. I hoped this would be a sanctuary, at least for a couple more years."

I was staring down at the table, still trying to make sense of the map, but out of the corner of my eye it seemed Andromeda wiped tears from her eyes.

"Maybe there is some way to control the particles, maybe push them back out into the deep ocean?" I said, lightly touching my hand to the side of her arm.

She seemed to laugh a little, perhaps at the absurdity of my suggestion.

"Maybe some large ships could be designed to scoop up the detritus. A future project for restoring the planet," I suggested.

She smiled wanly.

"Perhaps, but these are microscopic particles. It would be extremely difficult, an almost impossible task. If the earth is to be restored it will require more than large vessels for cleaning the water, it will require a complete change in economic behavior; a new mode, one that doesn't generate a super abundance of detritus." She looked up, and out to the waves breaking on the shore.

"We're losing a part of our being," she added almost under her breath.

"The being of the ocean?" I was reminded of what Gemina had said earlier.

"We're not separate. We are the ocean," she said quietly,

"It's terrible what's happening to the world." I said, touching my hand to her shoulder. It was hard for me to imagine such a beautiful and remote place touched by any sort of contamination.

She looked up toward me, the flickering light reflected in her eyes. In the reflecting pool of her eyes I recognized my silhouette. There was a moment suspended in time as we stood there. I thought of the evening in the church in Paris. I had the same feeling well up in me, a feeling of joy and warmth. I was almost ready to lean over and kiss her.

"What kind of system would kill the oceans, and poison the atmosphere?" She stared into my eyes, "Is that evil?"

"What is evil?" I wondered aloud, "Is it intentional or is it unconscious?"

"This is the heart of the problem. Some part of the system is intentional. There is certainly an intentional disregard for the being of nature. The system functions by dissembling and by fragmentation. The controlling agency is removed from our scrutiny, as if it was beyond question, opaque to our view." She paused a moment, turning away from me, "And yet all of us are implicated, in part, since the system is so all encompassing, it's almost impossible to escape."

"Why must the world be like this?" I looked out to the waves, "it could be organized so differently," I offered earnestly.

"Precisely, the elemental energies have been harnessed in such a crude and wasteful manner."

"The improper exploitation of the natural resources."

"Yes, but not just the earth energies." She looked out again to the sea, "even human energies and impulses have been harnessed and exploited."

I intuited something deeper lingering in her complaint.

"You mean the natural human drive for love, companionship, social connection, even a family?"

"Exactly, and the arbitrary structures twist and distort the natural impulses in the most obscene ways." She paused a moment, wistfully looking out to the sea. "How can we even bring children into a world like this?"

"I don't know."

"A world more and more controlled by the forces of death."

"It's disturbing."

"It may be too late for children, even." Andromeda stared out to sea.

"In what way?"

"It's different, now. There's no room, anymore."

"No room for childhood?" I almost said to myself, thinking about the freedom of my own childhood; the carefree, and indeterminate nature of my childhood, seemingly free to explore an endless realm of possibilities, endless days playing with friends, or out in nature. The world seemed more spacious, then, room for more possibilities.

"The absence of nature, would in some way, preclude the possibility of children," she said distantly.

"Yeah, but maybe in the future there will be some giant projects to cleanse the Earth, restore the forests, sift the sea to remove all the debris." I was fantasizing in away, a utopian vision of the planet, restored by some enlightened iteration of human culture.

"We can only hope there will be those prepared to undertake such enormous tasks."

She turned back toward me, and suddenly embraced me.

"It's been a long day." She rolled up the nautical chart.

"You must be tired." She seemed to study my face.

"I'd almost forgotten. I'm still adjusting to being here," I replied.

I wasn't sure if I was even making sense. Everything on the island had been such a new experience, and all so overwhelming, that I had almost forgotten that I had only just arrived. My senses seemed strangely overloaded, filled with images, colors, and light. Even my body felt touched by the impress of the solar radiation.

We walked back toward the entrance of the restaurant. "Tomas, I'll be working for the next few days," she informed me. "Mattheus and his family will take care of you." She then embraced me again, and we said good night.

I went back to my room and lay in bed listening to the sound of the wind and watched the flickering light of the moon on the waving palm fronds. In the background, I could hear the ocean. I imagined the island as a vessel traveling in the sea. My internal dialogue decoupled from its pictures. I fell into a deep and restful sleep.

5: Atlantean Fragments

I saw Gemina briefly the next morning. Before leaving on some unspecified task, she showed me the library, and left me to explore it on my own, saying "The weather is changing, watch for the change. Our plans may be altered."

Somehow, the library had escaped my attention on the first day. It was surrounded by a large growth of bougainvillea. The brilliant red and purple flowers concealed part of the structure. The building must have been designed by Andromeda since aspects of the structure reminded me of her other works. The base looked almost like a beached catamaran, with twin hulls that raised the structure off the ground to shoulder level. The shape of the outer form reminded me of the Sea Station. Inside, the spacious central room was completely surrounded by a ring of bookshelves, and several long tables were placed in the middle of the floor space. The structure of the wall, upon closer inspection, was unusual, consisting of innumerable capillaries spreading throughout the entire material. Connected to these were tiny pores in the surface that seemed to breathe out a cool and refreshing air, apparently ventilating the structure, for there were no visible air conditioning vents. There was also a certain variable translucency in the material that I noticed particularly in the late afternoon. The light transpired through the walls illuminating the interior.

On a table in the center of the room was a large globe, depicting the oceanic currents and land masses of the world. I paused a moment trying to determine in my present location, somewhere west of Dakhla. What was the longitude here?

I followed the North Equatorial current across the Atlantic to the West Indies; the Sargasso Sea, the Gulf Stream flowing northeast, the Labrador Current, and Greenland. There were no national borders, only major cities were marked on the globe. I found Paris and tried to imagine again in what physical direction it would lay from my present location. I then looked westward and found San Francisco on the edge of the Western continent. It was then that I noticed part of the globe was dark. I suddenly realized the globe was a dynamic object, showing the day and night regions of the planet in real time. I spent a long time standing there watching the almost imperceptible change in the light and dark areas, indicating the movement of the Earth eastward into the night. Again, I remembered the dream I had had in Florence. I visually traced the lines of longitude, emerging from the poles, diverging, crossing the equator, and then converging again at the opposite pole. The Earth moved under these longitudinal lines, rotating through the zones of time. For an allotted period of time we journeyed through morning, mid-day, afternoon and night. It was not the other way around, that day or night happens to us dwellers on Earth, but that we visit these times sequentially in some sort of passage through time. There was something about this realization, something just beyond my awareness that I couldn't quite compass.

Eventually, I broke away from the mesmerizing grip the globe had on me and surveyed the extensive book collection. Most of the books seemed to be in French or German, or even in Arabic, with only a smattering of English. I found some

English translations of Jean-Jacques Rousseau, a complete works of Thoreau, and a small volume by Oscar Wilde having to do with the soul of man. I stacked them up on a low table, and leisurely read them over the course of the next three days.

I would find from my readings that all these writers seemed to share common threads. I felt certain that they had read each other, particularly, Rousseau and Thoreau with their love of nature, and their insistence on the unfettered life. Even Wilde, with his emphasis on the individual seemed congruent with the others, and my own natural disposition.

The library was a good refuge from the sun and the heat. After a morning swim, I spent most of the afternoon in the library. My first task in this quiet sanctuary was to review the state of my project, and to formulate the work I was to present at the exhibition in San Francisco on the future of cities.

There was a couch in the back placed next to a window. I sat down and laid out some of my material. There were the notes I'd taken during the interview with Christopher Fields. There were some diagrams and notes that I had made in earlier. Before long I closed my eyes, and leaned back, drifting off into a light sleep, and a chain of reveries followed, one connected to another, a reverie that was like a weaving of many different patterns. A field of thought patterns, of which no single thought was I identified with. It was only when I opened my eyes that I realized that the singularity of my waking consciousness, was contrasted with, or was overlaid, or emerged out, of this field of thought patterns.

I resumed looking at my notes, and then drifted off again.

It was in this manner that I wiled away the hours of my second day, with no great inclination to accomplish anything. Perhaps, I was still adjusting to being on the island. Maybe, it was due to the tropical atmosphere, or the rhythm of the waves, and the breeze, that lulled me into such a relaxed condition.

The next three days followed much the same pattern. I went out early for a swim, walking even further down the beach than before. The colors of the morning were always more delicate than those produced by the intense midday sun, softer shades of blue in the sky, and clumps of pastel colored clouds floating low over the distant shore.

On one of these morning walks, I discovered a part of the beach where a twisted rock formation emerged from the sand and jutted out into the water. The rock was worn and eroded with hollows, and tidal pools, and in one place, nestled between the rocks and the beach there was a sheltered pool with a sandy bottom.

I carefully clambered over the outcroppings, attempting to climb to the top of the rough spine of rocks.

It was then I noticed, facing the shore, a large rounded hole, leading downward, partially filled with sand but still not flooded by the sea water. I stared into the dark tunnel, hesitating to venture into the wet sand to look more closely. Maybe ten or fifteen feet down the hole, buried between the sand and the rough rock, I could see the sharp angles of what appeared to be stone steps going downward. I listened for the sound of water coming from the dark hole. I turned around surveying the rest of the rock outcropping, tracing the rocks back toward the interior of the island, wondering what other secrets might be found. Perhaps, this was part of an old pier from the pirate days.

Later, walking back down the beach toward the hotel, I collected a host of shells, including another scallop shell. There was something about gathering the shells that triggered a memory inside of me, something else from my childhood, a free feeling, a memory of play, and joy.

When I returned to my room, I looked again at the form of the shell placed at the top of the mirror, and then stared again at the one I had retrieved from the beach. Something indefinable came to me, like a key opening a silent door inside. Later when I went to the library I began to write in my journal, at first just random reflections came to me.

I've been on the island for three days now...the ever-present breeze rustling the palms...the dark blue color of the sea beyond the reef...Mimosa and hibiscus and the purple bougainvillea. The scalloping of the beach mirroring the waves...the ripple pattern in the sand, and in the water...clouds drifting overhead, unimpeded...a sandy shoal of an island, a fragment of Atlantis... salt...imagination.

The train of thoughts, and the recollection of the images in my mind, again triggered the memory world of my childhood, a time before imagination had receded.

Had our capacity for imagination dwindled? I wondered. Hadn't the act of play itself, undirected activity, out in nature, with the wind and the waves surrounding me, unlocked an inner dimension? Then again, perhaps, the shells were magic keys to the realm of the imagination? I wondered. Each shell was a talisman, an artifact imbued with a numinous power, drawn from a source outside the circuit of technology. The shells were the key, since they contained the memories, imaginal memories; keys, for building a bridge to the imaginative realm.

Imaginopolis

I wrote the word in my journal and drew a picture of a shell. It wasn't a place per se. It was more a state of mind. To learn to play again, that is why art is the bridge to *Imaginopolis*.

I realized that the city of the future wasn't about mere physical buildings, or designing infrastructure, although, that would be necessary on some level. The present-day city seemed primitive to me. Particularly the housing arrangements and how everything was subverted to the automobile and culture of convenience. Certainly, relying on market forces was a recipe for disaster.

It was only through art that a livable future could be shaped. A new creative sensibility would have to permeate the whole culture, an artistic sensibility that would pervade the entire city, an antidote to the generic detritus of the current commercially dominated mistake. I had a picture in my mind of trees, a park, and the city interwoven into a park.

The details weren't important, though.

The real transformative impulse was going to be non-physical, since it was through technology that we had lost our autonomy. How to disengage from technology? We would have to break from the focus on the screen, and all other externalities, and come back to something inside.

That was the insidious thing; they had used something that was internal to us. Yes, the screen was a metaphor, a metaphor for something that was inside of us, something that was intrinsic to our human condition. The interface between the outer world and our inner world was the place where our true being was situated. We needed to come back to that interface, this inner place, and to reawaken to this place in our being. Here was where agency resided, and it was from here that we must engage the world, or we would never make sense of the conundrums facing humanity. We needed to expand and strengthen this dawning awareness before it was washed away in a tidal wave of digital distraction.

In the course of one of these reveries, I picked up the book by Rousseau. It was an old bound copy of *Emile,* and I opened it in the middle, since it was often difficult for me to read a book right from the beginning. I found that I got more interested in the subject when I read in this fashion, backwards, in part, as it were. And so, I randomly read different passages from the book for part of the afternoon. From the reading I could see that America had fallen into a situation that was completely antithetical to Rousseau's ideas. In fact, in the last 40 years it had reached the extreme point of not allowing the child to develop in a free manner. Like Andromeda had said, about nature and childhood, there was no space for childhood anymore. Certainly, we had violated the sanctity of childhood. Everything I read confirmed the intuitive sense I had felt for Rousseau back in Paris.

Leafing through the center of the volume I found numerous passages that resonated with my own views. "General and abstract ideas are the source of man's greatest errors." Obviously, in America we had descended into a realm of generalities. Even the way science was designated as the final arbiter of anything of value, encouraged this emphasis on the abstract, and the masses were continuously instructed in generalities by the media.

Continuing this line of thought Rousseau remarked, "And as soon as one wishes to enter into the details, the greatest wonder- the harmony and accord of the whole- is overlooked."

This was typical of much science journalism, such as I had remembered hearing on NPR, with their focus on minutia, without connecting the dots, without looking at the big picture. In fact, the whole focus on global warming, the increase in carbon emissions and the consequent rise in global temperatures was all wrong. It was too one dimensional, too flat, too reductive. What about the contrails crisscrossing the sky? What about the diesel emissions breathed in by pedestrians? What about the streams of plastic disgorging from the Mekong and the Yangtze? It wasn't only one factor; it was the whole picture that was significant.

I returned to the reading.

Rousseau even realized what distinguishes the human being from the rest of the animal kingdom, "...what being here on earth besides man is able to observe all the others."

He even condemns those who would reduce our status to no more than aeronautical primates. "What! I can observe and know the beings and their relations. I can sense what order, beauty and virtue are. I can contemplate the universe. I can love the good, and do it, and I would compare myself to the brutes?"

I marveled at Rousseau's insights made over two hundred years ago. Issues that he raised that we have been led to believe were broached only in recent times. Issues that we thought were strictly contemporary concerns, and senselessly were still being debated. I wondered what had happened in the intervening centuries, or what hadn't been integrated into our thinking. An entire worldview had been dismissed as irrelevant.

I began to sense more clearly that the structure of knowledge in the contemporary world was a lopsided arrangement, an asymmetric arrangement that deliberately obscured these important truths.

Rousseau echoed my own thoughts, "The picture of nature had presented me with only harmony and proportion; that of mankind presents me with only confusion and disorder!" I smiled to myself. Yes, the same situation as now. Nothing has changed in that respect.

Reading on, "The more I reflect on thought, and on the nature of the human mind, the more that I find the reasoning of a materialist resembles that of this deaf man." I laughed to myself. I should have read Rousseau years ago.

Reading further, even more importantly, he addressed the idea of freedom. The will is independent of the senses, and our judgement is part of will. Freedom, it seems, resides in the human capacity to make moral choices, differentiating between the good and the bad. Like a gift from the universe, we are given freedom to choose different courses of action.

Then my eye fell on another passage. Here, Jean-Jacques seemed to address me personally, "Something in you seeks to break the bonds constraining it. Space is not your measure; the whole universe is not big enough for you."

I leaned back and looked outward, up toward the ceiling. Something in this writing confirmed a deep presentiment inside of me. Why had American society turned its back on these ideas, obstinately refusing to accept and implement them?

Lost in thought, the book fell to my side, and I slipped into a deeper reverie, closing my eyes for a while. When I opened them again, I noticed a change in the light. Something had also changed in the quality of my being. Something that was tightened up was now loosened. Some part of myself that had been long forgotten had returned. Maybe it was the warm afternoon light. Yes, the earth had shifted, the movement eastward through the meridians, but there was more. The shadow from the trees outside angled across the floor. I watched the silhouette of the leaves swaying in the breeze, absorbed in this feeling of completeness.

Why was it so hard to find this quality in America? A peaceful place to watch the shadow and light, listen to the breeze, a sanctuary from the din and discord of modern society. Wouldn't this be the bare minimum for any future society?

There was a dream, or just a moment of it. I was looking out of a round window gazing at the blue white of planet earth as if I was positioned in orbit high above the surface.

"Thomas!" Gemina had appeared at the doorway of the library, "I see you've been meditating."

"Yes, I was." I was a bit startled by her entrance but was pleased nonetheless to see her.

"The weather has changed," she remarked.

Walking outside to join her, I immediately sensed the difference in the air. It was now drier, and more refreshing. Perhaps, that was why I felt different. Maybe the air pressure had even changed. Instead of the usual cumulus clouds, wispy cirrus clouds streaked across the deep blue of the sky. It hadn't even rained this afternoon, I realized.

"Andromeda has returned." She pointed down the beach.

In the cove in front of the hotel floated the gracefully shaped catamaran: The Sea Voyager. A portable dock had been installed and stretched out from the beach to meet the boat.

"Yes, the earth has changed," she said. I noticed something more insistent in her voice, and she continued in this manner as we walked down the beach.

"There are changes happening below the awareness of the global masses. Let's talk about America, since there is such a focus on technology there, but this also applies to the rest of the world. It's the focus of the whole society. The news is dominated by technology stories, like a banner they constantly wave. Such tremendous hubris. This constant promotion of technology is all a diversion, a diversion from the continual destruction of the earth, from the degradation of the earth, of the being of Natura. Is this the price we pay for so called progress? Sacrificing of Nature? Future generations won't even remember what the Earth was really like, with silent forests, and clean oceans."

She seemed incensed, and I was concerned that she might think I wasn't on board with her position, but I agreed with everything she said. It was all congruent with my own ruminations over the last week, if not years.

She continued, "This is an ethical test that we're facing as a species, and we're failing. Technology is a diversion from our true nature, our true human nature that will go fallow in the thralldom of technology."

We reached the portable dock that extended out into the water, and Gemina continued talking as we walked toward the moored Voyager.

"America used to be a leader in the world, in terms of freedom, now it leads only in promoting technology. I know America. It's become a toxic culture. People have been colonized by the corporate system. Corporate memes have been implanted into the consciousness of average Americans to an alarming degree, different in character, far more comprehensive than it was even forty years ago; technology, the opiate for the masses. Of course, the masses have always been subject to influences whether it was a divinely inspired ruler, or the aspects and conjunctions of the planets, or the moon."

Stepping on board the catamaran, I noticed Andromeda lying on the deck in the shadow of the mast.

"Tomas, welcome on board," Andromeda greeted me without rising.

She was wearing a shear single piece white swimsuit cut in a biomorphic design. One shoulder was exposed, and the opposite side had a wide crescent opening that exposed half of her belly. She had a pair of sunglasses on, and I couldn't tell if her eyes were open or closed. Gemina continued speaking seeming to ignore Andromeda's presence.

"The present culture has instilled in the masses a degraded sense of our human value and possibilities. There is a diminishment of the human being, our existence in the universe relegated to mere chance or accident."

I was agreeing with everything she said, but I was so distracted by Andromeda's presence, that I couldn't take my eyes off her body resting on the deck.

"Science says that freedom is not possible, that we're determined beings. Freedom, and with it, the moral quality is obscured, and devalued. The most important aspect of our being is blocked by the expansion of the technological apparatus, enabling the apparatus to integrate the human being into an artificial system. The market supposedly offers us endless choice, while denigrating the substance of our being to mere animalistic drives. They've lost Ariadne's thread."

"What about an individual breaking away from the masses?" I suggested, not trying to sound too defensive.

"There is no longer much talk of the individuality. It's all about Big Data, and the marketplace, isn't it?"

"I guess that's true. In the face of the market, one's individuality seems almost irrelevant," I admitted. The waves gently rocked the boat back and forth.

"They regard it as some sort of romantic notion," Andromeda said indolently.

"Yes. The validity of the individual has been called into question with the gospel of genetic determinism on one hand, and behavioral science on the other; survival of the fittest. The Neo-Liberal agenda is made to appear as an inevitable natural fact, part of nature. Their propaganda machine claims science has discovered these facts."

"Adam Smith says it is so," Andromeda added flatly, still lying immobile on the deck.

"Out of this, springs a disregard for nature. Even an unconscious loathing and dissatisfaction with being human, promoted insidiously by certain factions."

"There's a fascination with the dysfunctional in the American media," I said.

"You've noticed?" Gemina looked at me searchingly.

"I have. I try eliminate those influences from my life, but..." I responded, and then looked away momentarily, surveying the deck of the boat, and the aquamarine of the water.

"Part of the Western heritage woven into its culture from ancient times, it waxes and wanes in its power. It's not part of who we are as human beings, though," Gemina stated firmly.

"They want us to believe it's natural. They use fear to enforce a certain regime of behavior," Andromeda remarked flatly.

"There is even an addiction to fear. Yes, they have many ways of constructing an identity that is purported to be fixed, and permanent, assigning a false sense of individuality that is efficacious for their purposes. Of course, we're told we define ourselves by our consumer choices, nothing else is worthy of note," Gemina declared.

"Yeah," I agreed. "But more than that even. The pseudo individuality we're given seems to deny that we're all part of something worthwhile, something meaningful, a greater whole aside from mere consumer activity or data points." I looked out at the water again pondering some still submerged feeling,

"And what good is being an individual if no one recognizes who you really are, or no one will play with you," I continued, thinking about some of my earlier ruminations

"Exactly, Tomas," Andromeda responded more energetically than before, seeming to stir from her prone position.

"You find that you're assigned a role in the social Darwinian scheme, in the Neo-Liberal apparatus. If you object, or choose not to participate, you're marginalized, or even consigned to a worse fate," Gemina explained.

"I know," I acknowledged, "but these roles seem to be so one-dimensional, so deficient."

"The system makes everything we love seem meaningless," Andromeda said slipping back into an indolent tone.

Gemina looked down at Andromeda, finally seeming to acknowledge her prone position on the deck. "Andromeda has had a long day."

I stared again at her lying there, taking in the features of her body revealed by the sinuous cut of the swimsuit.

"We received a transmission from Andreas and Jacques," Andromeda remarked.

At the mention of the others, Gemina went below deck momentarily.

I looked down at Andromeda. She was still immobile. The golden sunlight was starting to move across her body. The catamaran rocked gently in the water.

"Thomas, the weather is changing. We might have to change our plans," Andromeda informed me calmly. There was a hint of wistfulness in her voice.

"When will you know?" I asked, feeling a tinge of uncertainty regarding my presence on the island. I looked around at the gentle swelling of the aquamarine water.

"Tonight, maybe tomorrow," she responded.

"How do you and Gemina, and Jacques communicate here? You don't have mobile phones," I asked, suddenly curious.

Andromeda laughed a bit. "No, that would be problematic since it would open up the possibility of being monitored. We agree on certain things, and we have other ways of communicating."

Just then Gemina, came back up on the deck.

"Jacques and Andreas will be returning sometime this evening. We should leave Andromeda here to rest for a while. Tomorrow will be another long day."

I looked back down at Andromeda, it seemed her eyes were now closed, but I couldn't tell for sure. Looking back up, I could see the sun was getting lower. The color of the sea was a deep ultramarine. Looking back to the shore, the waving palms were silhouetted against the golden light. The sun was starting to touch the horizon. The band of the sky where the atmosphere was thicker was suffused with glowing light.

I was reluctant to leave Andromeda behind, but I slowly followed Gemina back down the portable dock toward the shore. When we reached the restaurant, Gemina suggested I meet her a little later for dinner. I went back to my room and laid down for a while.

7: The Reading

Though I hadn't thought I was tired, I closed my eyes and one thought after another led me into a strange amorphous zone halfway between sleep and waking, filled with a train of ruminations. I realized my body was strangely paralyzed in this mode of consciousness. Then I slipped into unconsciousness.

I woke up and sat on the edge of the bed trying to compose my thoughts. I was slightly unsettled by the thought of having to leave the island. I was just starting to settle in, but more than that, I felt this lingering urge, something related to Andromeda. More than before, I felt some indefinable connection to her, and realized I didn't want to leave the island without discovering more about her.

I looked outside, toward the west, away from the beach. This was the first evening that the sky was really clear, and in the twilight of the sky I saw the evening star floating just above the horizon, Venus glittering against the deep blue.

I walked down to the restaurant and Gemina was seated at her favorite table on the edge of the platform. She had a couple candles lit and placed at the corners, and there was a tray of food placed next to the table.

"Thomas!" She greeted me warmly, seeming to be more relaxed than earlier. I noticed she had a bundle wrapped in a brilliant vermillion colored scarf placed on table in front of her.

"Have you noticed the star in the west?" She remarked, offering me a bowl of the conch soup

"I did." I felt a strange joy come alive inside of me at her remark. As if her noticing it as well, had confirmed something inside me, an unspoken understanding. The grogginess I felt from the nap, rapidly slipped away, and I took a few spoonsful of the soup, my body welcoming the sustenance. I felt a festive feeling coming over me, just her and I seated in this beautiful tropical setting. I wondered about Andromeda, and the possibility of seeing her later in the evening.

"In Paris, you expressed an interest in having your chart read."

"I did."

I thought back to that evening watching Venus through the window of her apartment. I realized I was now feeling the same sense of enchantment that I had felt on that night. Strangely, though, I had an image of a different place transposed over the rooftops of Paris. There were palm trees, yes, but it wasn't the island. Instead the picture in my mind was like a completely different world. There were some desert mountains illuminated in the moon light, an almost indescribable purple light suffused a still landscape. An oasis surrounded by palm trees, a lamp in the darkness. But this impression was all very momentary, and the picture quickly faded.

"I have your chart here." She pulled out a piece of paper, no larger than an envelope, and unfolded it in the middle of the table.

"You were born between two eclipses."

"Really?"

"Yes, a total solar eclipse a week before your birth."

The chart was hand drawn with a thick black ink, and the glyphs and symbols surrounding the circle were noted in the cursive Arabic writing.

"You have a T-square here, a powerful configuration." She pointed to a boldly outlined T shape spanning both ends of the zodiacal circle.

"On the left, you have Uranus squaring the sun, and opposing the moon. The Uranian archetype dominates this chart. Reading from left to right, around your sixteenth birthday the transiting planet would cross a cluster of planets surrounding your sun: in the fifth house, the house of creativity." She paused considering something. I thought back to my childhood.

"The inner world is churning inside you. Yes. I'm particularly interested in Neptune here, the dissolver of boundaries. Neptune is conjunct your sun in Scorpio, you see the world through a watery veil. Think of the dissolving power of the sea, the ocean. This is a very natural setting for you." She seemed to indicate with her hands the ocean behind her, "but more, much more, than the ocean, the entire dream world is open to you. I saw this earlier, and since tonight is the night of the full moon, I realized a mere chart would not be enough."

I watched as she unraveled the contents of the red scarf and pulled out a deck of tarot cards. Spreading the cloth on the table and anchoring it down with the candles. She shuffled the deck in front of me, and in turn handed me the deck to shuffle. I shuffled them three or four times and handed them back. She then laid ten cards down in the shape of a pyramid.

"The *tetractys*." I stared at the arrangement of cards, surprised at the reappearance of the form, and intrigued by the artwork on the back of the cards. The illustration depicted an incandescent colored scarab pushing the sun through a night sky, with a sparkling background of stars.

"Yes, of course, the magical triangle. All the possibilities of the universe are contained within its form."

She turned over the first card placed at the apex of the pyramid.

"Kerhet." She paused, studying the card with half closed eyes.

In the flickering candlelight I could barely make out the image on the card. I leaned forward and stared at the picture. It was a strange hybrid human animal figure, a woman's body, and a frog head. The frog woman held an ankh, but most prominently she raised one finger to her mouth.

"A secret?" I asked, puzzled by the image, and made uneasy by the incongruity of an amphibian head on a female body. There was something primordial in its frightening juxtaposition. I didn't know if it was good or bad.

"Yes," Gemina answered distantly, still pondering, and she was quiet for a while. I sat there suddenly conscious of the waves in background. The full moon was poised just above the horizon. I watched the glowing orb, wondering what Gemina was thinking.

Finally, after what seemed like five minutes or so, she continued.

"Yes. There is a secret, indicated here, a secret transmission," she almost whispered the last words.

I was mystified. Yet on another level, beyond words, the symbolic wisdom of the card was telling me something that circumvented my rational mind. The more I looked at the picture, the gesture, the combination of amphibian and human female, the hieroglyphs arrayed to the side, the ankh, something percolated into me, some unfathomable realization was dawning in me.

"Yes, with Neptune conjunct the Sun, I shouldn't be surprised. Kerhet is one of the primordial eight, the ancient *Ogdoad*. She stands in the primordial waters. This indicates a transformation, a metamorphosis, but no ordinary one," her voice trailed off into silence.

"What's the next card?" I asked after a while, a little bit excited about what else might be revealed.

She silently turned over the first card in the second tier of the pyramid.

"Bastet." Gemina seemed to smile.

The card represented another hybrid, part human, part cat. Bastet held a *sistrum* in one hand, a lotus stem in the other and a domestic feline sat by her side. I unexpectedly remembered I had dreamed about a cat the previous night.

"You are among the cat people." She seemed relieved, even joyful at this card.

"I always had a connection to cats, since I was very young. We got our first cat..."

Just then a gust of wind whipped through the patio, the candles flickered, and the cards were lifted off the table and scattered on the ground. Gemina grabbed the deck and leaped nimbly to the ground bending down on her hands and knees to pick up the loose cards one by one. With the burst of wind, I had reflexively slapped my hands down on the table to preserve the arrangement of cards. I could only hold the first two cards, and a third one, still face down at the base of the pyramid.

Gemina laughed as she returned to her seat, acting as if she had half expected the gust of wind. I sensed there was something else going on beneath her composed exterior, some thought pattern that was working itself internally.

"Apparently the secrets don't want to be revealed," she said.

I was still focused on holding the three cards down. "I saved these three." My arms were fixed, arched across the table, as if the cards were personal talismans of great importance. Now, the wind calmed down just as suddenly as it had risen.

"I see," she said straightening up the cards she held in her hand, while she looked at the table, "and what is the final card."

I turned it over.

"Ma'at," she said.

I could see the name written on the card. The goddess with the feather stuck in her headband.

"Truth and justice, higher laws influencing events; universal wisdom, the divine order of the universe," Gemina remarked thoughtfully.

"What does it mean for me?" I asked

"Have you seen Ma'at before?" She looked up to me.

"In Egyptian artwork; different tomb paintings; the scenes of weighing the soul of the deceased."

"Yes, the *psychostasia*. Of course, that is only one aspect. Ma'at also addresses a different level, more internal, more fundamental. Think of the idea of judgement. How does that principle come into play in respect to yourself?"

"You mean how do I use judgement? Judging, deciding." I was almost thinking out loud trying to hit upon something.

"Think of the scales."

"Weighing, deliberating." I faintly sensed some idea emerging from within. Still inchoate, something else, somewhere, I had seen that reminded me of the principle.

"Yes, we have this capacity inside of us, this ability to differentiate," she suggested

"Discriminating wisdom." I suddenly remembered the image of Manjusri, the Buddhist deity.

"Precisely, this is one of our attributes as human beings. It seems you are being called to recognize this or develop this quality in your own life; as we all are."

"I see," I acknowledged distractedly, still looking at the card. I was following a train of thoughts. I was trying to remember some other related thought; perhaps connected to some of the reading I had done in the library.

312

I relinquished my grip on the cards, and Gemina gathered them back together, and wrapped them again in the scarf.

"Yes, I think we've read enough tonight. Perhaps, it's best that certain secrets remained hidden. It's not for us to probe any further."

She suddenly seemed tired, though a warm smile faintly lingered on her face.

I didn't want Gemina to leave quite yet. It seemed too early, and there were still a host of unformed questions lingering in my mind. I was trying to think of something else that would delay her.

"What about the world? Can the cards be read for the future of the world?" The thought had come suddenly into my mind. I immediately regretted saying it, realizing it was asking too much.

She laughed a bit, "No. For tonight at least, that would be going too far. After the message we received from the wind tonight, that would be tempting fate. We have to know when to resist the temptation to know everything." She paused, and then with a more serious tone emphasizing the first word, "You have to resist the temptation to know everything. Yes, Thomas, there are limits. Listen to the wind."

She stood up, and softly bid me good night, touching me lightly on the shoulder as she walked by.

8: Freedom vs. Entropy

Since it seemed too early to go to sleep, I walked over to the library. The vegetation was brilliantly illuminated by the pearl light of the moon. I was still thinking of the Gemina's description of Ma'at, and I also wanted to reread some passages from Rousseau.

When I entered the library, the only light was from the interactive globe in the middle of the room. I walked up to the globe and studied the terminator line. In the moment, I couldn't detect any movement in the daylight falling across the globe; the two sides of the Earth: night and day. The Western Hemisphere was now dark. The line of daylight curved across the Eastern Hemisphere: daybreak in Malaysia. I sat down and watched the globe for a while trying to discern any sign of movement.

I must have fallen asleep. I awoke with a start. Looking at the globe, I could see now that it was daybreak in India. I jumped up, suddenly concerned that too much of the night was slipping by, and I hadn't seen Andromeda yet.

I walked back to the restaurant. All seemed dark, but I could hear muffled voices mixed in with the sound of the waves breaking on the shore. As I approached the veranda, I could see two figures silhouetted against the moonlight.

"Tomas, welcome to Splendent Cay," a jovial voice greeted me.

"Jacques. You've finally arrived. What are you doing out so late?"

"We were waiting for the rising of Sirius," he chuckled.

I now recognized Andreas standing off to the side, his bald head gleaming in the moon light.

"In truth, we were discussing the origin of the universe, as we know it." It was Gemina, lying back on a reclining chair staring up at the sky.

"A stupendous night here on Splendent Cay," Jacques remarked staring up at the luminous sky.

"Where have you been?" Gemina asked, "Andromeda has been looking for you."

"I was in the library," I responded wondering how I could have missed Andromeda, and why she wasn't here with the others. I couldn't quite formulate an appropriate question before Andreas moved the conversation on.

"Actually, we were just discussing the second law of Thermodynamics. Are you familiar with it?" He asked in his precisely articulated English.

"Entropy: the universe cooling down," I answered.

"*Exactement*," Jacques said. My eyes were gradually adjusted to the setting, and I could see they had a telescope set up on the deck as well.

"If I remember correctly, the model is based on a closed system, but is the universe really closed?" I asked.

"Theoretically, there are no closed systems," Andreas stated.

"Yes, only the model itself is closed in its ability to describe the universe," Jacques noted.

"It presents a conundrum of sorts. In this model, the universe would be fated to an inevitable heat death," Andreas explained.

"This had a tremendous impact on philosophical thought in the 19th century, as you might imagine," Jacques said.

"The universe as a heat engine," Andreas added.

"Consciousness was limited by this false view," Gemina interjected."

"The mechanical model, yes," Jacques acknowledged,

"...And other deterministic analogies, such as optimization, and the invisible hand," Gemina continued.

"Without question, these were powerful and transformative ideas whose effect was sometimes for the worse," Jacques commented, slowly nodding his head.

"The Romantics recognized the intrinsic poverty of all these models," Gemina added.

"However," Andreas resumed, "we now understand there is a counter tendency to the second law."

"What some have called *cosmogenesis*," Jacques affirmed.

"Exactly, a complementary principle to explain the miraculous emergence of life, and structure in the universe," Andreas explained.

"A cosmic invisible hand, so to speak," Jacques laughed to himself. "We find density waves moving through the galaxy creating star systems, counteracting the descent to entropy."

"In truth, it's much more than just star creation," Andreas continued, "Inside of our own being we continually recreate ourselves in each moment; the being of our Self places itself into the field of awareness in a dynamic ongoing process. Out of the vast realm of the universe, we collapse ourselves down into conscious awareness."

"In each moment, from outside of time and space, the Self places itself into the space time continuum. A completely free act of instantaneous genesis," Jacques added

"A continuum of potential?" I asked.

"Yes, unlimited. Pure self-creative autonomy in each moment," Jacques affirmed.

"We are not determined. We're not bound to past structures. We're free in the sense that each moment is an open act of creation. The feeling of dynamic, ongoing creation engenders a sense of freedom, a sense of freshness in each moment in time, drawing our attention to the fountainhead of creation in each present moment," Gemina interjected.

"We must keep in mind, that our conscious being is not a thing, but a process, a continual reassertion of our being," Andreas explained.

"Our very thoughts are the leading edge of the cosmos, the self-reflective emerging consciousness of the universe," Jacques continued.

My mind felt like an intersection of multiple trains of thought. I was trying to reconcile this new information with what I had recently read. Hadn't Rousseau indicated that space is not your measure, that the whole universe is not big enough to contain you? Strangely my mind was also thrown back to the day I met Monsieur Sind in the Luxembourg garden, something about time, and breaking free from clock time. There was part of our being that was not bound by space and time. An internal escape hatch seemed to open up allowing us to escape the deterministic laws.

"When we were at Le Bourget, what did you say about the holographic nature of the universe?" I asked thinking back to the questions that had been raised in my mind on that afternoon.

"Did we speak of a holographic universe?" Jacques looked over to Andreas.

"In respect to light, each point in space carries an image of the whole," Andreas affirmed.

"Ah, yes. The ancients believed that we hold a model of the universe inside our being, a microcosm. A living image of the universe, but image may not be the right word. A living reflection, a model, yes, but all these are just metaphors, since we recreate ourselves out of the universe..."

"We encompass the whole," Andreas added.

"The intelligence of the heart opens a door to the infinite," Gemina interjected again.

"Yes. Remember the two types of mind. The intelligence of the heart, as opposed to the analytical, rational mind, the mind of science," Jacques added.

"The Sethian mind binds us to the finite, and the fixed, allowing no understanding for the irrational nature of the origin. Relegated to this analytic mind we are only a fraction of ourselves, a diminished being. Modern science would like to erode our agency and cast doubt on our ability to discern the order of the universe in any way. Thereby alienating us further from Nature, forcing us to rely on the abstractions of an opaque science," Gemina explained.

"The scientific accomplishments of the last two hundred years have even called into question our status as beings able to grasp anything conclusive about the nature of the universe," Jacques explained.

"Even science is called into question. The conclusions of less than fifty years ago are now discredited or disputed. New more sophisticated technology erodes previous findings; even the same studies cannot be duplicated. New theories re-interpret old data, and it will go on and on," Gemina added.

"Rational intelligence is only able to grasp the particular, the specific, the enumerated. While the intelligence of the heart takes in the infinite. The scientific mind will fill in the details, the quantitative information; but the knowledge of science seems to be an ever- increasing denominator placed against the mystery of the whole. It's only through art that we can advance human consciousness," Andreas explained.

"*Exactement*. The immensity of the universe astonishes us. The wonder of our embodied experience evokes ever greater levels of awareness. Astronomers can measure the vast cosmic distances, and map the patterns of galaxies, but how do we account for our presence here on the planet? No, this is something that is still beyond the realm of mortal comprehension. How do we explain the intricacies of the mind, even the origin of language, the nature of our consciousness, our position here in the depths of space? It beggars the imagination," Jacques said excitedly.

"We are not entirely bound by space and time. In creative action we open a free space, allowing us to escape the determinism of the natural world," Andreas added.

"Yes, but the essence of the universe will remain one step beyond our grasp, like an asymptote always beckoning. The cosmic trickster luring us onward," Jacques remarked chuckling to himself.

"Thomas," Gemina stood up from her reclining chair, "Mankind has unleashed a powerful autonomous force on the world. The science project is beyond our control, for better or worse."

"Yes, I'm afraid we are like passengers on a run a way freight train. The question is how we respond to this opportunity: life," Jacques added emphasizing the last word.

As Gemina walked across the platform, I remembered the question I was trying to ask earlier, "Where did Andromeda go?"

"She's on one of her long walks tonight."

Gemina pointed down the shore toward the west where the strand of the beach curved off in the distance.

"It's been a pleasure seeing you, again." Jacques shook my hand, "Enjoy the remainder of this splendid evening." Following Gemina, he walked slowly away toward the lodge.

I stood there for a moment with Andreas, listening to the palm trees rustling in the breeze and the sound of the waves touching the shore. It seemed the surf had quieted down, since the sound of the waves trailed off into the distance. Gazing at the moonlight reflected on the water, I tried to imagine each droplet of luminous water reflecting the whole, even the folded palm fronds glinting in the lunar light, each facet capturing an image of the whole. Each invisible point in space potentially contained the light image of the whole. It was almost beyond my imagination.

I turned to look at the disk of moon itself, the great reflector. Strangely, it seemed the yellow light of the moon had a greenish tinge; it was so bright, I could barely look directly at it. The entire shore was drenched in a luminous purple light. I looked way down the beach wondering if Andromeda was somewhere down there. There were many questions I could have asked Andreas about light, about the holographic universe, about the inexplicable experience I had at the Palais de Tokyo, but I felt a growing feeling of impatience, wanting to find Andromeda before even more of the night had passed.

"Without the moon, life on Earth would be impossible," Andreas commented.

"You mean the tides?" I felt there was some unfathomable ancient connection between the moon and the sea.

"Yes, that's part of it. The gravitational pull establishes exactly the right amount of disequilibrium for the Earth system. Even our consciousness is dependent on just the right disequilibrium, an important asymmetry."

The moon seemed like a giant radiant eye. The eye of Horus, or a colossal reflecting device set up in orbit around the earth. I thought of the light experiments in the hanger at Le Bourget, and how the light was projected through the round holes of the screen, maybe space was some sort of screen.

"When I was at the Palais de Tokyo, I felt like the universe was floating on a cushion of photons, photons filling the entire universe. How is it possible for photons to travel across the galaxy or the universe? I mean, there must be billions and trillions of photons, going back and forth, crisscrossing the galaxy."

I turned around looking back toward the west, down the beach where the constellation Leo was still visible just above the horizon. "Like, the light from Regulus, how is it possible those photons can actually reach us? How come they don't collide into other photons?"

I looked down the beach, wondering if at any moment I would see Andromeda walking towards the lodge.

"Astonishing isn't it?" Andreas responded distantly. "An ocean of infinitesimal particles, traveling through space, like waves moving over water, or the wind flowing through air, waves of light travel on a sea of light." He seemed to be lost in the contemplation of this thought, his head tilted up looking into space.

Andreas must have intuited my eagerness to find Andromeda, for he then turned toward me, shook my hand, and quietly bid me good night.

9: A Nocturne in Aquamarine

As I walked down the moonlit beach, I looked far ahead, all along the shoreline for any sign of Andromeda. Floating above the long curve of the coastline, I could see the constellation Leo, tilted downwards, as if the lion was ready to plunge into the waters of the west.

The ocean seemed unusually calm tonight. The surf gently lapped at the shore, and then drew back, the sound stretched off into the distance, almost into infinity.

Way down the beach I could now see the rock formation where I had discovered the small pool. Then, off in the distance, just beyond the rocks, I faintly saw a figure. It was Andromeda.

The moon light reflected off her white bathing suit. I picked up my pace and quickly reached the rocks. I could see her walking in the surf now. I went past the rocks, and we now approached each other.

Andromeda seemed to be stopped, preoccupied with looking down into the foaming sea water when I reached her.

"Andromeda," I cried out.

She looked up, stepping backwards before the incoming waves, and then ran over to me.

"Tomas, I was waiting for you." She embraced me, her body felt damp, and warm.

At first, I thought she was just referring to just this night, but then for some reason I started to think of the broader context. Did she mean she had been waiting for me for all these years? It was strange thought, since in some crucial way, only now after these last few weeks, and particularly the last few days, did I really feel myself fully come into my being. The full complement of who I was had finally emerged out of the foggy mists of my psyche.

"I was afraid, I wasn't going to see you tonight," I said.

"Ha." she smiled, and then added, "I didn't want to spend the whole night at the lodge, with the others." She hesitated for a moment, "I did want to tell you something. I was thinking about your project."

"The future of cities?" It seemed like a distant subject now, even though I had spent the last three days writing down my ideas for the exhibit.

"This idea of the future city is usually conceptualized in the wrong way, I'm afraid. Material conditions don't lead to evolution. Changing the physical structure of the city won't work. It's something that comes from another level that drives our evolution. The more technologically advanced we become the inverse happens in terms of social behavior, we become less advance. In fact, there is now a dominating regressive influence that is operating throughout the world, counter-acting all the tendencies that we would hope to nourish. This is an extraordinary threat to humanity, to even being human. We've lost our connections to nature, to our bodies, to our souls. We no longer understand the full meaning of Eros in all its richness." She paused looking out toward the moonlit sea, and then she continued, "The system is programmed to destroy nature."

"How can we stop it?"

"It might not be possible, any longer. We've passed too many critical thresholds."

"What can we do, then?"

It came back to me how radically different our paths through life had been, and how it was almost miraculous that we had finally come together.

"It may be enough for the universe to experience this night through you and me."

"We're the eyes of the universe," I suggested.

"Not only that, but the natural world is our nature."

She looked out at the waters surging under the moon.

"Tonight, I wanted to be close to the sea, as close as possible."

"This is really beautiful," I exclaimed, looking at her and all around me at once.

There seemed to be something different about Andromeda tonight, more free and, relaxed, yet at the same time more intense, and insistent than before, maybe because it was the night, the moon, or the sheer beauty of the evening walking by the surf. I remembered reading about how the ozone by the sea, or by waterfalls, alters something inside our bodies, perhaps it was something like this that affected her, and me.

I suddenly felt a tremendous sense of relief, and even joy, realizing this was where I needed to be, now, more than anywhere else in the world; the breeze, the gentle sound of the surf, the liquid moonlight, the expanse of the deserted shoreline, and Andromeda.

For a moment, our eyes met, the pearl light glimmering in her eyes.

"The Atlantic Ocean," she declared, turning to face the water. I then noticed she had a backpack on.

"We might not get to come here again. This ocean might never be the same. I wanted to spend the whole night on the beach, in the water."

"The full moon," I acknowledged.

"Yes. The weather will change tomorrow, and we'll have to leave soon."

It seemed like such a distant and improbable reality. I had lost touch with any sense of my own future. I was so absorbed in being in the moment on the beach.

"What will happen?" I asked.

"Too many things, the world is changing before our eyes. The next several years will be a difficult period for the entire planet. The catastrophic pollution, the ocean acidification, even our Atlantis Station might not be permanent. We might not always be here." She looked out to the ocean. For a moment there seemed to be a look of regret passing over her face, but then it disappeared, and she looked back toward me.

"We have no time to lose." Andromeda seemed to be excited about something, "We might not get this opportunity, again. Once a year the moon is in the perfect position, it lights up the sea along this beach in a very special way." She pointed down the beach to the rock formation. "Let me show you something, my favorite secret here on the beach."

We quickly walked down to the rocks, where we stopped momentarily, silently taking in the setting. Two twisted rock formations partially blocked the surf, and in the in-between area there was a sheltered pool with a sandy bottom.

It was a sublimely beautiful scene, the water pooled between the rocks, swelling and swaying with inflows of sea water, moonlit swirls shifting in an ever-changing pattern of light and shadow. The gentle sound of the water gurgling, and sighing, a subtle undertone to the louder surf receding off in the distance. The rocks also formed a dark silhouette against the sky, glistening here and there with reflected moon light. Looking above the water and the rocks, a necklace of clouds hung just below the moon, seeming to merge and dissipate in mere moments as we stood there.

"I brought some snorkeling gear, but we won't need it now," Andromeda took off her backpack, and bent down to the ground and unzipped it. "We can go out to the coral. There's a secret passage, I'll show you."

Andromeda took my shirt and put all our loose things in the pack and placed it higher up on the beach sands, and then we waded into the pool. I noticed that she had a tube, or transparent band filled with a green phosphorescent liquid wrapped around her wrist, and another one held in her hand. Standing up to our waists in the water, she paused, pointing to her wrist.

"You'll need to wear one of these." She took my hand and wrapped the phosphorescent band around my wrist.

"Underwater you'll see the light from my luminescence. Follow me, closely. Timing is really important. We have to go down under a hole in the rocks."

Although, I was a good swimmer, used to holding my breath for extended periods of time, with anyone else but Andromeda, this sort of call to adventure would have seemed crazy.

We dived into the warm and viscous waters. Right away I could see the green light on Andromeda's wrist moving ahead of me, yet the light from the moon also vividly illuminated the sea floor with a pale blue light. We swam ahead for fifteen or twenty yards, until the water was maybe ten or fifteen feet deep. Through the clear water below, I could still see the pattern of perfectly even sandy ridges marching across the bottom toward the shore.

We surfaced in front of a cluster of rocks, holding on to them as the water swelled around us. Andromeda gestured ahead, and said, "We're going down into the passage now, it will take about ten seconds to swim through it, Are you ready?"

"Yeah," I responded.

"Take a deep breath. Follow me closely."

We dived down. This time Andromeda swam about ten feet below the surface. I could feel the increased pressure in my ears even at that depth. Ahead of me the green luminescent light marked her movement.

I could see the opening of a passage ahead of her, an even darker opening in the dark rock. The moon illuminated the pale aqua colored sands below us, framing the bottom of the underwater rock formation. She slipped into the dark opening and I followed closely behind her.

The passage itself seemed to be about ten feet wide. The green phosphorescence reflected off the rough texture of the passage creating an indescribable mixture of colors, emerald, lime green, violet, glints of red.

Swimming behind Andromeda, I counted to myself, "1...2...3...4..." For a moment my attention was diverted by a cluster of tiny fish darting off in all directions disturbed by our movement through passage. I resumed counting, "...5...6...7..." I could now see Andromeda's body framed by moon lit water. She was out of the passage, and then she quickly swam upward. I followed her, and we surfaced.

I was almost out of breath. I gasped for air, refilling my lungs with deep breaths.

"Are you ok?" She asked.

"Yeah, I'm alright," I responded, catching my breath. I rocked backward and floated on my back staring up at the moon.

Staying on the surface, Andromeda slowly swam ahead of me for twenty yards or so.

I followed after her, swimming on my side, taking in the setting. We had left most of the larger rocks behind, yet the area still seemed protected from the open ocean, the water almost placid, swirled slowly in moon lit patterns. We rested on a terrace of rocks that sat just below the surface. Back and forth the gentle flowing of the water pushed our bodies together in an intermittent and repetitive motion. We had to hold onto each other to stay on the rock. We laughed a little bit together. I felt exhilarated by the physical activity of swimming, but the water itself, the sea water seemed to enhance all my senses. It was more pleasurable to swim in the moonlight than in the intense daylight of the tropical sun.

The water around us was deeper, maybe twenty feet or so. I still could clearly see the bottom, but here there were varied rocks and coral formations mixed with sandy areas, and even some strange marine plants slowly waving below. Once I got my breath back, we swam around the area for a while. Under the water, the brilliant moon light created a spectral illumination. An indescribable shade of pearl blue suffused the entire scene.

Andromeda dove down deeper to touch the floor of the pool, bringing back a fragment of coral, a branch like pattern with an encrusted texture glistening in the light. Only when she held up her phosphorescent band did the coral reveal its color, a deep red purple, otherwise it was bathed in the blue light of the moon. I ran my hands over its rough surface and then she released it back into the water.

We went underwater again moving on from our rock terrace, this time I felt like I was more adapted, and my rhythm of breathing matched Andromeda's. We slowly swam along gazing at the sea gardens, intermittently surfacing for air, and then diving down again, marveling at the different shapes and colors of the coral. Andromeda would pause down at the bottom and illuminate the coral forms with her wrist band. I started to notice more fish swimming off on the edge of my field of vision, mostly dispersing at our presence, some curious, lingering in front of me, or nibbling at my feet. We moved along until we came to another rocky form that emerged out of the water.

"One more underwater passage, this one is much shorter."

"Ok."

"Ready?"

"Yeah."

We dived down again, this time I followed Andromeda with more ease. We slipped into the passage. This passage seemed darker than before, but the light from our luminescent wrist bands illuminated the rough walls of the passage.

I counted, "1...2...3....4.....5." I then noticed some light coming down from above, and Andromeda quickly swam upward, and surfaced. I emerged right after her. Instead of coming into a wide-open area like before, it seemed we emerged into a sheltered grotto, open to the sky by a small portal above, an oculus. The moon was almost directly overhead. All around on the faceted sides of the rock grotto the moon light was reflected in different ways. It was like being inside a giant shell.

The unexpected setting left me speechless. I looked over at Andromeda sitting next to me looking up, the moonlight glistening on her wet skin. I suddenly was overwhelmed by emotion. A feeling welled up inside of me.

"Andromeda," I said, my arm reached around her side.

She turned and kissed me, her lips finding mine. In some indescribable place we were lost for few moments, the muffled sound of the sea all around us.

"One more passage, are you ready?"

"Yes." We disengaged, and she slipped down into the water.

I went down following her luminescent glow, the passage bent around a corner. I counted again "1...2...3...4...5" and then we came back into the light. Andromeda gradually swam upward breaking the surface of the water, I could see the ripples spreading out from her body.

Emerging from the water, I could see one more rock formation just barely rising out of the water. Here the bottom was only a few feet deep and my feet touched the sandy bottom.

Andromeda rose out of the water and stood in front of a sandy cove no bigger than a bed nestled in the lee of the rock. I swam after her. I could see just behind the rock, the edge of the reef where the ocean waves were breaking against the coral structure, the foam and spray glowed in the moonlight, the mist sprayed over the rock, almost forming an aura of liquid light around Andromeda's silhouette.

"Isn't this amazing?" She walked on to spit of sand that wrapped around the rock.

"Totally."

"Yes. We might never be able to see this again. The world might not come together in the same way for us as it is tonight."

"This is incredible."

"The ocean, the living ocean," she seemed to gesture out to the spray of the surf foaming in the pearl light of the moon. "It's like a coming home, to our place of origin."

"Yes, I feel it too."

I felt this indescribable feeling, more than ever before, a living connection to the surging water, like the water in me was the same water as outside.

"We're not divided from the sea, we're part of this...amniotic ocean," and she paused coming closer to me, "and we're not divided from each other."

I felt this deeper magnetism drawing me closer to her. I looked into her eyes, into her being, like I was falling into some deeper place. I'm not sure if I put my arm around her waist or her leg wrapped around mine, but we slipped down into the soft sand, kissing her all over, she kissing me all over, her neck, my lips, softness, salt taste in my mouth; Her lips, her tongue touching my tongue, wetness. The top of her bathing suit slipped away, and I held her body close to me, the sound of the sea surging in the background.

330

In the light of the moon, what color was her skin? It was a strangely disconnected thought. The crash of the waves resounded in my ears.

"Listen to the waves," Andromeda whispered. A world of memories flooded into my awareness. The sound merged with my feelings, my body, her body, collapsing into one organic whole.

"Who are we?" I said.

"We are the moon and the tides, tonight," she said. I kissed her lips again, sliding forward, tasting the sea salt on her mouth. My eyes closed; the sound of the sea, the feel of her, her body and mine. The beach seemed to quiver with each crash of the waves, the vibrations traveling into our bodies. I looked into her eyes, opening slowly, the moon reflected there, I lost myself for some moments gazing there. A large wave washed over us. She shifted her body, pivoting, her thighs wrapped around me, pulling me inward. In the surprising coolness of the water I shuddered suddenly.

There seemed to be the sound of musical notes coming from the sea. Resounding tones, like the sound of gigantic oceanic chords being strummed, notes rising up from the depths of the sea. For some moments, my vision ceased. I could just feel her warmth, enclosing me, moving, pulling in. There was a place we reached that was beyond words. Even beyond my conscious recollection.

After a long time, we rested in each other's arms, and then sat together gazing out to the north, over the surging ocean. We looked up into the sky and identified the constellations Cygnus, and Cassiopeia descending into the sea. The moon had by now moved across much of the sky.

The Earth had turned eastward, and we left the sheltered spit of sand and swam back to the shore. This time we took a quicker and easier route avoiding the underwater passages. Gently flowing back to the shore, we let the waves bring us in to the beach. The eastern sky was just rimmed with the first sign of light.

I was exhausted. We kissed on the edge of the surf, and then walked along the beach to retrieve her backpack. The waves seemed stronger now, the surf surging up higher than earlier in the evening. Off to the north I could see a cloud bank running along the entire length of the horizon.

PART THREE: Imaginopolis

1: The Ophthalmologist

Dr. Jaffe seemed to be in his seventies, originally from South Africa, soft spoken, but energetic. His office was not far from Euston Station, located just off Gower Street, and he was affiliated with the nearby University College. At Gemina's bidding he had found a way of fitting me into his busy schedule.

I explained the abrupt departure from the island, and the circumstances surrounding my discovery of the problem. I described the fuzzy brown spot on my field of vision, almost like a burn mark. He quickly dismissed any notion that it had been the intense tropical sun that would have been responsible for the onset of the condition.

My eyes were dilated, and what followed was a typical preliminary examination. With my chin resting on a metal apparatus, staring at an eye chart on the wall, I read several rows of ever diminishing sized letters, first with one eye closed, then the other. Several different lenses were placed over my eyes, and I read the letters again. With my right eye, I struggled to see anything even in the first row.

Then, he positioned himself in front of me, and peered into the interior of my eyes with his ophthalmoscope. In particular, he studied my right eye intently for a while. Setting this aside, he then took out a small flashlight and shined it into my eyes, quietly looking for a moment.

"The good news is you don't have a detached retina. We'll have to do more tests before I can say anything definitive."

I was led into another room where one of his assistants prepared me for a more advanced test.

A florescent dye was injected into my bloodstream, and after waiting for a few minutes, my head was again locked into an apparatus and pressed up against the front of a faintly lit space. I peered into the insides of a pale white sphere.

I was then instructed to note the appearance of different flashes of colored light. Some of the flashes were on the extreme edge of my field of vision, others seemed barely visible, or came so rapidly I wasn't sure if I actually saw anything. After a few minutes I became fatigued, straining to note the brief appearance of the stars of light, and struggling even to keep my eyes open. Finally, the examination was completed.

Afterwards, with my eyes still dilated, I returned to the first examination room, where Dr. Jaffe explained the nature of my condition while holding a sculpted model of the eye.

"Light passes through the cornea, the lens, the vitreous humor, back to the retina, and finally there is the optic nerve leading to the brain. Here, is the problem," he finished speaking by pointing to the optic nerve on the model.

"You have optic neuritis," he stated plainly.

"Optic neuritis?" I asked, not sure if I had even heard of such a condition before.

"Yes, inflammation of the optic nerve. The outer covering of the nerve has been stripped away, a process called demyelination, possibly caused by an immunological response to a viral infection; an auto-immune response."

"Really?" I was dubious, even confounded.

"Yes, a myelin sheath covers many nerve fibers. Damage to the myelin effects the nerve transmission."

"So, something is eating away at the myelin?" Some agent had invaded my eyes and attacked the optic nerves, I thought.

"Not exactly, however I can't say anything definite at this stage. You'll need to undergo more testing."

"What sort of treatment is available?"

"Very limited; with any luck you will have a spontaneous remission after six to eight months, your vision might return to normal. Sometimes it takes longer."

"Is there any treatment?" I asked again.

"Nothing I would recommend, I'm afraid. Formerly, corticosteroids were prescribed, however the latest research shows they don't affect the outcome."

"Nothing?"

"I'm sorry. I recommend you avoid fatigue, over exertion, and overheating."

"Is there anything I can do?"

"Yes. You need to come in for further tests to make a more complete diagnosis."

He seemed to be in a hurry, but he shook my hand before he departed, and briefly gazed at me with a concerned expression.

This shouldn't be happening to me, I reflected. The whole idea of an auto-immune response sounded absurd, an unlikely scenario, some excuse for a medical uncertainty. What could have happened on the islands to cause me to be vulnerable to this condition? Dr. Jaffe had dismissed the intensity of the sun, but what if it had been the cosmic radiation, now flooding into the planet during the solar minimum; high frequency cosmic radiation, that had damaged my optic nerve. There was the cycle of solar maximums and minimums and the consequent ebb and flow of cosmic radiation. Only the heliosphere shielded the planet against the cosmic rays; and with each cycle more of the damaging cosmic rays entered the earth, incrementally my body was broken down by these extra-terrestrial radiations, in an almost clocklike exposure, and then reprieve. Waves from the greater universe, eating away at my optical nerve, eating away at my life.

I hoped for the natural healing process to counteract the galactic influence. The doctor had indicated my vision would probably not get any worse. And after a few days I did start to feel better; the eye was no longer sore, and my vision gradually improved to some degree, but I waited futilely for the promised complete restoration of vision.

And so, during the first week in London, I barely had time to digest the events of my stay on the islands. Everything that had happened on Splendent Cay quickly receded into the past, and seemed almost like a dream, especially contrasted to the hectic nature of life in the city of London.

As I reflected on my memories of the island, I noticed already a distortion, an alteration in their integrity. What had seemingly been the most intense experiences were now only disjointed fragments, partially faded away, as if the color had been drained from them, as if the incessant ocean waves diluted the integrity of memory. Whereas other, more incidental events, persisted visually intact in my mind.

I still remembered following Andromeda through the underwater tunnel, holding my breath, with the green light from her luminescent wristband illuminating her body and the surrounding rocks. And when we reached the edge of the reef, I still vividly remembered her standing there, her face in the moonlight, the spray of the ocean behind her.

Many of the other moments of that night were just blurred together in an almost dream like sequence of moonlit water, coral, and the physical feel of the push and pull of the waves, the tide surging in my body. The climax of the night, when we fell together on the wet sand was now mostly a blur, only a visceral memory; the feel of her body, the warmth and moistness of her skin, these were the only sensations that remained in my memory.

Another earlier memory also came back to me quite vividly, on the first day, after our long walk down the beach we had stopped to smell a cascade of jasmine flowers. I remembered the sweet smell of the flowers, and her face bending over, seemingly with a tired smile, surrounded by all the tiny white flowers. As for what we had touched on in our conversations, most of that was now just a jumble of disjointed fragments.

For lodging in London, I rented a small room just a few blocks from High Holborn on Theobald Road. The room was a sparsely furnished meditation space located on the second floor of a holistic healing center. Despite its location in central London, it was a remarkably quiet space since it faced away from the street, looking north over the roofs of various old brick buildings. In the evening I would look out at the crenelated row of buildings silhouetted against the sky, gazing at the long twilight of the northern latitude, thinking about the events of the last few weeks.

At night, closing my eyes in the dark, I could observe a persistent afterimage, a pattern of spectral incandescence, sometimes orange, sometimes green, or violet, that seemed to waver and flow, swimming inside the inner darkness of my eye; the so called pathological colors.

2: The Internship

I realized the refreshing climate of England appealed to me and was a welcome relief after the tropical heat of the island. The weather was quite breezy, with intermittent rain showers; and often flotillas of clouds would rapidly sail across the sky imparting a varied and dynamic quality to the atmosphere.

I reconnected via email with the architect Christopher Fields, and accepted his internship offer. I started working part time within a week of my arrival, and usually arrived at his office later in the afternoon, and worked into the evening, five days a week. And even though I didn't actually see Christopher for several weeks into my stay, in handwritten notes rendered in a precise and rectilinear fashion, he provided explicit step by step instructions on how to carry out the tasks I was to perform. It was all digital work, mostly using Photoshop. My primary task was to open texture files, and make subtle tonal corrections to the images, adjusting the exposure, contrast, and sometimes color, resizing the images, and then saving the files in a new folder.

My afternoons would include a long leisurely walkabout London, eventually leading to his architectural office in Southwark. Located on the top floor of a nondescript brick building, the office had a view looking north across the river, toward the dome of St. Paul's, partially visible through a large window. By the time I arrived, most of the other staff had departed.

The work quickly became monotonous. My first week consisted of opening, and adjusting hundreds of images of stone pavers, running the gamut of materials and shapes, from squares, to quatrefoils, to octagons, a rainbow of browns and shades of grey, in different textures ranging from smooth to rough, labeled with evocative names like Caledonia gold, and Hibernia sea mist.

An obsessional state of mind seemed to possess me as I made these minute adjustments to the tonal contrast of material. The tedium of this repetitive digital manipulation was coupled with the cold temperature of the office interior, and this along with a lack of social interaction, prompted me to fall into an almost autistic frame of mind, my attention fixed by the glow of the computer screen. It was only by liberally staring out the windows, that even four hours of work was tolerable. As a further diversion, I would aimlessly walk around the capacious office looking for any random visual stimulation, such as interesting journals or diagrams left lying about in the open.

Indeed, some of my most creative moments were those free minutes gazing off into the distance at the Thames, taking in a fragmentary glimpse of the skyline. In many ways it was an apropos environment for me to conjure up my own distinct approach to the future city, as an antidote to an imperfect present.

London seemed to be mobbed by many more summer visitors than ever before. There were hordes of people, especially on the weekends, throngs of obnoxious tourists, many of them with selfie-sticks. They weren't just the quintessential ugly Americans either they seemed to run the complete gamut: Chinese, Indians, Russians, Brazilians, Europeans and other undefined nationalities all converging on the city of London. Trafalgar Square on the weekends was impossible. I usually tried to skirt the major thoroughfares, and I avoided the underground like the plague.

It occurred to me that the flood of visitors and migrants was part of a plan to draw in more capital to London. The constant influx of money and talent generated a tremendous creative energy to the city. The policy wasn't really a generous open door to former colonials, or other foreigners, but a calculated move to keep the pound strong and insure London's reputation as a safe haven for all their money, and to maintain its prominence as the global destination for capital.

As a corollary to these circumstances, London could lay claim to being "Capital of the World". Of all the cities in Europe, London was easily the most dynamic. What city had comparable airline connection to every corner of the world? Every time I looked up into the sky one jumbo jet after another was bringing hundreds more to London. And what city in the world had downplayed its own native culture in order to welcome the global masses? This was the secret engine for growth and innovation; here was the technique par excellence for creating a vital city.

New York City had filled a similar role in the United States, and historically the model had been followed by all the major American metropolitan areas: Detroit, Chicago, San Francisco, and of course Los Angeles. And to the north in Canada, Toronto and Vancouver were perfect examples of this model. Yet, London could more legitimately claim the mantel of "Capital of the World" than any other city.

The Asian cities were too ethnocentric. Shanghai, Tokyo, Mumbai, all provincial colossi. Landlocked Berlin was too German. Paris was still too French. The American cities would always be too American; separated from the Eurasian landmass. Something had happened in London, a diminution of the national character, a certain distance, a certain accommodation just sufficient to allow the global citizen to make themselves a home. Maybe it had been the colonial legacy. Maybe it was the English language. All Londoners were born citizens of the world. Olde London became the container for the new international city, the first truly global city- a New Atlantis.

Then, in a formal sense, there were many things I liked about London. The density, the parks, the organic structure, the way the historical still seemed be a persisting template for the present city, and how this older form acted as a physical memory of the past coexisting with the new steel and glass shards that erupted sporadically out of the urban fabric.

And only in Europe could I conceptualize a city without automobiles; at least the structure was here for a car-less society. I couldn't imagine such circumstances in America, the nature of the land was so much more expansive. But more significantly, car ownership was such an ingrained feature of the American social temperament.

One night I used a combination of bus and the underground to return to my room. The experience prompted a realization that was similar to the one I had in Paris, I had the distinct feeling that by shifting modes of transit, changing trains and stations, calculating what route to take, I was somehow unlocking a higher level of consciousness.

Looking at the map of the bus routes and then overlaying that on my physical experience of traveling through the streets of the city required of me some sort of leap of consciousness, or a novel combination of different modes of cognition and perception.

One mode was the abstract representation of the map, the other the actual embodied experience of traveling down the street. This prompted a shift in my level of awareness. From this realization followed a chain of other associations, cascading one after another like a dream interlude.

On one level there was the specific person navigating through the city. Then on the other, there was the level of the masses. From a higher perspective the masses seemed to be moved independent of any individual volition. The nominally free individual was nested within the higher order of the will of the city.

These ruminations, and the actual work environment, began to seep into my unconscious, and one night after returning from work, I dreamt of London as a sepia toned animation; the dome of St. Paul's Cathedral, slid open, revealing another city inside, structures within structures, nested like a Russian egg. Inside, even deeper down, there was the strange intimation of an enormous cache of gold buried underground.

3: Shifting Paradigms

When I finally saw Christopher again, it was a sunny Saturday afternoon, and we met at a pub just across from Blackfriars Bridge. We ordered a couple of dark English beers and sat outside, where a few small tables were placed off to the side.

Christopher seemed in good spirits. He didn't talk at all about my work at the firm. Apparently, everything was fine with the textures. I had moved on from pavers, to bricks, and now was editing images of vegetation. He seemed keenly interested in my own project, and the conversation soon drifted into the more philosophical implications of urban design.

"There is an inherent disjunction between what it means to be a human, and the Neo-Liberal system," I said, sketching out my vision of the current state of affairs. "The self is trivialized, reduced down to just a locus of desire. There is so much that is hidden from our view. The system relies on disinterest or ignorance to perpetuate a false picture of the world, even a false view of economics."

He laughed a bit, not unsympathetically it seemed.

"Yes, but it's not just the Neo-Liberal system, an entire paradigm has been constructed to justify this particular ordering of the world," he remarked jovially.

"Skeptical empiricism, you mean," I said.

"Indeed, that's part of it, and we can thank philosophers such as Locke and Hume for all this," he added.

"That's why I started to think that it wasn't buildings that needed to be designed, but a new paradigm that needed to be shaped. There isn't any way to modify or alter the existing structure that would rescue the world," I ventured.

"Yes, there is something intrinsic in Western consciousness that leads to these errors of apperception. Unless the flaw is addressed, any new paradigm will have the same or similar errors. Aren't you yourself a product of the West?" He added, smiling mischievously.

"Yeah, but..." I protested. Inexplicably, didn't I see myself as an exception, somehow set apart from the rest of the West?

I continued to outline my critique of the existing structure.

"The Neo-Liberal system positions itself as the only solid structure in an ever shifting, groundless world."

"So, outwardly then we have this functional, directed instrumentality, over a layer of incoherence, and impermanence."

"That's how things are presented to us. Nothing else but practical matters, or empirical scientific data, is certain, or of value. All else is dismissed as unreliable, subjective, yet that subjective quotient is what makes us human."

"You must be a Romantic," he said.

"Thanatos has eclipsed Eros," I complained.

"Indeed. There is a preoccupation with the pathological in the cultural world."

"How do we explain this?"

"The emergence of the repressed, I suppose." He looked down briefly into the pint glass; it was slightly more than half finished.

"The system denies nature, even human nature, unless it's something that can be quantified, and exploited," I continued.

346

"It's true, nature is being irretrievably altered, and even the nature of the human body is being transformed by hormonal engineering, serotonin uptake inhibitors, endocrine disruptors like phthalates, it's quite disturbing, particularly if you have children. And no one can say definitively how extensive these alterations already are," he said seriously.

"What kind of childhood can you have without nature?"

"You sound like Jean-Jacques Rousseau," he said, laughing a bit.

"Actually, I've been reading Rousseau."

"Influenced by your stay in France, I can see."

"Perhaps, but I feel an affinity for Rousseau."

"He hated Paris, you know, abhorred it."

"You know, he had this great idea of reducing political entities down to the city state level, kind of like the cantons in Switzerland, loose affiliations, where everyone still felt a connection to the decision making process," I explained.

"What a contrarian. He was absolutely right, but highly impractical. You don't think the will to power could stop at the canton level?"

"Things would function better at that scale," I suggested.

"So, Rousseau is your patron saint."

"Yes" I laughed, "I'm solidly in the Romantic camp." I sipped more of my beer, and then continued, "The Post-Modern turn left a vacuum, into which the Neo-Liberal system asserted itself as the only firm reality. The predicament the planet faces is due to this distortion, a horrendous fragmentation. In the 19th century we lost something. They dismissed the most important aspects of being human."

"Threw out the baby with the bath water, so to speak."

"Exactly, Post-Modernism is the inevitable culmination of a long development toward fragmentation, and a final ceding of agency to autonomous forces like technology and business." I paused to take another sip of my beer, "We need a picture of the whole again, we need to have confidence in our ability to forge a new meta-narrative, otherwise we're paralyzed, and the Neo-Liberal machine assumes control."

"So, you're going back for the future, so to speak?"

"No. Forward. Consciousness evolves. Post-Modernism seems like an interim, or terminal phase of an older paradigm. It's time to move beyond the Post-Modern impasse, beyond this unwillingness to picture a future. I think we're implicitly seeing this, in your work and in others, the architecture of a new paradigm."

"It's a beginning, certainly." He finished his beer and ordered a second one.

"There seems to be a correlation between the advent of Post-Modernism and the increase in income inequality starting in the Seventies." I claimed, continuing my analysis of the Post-Modern condition.

"Yes, that is interesting. Things were so different, even forty years ago." He mused, looking past me, "For one, the Tate Modern was still a power station." He seemed lost in thought for a moment.

I thought back to my first visit to London. I had stayed in a youth hostel of sorts. Called Tent City, it was located on the edge of Wormwood Scrubs, a large barren open space enclosed by the surrounding city. The place had an improvised feel, with cots lined up in rows underneath large canvas tents and was adjacent to a dreary working-class neighborhood called East Acton. The memories from that trip still seemed so vivid. I had a feeling well up in me, a nostalgia of sorts for that lost time. I felt, I had left something behind of myself, back there. It seemed the entire structure of time had been altered in the intervening years, maybe even multiple times, as if some giant cracked crystalline lens clicked into different settings, irrevocably changing the world. London now seemed like an entirely different city.

"What made 1960's London such a creative place, do you think?" I asked breaking the momentary silence.

"There were many factors. Certainly, things were more open, or at least more open than the rigid pre-war years. Class barriers were loosening up; there was a sense of informality, more freedom, an excitement about the future. Influences from the larger world, particularly all the American influences were energizing England, together with rising affluence. It was definitely an economically expansive time." He sipped his beer again, and then resumed, "London was like a large village then, you could know, even run into all the important creative people."

"Scale, then?"

"Yes, the scale of the city was entirely different back then. There was an openness, a conjunction of different cultures, a confluence of new ideas, everything, and anything seemed possible. I think it was an interlude before the structure solidified. Before the Neo-Liberal institution asserted complete control. England changed in earnest with Thatcher, of course."

"The same thing happened in America with Reagan."

"The 80's represented a restoration of sorts, a return to order after the seeming disorder of the immediate post-War period."

"And now we're almost in a post-historical period," I suggested.

"You think so?"

"In a way you could say disorder is history," I speculated.

"And with the institution of order, nothing substantive changes," he remarked.

"Exactly, there's this sense of history being put on hold, cycling of the same events, repeating endlessly. You barely need to listen to the news anymore, everything seems to be repeating. We used to see major events reaching some final conclusion, think about the wars of the 20th century, the Second World War lasted only five years, the Korean, three or four, Vietnam ended after ten years, but now we have war without end. The United States seems like it's in on permanent war footing."

"Yes, it's like a chronic illness. A low-grade fever that won't abate," he nodded.

"Technology is the only thing that seems to change. More sophisticated tools for controlling the masses. Attention is fixed, almost everyone with their smart phones. It's not just the content of what they're looking at, it's how their attention is regulated. Social attention is channeled."

"Yes, that's true. Yet, at the same time there are so many possibilities, so much potential, for creativity, for even getting your work out there."

He took another sip of his beer, looking over his glass at me.

"I know. It's a paradox in a way. I feel that the masses are being directed, but as an individual, if you can assert agency, there is an infinite range of possible avenues to explore."

"It can be paralyzing, I know. But if you're free, things open up."

"I guess that's the problem. Sometimes, I don't feel entirely free. Like, I'm trapped by a web of circumstances."

We had suddenly touched a lingering point of uncertainty that I still felt, even after, or maybe because of meeting Andromeda, and Jacques, and Gemina, and the others. In a way the extraordinary events of the last few weeks had highlighted the insignificance of my own life, at the same time opening a new realm of possibility.

"Let's go back to the paradigms. Yes, there is the broader cultural paradigm that we live within. Everything you've said about this is largely true. Yet, it's your personal paradigm that influences the unfolding of your life possibilities. The greater the level of complexity you can integrate, and the more you can break free from any ideological constraints, or even psychological inhibitions, the more you can open things up."

350

"Yeah, I know. In each moment we recreate ourselves." I remembered what Andreas had said, but there was the question of how to integrate this awareness.

"Metaphorically speaking, yes; radical self-definition, if you choose, and therein lies your freedom, and agency."

He finished his beer and looked down at his watch.

"Well, Thomas, it's been a wonderful conversation." He stood up and shook my hand. I had just about finished my single beer, so I was ready to leave as well.

"Let me know if there is anything I can do to help with your exhibition in San Francisco," he added, as he left.

4: Hampstead Heath

The next day, a Sunday, I finally reconnected with Gemina. I took one of the red double decker buses out to green and leafy North London.

On the bus, I tried to recollect the many things we had conversed about on the island, and in Paris, even the things that Jacques and Andreas had said and the conversations I had had with Andromeda, all in an effort to recollect the breadth and width of everything that had been transmitted to me. Even what I was doing in London was further enhancing my picture of the world, adding to the experiences of the last few weeks. I was trying to gather together all these thoughts in some comprehensive way, perhaps even to benefit my own project on the future of cities.

Her place was located on a quiet side street, a modest apartment that opened out onto a backyard garden. On my first visit the room was filled with packing boxes stacked up along the walls. There were a few upholstered chairs, a table, and record player. While I waited for Gemina to get ready, she had left an old vinyl record playing, an album of Arabic music.

The music was evocative of a whole world to me, an exotic fantasy of the Middle East, connecting back to my childhood fascination with the Arabic world. The female singer dominated the music, with the strings in the background following her lead, the voice rising higher, the strings swirling, the voice stretching out, holding a long sustained note. The sound even reminded me of the swirling visual arabesques of Arabic script. There was a plaintive, yearning quality to the voice. I suddenly fell into the mood of song. My feeling self was drawn up by the rising melody, the articulation of the voice, swirling around a spiral, and then back out again. I pictured the singer in my mind, vaguely, maybe she looked like Andromeda. And I suddenly wondered, why did Andromeda seem so alone to me?

Gemina returned carrying a small packet, "Andromeda sent this to you." It was wrapped in brown paper, and I slowly tore the paper off revealing a flat box no bigger than an envelope, the contents rattling slightly. I smiled as I opened the box, inside were an assortment of small shells, almost like amulets, from pearly white scallops with their ray like patterns, to spiral cones with different colored bands converging to a point. In my rush to leave the island I had forgotten to bring any shells back. Inside was a handwritten note.

"Exiled to the ends of the earth, separated by the seven seas, still our hearts are held together outside of space and time."

"That's beautiful," I said after a moment, pausing to soak up the message. For the last few weeks, part of me had been in suspended animation, not sure about the reality of me and Andromeda's coming together on the island. The message and the shells were a confirmation of a hidden hope inside of me.

"She sent this last week from Trinidad," Gemina remarked.

"Where is she now?"

"Java. She's working on the design for a Buddhist healing center and retreat in the mountains outside of Yogyakarta."

My elation at receiving the package suddenly faded thinking about Andromeda being so distant, and there seemingly being no way for me to influence the direction of our friendship. An unexpected sense of worry and concern welled up inside me, a fear that I could lose Andromeda somehow. I then remembered that Gemina could probably read my thoughts. I felt a little embarrassed at how quickly my emotions had veered off in a different direction, and I tried to return to the warm feelings I had felt while reading Andromeda's note.

"Yes." Gemina continued," There is no script for you and Andromeda. It's your destiny to find a new path. Things are so different now, more uncertain, from when Jacques and I were young. Nature has been subverted, and the predicament you and Andromeda find yourself in is a product of this distortion." She paused for a moment, looking out the window.

"How can I reach her?" I asked.

"I can send her a letter for you. You could tell her about your project. She would be very interested to hear about your work. She would be glad to hear from you."

"What about email?"

"No. She doesn't normally use email, and now she doesn't even have access to email. At least for a month, until late July probably, and then she'll be returning to London."

"Late July!" I exclaimed, it seemed like a long time, even though it was little more than a month away.

"It will probably be the first week of August before she actually arrives back," she informed me.

While Gemina prepared for our walk, my mood was buoyed by the thought that Andromeda would at least be returning to London once this summer.

It was one of those rare and exceptional English days, sunny with a perfect breeze, with just a few puffy cumulus clouds floating on the edges of a clear blue sky. Gemina suggested we walk to nearby Hampstead Heath. As we began our walk, she seemed to project a sense of urgency, as if there was something important that she needed to convey to me within a limited amount of time.

We revisited many of the same strands of thought from the previous weeks as we walked through the quiet back streets on the way to Hampstead Heath.

She spoke about the trap Western thinking had fallen into, how humanity had been separated from nature, and the true source our true psychic being, isolated in a sterile cubicle, so to speak, separated from the restorative being of nature, and subject to great unseen forces and energies that operate just beyond our conscious purview.

Forces, and even beings, that operate on our conscious minds without our cognizance. She described these beings as archetypal energies, otherworldly forces that drive human history and human behavior. Caught between these extraterrestrial energies, and other entities that would manipulate the masses of humanity, exploiting a disjunction between the old paradigm and the new, for profit, the individual human being was subject to tremendous pressures, a karmic challenge or even a test confronted all those incarnated during this time. Each human being was called on to develop higher capacities, higher cognitive organs to counteract and vouchsafe their individual integrity and even insure the future of the world. At one point, I asked Gemina to tell me more about the role of the intelligence of the heart.

"The intelligence of the heart is the highest consciousness we can experience as human beings. Like a ray of light, the Ma'at consciousness comes into our being. If we can receive it, a ray of the universal consciousness enters our heart. However, we can only receive a small portion of this consciousness at any given time. We have to make ourselves receptive to it."

"There is a contrast between Ma'at and Set?"

"Indeed, even a conflict, a tension between these two energies. Ma'at is an infinitely expansive consciousness; Set is the contractive tendency, drawing us down to the material; a fragmenting force, a two-dimensional thinking compared to the spatial intelligence of the heart."

"Intuitive thinking?"

"Yes, an intuition of the whole, a direct perception, as opposed to the Sethian analytic approach."

"Then, how does one cultivate the intelligence of the heart?"

"Love is the key."

"Yeah, I should have known," I responded a little embarrassed at my obtuseness.

"Of course, there are special techniques. We can take advantage of circumstances. Even natural energies can open us up to these higher energies. Remember the keynotes, a special moment, even the color of a sunset or the fragrance of a flower, can shift us away from the fixed intelligence and transform our consciousness."

"Yes, I remember now." I thought back to the night at Gemina's apartment in Paris. The memory seemed to stir something inside of me, a recollection.

"In fact, we can try an experiment."

Gemina didn't explain what she meant, but we altered our course slightly. We had passed by the house where the poet John Keats had lived in the town of Hampstead, and then crossed over a busy road into the heath proper. Since it was Sunday there were crowds of people walking throughout the park and sitting in groups on the grass. Many of them were teenagers, laughing and running around, as well as families with younger children playing in the grass. There was even an exuberant group of bathers on the far edge of a small pond, causing a commotion, shouting, and diving into the water.

The path took us higher, into a more wooded area where the red leafed beech, the dark green holly, and luxuriant elms shaded the way. The steady breeze rustling the leaves accompanied us into the heart of the park. I sensed something indefinably magical about the atmosphere on this day. I marveled at the different colors of green foliage set against the bright blue sky. Further into the woods we passed by several ancient oaks towering over the trail, and even further on we descended into a valley where an old stone bridge crossed over the edge of a larger pond.

Up on the hill, I could see our destination, Kenwood House. The building was a well preserved 17th century manor on the northern edge of the park. Even though it was late spring there was still a profusion of flowering shrubs near the manor. Large rhododendrons and azaleas with clusters of flowers tumbling onto the ground, in many different shades of red, magenta, pink, and white, even some yellow. We paused in front of a cascade of color, a sweet fragrance emanated from the white flowers. I placed my nose into the redolent petals, closing my eyes while inhaling deeply its aroma. I laughed to myself at the sheer pleasure of this sensuous act.

"Imagine there is a whole universe inside the cup of the flower," Gemina suggested.

I leaned my face into the heart of another flower, a heavenly trumpet of vivid reds and pinks filled my field of vision.

"A magenta dimension," she added, "where time has slowed down, magenta healing energy filling your entire being. You feel it now, don't you?"

"I feel something. I do." I gazed at the different tones of magenta and red, and then counted out ten of the stamen.

"Our olfactory senses are the most primordial," she added, "think of the times when a smell triggered an old memory."

I breathed in the sweet fragrance again, laughing a little, like I'd just released a burden. For some reason I felt like a child again, perhaps remembering times when I had imagined a fairy world inside the flower bulb. I stepped back for a moment to enjoy the play of colors, the light of the sun creating highlights and shadows.

Gemina had brought a small blanket and a thermos, with two cups for tea. She spread the blanket on the grass, and we sat down cross legged, all the while facing the wall of flowers.

"Now, study the colors. How many different shades of red do you see?"

I looked up at the mass of flowers, trying to differentiate between the pinks, and the magentas, the fuchsia, and the purple pinks. The way the sunlight hit the petals changed the value of the color, and my eye passed over the different tones like a paint brush.

I closed my left eye, trying to test the vision in my right eye. There was still a blurry spot on the edge of my vision. Nothing had changed, it seemed. I had become more attentive to the act of seeing now, always checking my vision. I opened my left eye again, and gradually re-focused on the flowers.

"I'm not sure I can count them."

"Yes. However, try to keep them separate. Then close your eyes and call them back to your memory."

I sat back on my elbows and closed my eyes. I tried to separate the different reds, maybe two or three shades, from the pink, and then the bright magenta contrasted to the fuchsia, and then there were the white flowers each with a traces of pink and yellow.

After a while she intoned softly, "Remember these colors tonight before you go to sleep. They are healing colors."

I opened my eyes again, and Gemina had poured the tea from the thermos into the two cups. It was a dark golden colored tea with a rich malty taste. We sipped the tea for a while, silently gazing at the flowers. Gemina seemed to be meditating, her eyes partially closed. Around us other people were gathered about, talking, even laughing. Since we were facing away from them, I could ignore them to a certain extent, but part of me wished they were gone, or at least that there were fewer of them. I was partially distracted by the voices, but continued to look at the flowers, but my eyes started to feel heavy and I closed them, opened them, and then closed them again. For a while I was suspended in some in-between place.

"You love Andromeda?" Gemina said unexpectedly. I was startled out of my stupor.

Was it a question, even? I had opened my eyes, still gazing into the different shades of red and pink, dappled by shadow and light.

"I do," I exclaimed, "at least I think I do...but what I mean. I don't know. It's been so long since I had feelings like this that I don't know what to make of them anymore." I felt like I was stammering incoherently.

She was silent for a moment, her eyes still partially closed, "Yes, it might have been different years ago."

"I suppose my natural inclinations were foiled so many times, that I don't trust my own feelings anymore."

"The natural order of things has been distorted. Both of you have lived outside the norms of society for so long." She paused, and then added in a seemingly different tone.

"Andromeda was stubborn. She didn't want just any man. And now, things are very late for her."

"Really?" I responded, wondering more than ever about Andromeda's past, but uncertain how to articulate an appropriate question.

Gemina was silent for a while, presumably meditating and then she resumed speaking.

"You mentioned once that you had a feeling for cats."

"Yes. I do. We always had a cat when I was a child," I responded. An image of the past resurfaced. I remembered vividly the day our first cat arrived.

"Andromeda's cat, Attabiya, is still in Paris. We need someone to retrieve the cat and return back here to London."

"What would be involved?" I asked.

"It will be complicated." Her eyes were still partially closed, then she added, "You should get to know Attabiya, it could help you."

Gemina then went on to explain that Attabiya needed to be picked up in Paris and personally escorted by land from Paris back to London, all in one day. Flying was not an option. It would be a long and strenuous day of traveling back and forth.

"Would you be willing to do this?" She asked me, staring closely at me.

"I think so," I responded tentatively.

"The major difficulty is that Eurostar doesn't allow cats on their trains, not even in pet containers. Instead you'll have to take a train to Calais, and then travel by taxi through the Eurotunnel route, otherwise it won't be possible."

"The Eurotunnel?" I was hesitant, but I could hardly refuse Gemina's request.

"Yes, it's different than Eurostar. It's a train that takes passenger cars and freight underneath the channel. It stops in Calais."

"Hmm," I mused, trying to visualize all the different steps and what would be required of me to bring the cat back to London. "When would this need to happen?" I asked.

"This Wednesday, you'll need to depart from St. Pancras quite early, and arrive in Paris at least by noon."

5: Attabiya

Gemina made all the arrangements. Very early Wednesday morning, I went to the Eurostar terminus at St.Pancras station. Waking up at such an early hour was probably the most difficult part of the trip. It was daylight though; a kind of wan grey light illuminated the overcast sky. By the time the train left the station it was raining, but we quickly went underground, crossing below the city, and the Thames, and then emerged above ground in a nondescript southern part of metropolitan London. I leaned my head against the side of the seat, closed my eyes, and drifted into a semi-somnolent state. I heard the drone of the train, and vaguely registered on the edge of my attention people entering the compartment, placing their bags in the racks above, and even a couple people sitting down in my row.

Some minutes later, I opened my eyes briefly as we approached Ashford, drops of rain streamed across the window. The man seated across from me was intently focused on his digital device, ear buds in place. He was maybe in his late twenties, with a closely cropped black beard, well-groomed hair, wearing a dark blue sports warm-up jacket, and jeans. I closed my eyes again, and we shortly entered the channel tunnel. The drone of the train was louder in the tunnel, and I focused my attention on the interlocking patterns and rhythms of the train's passage beneath the channel.

Maybe twenty minutes passed, and I opened my eyes. Testing my vision again, I opened only my right eye. The man across from me was still focused on his digital device. I closed my eye. I felt constricted. The seats in this class were really cramped, and only a metal post separated my knees from the man facing me. In this tight arrangement, the circulation to my legs was being cut off. I opened my eyes again, feeling restless and irritable.

Without any warning, the train suddenly exited the tunnel, and we emerged into French territory. I decided to get up and head down to the cafe car, in order to stretch my legs and buy a cup of tea.

When I came back the man was still engrossed with his digital device, periodically dragging his thumb across the screen. I looked out the window at the mostly monotonous landscape of Northern France, a predominately agricultural region, with long open vistas of green fields. Clumps of trees, and small villages periodically swept by the window, and here and there two-lane roads and highways crossed or paralleled the train track. I noticed the trucks or cars traveled at a markedly slower rate than our train. The trucks were short, and tall for their size, with a compressed cab, different from the typical American semis with their long trailers and enormous cabs. The tea might have helped me feel more alert, so I turned to face my seat mate and ventured a comment.

"Beautiful landscape." I wasn't being sarcastic; there was indeed something pleasant, even satisfying about the neatly organized patterns of green, and brown, the clumps of trees, the roads and villages.

"I'm sorry," he responded, taking his earbuds out.

"Nice landscape. Picardy."

"Yeah." He looked out the window for a moment as if weighing the truth of my statement, and then returned to his digital device. He didn't seem English to me, some intuitive sense made me think he was an American.

"Are you on vacation?" I asked.

"Oh. No." He stopped looking at his device, but touched something on the screen, and then looked up, and said, "No, we're launching an app in Paris." I was now certain he was an American.

"What sort of app is it?"

He hesitated a bit, touching the screen again, and then responded, "It's for Americans who are looking to invest in Parisian properties."

I laughed a little to myself.

"Really?"

"Yeah, there's a big market for Americans looking for a vacation home, or an investment property in Paris."

"Amazing."

It was a clever idea, but something about it seemed wrong to me.

"We're in a crunch mode, now, two weeks to get the prototype up and running."

I thought about wealthy Americans flooding Paris, using the app to score their dream apartment.

"Will this bid the prices up in the market? All that American money, you know. Sometimes it seems to me like the internet, like Craigslist, caused rental prices to go up?"

"I don't know about that," he responded politely. "It gives people more choices."

"I'm kind of a Luddite, I guess." I laughed a little.

"Are you?" He laughed too, and then added, "You know they used to shoot those people."

"Yeah, I remember reading that," I acknowledged, laughing at his comment. "I guess we've advanced a little bit since then.

It's just that I have an issue with this whole paradigm, using data, and algorithms to structure all our lives."

"It's the future. Instead of using intuition, we can be more scientific now, using data and analytics to make a better life."

"That's just the problem. I have a problem with algorithms determining the course of my life."

"Nature uses algorithms," he said confidently.

"That's not true," I said assertively. "Algorithms are abstractions, computational formulas for solving a problem. I don't think nature works like that. What about chance and improvisation?"

"The world needs efficient solutions. We can't wait for chance anymore." He seemed serious.

'Sure, I guess there's a place for algorithmic solutions," I acknowledged, trying not to seem totally inflexible. "But when they invade our social lives; the spontaneity, the magic of life is lost. Don't you think?"

"Maybe," he mused for a moment looking out the window. "Maybe things used to be like that, but those ideas aren't really relevant today."

I looked out the window again. The clouds hung low over the passing countryside. I was sure we were nearing Paris. Wasn't this train a wonder of technology? I thought to myself. To make the underground crossing of the English Channel was a marvel of engineering. This part of technology I accepted, didn't I? And except for the cramped seating, it was an entirely satisfactory experience. But then, I wondered, what sort of algorithm had been employed by Eurostar to insure the maximum exploitation of seating possibilities for the train carriage, an algorithm contributing to the cramped conditions.

In truth, I didn't really mean to be overly disparaging about the American's project. Really, it was an ingenuous marketing idea. Once again, I reflected on the type of Americans I was meeting during my travels abroad. Probably, only the wealthy could even afford to take a trip to Europe these days, what with airfares going up constantly. How many dissenters to the prevailing culture would even be traveling on the Eurostar, anyway? In the window I studied the reflection of the other passengers. Everyone seemed relatively prosperous, with laptops, cell phones, fashionable clothes, expensive luggage, for a moment I felt strangely out of place.

We came upon Paris suddenly. I craned my neck around briefly getting a glimpse of the Eiffel tower silhouetted against the grey sky, and then it was gone. The landscape approaching Paris was unremarkable, and the urban fringe was equally nondescript, a cluster of high-rise apartments, and the usual graffiti unfurling along concrete block walls.

The train slowed down, signaling our arrival into the city, and we slowly rolled into Gare du Nord, coming to a halt beneath its great cast iron roof. I felt a funny sense of excitement, even anxiousness come over me, suddenly realizing that the strangely lulling experience of travel was over, and I would have to disembark.

When the train stopped, the app developer quickly jumped up and grabbed his bags, shaking my hand warmly, with a slight glint of amusement in his eyes. He wished me a good stay in Paris, and then walked down the aisle. He wasn't an unpleasant person. He was polite, stylish, even smart, if somewhat misinformed. I wondered why he hadn't asked me anything about myself, as if he wasn't curious.

Attabiya was being housed at Chat Heureaux, a temporary residence for cats in Bercy. After exiting the train, I made my way through the bustling hall, and downstairs to the Métro station. I took the number 5 train headed toward Place d'Italie, and got off at Bastille, then changed to number 8 headed in the direction of Creteil-Prefecture, and after a few stops I disembarked at Montgallet.

Inside Chat Heureux, I recognized Attabiya right away, and the orange tabby seemed to know me as well, approaching tentatively, sniffing my finger when I extended it, and then rubbing against my legs. We had a few moments to get reacquainted while the staff put together all the necessary documents, records of vaccinations, and the cat passport for entrance into Great Britain. Attabiya was placed inside a cat carrying box, a taxi was called, and shortly we drove back to Gare du Nord.

By early afternoon, the cat and I were on board a TGV, headed to Calais. Since I was famished from the morning trip, I had purchased something to eat in the station prior to our departure. The only thing that seemed palatable to me was a Monsieur Croque, a generic cheese sandwich on an elongated piece of French bread. I broke off pieces of cheese and dropped them into Attabiya's container. I was reluctant to leave Attabiya alone, so I spent the entire two-hour trip seated next to the baggage racks in a section between the two carriages, attempting to communicate with the cat. Periodically the cat meowed, and I meowed back. My efforts at communication were an attempt to voice some reassurance to the cat, and when I periodically peered into the container the cat glowered up at me.

Calais-Frethun was the modern station on the outskirts of Calais. After disembarking from the train, I briefly stopped in front of station to look at the sky. A gash of blue had opened up in the grey overcast, and I wondered at our proximity to the channel. I tried to imagine the sea just beyond the horizon to my west. Was there anything in this altered environment to remind me of the nearby body of water?

Gemina had arranged for a Folkestone based taxi to meet me immediately in front of the station. I searched the gathered vehicles and sighted a black taxi with the words "Folkestone Gold" emblazoned across its side. I raised my arm and waved.

The taxi was an older sedan, almost antique in its style. The driver was a Sikh, bearded, wearing a saffron colored turban. He warmly greeted me as he jumped out of the car, hurrying to open the back door.

The hardest part of the trip was over now, and I settled into the back seat with Attabiya in the cat carrier. I needed to give the cat some water. So, prior to boarding the Eurotunnel train we stopped, and I improvised a water basin from a paper cup and gave the cat a chance to drink.

Entering the Eurotunnel embarkation zone, we were casually waved through by French customs officials, and joined a column of cars entering the double decker train carriages. The interior of the train was almost like a spaceship, surrounded by metal walls, with small rectangular windows. The line of cars slowed, the car ahead of us stopped, and the taxi finally came to a halt in its allotted space. We were locked into our compartment, the metal doors closing ahead of us in preparation for the journey under the channel. The train started to move, and I gradually slipped into a somnolent state, with my head heavy, leaning against the window, I closed my eyes, and listened to the rhythm of the train.

I fell into a series of dreams. First, I dreamt I was looking at a line of words passing before me, and as each word would pause, I would inject the word with color, first green, then red. Then another word would arrive in front of me, and I would carry out the process again with another set of colors, with each successive word I would inject more enhanced colors, radiant magenta, and then a brilliant living green.

I woke up briefly, my eyes still closed, listening to the trains sounds, still deep inside the tunnel, I remember looking at the colored pattern inside of my eye, the shifting, liquid, form that seemed to change as I watched it, the pathological colors and patterns, a result of my eye condition.

The second dream sequence was different. I saw Attabiya walking ahead of me, seeming to call me to follow. The space was a great interior with many paths, and rooms or chambers, a dimly lit nocturnal scene, a forest with different canopies. I followed the cat up higher, and now it was like I was a cat too, with the same agility, and ability to climb up into the heights. We climbed out on to branches of large trees, jumping up, higher and higher, so that I now looked down through the branches at glimpses of a landscape far below. The cat was meowing to me, communicating, something I couldn't make out for sure. Then the dream faded, and I woke up. We were no longer in the Eurotunnel train. I had completely slept through the disembarkation process. The taxi had stopped in front of the customs booth, and the taxi driver was talking to the customs agent. We were being asked for our passports, I rummaged through my bag to find my passport, and Attabiya's cat passport. The custom agent seemed miffed about something, even suspicious of our purpose.

"How long will you be staying in the United Kingdom?" He asked.

"Two months."

"And what is the purpose of your visit?"

"I'm an artist, and I'm doing research for an exhibition on cities of the future."

He looked incredulous his mouth half open.

"Where are you staying?"

"In London."

"And the cat?"

"I'm transporting the cat for a friend of mine who lives in London."

There was a look of astonishment coupled with irritation on his face. He looked back down at the documents, and then looked over at his computer monitor as if studying something on the screen.

He looked back at me, and then shuffled the papers back and forth, apparently checking the cat's vaccination record. He looked up again, behind our car, and again looked back down at the papers. Then he quickly stamped our passports and handed back the documents, silently waving us through.

I slept for the rest of the trip back to Gemina's place in north London. When we returned it was quite late; Gemina let me spend the night at her place, and I slept on a daybed by the window in her living room, surrounded by all the packing boxes. The next morning, I woke up early. I had had an unusually deep sleep, and felt well rested, and the bright sunlight entered the room waking me. I looked up, and not far from where I lay my head, Attabiya was seated on the windowsill staring down at me.

6: Return to Hampstead Heath

The next weekend I visited Gemina again. Most of the boxes had now been removed. While I was waiting for her to get ready, I had a chance to inspect the book collection.

There were many old bound volumes mostly in Arabic, and French, and even a few in German. I was intrigued by the arcane bindings and the marbled covers of some of the volumes, but I was hesitant to pull any of the books out and look at them.

Placed among the books, inside a larger niche, were an assortment of old record albums. Among the obscure Middle Eastern music that I wasn't familiar with, I noticed some music I did recognize. Here was a Beatles album, *Magical Mystery Tour*. Here was Miles Davis, *Filles de Kiliminjaro*, there a Jimi Hendrix album, a Soft Machine album, a Ravi Shankar. I suddenly realized that Gemina and Jacques were part of that generation.

They both had been at the perfect age to experience the 1960s culture, whereas, I had seemed to receive this cultural transmission obliquely, a buffered version, mediated in the sheltered suburbia of America.

I thought of the ebullience that had attended this period, even despite the many countervailing tendencies. I remembered the joy and hopefulness that filled the sounds of this period. How could there have been such a rebirth of innocence after the catastrophe of World War Two, after the holocaust, after the dropping of the atom bomb, the Korean War, the cold war, the assassination of Kennedy; and on and on, one crisis after another like an avalanche of social disruption.

I thought back to my childhood. An image of the late afternoon light flooding into the living room came back to me. Yes, there were the tumultuous events of the decade, but there was something unexplained. There had been a change of the guard, a shifting in allegiances. Something had happened behind the scenes; unremarked upon events, felt but not understood. And now we had lost the thread, or the thread was hidden.

I drifted away from the bookshelves, thinking about that distant period, preserved in images, memories, but more so in the music. There was a large detailed map of Egypt placed on the opposite wall. I stopped in front of it studying the course of the Nile through the surrounding deserts. I was lost in thought for a few moments, before Gemina reappeared.

"Why did you leave Egypt?" I asked.

"Everything changed once Nasser built the high dam."

"Yes, I remember seeing pictures of that." I thought back to some of the old National Geographic magazines I had seen as a child. The one issue that stuck in my mind showcased the project to move the colossal statues at Abu Simbel before the rising waters of the dammed Nile.

"It was a disaster. It changed the ancient flow of the Nile."

"The seasonal inundation of the waters, you mean?"

"Yes, the natural rhythm was disrupted, a fatal break with the rhythm of the earth. There was also much destruction; many people were forced to leave their homes. We returned for a while, several years later, when Andromeda was a child. The

371

whole event was another example of the hubris, the arrogance of modern technological society."

"I remember seeing pictures of Abu Simbel being moved to higher ground."

"Yes. We lived north of there, near Syene."

"Why did they build such colossal statues?"

"The pharaoh was an incarnation the divine. A colossal statue symbolized the cosmic dimension of the human, symbolic of the human being as the epitome of cosmos, the final product of creation, a representation of all the universal functions, the crown of creation, if you will."

"So, then each of us is also a symbol of that, as well."

"Yes, at least in potential."

"Then, these were not just political, propagandistic statues, to impress the masses with the power of the pharaoh."

"No, that's a mistaken view, a modern projection. These colossal statues were much more, they were religious, spiritual symbols, meant to remind those who were awake, the initiate, that the human body was the embodiment of all the cosmic functions, the supreme vehicle, for enlightenment, as it were."

It was another unbelievably beautiful day, even better than the weekend before. There was a refreshing breeze, and puffy white clouds appeared in a deep blue sky; a glorious day that might be remembered many years later.

Gemina had asked me to bring some drawing materials, a pad of paper, and some pencils for the afternoon walk to the nearby Heath. It was just as busy as before, and we took slightly different route into the park. This time we walked to a section of the park that looked toward the south and the east, with a tremendous view of the London skyline. We found a bench at the top of a hill, a long sloping sward of grass, speckled with flowers spread out below us. To the northeast, on a wooded hill, was a small village marked by a steepled church. I looked to the southeast over the Thames valley, entranced by the modern skyscrapers that were transforming the London skyline. I could see multiple construction cranes, some yellow, some red, arrayed across the horizon, marking the site of new building projects. Beyond, the lighter blue of the distant sky, hinted, to my imagination at least, the location of the North Sea, and continental Europe further beyond. There was the smell of thick unmoved grass in the air, and the high-pitched call of birds echoed across the meadow. Intruding into the blissful natural setting, every minute or so, was the sound of a large jet airliner, wheeling overhead on its approach to Heathrow.

Gemina had devised some sort of drawing exercise for me, and so when we were seated on the bench, she directed me to retrieve my pad of paper and pencil, and proceed to sketch the changing shapes of the clouds. At first, I tentatively looked up at the sky, and then back down at the paper, clumsily connecting the drawn lines with the seen clouds. But gradually, I developed a more coordinated flow, capturing the rounded shapes, shading in the darker undersides. After I had accumulated a few pages of drawings, she insisted that I watch just one cloud, and then keep redrawing it as it slowly changed. This required both erasing, and drawing, for no sooner had I drawn the outline of the cloud, than it changed slightly, and so I spent a half an hour on just one cloud, gradually recording, and then erasing the metamorphosis of its form.

After a while I realized that it wasn't really the particular cloud shape in any given instant of time that she wanted me to capture, but rather, that I should become aware of the dynamic form of the cloud itself over time. I entered a sort of zone, responding to the changing flow, and wondering about the wind sculpting the clouds. Wondering about how clouds materialized out of almost nothing, manifesting out of thin air. It was remarkable notion, for I didn't know what caused water vapor to suddenly become cloud matter.

I then suddenly recalled something Jacques and Andreas had said about the universe. In each moment we re-create ourselves. Here, the cloud was a metaphor for this principle. I also recalled something I had heard about the quantum field, how high energy sub-atomic particles briefly materialized out of seemingly nowhere, briefly bonding with other extant sub-atomic particles, then dissolving away, only to be replaced by another multitude of sub-atomic particle. In every instant, all across the universe, an infinitude of sub-atomic particles, appearing, joining, dissolving, appearing, joining, dissolving, a perpetual dance of creation. I suddenly had a vision of the utterly dynamic nature of the universe. I laughed a little to myself, and stopped drawing, remembering a further question I had wanted to ask Gemina.

"What about the macrocosm? microcosm? How is it we are a microcosm of the universe?"

All the while I was drawing Gemina had seemed to be in a meditative state, and she responded slowly, almost as if she was speaking from a distance.

"The human being is a synthesis of all the universal functions. Our heart is like the sun. All our internal organs correspond with heavenly bodies, the liver with Jupiter, the spleen with Saturn. Look at the forms of your body, the pattern of the veins, aren't they like those of a leaf? Everything in our body is a reflection of a universal processes. The way the lungs bring in oxygen, the fire of Ptah that makes the blood red. The inhalation and the exhalation reflect universal principles. Even the eyes are like orbs, solar and lunar. The eye of Ra, and the eye of Horus. Our vision allows us to reach out into space, measuring the volume of our world. Our sense of hearing brings the outer world inside to our inner being."

I closed my left eye and looked up into the sky. A blurry brown patch, the size of a match head, was still burned into the middle of my field of vision. I opened my left eye again, and focused on the distant horizon, beyond the towers of London stretching east. With my eyes, I probed the vastness of that airy space, trying to encompass the limits of my perception. In that blue distance, I could see faint armadas of clouds receding into invisibility.

"Leonardo privileged the sense of sight."

"Yes, of course, he would have. Sight is the most conceptual of senses. Vision and the idea are intimately connected. Even etymologically. Idea, means to see. Ideas are revealed to our inner sight. We see an idea, and our ideas allow us to see, whereas, hearing enters the world of feeling, transforming our emotions. That's why song and melody are so vital to our souls. However, if we apprehend these matters merely as intellectual ideas, we lose the full spectrum of the experience. We need to connect this knowledge with our heart intelligence, something innate in our being that resonates with these truths. That's why the numinous is so important. It can provide an opening that breaks through the rigid confines of the intellectual mode of experience. With our normal waking consciousness, we're limited...only through the numinous experience can we hope to see the other level."

7: Shiva Nataraj

Two weeks later, we arranged to rendezvous at an Indian restaurant not too far from where I was staying. The place was located down a pleasant and quiet side street, a few blocks north of Theobald road. The late afternoon light was slanting through the windows when I entered the restaurant. I had arrived a little early, and there was no one else there. The aroma of Indian food filled the restaurant.

While I waited for the staff to arrive, I stared at a statue of Shiva placed on a podium just inside the entrance. Shiva Nataraj, the arms holding the characteristic implements, the hand drum, and the flame, one leg lifted impossibly, surrounded by a ring of fire, dancing the creation and destruction of the universe, dancing at the gate of creation. In each instant we recreate ourselves, I remembered. The entire universe; a perpetual dynamic creation; an infinitude of sub-atomic particles appearing, and then disappearing into the immaterial substrata over, and over again. Energy, appearing, seemingly, out of nothing, but this seeming emptiness, was The Source. The source of everything, like an eternal spring, ever welling up: Shiva dancing at the source.

I had seen Shiva, before, in my youth, in another hypnagogic interlude, that was cut out of the cloth of time. Inside my mind there had been a still place, removed from the world, inside a pebbled niche, and an apparition of Shiva, or the sculpted form. And then the vision dissolved.

Gemina arrived, and the maître d' appeared from the back, and we were seated at a four-top table near the front window. Aside from the staff, we were still alone in the restaurant. The decor of the restaurant was all white, and the late afternoon light, lent a pure ethereal quality to the interior. I mentioned my connection to the statue of Shiva, and Gemina smiled.

"I remember the placement of Uranus in your chart. By age sixteen you would have been right in the middle of a Uranus transit, crossing the stellium in the fifth house. Yes, that would have been tumultuous."

I thought back now to those days. I had never previously considered the effect of the Uranus transit in my life, how it triggered certain experiences, a certain disposition, coinciding perfectly with my teenage years.

"It was like an insurrection, inside my head."

"Then, tell me about your childhood," she asked.

I thought back, again, to the submerged continent of images and memories, that Atlantis of my soul, with all its buried treasurers and drowned cities, filled with pictures and words. Weren't they like lost cities, or networks of nerve endings, now myelinated, disposing with those past experiences?

The waiter brought some tea, and I ordered a *nimbu pani*, as well.

"Everything seemed really good. I have many memories of sunny days, playing outside, playing in the field behind our house, in the woods."

"A field?"

"Yeah, we lived outside of Detroit, kind of a partially developed subdivision. Old fallow farms, lots of trees, woods, even a lake in a hidden valley. The back of our house faced one of these fields, or meadows. I remember playing there a lot; all the different plants, like a miniature forest, a place to enact my childhood fantasies. I remember the afternoon light streaming into our living room. The light, a warm light, glowing, even in winter." I paused to sip the *nimbu pani*, then continued reminiscing.

"I remember being intrigued with pictures of faraway countries, particularly the Middle East. Arabia, Egypt, Libya, and Algeria. There was one picture I remember, of a nomad, a Tuareg, in the Sahara. Wrapped in dark blue indigo robes, you could only see his eyes, and hanging from his neck were some magic amulets, magical pictures."

"I loved books, and the maps. I guess that was the beginning of my bibliophilia."

"Do you still have those books?"

"Some of them, they're in a storage facility in South San Francisco." I sipped some of the tea now, and then continued.

"One day, I remember vividly, it was a clear late November day, all the trees were bare, and it was cold. I was playing in the back, near a line of trees. It was just after the sun had set, and I was by myself. I suddenly heard a sound, like a roar, or a rush, and I looked up into the pale twilight sky and I saw something burning, like a burning rock moving across the sky."

"Such an unusual experience."

"It was about the size of a car, moving from west to east, right over our house."

Just then out of the corner of my eye, I noticed someone else seated in the restaurant. I turned my head briefly to look, a bearded man who wore a dark purple colored turban. He was turned slightly, looking directly at me, his eyes glimmering, almost smiling at me. In the center of the table, a candle burned with a rising flame, and a tendril of smoke climbed upward. Strangely, his face was painted with ashes. I wasn't sure, but for a moment I thought I recognized him.

"Monsieur Sind," I said, turning back to Gemina.

378

"Yes," she replied in a distant sort of way, almost like she was meditating.

I turned back to the table, but the Monsieur Sind was gone. The table was bare, a white tablecloth only, as if there had been no one seated there at all, as if I was merely hallucinating.

"Wait," I said momentarily flustered, staring at the table in the corner, almost laughing to myself at the strangeness of the apparition. It couldn't have been my imagination? I thought. I hadn't even been thinking of Monsieur Sind.

"Yes?" Gemina responded, as if to prompt me further.

"What happened? Where is Monsieur Sind?" I asked.

"He should be with us momentarily. I invited him to meet us here, and, as usual, he's late."

"Where's he coming from?"

"He's flying in from Delhi."

Just then a party of four people entered the restaurant, and a couple followed closely on after them. Two of the staff materialized from the back of the restaurant, one of them brought us an appetizer, a dish of garlic naan, along with some condiments.

"This experience you had as child, this burning rock. What then was it?" She addressed me again.

"I guess it was a meteor. Later that evening I remember we heard some reports on the news that other people had seen it, that there were even reports of finding fragments of the meteorite."

"It was real, then."

"Yeah, it was a real event, verified by the news media. But still the question remained in my mind. What was it, really?"

"And why?"

"Yes, and why? The timing of it all, what it meant for me, in my life, to suddenly see this object hurtling through the sky: a sign from the universe. The mystery of the world, that the complete unexpected could happen at any time; a sense of wonder that was a visceral tangible thing for me; the wonder of the sky; the world of nature. It wasn't incongruous with that sense of wonder, the sense of unlimited possibility that was part of childhood, part of my world view, back then at least."

"Yes, we all experienced that in varying degrees. The wonder all around us.." she paused, and for a moment I had another vision, this time opening to my inner eye, something like a beautiful evening in the mountains with tall trees around, looking down from a great height, over the sea, the crescent of a new moon hanging in the green blue sky, the breeze wafting through the trees, the sighing of the wind; a feeling of great joy and expectation.

"And then that world seems to fade, we discover things aren't what we supposed them to be, or our experience is contracted down to a fixed point. And even now the world is contracting further, by design." Her eyes were cast down briefly, then she looked up smiling.

"Ah, there he is."

I turned to see Monsieur Sind calmly approaching our table. He seated himself next to Gemina without any word of explanation. He was dressed as I had seen him on that day in the Luxembourg Garden. There were no ashes painted on his face.

"Thomas was just discussing his childhood, some important events"

"Ah, yes," Monsieur Sind nodded, pouring himself a cup of tea.

"Uranus square the sun, transiting the sun during his teenage years."

"Yes," he nodded again, looking at me affirmatively, as if he was already apprised, as if he had already looked into the subject of my life.

I thought back to the years of my childhood, what had seemed like such a long time at the time, especially compared to the careless unraveling of the years that followed. The different houses we had lived in, the sequence of different cities; each place segmenting or separating discrete periods of time. Each a self-contained phase, like an eternity to itself. Only ten years between the meteorite and the vision of the Shiva statue. What had Monsieur Sind seen? Had he already seen this vision? It was an unreasonable notion, just a strange assumption that had entered my mind. After all, how could he know? But, I felt an uncanny feeling, there was something in my mind insisting that he already knew, that he had actually even been there, and that the hallucinatory interlude wasn't something in the past, but something outside of time and space that could be reentered.

"Neptune conjunct the sun, as well," Gemina remarked

"Neptune, a door to the transpersonal," Sind nodded, with eyes half closed.

"Continue with the story of your childhood, then."

"Well, it all seemed to come to a head, between the ages of twelve and sixteen. I was reading the Romantic poets, Tolkien, the Surrealists, there was the discovery of art, the music. It felt like the final extension of great historical movement, like I was being handed the torch, almost like a wave crashing against the shore, and then it all seemed to slip away, into these disparate elements." I stopped for a moment. What was I trying to get at here? Wasn't there something terribly important held back in these memories, the pieces of a puzzle, inert, waiting to be placed together.

I continued, "Now, it seems like you can't see the forest for the trees. We're plunged into this situation where we have no perspective, lost in the flotsam and jetsam of the technological world, where the vanishing point is the smart phone held in your hand."

"Yes, something has been deferred, for all of us," Gemina acknowledged. "The post war period was a brief interlude, a window, before the Neo-Liberal system asserted total control over all aspects of life, an interlude before the system drew the rest of the world into its maw."

"Relegated to the narrow band of ego consciousness, one can barely comprehend the entire scope of our universal being," Monsieur Sind interjected.

"The connection between the microcosm and the macrocosm is implicitly dismissed by the reigning paradigm. What seemed obvious to you as a child, suddenly loses validity, substantiality, fading like a dream," Gemina added.

"The Western way of life blocks access to these other dimensions of experience," Sind said.

"Particularly in America, with its lack of self-reflection, its ahistorical consciousness," Gemina added.

"There are limits to our present stage of consciousness. We're locked into a particular setting at this level, for very definite reasons. We're placed into this particular stage, one stage within a larger array of levels. Even so, the scope of what is offered to us is rarely developed. The larger culture obscures these possibilities with its diversions, and literalisms, leaving one with an impoverished sense of self."

"Knock and you shall enter," I said, remembering the biblical passage.

"Yes," Monsieur Sind replied. "Yet it requires more than breathing exercises, or concentrative meditations." He seemed to address the following to me specifically, "Our waking consciousness is like a stage set. The parameters of the stage set are apparently pre-determined. Different actors appear and disappear seemingly of their own accord."

"The archetypal beings," Gemina added.

"The actors dominate our attention. We become identified with them, we lose ourselves in them, like with anger or some other passion that suddenly captures our whole being, and we lose ourselves."

382

"Aren't these actors part of us?" I asked.

"The experience of their presence shapes us, like colored glass tinting the sunlight."

"Are we one or many?" I asked.

"It's a paradox; simultaneously one and many. Think about the experience of seeing a play, or a movie, but you aren't the play or movie."

"Am I not my experiences, don't they all mean something? Or am I just an eternal essence?" Again, I was trying to make sense of all the events of my past, all the memories that had receded, and were continuing to recede further into the past. Weren't these experiences real, something more than just passing dreams?

"Although, you are only passing through the events of your life, falling through time, there is an important relationship between you and these experiences. Yet, this is all beyond our present comprehension, we can only intimate such matters," he explained patiently, seeming to intuit my feelings.

"One must remember the contingent quality to our being," Gemina remarked

"Yes, we are dependent on the strength of our presence in each given moment. Moreover, you must learn to differentiate yourself from these actors. Differentiate the figures from the ground. Your true self, your psyche is the ground; discover in yourself the secret watcher."

"The watcher?"

"Yes, the secret watcher. Imagine yourself placed on a high hilltop. From there you will observe the coming and the going. To the degree that you remember the watcher, to that extent you will discover the presence of your true being, but it is very difficult to remember yourself."

"What about the hierarchies?" I asked, remembering something Gemina had mentioned in Paris.

"There are hierarchies. The angels and archangels, and others, but as we're normally constituted, we can't know these levels, except indirectly. They would be too intense for our being, too bright for our vision, they would overwhelm us, drown us in their radiance. No, the most important thing is to differentiate the figures from the ground of your being, and gradually you will come to recognize the entities that press into your being, that cloud the psyche. They are like passing clouds. You will see through them, and then you will recognize the ground of your being. The clouds will drift by, leaving behind your true being, like a pure, crystal clear blue sky."

"The spiritual witness."

"The universal consciousness. A drop of which is in each of us."

"Ma'at."

8: A Day in the Countryside

Andromeda returned in August for a brief visit to England. On a Saturday we rented a car for a day trip into the countryside, Andromeda drove since I didn't have any experience with driving on the left-hand side of the road. We started early, heading west with no destination in mind. It had rained the previous night, but the clouds had broken by morning, the sun was shining brilliantly, and the atmosphere had an almost spring like, indefinable freshness in the air. We took the M4, past Windsor, past Reading, and near Hungerford, we exited the motor way, and randomly chose roads that seemed to lead us deeper into the heart of the country, into the hills of the West Country.

On our way out of the city, Andromeda thanked me again for retrieving Attabiya, and enduring the tedious journey back to London. She also related details of her two-month stint in Indonesia, complaining about the incessant rain, and the oppressive humidity.

However, the work site was located on a spectacular hilltop, and the wealthy Buddhist sangha who were building the retreat were generous and had provided her with pristine and comfortable accommodations. She was eager to hear about my project, and how my creative ideas were unfolding. I told her about my experience working with Christopher Fields, and how living in London had influenced my ideas in some unexpected ways. I was scheduled to fly back to America in three weeks, returning to San Francisco just after the Labor Day holiday. I also mentioned meeting her mother and Monsieur Sind for dinner at Salaam Namaste. She nodded her head thoughtfully at the mention of Monsieur Sind, but mostly she smiled at my recounting of my time in London.

Somewhere further west, we diverged off the main roads altogether, and stated to drive down even more deserted and narrow country lanes. The sun shone across the green landscape. The sky was a brilliant blue, and a few puffy white clouds with bright highlights sailed across the sky. We pulled the car over at the bottom of a small valley, a hollow in the hills, where a tiny stream gently spilled down through a wild meadow, and a few clumps of trees were scattered here and there across the hills.

The stream was narrow, no wider than the soles of our shoes, and walking along the path, we paused several times to crouch over the flowing water, and study the moving current, looking closely at the plants that grew along the course.

Andromeda picked up a hollow seed pod, and placed it in the current, and we followed its progress down the stream away. She found another one, this time it was a little bigger, more oval shaped, and placed it once again in the current. The pod had the appearance of a boat, and at one point it got hung up on a stem that straddled part of the stream.

"It's docking to unload passengers," I said.

Andromeda laughed.

"This could be the design for a new type of vessel," she remarked.

"Yeah, designed by Hieronymus Bosch."

She laughed again, and then found another one of the seed pods, studied it closely like it was a gem, and then placed it again into the flowing water. I found some hollow stems and also placed them in the water, watching them drift downward. They were more like rafts, than boats. We played like this for a while, absorbed in the miniature world of the stream.

Suddenly, a beautiful blue butterfly swooped down low over the stream in front of us, and then swung around behind us.

"A butterfly!" Andromeda exclaimed.

She jumped up and started to run along the path chasing after the butterfly. I followed behind her.

The butterfly remained just out of our reach, and then at one point swerved higher up and disappeared into the sky. Andromeda stopped in the path.

"That was a Chalk Hill blue," she said panting a little, winded from the exertion.

"Really."

Just then another butterfly swooped down, and circled over the stream, seeming to hover for a moment just above the water, and then it also swerved onward following the stream.

Andromeda ran off again following the butterfly higher up the hill. I followed her, and we climbed higher and higher up the gentle slope, until we finally came near a clump of trees, and we stopped, both of us laughing.

The meadow now spread out all around us, gently swaying in the breeze. The butterfly was nowhere to be seen. There was a smattering of flowers, mostly red poppies, and some white flowers that reminded me of Queen Anne's lace, and amongst them were scattered many tiny blue flowers. In the shade of the clump of trees, we decided to stop for a while. In her backpack, Andromeda had included a yoga mat on which we could lay. She unfurled it, and we lay down, with just enough room for both of us, our heads leaning together, looking up to the sky, watching the clouds pass by.

We watched the clouds for quite a while. It was supremely relaxing and reminded me of the kind of things I would do as a child. We imagined what the different shapes reminded us of. At first, they were quite simple, but then they became more elaborate.

"I see a face looking up into the sky."

"A man looking up, leaning back on some sort of cushioned recliner."

"A rabbit."

"A rabbit with a roll on its head."

"Look at that one," she pointed.

"A basket with a head of cauliflower, and a rabbit inside."

"A baboon head, lying in a canoe on its back."

"Two heads looking up into the sky reclining."

"That's us. It's a reflection of us in the clouds."

We laughed.

She rummaged around in her backpack, "While I was away, I was thinking about your eye. Is it any better?"

"It's about the same, I think."

I closed my left eye and looked out into the sky with only my right one open. It was hard to tell. There still seemed to be small blurry spot in the field of vision.

"What did they say caused the inflammation?'

"They're not sure."

"Yes. That's to be expected. I'm afraid we might see more of these unexplained conditions along with the Earth changes, especially the change in the atmosphere."

"That's right. The air isn't even the same anymore."

"Yes."

She looked into my eyes, studying them for signs; her blue-green eyes looking down into mine, seeming to get bigger, looking deeper into me, reading something inside of me.

"I want to try a special treatment, something to heal your eye." She paused to garb her backpack.

"An essential oil therapy."

She pulled out a clean white silk bandanna from her backpack, which she proceeded to scent with droplets from a bottle of essential oil, and then placed it over my eyes, almost like a compress.

"What kind of fragrance is this?" I asked. It was sweet and pleasant to smell.

"The essence of magnolia flowers; a special tree, very ancient, the trees once covered most of the earth with their heavenly fragrance. Now they're limited to parts of Asia and North America." She paused adjusting the bandanna, and then added, "Relax, and slowly breath in the essence of magnolia, the healing essence," she softly intoned next to my right ear, ending on almost a whisper.

I lay there still, listening to the wind sighing through the meadow, the leaves of the trees rustling every now and then, and slowly it seemed I heard Andromeda very softly humming a melody. We lay there for a while, me just listening, and Andromeda humming.

Maybe we stayed like that for half an hour, or maybe an hour. It was hard to say. I had entered a completely relaxed state.

"Now, imagine a beautiful white magnolia flower on your head. Inside this flower a magical genie with golden light that shines all around him. Golden light is radiating all around him. He is a very powerful magical genie. He knows all things. His body is filled with healing and restorative energy. Inside of his body is an unending source of healing nectar. From his big right toe a stream of healing nectar flows down into your head, into your whole body, filling you up, filling you up entirely. All the impurities in your body are channeled out, flowing out, draining out to the bottom of your body, a charcoal colored liquid flows down into the ground, leaving you. The flower and the genie dissolve into the essence, the essence dissolves into you. Your body is now like a clear transparent crystal, filled with pure healing golden nectar."

She then chanted, in a melodic sort of way, a long series of what seemed to be Sanskrit words. Some of the words were repeated in a rhythmic pattern. She finished by chanting lower and lower, whispering in a deep throaty voice, and then she was quiet.

It was quiet, just the soft sighing of the field. I could feel the warmth of her body, next to mine, her slow steady breathing, my heartbeat, her heartbeat on my side, the sound of my breathing coming into the hollow of my body. We lie like that for a while.

Some time elapsed, and she removed the silk bandanna from my eyes. It was by now later in the afternoon. I felt strangely altered, different than I had felt ever before. Andromeda seemed to have entered a quiet mood, even introspective. We sat up and surveyed the landscape. The colors of the landscape had taken on a rich warm tone, the shadows almost blue violet. I felt a certain feeling, a connection to this earth, this part of the earth, these green hills and pleasant meadows.

Later, on our way back, Andromeda said, "I've decided to visit you in San Francisco. The project in Indonesia will soon be completed, and I'll have a layover on the way back to Europe."

9: Trans-Oceanic Flight

In early September, I left England bound for San Francisco. The midday flight out of Heathrow quickly lifted above a few scattered clouds, and as the plane banked to the north, I caught a glimpse of greater London spread out to the east. I traced the path of the winding Thames and could faintly make out some of the taller buildings in the city before the plane banked, heading west by north west, over the green fields of western England.

Shortly we crossed over the more rugged terrain of Wales, then over the sea, and soon we were flying over Ireland. The entire expanse of the green isle was visible from my elevated perspective. Ireland seemed like it was cut from a different cloth than England, a different, unrelated puzzle piece, a geological fragment from another continent. The land was parceled up in long vertical strips, and elongated lakes stretched across the inner heart of the island. I had a vague intimation of a northerly land, formed under the imprint of the ice age. The western coast was a jagged edge of cliffs, and long curved beaches, brilliantly illuminated in the sun, and then, the endless sea.

Great Britain was now behind us moving ever eastward into another time zone. Our plane was keeping pace with the apparent movement of day, a perpetual noontime that raced across the Atlantic Ocean.

I sat back for a moment. The moving panorama of the British Isles had been exhilarating. However, inside, I felt a muffled sense of regret at leaving England. I was slighted miffed even, irritated at having to return to America. I had lost almost any desire to be part of the Different Futures exhibit in San Francisco. During course of the summer, with all my travels, something of my old direction and preoccupations had faded behind.

It was sunny for quite a way into the Atlantic. The high-altitude sun light pored through my window. From this great perspective, I watched the intricate ripple patterns on the water far below, the ever changing pattern moving westward, and I watched the wispy white of the clouds drifting by, and the dark blue of the deep ocean, the sunlight glistening on the ever moving surface.

The effect of flying seemed to accentuate all my reflections, shifting something inside me. I was looking over the whole world, it seemed, my eye touching the far distance, trying to take in the curve of the earth, and touching the hazy white edges of the horizon. Perhaps the inner shift I felt was a result of my actual physical overview of the planet, or perhaps the rarefied atmosphere of the airplane cabin had contributed to a subtle change in my awareness. The seat next to me was vacant, setting me apart from the rest of the passengers, further adding to a certain lightness and freedom that I felt.

Sitting there looking out, the pure high-altitude light poring through the window, I could almost feel how my mind was constituted, structured, and enforced by the routines of perception. I sensed the edge of my awareness. At the edges, it seemed, I caught a glimpse of how the settings of the mind were held in place. I could also see how shifting the placeholder of consciousness, the bookmark of attention, would take me into different territory. I could see that relegated to the narrow band of normal ego consciousness we could never fully grasp the notion of the microcosm and macrocosm.

I looked out immersed in the light and in my thoughts. The plane continued along a northwesterly course. I thought about the longitude lines of the earth, drawing closer together at this latitude, converging toward the pole, the time zones closer together. Time more compressed. Here at the extremes of the globe the parameters of reality were altered.

After some time, a cloud bank appeared on the horizon, and the ocean was obscured. Now the planet was covered in a gauzy white blanket. I watched, peering ahead, over the wing for signs of land ahead. Soon, my eyes became heavy and I leaned my head against the cool window.

When I opened my eyes again looking ahead. I could see a dark form emerging out of the white clouds. The closer we approached the more certain I was that it was land. The plane moved ahead, and I could now see that these dark forms were mountains breaking out of the clouds. It was Greenland. The clouds seemed to break open behind the bulwark of mountains, revealing a panorama of desolate rock and ice. Looking down I could see the mountains rise precipitously above fjord like inlets, areas of ice-free water, narrow streams flowing out of the icy heights, and then glacial lakes, and barren expanses of earth mixed with ice floes. Then more clouds, and intermittently icy peaks emerging from the white. Then more clouds obscured my view of the earth below for a longer period.

More time elapsed, again the clouds parted again, and I could see a long prominent form illuminated in the distance far ahead. The plane approached, and I could discern a headland, a snow-covered plateau, a long line of cliffs running along the sea. Perhaps this was Labrador or northern Quebec. This feature soon receded from view, and we entered a vast area of water, intermittently covered with islands of floating ice. The irregular white shapes were like pieces of a giant jigsaw puzzle randomly dispersed over the arctic waters, seeming to extend all the way to the fuzzy edge of the horizon. I looked south toward the American continent, trying to imagine the great swath of civilization in those hazy latitudes. I studied the pattern of ice for a while, taking in the different sizes of ice, mindful of the shift in scale from small to large.

After a while, I became distracted, maybe even bored by the monotony of the scene, and pulled a magazine out of the seat pocket. I randomly opened to an article about some entrepreneurs in San Francisco. The story described in glowing terms the saga of three or four guys who received seed money from investors and had then rented a one-bedroom apartment in the Tenderloin in which to incubate their ideas. Months passed, and their initial idea wasn't bearing fruit. They were living on fast food and Gatorade, in a filthy dump of an apartment, staying up all night hunched over their laptops, when suddenly they stumbled on the next great idea. What the world needed was a new drink, a beverage that would be packed with all the vitamins and nutrients humans could possibly want, eliminating the need to eat any meals. They pitched their new idea and received a second transfusion of money from their Venture capitalists and were soon taking the product to market.

I closed the magazine and looked out into the expanse of arctic landscape. Perhaps we were now flying over the western edge of Hudson Bay, approaching the northernmost stretches of Manitoba. The great expanse of the Canadian Shield was coming into view, with its endless lakes stretching far out to the edge of the horizon, a vast wilderness of seemingly undeveloped earth, a repository of untold natural treasures, and for the Neo-Liberal economy, a zone of resource extraction, outside of the frame of most of the habitable world. I thought about the possible mineral and oil reserves, I thought of the flowing streams and pristine lakes, from the perspective of 35,000 feet seemingly untouched by human hands. Here looking over the great expanse of the north, I felt like I could grasp a sense of where the future of humanity was going.

There is a proportional relationship between technology and the destruction of the Earth; a causal relationship, whereby science provides the tools for technology, with no moral governor to soften the blow. The petroleum-based economy was like a dragon ravaging the earth, an insatiable beast breaking open the sacred seals of the natural world: cars, plastics, fertilizers. The titanic scale of consumption, unleashed across the planet, triggering the law of unintended consequences, was a machine unchecked. We sold our patrimony for the accoutrements of consumerism and technology. The source of our human being-ness had been covered over, obscured by the rigid artificial cladding of the technological apparatus. The terms had been established to describe our world of possibilities, and now seemed to be irrevocable. The world of possibilities was arrayed before us; and supposedly all things were possible, thereby making nothing possible. The financial institutions and corporations made all the decisions, whether there was grapefruit juice or kombucha on the store shelves, or what kind of clothes you wore, what your house looked like, even whether you were worthy to live in this place or that place. All the while claiming the market demands this or that, deferring authority to the abstract spectral agent of the market.

Implicitly, all individuals were rendered redundant to the tyranny of the market. Implicitly the individual is told they are not relevant, that the unaided human mind is incapable of discerning the complexities of the world or the universe, matters best left to the technicians and marketers. The individual is given a consolation prize, an impotent voice, one of billions, to speak their minds on the ubiquitous platform of digital media.

Yes, the capitalist system was a colossal sleight of hand, on a massive planetary scale, structurally designed to perpetuate inequalities, in its DNA, so to speak, to create a global imbalance. Wealth increases wealth, a positive feedback loop that increases the benefits, and the privilege, to the holders of capital. As blatant an immorality as slavery was, in fact, in extremis, capitalism was a form of bondage, with its debt instruments, and the necessity of credit, for anything, really. I stared out the window, tracing some solitary road or pipeline etched out of the wilderness. The sign of capital on the face of the earth, a mark of linearity, cut into the organic pattern of lakes and streams.

Up ahead on the horizon, I noticed a large body of clouds fanning out from close to the ground. As the plane approached closer, I realized it was a large plume of smoke, tinged by orange and red, trailing off into the distance. Approaching even closer, I peered down at the burning perimeter of a fire snaking across the forested landscape.

Soon we crossed over the cloud and another viewpoint opened up to me.

I was looking over a vast expanse of land, maybe hundreds of square miles of northern Saskatchewan. I now realized the first plume was only part of a much larger conflagration. And even farther ahead, maybe 30 or 40 miles, I could see another smoke plume trailing off into the distance. Was this another fire, or was it part of the same fire? I couldn't tell for sure since the airplane window limited my view.

The stewardess leaned over the seat and informed me that one of the passengers had complained that my open window was preventing them from sleeping, and would I please be able to pull down the window shade.

Reflexively, I resented the intrusion into my meditative space. Wasn't I paying for a window seat? Didn't I have a right to look out the window? I looked around and realized that almost everyone else had drawn their shades and were either sleeping or watching a movie. Over the drone of the aircraft, I explained to the stewardess that I was viewing the Earth. She walked away without any comment.

I looked back out the window, thinking I would see the forest fire again, but the ground was now completely obscured by clouds.

A few moments later, a man, shifting seats from the back, moved into the vacant aisle seat on my row.

"You don't mind the window?" I said looking over at him.

"No," he responded in a neutral manner. He was maybe in his mid-forties, with wire frame glasses, his hair cut almost like Steven Jobs, and a laptop placed on the tray table.

"How often do you get to see the Canadian Arctic?" I remarked, not sure if he could even here me over the drone of noise.

He laughed, looking toward me, out the window.

"Are you from San Francisco?" He asked.

"Not really, I'm originally from Michigan."

Perhaps, I looked like a certain San Franciscan type. I gazed out the window again looking for Lake Winnipeg to the east, trying to imagine the Great Lakes somewhere out there on the distant horizon.

"In the tech industry?" He asked.

"No. Just the opposite," I laughed to myself. It was a likely assumption, being that San Francisco was such a focus of technology.

"Actually," I continued, "The more we go into big data the more imbalanced humanity will become."

"Really, now?" He stared at me, for a moment, and then seemed to look out beyond through the window, "Most people believe just the opposite, that technology, and science will now be able to make our lives better."

"That's the general consensus, of sorts...but. Science is contingent. The deeper you get into the scientific evidence the less certain it seems. Science, or the body of evidence we call science, is a subset of the known, the known unknown." I laughed emphasizing the last words, then continued, "Conditions change, instrumentation changes, paradigms change, the way we interpret the evidence changes, all based on the level of our ideas. And science isn't able to account for consciousness, the most obvious mystery, and the role consciousness plays in structuring reality."

"Without quantum theory we wouldn't have transistors or lasers, or many of the current technology."

"Yeah. I know, but quantum theory is an abstraction, a descriptive shorthand for something that the researchers still don't completely understand."

"It works, it has functionality. You can't argue that."

"Of course," I acknowledged. "The problem is we take these things as literal truths, instead of as ifs, and then these structures are applied to human experience, to our lives. Didn't Hume show that inductive reason is fallible? You can't draw conclusions about the whole from small parts, an infinite whole. It calls into question the entire scientific program, particularly its application to our lives. Sample sets, statistical averages, demographics. That's not who we really are, they're abstractions, we don't live in statistics. I'm more than what shoes I wear, or what books I purchase on Amazon."

"Statistics are a tremendous tool for understanding society."

"It's used to manipulate the masses."

"It's called marketing."

I laughed.

"I suppose it's not as austere as Orwell's vision," I conceded.

"It's necessary to manage a world of six billion people, otherwise it would be chaos."

"Perhaps, at the scale we've reached, this is inevitable," I looked out the window for a moment, "but don't you think it's interesting that the psyche, meaning the soul, is denied in conventional thinking, but on the other hand there is such a focus on figuring out the psychology of the consumer by marketers."

"There's a contradiction?"

"Yeah, to deny the validity of soul, but then try to quantify it."

"Most educated people don't believe in the existence of a soul, anymore."

"That's just the problem; in psychology that's called denial."

"Anyway, how do you define soul?"

"That's a good question, and I think it points to the general confusion of our time."

"It's an abstraction, isn't it? One of the superstitions we've left behind?"

"Just because it can't be quantified, doesn't mean it doesn't exist."

"Hmm."

He looked blank for a moment, staring down the aisle as if he was expecting cabin crew to bring drinks or some food. Perhaps, he was tired of our conversation.

"I'm troubled by the way statistics are manipulated by corporations and the big financials," I continued.

"Are you?" He looked back at me, smiling a little.

"There's a lack of transparency in the corporate world. Common wisdom about the real economic situation is often wrong. False perceptions are rife. It's like a deliberate smokescreen, a camouflage that the media generates to create a false picture."

"For example?"

"What about the 700 trillion plus global derivative market, the unacknowledged dark matter of the economic universe, a potentially huge destabilizing factor. Are those derivatives on anyone's books? Does anyone even think about derivatives anymore? If it wasn't for the financial meltdown, it would have remained an esoteric footnote."

"700 trillion, are you sure?"

"At least. Look it up on Google."

He laughed.

"Or what about China?" I continued. "Everyone in America thinks they're going to eat our lunch, that they're, already, Number One," I emphasized the last two words, since the view of global economics seemed rife with sports metaphors.

"Have you been to Shanghai?"

"Do I need to? Is there anything really new coming out of China?"

"There might be. Over a billion people." He looked down at his laptop.

"The statistics show that our economy is still much larger, but most people don't bother to look at the facts. And anyway, we still seem to have the creativity, if you want to look at things from that perspective."

"Silicon Valley, you mean?"

"Yeah, San Francisco seems to be the innovative center, the cutting edge of the world, still."

"Well, you've come full circle. And you say you're not with the tech industry?"

We both laughed for a while. He caught me. I was suddenly face to face with one of my own internal contradictions. I guess I was more of an American than I thought. I was at times a proponent or spokesman for our technological prowess. I looked out the window to deflect a slight bit of embarrassment I felt, still laughing to myself.

Soon, the cabin crew came down the aisle with the food cart. We were only an hour or so out from San Francisco. We must have crossed into the United States. Looking out the window it was mostly cloudy. Here and there I caught glimpses of a mountainous landscape, intermixed with dry barren looking plains. It still seemed to be a vast wilderness, with no signs of substantial development.

About an hour later, the clouds broke apart, and I recognized the golden hills of northern California. The sunlight was now much brighter, the warm afternoon light of the west coast. We were somewhere south of Mt. Shasta, and I felt a palpable sense of expectation, even excitement. I studied the different mountain ranges, forests and valleys, and a vast reservoir reaching into the folded creases of the earth. Other signs of human habitation appeared: farms, roads, towns.

We continued south, the land seemed to become drier, the golden brown of California dominating the landscape. We crossed over a large lake: Clear Lake, and down over another range of mountains, golden hills, and more golden hills.

The plane banked to the west, I could see part of the bay ahead in the haze, and then we went out over the ocean, banked again, and Mount Tamalpais came into view. Then we crossed in front of the Golden Gate Bridge, an armada of sailboats floating in the bay, the white sails set off against the deep blue waters.

Then, San Francisco, the white buildings perched on the hills brilliantly illuminated by the afternoon sun. San Francisco was like a fairy tale city, at the end of the Western world. Within moments we came in for the approach and landed at SFO. I looked out the window as we taxied to the terminal.

There was something refreshing, even effervescent in this view of San Francisco Bay, a promise of refreshing breezes, comfortable temperatures, cooled by the ocean. I could see the line of hills behind the East Bay cities, in the atmospheric haze they took on a blue color, and the waters of the bay were an even deeper blue.

10: The New San Francisco

I boarded the elevated airport train, and headed for the rental car facilities at the end of the line, all the while staring at the azure waters of the bay, and looking at the liveries of the many international airliners parked on the tarmac. Large 777s, and 747s. Air New Zealand, ANA, Lufthansa, Delta. The train went past the cargo hangers, and finally arrived at the rental car station at the end of the line. There was a long line of people waiting at the rental counters, and others seated with stacks of luggage. After the ten-hour flight, I barely had any patience for understaffed facilities. Finally, my reservation was processed, and I walked down to the parking garage level.

I had rented a car, at least for the first few days, since I would have to pick up some of my art works that were being shipped separately; and also to pick up some things at a storage facility just north of the airport, off the 101 freeway.

I drove north on the airport road, gazing up at the hills that separated South San Francisco from San Francisco proper. A tongue of fog lapped up on the western edge of hills. They were bare, almost completely devoid of any green vegetation. Transmission towers marched up the hill and over, a few housing developments crept up the lower elevations of the hill, and a cluster of office towers stood off to the bayside of the freeway, tech companies. I could feel the breeze rock the small economy car as I drove up the 101.

The storage facility in South San Francisco was like a home for me. It was the repository of all my worldly possessions, clothes, a few household items, but mostly books and artwork that I had carried with me for decades, and they were now packed into a partitioned metal shed. I pulled up in front of my space and unlocked the shed. Lifting the metal door, and gazing in at my familiar boxes, a motley collection of newer white banker boxes, and older brown boxes, stacked up, filling the entire space. Some of the boxes were more than 30 years old. It was like the discovery of a personal archaeological site.

Reflexively, I rummaged through one of the boxes and came across an old album of photographs. These were pictures from my childhood. I opened it up briefly, but it wasn't the main object of my search. I came to an old picture of myself from a family trip to Chicago.

There I was in downtown Chicago, Michigan Avenue. The Wrigley building, its white stone tower at the end of the street. I was age 12, wearing an orange shirt, and plaid shorts, posing contrapposto style, one knee bent. My head tilted, smiling. There was a look in my eye, beyond the smile; there was something else hidden.

I stared at the picture. Again, I connected to the lost time of my childhood. A world seemed to open up to me, a living feeling came back to me, filled with a multitude of memories and images. A chapter in my life, a section of time that seemed almost entirely disconnected from the present. Which me was the real me, here? That distant time captured in the family snapshot, or the present me looking at the old pictures?

What was I trying to unravel here? What was the past trying to tell me? What did I know or sense in that distant sunny August day?

This was more than just a picture of my young self, more than just a picture of a twelve- year old boy on the brink of adolescence. Although, I was insulated in the dreams of childhood, it seemed that some part of me intuited an uncontainable change looming ahead. A dawning realization that the world wasn't all it appeared to be, that the trailing clouds of childhood were about to be dispersed.

There was more, though, something was telling me now. This wasn't just about me. I was part of a whole, the greater whole of the world. I should be able to read the course of the world in this picture, like Goethe gauging the weather by looking out his window.

What would a visitor from another planet say of this world, this moment in time from the evidence of the picture? Weren't all the elements present here, just in this snapshot, elements signaling some incipient transformations just beyond the frame, the sense that we were passing through a threshold, through the eye of a needle? Some things were left behind, and other things were enjoined, in the rush forward, into an irretrievable alteration in the world.

I closed the book. I grabbed some clean clothes, some paint brushes, and my old 35mm camera, and after taking one last look at the boxes, I closed the shed.

It was by now late afternoon. The coastal fog was now flowing over the mountains; a meta-layer of the ocean was reclaiming San Francisco for the night. The East side of the peninsula was still clear, golden sunlight illuminating the dry hills. I drove north up the 101 heading for the Bay Bridge. The exits passed by. Brisbane, the Cow Palace, Candlestick, Cesar Chavez, Vermont. I kept my eye open for the signs pointing to I-80 north, and to the bridge, jockeying position to make sure I was in the right lane.

On a bridge crossing over the freeway someone had put up a banner, "Save the Planet."

Some of the few remaining San Francisco dissidents, I thought.

The elevated freeways looping over and under me seemed like giant concrete dinosaurs, artifacts from a different era, still snaking across the city even in this digital era.

Contrasted with these relics of the twentieth century were the numerous Apple billboards I passed. Clean design. Sleek images advertising the latest iPhone, horizontal, tilted slightly, on a lime green background. On the way north, every few miles it seemed there was another iPhone billboard, each one in a different color, here magenta, there lemon yellow, here orange. The future presented in the billboards seemed so colorful, bright, and fun.

Now, I could see the towers of downtown San Francisco splayed across the hills, the buildings burnished in the late afternoon light, the Bank of America building like a dark sarcophagus, a monolith; The Transamerica tower, only its pyramid point visible; an American ben-ben stone waiting at the end of the Western world. Then I approached the gleaming new high-rise tower rising just before the bridge entrance. In a few moments, I shot by the whole scene, barely enough time to encompass the spectacular setting of the city on the bay, and then I was closed in by the lower deck of the bridge.

A few moments later, I hurtled through the tunnel on forested Yerba Buena island, and then out into the open again, the hills of Berkeley stretching across the horizon. I quickly glanced out at the water of the bay, and up at the new cantilevered suspension bridge, its white towers glowing orange in the sunset light. I was heading to Berkeley, first to have dinner at a favorite Indian restaurant, and then to locate the room I had rented for the first week of my stay.

By the time I finished dinner, it was late, and I was almost completely exhausted. The jet lag had finally overtaken the initial exhilaration I felt at being back in San Francisco.

Several times, I circled around a quiet leafy neighborhood just off Shattuck peering at street signs and house numbers trying to locate my lodging. The house lights were sporadic, and my eyes were losing their ability to focus, guessing that I was in the vicinity of the house, I decided to park the car. Grabbing my backpack, and the printout I had made in London with instructions on how to locate the rental, I set off on foot.

11: Cedar Hollow

The place was called Cedar Hollow, and the deeply shadowed front was overgrown with vegetation. A small wooden gate was partially open, and I walked into the front yard, the house lights glowing up ahead. At the door, I entered the security code into a keypad, and walked into the front room.

The place had a rustic quality, like a cabin up in the Sierras. All about the room were musical instruments: several guitars, a drum set, a saxophone, and few small bookshelves. I walked in and found the host working on his laptop at the kitchen table.

His name was Cody. He seemed to be about fifty, a young fifty though, tall, and tanned, bespectacled with a mustache. Cordial, and intelligent, he had a certain easy familiarity to his manner, a Californian laid back openness, and we shortly began a wide-ranging conversation briefly touching on art, music, cities, and technology.

He offered me a beer, and we sat down in the music room. I happened to glance over at his bookshelf and noticed an old paperback copy of Huxley's "Doors of Perception" and then mentioned that I had been thinking a lot about perception lately, particularly visual perception. I didn't want to mention the reasons for my recent interest, my case of optic neuritis, since at this point, I was still hopeful that it might be only a passing condition.

"The question I've been pondering is, where is the image we actually see? It can't be in the eye, nor in retina, since that would be upside down. So, it must be elsewhere," I remarked, sipping the beer.

"Vision is non-local," he said thoughtfully.

"Apparently our perceptual apparatus is holonomic," I added.

"I've heard the brain itself is like a hologram," he replied, seeming to be fully conversant about this subject.

"Potentially, any point in space has an image of the entire scene enfolded into it." I was remembering seeing multiple water droplets spread across a surface, each reflecting an image of the scene, each a tiny lens capturing the world.

"What's really out there is just electromagnetic energy."

"Everywhere," I said gesturing around the room.

"Yeah, just scattered light rays bouncing off surfaces and objects. Entirely different than the picture we finally create with our own vision."

"I know." I looked around the room, studying the light, "The lens and the pupil actually create an image out of the dispersed reflected light. Of course, then it goes on to the retina, and the brain."

"And there's a crucial role played by the intervening space between the lens and the retina, just that minute difference allows the eye to read three dimensional forms and shapes."

"Right, the parallax effect, plus the shape of the retina is actually curved, so it's not just a flat two-dimensional surface like a camera." I took another drink from the beer.

"Are you familiar with visual purple?" Cody asked.

"Oh, yeah: rhodopsin, in low light situations the bio-pigment that absorbs the green blue light."

"Once exposed to light, it becomes exhausted, and takes about 45 minutes to be replaced."

"The eye is remarkable, isn't it?" The beer was starting to take effect. I was straining to keep my eyes open. The fatigue from the long Trans-Atlantic flight was finally catching up with me.

"Sometimes the photoreceptors randomly fire, even though quanta don't impact."

"I know."

I almost felt like I was seeing little sparks of light on the edge of my vision.

"The noise to signal issue. I think Goethe mentioned these, the physiological colors," I said.

"The light quanta strike the individual photoreceptors, and then an electrical charge is transmitted through the optic nerve to the brain."

"Yeah, I know."

What then happened to the light quanta? Do they just disappear, dematerialize, or bounce back out of the eye? I wondered. How could one particle of light be separate from another? What an absurdity. Can light quanta just dissolve back into the cosmic space? I was imagining the process taking place in my own eye, some part of the signal wasn't being transmitted. After the quanta made their impact, was the signal halted somewhere in my optical nerve? I hadn't found convincing answers to these intricacies of the visual apparatus.

"The eye is a digital apparatus," he remarked.

"I don't know about that," I countered, suddenly feeling more engaged, "I think it's more complicated than that."

"You have the action potential."

"Yeah, I know about that." I was getting a little tired, maybe I was sounding irritated.

"The transmission of the electrical charge is an all or nothing, kind of like an on and off."

"Well, that's not zeros and ones," I countered.

"Look at this."

He had picked up his iPhone from the table and his fingers flicked across the device.

"The digital model is an abstraction, a metaphor of sorts," I responded somewhat laconically.

"Ok. Check this out."

Holding his iPhone up and pointing it toward the wall, a beam of light emerged from the device projecting an animation on the blank wall.

"Here's the spike of the action potential, it's an all or nothing thing."

The animation showed little square blocks traveling down a pathway to the gates. The squares approached one of the gates, stacking up. First one, then two, then the third square, and the ganglion cell became de-polarized and the gate opened.

He turned off the animation.

"There you are." He said confidently.

"That's just an abstraction. I think it's more complicated than all that. As I understand it, with the photoreceptors in the retina, the photons are registered in a graduated way. Then following that, the retinal ganglion cells fire a signal. The action potential is about chemical changes in the cell, and gates open, several gates in fact. So, it's more multi-dimensional."

"Quanta are digital," he insisted.

"I have a problem with this reduction of things to the digital model. The world is analog isn't it? You know, when you think about the old radio dials, where you could tune into those in-between stations. Now with the digital tuners, you lose that possibility. You can't dial in something, it moves in these steps, so you miss something."

"Sensory inputs come in as discrete impulses."

"In a way, but it's part of a field effect. We interpret these impulses as a whole system. In an analog way. We live in an analog world. We live on a surface, an interface."

Our presence was pressed to the periphery of the body, stationed at the orifices of sense perception? What was inside? Chains of symbolic representation: trains of pictures and words? Flowing feelings, emotions, and surging passions; the heart beating; then a warm reddish interior?

I was struggling to keep my eyes open, but I continued, "And then, the way these cells fire their signals, it's more complicated than a simple yes, and no, on or off, it's part of process of inhibition and excitement, changes in chemistry." I laughed a little bit, starting to wonder if I was even making sense to myself.

Cody acted like he suddenly realized that I was no longer able to completely articulate all the nuances of visual perception, and he stood up, ready to call it a night. I had a funny intuition that he had really been testing me all along, pushing me to my limits, trying to gauge to what level I was able to maintain some coherence.

"This has been a fascinating conversation. I'm not sure if we can even resolve these questions, but I really enjoy discussing them, it puts me in a certain frame of mind."

"I agree. I think I've reached the limit of my consciousness. I've had a long day of travel."

"I understand."

Cody gave me a quick tour of the house, showing me the kitchen, and the facilities, and we said good night. I went upstairs, and he walked outside to an external open-air structure where he slept under the California stars.

***

The next morning was another glorious California day. There was a spring-like effervescence in the air. From the kitchen, I looked out the window on the yard. It seemed partially overgrown, like it hadn't been tended in several months. A wheelbarrow lay tipped over in the overgrown grass. My view was framed by a cluster of tall cedars, and another tall tree with a cascade of brilliant orange flowers, all standing against a pure blue sky. I didn't have the sense I was situated in a dense urban area at all, rather in a peaceful country hollow ringed by trees, swaying in the light breeze.

In the corner of the yard I spotted Cody, seated in his open-air office working on a laptop. Cody was emblematic of the new San Francisco, laid back, articulate, technologically adept, and a musician. After I had finished breakfast, he came back inside, and started to brew some coffee. I commented on his natural work environment.

"City of the future," I remarked, gesturing outside referring to his outdoor working arrangement.

"Just a freelance gig, mostly coding."

"I did some freelance work, for a while, at least, this Sunnyvale company, writing biographies for business executives concerned about their internet reputations."

He nodded, as if he was familiar with all that I was talking about.

"Virtual identities are huge," he said.

"These weren't virtual people. They were real, it least I thought they were. I did several pieces on the same individual, in each piece I was supposed to bring out a different facet of their biography."

"I'm sure, but there are people who are paid to create fake profiles; bots, and they trawl throughout the digital world, raising search engine results, beefing up social media accounts."

"What do you mean?"

"Virtual identities that hit on or respond to different sites."

For a moment, I was dumbfounded. Momentarily, I wondered if some of the people I had written about might not have been entirely real.

"Fake digital identities?"

"Right. They generate ad revenue. It's a massive part of the internet."

"How massive?" I asked.

"About a third of all traffic."

"Millions of fake identities?"

"At least, maybe more, particularly when you consider Facebook has several billion users. There are probably billions of bots operating out there."

"This seems kind of deceptive."

"You think so?"

"I mean, are these completely fabricated profiles?"

"In some cases."

"Could they be sampled from real profiles? Compositing of identities, some part real, some part fake, cut and paste identity, a real picture of someone, with false information?"

"That's entirely possible."

I was forming a picture in my mind, almost like a cubist or surreal collage of a persona, formed from random elements juxtaposed together, and then released, autonomously trawling through the internet; anonymous identities that one might interact with and never know whether they were real or not real. It was a depressing and sterile vision of the future.

"Why is this tolerated?" I asked.

"It's too important for the entire system. I don't think there is a way of addressing it really."

"There's something nefarious about all this. It's unethical."

414

"The system is trying to filter bots out. You're familiar with Captcha?" He seemed unconcerned about the moral dimension of it all.

"What?"

"Captcha. Distorted letters and numbers you encounter on certain sites. You have to decipher them before you're granted access."

"Oh, yeah."

"It's a protocol to differentiate humans from machines." he said casually.

Cody finished brewing his coffee, excused himself, and returned outside to his open-air office. There was still something that troubled me about the entire subject. Bots, fake identities, all trawling through the internet. Who manufactured the bots? Wasn't it the same tech bros, the disconnected left hand of the tech sector? I wanted Cody to tell me more, provide more information, so I could fully absorb this peculiar revelation of the technological world, but he had seemed somewhat disengaged, as if the topic hadn't really interested him as much as our conversation the night before.

12: Imaginopolis

For the next two weeks I remained in Berkeley, commuting daily into San Francisco to work on my contribution to the exhibit at the Yerba Buena Center for the Arts.

Cody's outdoor living arrangement was inspiring, and consonant with the ideas I had developed for my vision of the future city.

I was partially drawing from my past experiences of living in Ann Arbor, as well as many visits to Cranbrook in suburban Detroit. In these examples, nature was integrated with the city, and there was a deliberate shaping of the natural environment, interspersed with cultural centers and living arrangements.

The idea of the university campus seemed ideal. Certainly, Berkeley was a great town, but Ann Arbor was a better model to my mind, more compact and integral with its verdant landscaping, bookstores, cafes, and theaters right across the street from the university and its museums and libraries; all integrated into a green natural environment.

There were parts of London that inspired me in that way. Again, the integration of parks with the city was key; the mix of low rise and high rise, narrow streets, smaller cars: a pedestrian friendly scale. This was the most desirable vision of the future city.

I made a map of *Imaginopolis*. The imaginary city was full of parks, and branching street patterns. I painted more detailed renderings that captured the look of these arboreal cities. I included housing modules nestled in buildings that were built like trees, apartments that were more like tree houses on elevated platforms, and walkways that were placed amid the trees, and rooftop decks with space for planting trees, or stargazing. Some of the paintings were close ups of trees, all trunks and branches, against a leafy background, and hidden amongst these sylvan depictions, I added tiny dwellings lit by lanterns and reached by ladders, almost like a vision from Tolkien's *Lothlórien*.

I wanted to foil the utilitarian impulse, so I created one-way streets that terminated in pocket size parks. Garden zones, inside the city were linked by walking paths into larger park areas, and these extended out into more extensive wilderness areas, giving the residents the opportunity to access the full spectrum of natural experience without getting into their automobiles.

Importantly, the plans for my future city included physical spaces that promoted reflection, down time, non-useful, and meditative interludes, spaces that were insulated from the hubbub and din of transportation corridors. There were pools of water to capture the changing light and shadows of the day, and night. I wanted to evoke nature, even with a fantasy component.

In the city of the future: *Imaginopolis*, I wanted to emphasize creativity as opposed to commerce. I wanted to suggest a path forward that phased out business as the dominant force in society, a society that emphasized art, education and research, and small-scale prototype production, instead of mass consumption, and production. I diagrammed a flow chart for this more innovative social economy, one where continual learning and creative exploration were the rule instead of the exception.

A week before the exhibit opened, Andromeda arrived for a short visit on her way back to London from Indonesia. She was making a temporary exception to her prohibition on visiting America, only because of my exhibit, and then because San Francisco sometimes seemed like it was not part of America.

13: Tamalpais Vision

In the afternoon we drove out of the city, north on the 101. Over San Francisco the sky was a deep blue, but as we approached the Golden Gate, we could see wispy tendrils of fog drifting through the towers of the bridge entering the bay. Parts of the bridge were in sunshine, parts were wreathed in fog, and while crossing the span, the gusty wind blowing off the ocean rocked the tiny rental car.

We drove north into Marin, exiting the 101 at Mill Valley, taking the winding road that led up through housing developments and eucalyptus groves, toward the top of Mount Tamalpais. At each fork in the road we chose the higher road.

Stopping at Pan Toll Ranger Station, we parked, and began to hike up the mountain. We followed a steep trail that wound upward through the forest of oak and fir, through the fields of waving golden grass. Higher and higher we climbed, until we found a broad opening on the shoulders of the mountain. Here in a wide meadow, we had a panoramic view looking far west out over the ocean.

The marine layer came right up to the foot of the mountain and stretched out to the edge of the western horizon. The oceanic clouds were brilliantly illuminated by the afternoon sun. In my mind's eye, I could imagine the continent of clouds stretching over the horizon a thousand miles to the southwest.

Turning around to look south, we could see one of the towers of the Golden Gate rising above the fog, and San Francisco itself, appearing like a toy city, with the tops of its buildings poking through the clouds. To the east we could see the bridge to Oakland, and the Berkeley hills still in the sunshine, and even further beyond, Mount Diablo.

Looking west, I searched the edge of the horizon, trying to find a limit to the immensity of my view. The white blanket of clouds seemed to move ever so slightly as if it too was a part of the dynamic flow that moved the ocean. Far off, in among the clouds, I thought I spotted a tiny landform barely jutting out above the marine layer.

"The Farallons," I said pointing out to the west.

"I see," Andromeda responded.

Up on the windy aerie, I could sense the rotation of the planet, the turning of the globe ever eastward; we were riding on the edge of time.

The awareness of my being, my attention had moved from the periphery of my body and now extended out into the space that was opened to my view, my being was now coterminous with the vast space over the Pacific Ocean.

"I have this far away feeling up here, like I'm at the end of the world."

The breeze swirled around our position on the edge of the hill. Down on the lower flanks of the mountain, I could see the grasses silently blown into patterns, sweeping first this way, and then that way.

"Yes. It's a remarkable," she answered dreamily, "Physically removed from the world, but observing it from a distance, like watchers in some sort of Earth station."

Hadn't Gemina mentioned a watcher inside? I realized that being in a specific physical location, like this mountain with its high perspective, could place one into a special state of mind; a reflective, meditative mind.

"We're on the edge of the western world, the whole American continent is behind us, and Asia is somewhere way out there, over the horizon," I remarked, sweeping my hand along the rim of the sky.

"Yes. It's incredible to ponder that notion, the transition between west and east." Andromeda seemed in a dreamy, distant state of mind.

"Yet, it's such an immense transition; the whole Pacific Ocean."

"The world ocean; where the spirits of the dead go." It was a strange comment, almost like something Gemina would have said.

"Really?"

"Yes, on their way to the moon," she added.

I remembered seeing the sliver of the new moon the night before and tried to imagine the spirits swirling above the vast immensity of the ocean, waiting to embark on their journey upward. In my mind's eye it appeared rendered like some of the beautiful Japanese lacquerware we had seen in Paris.

The breeze swept over our position again.

Andromeda had brought her backpack and she removed a blanket for us to sit on, and a thermos with some tea. Sitting cross legged we gazed out over the ocean drinking our tea.

"How far do you think we can see?" I asked.

"How far are the islands?"

"Maybe 35 miles."

"Then the edge of our horizon is perhaps 75 miles," she answered.

"I've heard that on really clear days the Sierra Nevada are visible to the East, and that's at least a hundred miles."

"Yes, if the conditions are clear we can see light years away."

"Of course," I laughed at myself.

"However, even from this mountain we're still looking through the atmosphere. But we have a certain radius of vision, perhaps a hundred miles in every direction," she explained.

"I was thinking about Japan, way out there over the horizon." I pointed to the northwest out beyond Point Reyes.

"Some 4000 miles if we follow the curve of the earth."

"I was trying to imagine how far it would be compared to what we can see right now."

"I see." She seemed to be mentally calculating something, and then continued, "Think about this. Try to imagine ten times the distance you can see right now, and then ten times again, and then again, and then once again, and then you'll be in Japan."

We both laughed at the absurdity of such a grand visualization.

"Or what about this," I suggested, "What about the entire area of the Pacific Ocean." I swept my arm across western horizon.

"Some sixty million square miles," she remarked gazing out into the distance.

"Yeah, try to imagine. I mean, take what I can see right now, my entire field of vision. How many times would that fit into the immensity of the Pacific?"

Andromeda paused a moment seeming to calculate, and then answered, "To make it easy, let's say we can see 100 miles in each direction. We square that number to get 10,000. Then multiply that by pi to get about 31,000 square miles. That's the possible field of your vision. Take half of that to represent what we can see looking to the west over the ocean. Let's say that's 15,000 square miles. Then try to fit that in to sixty million."

"That's going to be difficult," I conceded, laughing.

"Break it down into parts," she insisted.

"Ok." I looked out into the vastness of the ocean, trying to make an approximate calculation, "Fifteen into thirty; twice times three is six, add a little extra, times ten," I paused a moment.

"Yes, close. We could say roughly that for every million square miles, there will be seventy fields of vision equivalent to what we see right before us."

"So, seventy of this," I swept my hand across the horizon, "Sixty times," I laughed.

Andromeda smiled at me.

"Try to visualize it. See where you come to."

I had to close my eyes, and picture myself above the earth, as if I was on a higher mountain that looked over an even greater swath of the California coast. Then I placed the sectors of vision into that wider perspective, transposing my present field of view onto this larger area. Then I placed myself into an even higher and larger perspective, taking in more of the Pacific Ocean, trying to map the field of vision out further, but I faltered at this point.

"I can't do it. At one point I lose track."

"Yes, those are the limits of our powers of conceptualization."

"I need to draw it out. I think."

"That might help."

It was starting to get late, the earth was turning, and the light had shifted to the golden light of late afternoon so typical of the California coast. We decided to hike around some more before working our way back down the mountain, following the trails ever downward, and gradually approach the area where we had parked the car.

Before we had descended too far, I heard a distracting whining sound encroaching on the natural silence of the mountainside. The sound vaguely reminded me of a weed wacker or some other sort of landscaping tool. The sound seemed to approach closer to us, emanating from the air above us.

Looking up into the sky, we spotted the source of the annoying sound. Hovering only thirty feet above us was the inexplicable object, generating a whirring sound with an assembly of rotating propeller blades.

"A drone," I muttered.

We were both momentarily frozen in our tracks. It seemed to be holding formation directly over us, tilted at a slight angle, as if specifically investigating and monitoring our presence.

"Even here on Mount Tamalpais?" I asked.

"Even here the military state has made its incursion. There's no pretense anymore. They don't care," Andromeda said severely.

Wordlessly, we both hurried down the trail. The covering of the trees intermittently blocked our view, but the sound of the drone followed us down the trail. Trying to escape the drone's view, we left the trail and darted into a denser stand of trees.

In an opening between the branches I could see the drone still hovering over us. In that moment of looking up, I lost my footing and slipped down the slope, rolling onto my side among the fallen leaves and branches. Andromeda ran down to me and helped me get back on my feet. The sound of the drone continued overhead as if it was deliberately following us downward. The thing was still hovering above, maybe only 30 feet over head, the whirling blades generating an even louder annoying sound.

Andromeda bent down to the ground to pick up a stone, and in one graceful motion hurled it upward toward the machine. It must have fallen short by several feet, but the machine appeared to buck upwards, and then it plunged down lower almost into the trees as if to retaliate against us.

We darted back under the trees and carefully weaved our way down the steep hillside, zigzagging under cover of the denser foliage until we came to the main road. We crossed the road and rejoined the trail. We seemed to have lost the drone.

It was now getting quite dark. Through an opening in the trees, we caught a glimpse of the end of the sunset. And a few moments later we also noticed the thin crescent of the moon hanging just above the orange horizon in the indigo vault of the sky.

14: Muir Beach Cabin

We drove back down the mountain, descending below the cloud layer, following the winding road until we came to the fork that led us further to the west, down toward the sea, down to Muir Beach. Andromeda had wanted to spend a night by the ocean. So, we had made some arrangements to rent a cabin close enough to the water to hear the waves that night.

The cabin was rustic, and the atmosphere of the sea seeped into the single room structure. The walls seemed like they were made from planks of old driftwood. The bed was more of a day bed, comfortable, but barely large enough for both of us. There was an old-fashioned lantern we lit and placed on the table. I had brought some food, and Andromeda made some more tea. I had also brought a few of my old photographs, pictures from my childhood that I had wanted to show Andromeda. And after looking at them, we laid in bed, talking for a little while and then just listening to the sound of the sea. Andromeda on her back, I was on my side facing the inside of the room.

I tried to explain the mystery of the photographs, the seemingly unanswered question that still haunted me.

I showed her an old postcard view of downtown Detroit. It was a nighttime picture of the skyline taken from across the river in Canada.

There was something magical about the image. I recognized the distinctive Penobscot building with its stepped tiers leading up to the brightly lit beacon, and then the modern looking Michigan Consolidated Gas building in the foreground. The entire scene of glittering lights was reflected in the river. The image seemed to capture something indefinable, giving me a sense of the expansive energy of the early 1960s.

"The pictures are like evidence that remind me that this time really did happen. That it was more than just a dream. Everything seems so different now, almost like we're on a different planet."

"I know," she said softly, "it's one of the strange distortions of time. Our past seems incomprehensible to our present being."

"But the pictures refer to something more, something greater, larger; a whole realm of inner pictures, like a submerged continent."

"How do you feel when you see these inner pictures?" She had placed her arm around me, holding me closer.

"I feel this sense of great expectations, a joy, an aliveness; the universe is bigger, wider, more open. The colors are richer, purer, filled with deeper hues."

"Yes. Can you give me an example?"

"Yes. We lived in suburban Detroit. It was summer, one night. I remember riding in car, in the backseat, the window was down; a summer evening, after the heat of the day, the fresh night air, the trees, all around, arching over the road, dark lush foliage, soft. There was a sound like whispering, like the trees were whispering. The leaves were rustling, or maybe there were crickets. The night sky was almost like velvet purple, a deep shade of violet. The stars were sharp, bright."

"Where were you going?"

"I'm not sure, but I think we were going to some school. I remember a gymnasium like room. It's strange since we wouldn't normally go to a school at night, or in summer."

"Then what happened?"

"For some reason, I remember a lot of people being there, a large group. I think, they were giving out sugar cubes."

"Polio vaccine."

"Yeah, that's probably right, but there was something more going on."

I thought back, I could still feel the flavor of that time. Something was more potent about that moment in time. So much mystery was still wrapped up in that particular moment of time.

"Perhaps, that evening you crossed a certain threshold of awareness, and that's why you remember it so vividly now," she paused, pulling me closer.

"It's when we reflect on these memories that we weave the raiment of our soul. You're joining together with your soul to fashion your soul body."

"Where is the soul?"

"Yes. That's always the question that is asked, and as long as we're not trying to find a literal location it will always leads us inward, to reflect. The soul is inside. In the Egyptian tradition, we speak of the Ba and the Ka. It's complicated, but in a way our soul is formed from the coming together of spirit and body. There are intermediate stages. The Ka has many different aspects."

"Is it like an interface, between two different realms?"

"Yes, you might say that. It forms in the in-between that is our life. This intermediate place we call life."

"Like the soul is visiting us?"

"More, than that, it joins the physical body even before birth. There would be no you without this coming together of soul and body. There are certain affinities that draw it to your physical form."

She paused looking out to the window.

"The Ka is a drop of the divine inside our being, the only part of us not subject to the laws of the physical universe."

In that moment I could hear the waves breaking against the shore.

"It's hard for us modern people to differentiate the different parts of the soul. A simplification, a literalness, has spread throughout the whole of Western civilization, a perspective that doesn't even recognize the soul."

"Scientific materialism."

"Yes."

She held me tighter, staring into my eyes, almost whispering, "It's worse than that. They want to thwart the conscious weaving of your soul. They want to block your soul reflections. They want to control your imagination, even enter into your dream world."

She shivered, and I pulled the blanket closer over her body. We lay still there for a while, listening to the waves. The light in the lantern was getting lower, dimmer.

"It's going to get worse."

She resumed, speaking a little louder. "The next ten years will be a difficult time for the planet. The planetary aspects indicate this. According to my mother, there is a tension between contrasting archetypal energies, and humanity is placed in between these forces. She has been studying the astrological geography looking for the most secure place. Even Andreas agrees, with his models, predicting the global tendencies, the demographics, the flow of capital, the distribution of resources, the change in the atmosphere, the change in the sun. We don't have much time. Soon, the world will become even more contaminated." She paused, looking up into my eyes.

"You and I don't have much time."

"You're leaving to go back to Europe, I know, but then, what?" What was she trying to say? I hadn't really considered what would happen after my exhibit was installed. Would I return to working as an adjunct faculty? Or if not, would I be able to return to Europe and join Andromeda?

"Yes, more than that. For us there is a short window of time."

Her arm wrapped tighter around me.

"I remember something you said on the island. The first night I was there."

"Yes. I was trying to suggest something, something about us, our future."

She paused again for a moment, "I can't live in America. Even in San Francisco, or even, especially in San Francisco."

"Then where?"

"I don't know, yet. I'll know more after I return to London."

15: Different Futures

It was another beautiful day in San Francisco. A Saturday afternoon, the day after the opening, and the exhibition organizers were hosting a conversation with the artists. I was invited to talk about my artistic inspirations. I took BART into the city since I had returned the rental car after Andromeda's departure.

When I boarded the train at the Rockridge Station, the carriages were already filled with passengers. For a moment, I stood facing the doors, gazing out at the panorama of the city and the bay. A jumble of forms intervened between my eyes and a clear view of downtown San Francisco. In the foreground were the giant shipping cranes of the Oakland harbor; and then the white towers of the new Bay Bridge, like ladders reaching skyward.

The Transamerica tower drew my gaze, and looking beyond, I could see the Pacific Ocean indicated by a soft horizontal line, blue against blue. It was an incredible perspective from which to take in San Francisco's physical placement on the coast, perched on the edge of the American continent. Here I could suddenly grasp my position in the world, on the edge of the western world; on the edge of time itself.

Was there something more to San Francisco than just an aggregation of people and culture over time? Was there something geo-physical about this place, a certain alignment of energies that contributed to what I felt here? I wondered.

This propitious view lasted only a few moments before the train dropped down into the flat lands of Oakland, and eventually down into the darkness of the Transbay Tunnel.

***

I emerged from the BART station amid crowds of people. The sunlight was bright and sharp, the sky overhead a crisp blue. A steady breeze funneled down the streets to the bay. I paused on the corner gazing west up Market Street, looking between the skyscrapers. The sky was a brilliant white at the horizon where the coastal cloud layer floated. There was something about this atmospheric effect that intrigued me. It was a signal of our proximity to the world ocean.

I walked the few blocks from Market to the Yerba Buena Center meditating on the nature of the present-day city, going over the main ideas I wanted to express. Pondering how the social structure had been irrevocably distorted by the Neo-Darwinian and Neo-Liberal programs, no amount of infrastructural adjustments would alter that fact.

San Francisco, and London were glaring examples of the failure of the Neo-Liberal system, exacerbated by digital media, both cities had become zones of exclusion, and exclusivity. More than ever, I could see how we were framed, limited by the dominate ideologies here in America, especially in San Francisco. Even rebellion, was limited to a handful of sanctioned tropes, and even the act of rebellion was turned into a cliché. I had sadly come to the realization that the destruction of the natural world, or at least a downgrading of its former natural potency, was fated. I grieved for the world, for the mutilated dolphins washing up on the beaches, the plastic micro-particles invading every available body of water, the diesel exhaust inhaled into out lungs, the egregious noise pollution assaulting our ears, the contrails and satellites incessantly cocooning our planet. Out of a sense of conscience, I still felt the need to at least advise or recommend, for whoever might listen, a possible path or escape from this insane fate. That's why I was here in San Francisco.

San Francisco was already destroyed, or at least the San Francisco I had known; the vital energy of the place behind the façade of the buildings and bridges. Even an earthquake couldn't destroy San Francisco more than it already was destroyed.

Still, it offered me a platform on which to gaze into the Pacific and view the edge of the world, from this most advanced iteration and outpost of technological humanity ensconced on the bay.

Like the rest of America, the muscle cars were here too, as well as the hulking SUVs, and super-size pick-up trucks. Their front grills like military masks, evil masks, black magician masks, like the helmets of Star Wars storm troopers. Was it aggressive or just passive aggressive? Did it matter anymore? Had we become so inured to these aggressive projections that we didn't even notice it anymore? It wasn't about fun or style anymore; it was just about power, horsepower, and motorized testosterone, the drivers of these vehicles descending into some bestial level of social display.

I crossed Mission Street and paused to take in the surroundings, particularly the way the Yerba Buena Center formed a sanctuary in the midst of a forest of urban high rises.

I continued further along Third Street approaching a side entrance to the art center. On my left someone had just parked their car, and as they walked away, they locked it by tooting their horn loudly in my left ear as I walked by.

This was a habit I hadn't noticed in Europe. It seemed to be a particularly American way of insuring that their automobile was securely locked; another example of mindless convenience culture gone amok. What did it say about the American psyche? I remembered that both Rousseau and Voltaire had hated the city.

I turned into the center, running up the stairs. The plaza inside the Yerba Buena Center was a peaceful oasis, but I didn't have time to enjoy it today. I sensed that I was running a few minutes late.

The conference room was filled with people and the other artists were already seated at a long table placed in front of a blue screen backdrop. The room had a sterile institutional look. The dominant color seemed to be a dark grey. The only traces of color were the refreshments staged on one side of the room; plastic cups filled with orange juice arrayed on a table.

I made eye contact with one of the curators who I had met before, and she gestured for me to take the remaining open seat at the end of the front table. Apparently, I had missed the introductory remarks, for the artist speaking was now describing his creative process.

At first, I felt distracted sitting there. The commotion of the busy downtown streets was still reverberating in my head. I looked around the room observing the audience, I glanced out the window. I gazed at the pure white sunlight illuminating the edge of the windowsill. There was a truncated view of the surrounding high rises. Gradually, I hooked into the ongoing presentation.

The artist was talking about repurposing and redeploying the urban debris.

"Part of my practice as an artist is to build a repository for discarded technology."

He went on talking about the massive amounts of technological waste, particularly here in San Francisco. The rate of planned obsolescence was acute in the tech industry, and old discarded electronic waste was readily available. He spoke about mountains of crushed PC towers, and tons of old monitors. He had filmed e-waste facilities in China and California, and he showed some of these images on the screen. I think I remembered seeing his work in the gallery, but it hadn't made an impression on me.

The following artist was introduced and began speaking about his practice. He talked about programmable matter and molecular structures. It seemed the main focus of his talk was on technology, not cities.

"The anthropocentric narrative won't help us survive the future..."

The next artist presented an opposing narrative, speaking about communally driven architecture, earth ships built from bundles of millet.

Then another artist was introduced and talked about medical machines that can imitate human organs.

"What is our relationship to these machines? Who has access to these technologies?"

A little bit of discourse started between the panel members, comments interjected here and there. I was still silent, looking for an opening.

"Cities are objects. You can never know everything about an object. Humans are artifacts..."

"Cities are organisms," someone on the panel countered.

I nodded in agreement.

"We as a community need to be closer to our garbage."

A murmur of laughter moved through the audience.

The next artist was more interesting. She seemed to be on the same page as me.

"San Francisco is inaccessible to 80% of the people in the country. There are no longer people working in factories. It is not a real city. It's a really weird city."

"London is much the same," one of the artists agreed, he was English.

"Who is the city for?" Someone from the audience asked.

The answer seemed obvious, but no one connected the dots, at least verbally. I wanted to interject a comment, but I hadn't been introduced yet. I even wondered if my ideas were too contentious to be aired in this reserved and polite company. And plus, the emphasis here was so strongly on technology. My approach was just the opposite.

Finally, I was introduced.

"Our last speaker is Thomas Moore, the creator of *Imaginopolis: The Future City.*"

I walked up to the podium and had to search a moment around the side of the computer before I could insert my flash drive. I decided not to mention the egregious noise pollution that had assaulted me right in front of the Yerba Buena Center. I wanted to speak about the need for more equitable housing, and then lead further into the idea of making a city more natural, bringing the natural element into the city, toning down, and muffling even those egregious audio assaults.

I started the PowerPoint with a satellite image of the Bay Area.

"Have we reached the limits of free-market capitalism? In San Francisco, and other West Coast cities, we're seeing the complete failure of the free market system. Silicon Valley has figured out how to make a gamut of digital devices, but affordable housing is still a challenge. To solve this problem, we need a complete transformation of the economic model, not just here in the United Sates, but in the whole world. Otherwise, the capacities of the free market model are going to be exceeded everywhere with negative impacts on the quality of life."

"In fact, much of the housing in San Francisco is actually sub-standard. We need a complete revolution in terms of design, materials, energy efficiency, and affordability, even seemingly mundane issues like plumbing, ventilation, and natural light need to be completely re-evaluated. There needs to be a massive capital investment in affordable housing in cities like San Francisco, so those of moderate income can continue to live in the heart of the city."

"One current problem now, is that much of the new housing is pitched to the high end of the market: condominiums with marble counter tops and Gaggenau ranges. Left to their own devices, developers will build luxury units, so they can maximize their profits. What few low-end units that come onto the market are built on the cheap. Again, so developers can cut a greater profit."

"We can't wait any longer for the market to solve this problem. In the case of San Francisco, there is a need for maybe half a million units of affordable housing. It's not even enough to change zoning codes, to allow higher density housing, or to build high density housing near transit stations. The problem won't be solved by building pencil tower apartments in Palo Alto."

I switched the picture now to a map of Europe. Followed up by pictures of housing developments in Vienna during the 1920s.

"We should look to Vienna as a model. Red Vienna, during the interwar period, when the government built modern, well designed, and affordable housing. In the Vienna model, the price of housing is not determined by the market." There was a murmur of agreement the crowd.

"There is a whole history of successful social housing in the German speaking world that Americans conveniently ignore.

437

Starting in the early years of the Twentieth Century we have the International Building Exhibitions that presented modern solutions to housing for a new century. Here is a picture of the Weissenhof Estate in Stuttgart built in 1927. This project included designs by many of the most prominent architects of the time, including Le Corbusier, Mies Van Der Rohe, Walter Gropius, and others."

I switched back to an image of California.

"I propose a similar initiative, starting with the establishment of a non-governmental independent California housing authority, affiliated with the local and state governments, tasked with building affordable non-market housing; well designed, quality, social housing with rents much lower than the current market rates. The southeast corner of San Francisco is ripe for this type of development; Islais Creek, Indian Basin, Hunters Point. All of this should follow the IBA model, where multiple international architects would be invited to submit proposals for innovative housing. An IBA San Francisco would be a way to avoid cookie cutter solutions, and deficient design. Each architect would present their own unique solution to the challenge of building affordable quality housing."

"Who would pay for all this?" A man in the front row remarked.

"Let's look toward the technology industry. Apple had a net income of $59 billion, Facebook, $22 billion. San Francisco could form a partnership with the technology sector, and then purchase land on the behalf of the new housing authority."

I continued. "Moreover, to sustain the affordability of housing, and arrest the upward spiral of housing costs, we need to change the tax code, shifting the burden of taxpaying to the landlord class, charging more aggressive taxes based on the assessed value of the property; this would discourage the upward spiral in housing costs." An incoherent rumble of

438

voices from the crowd seemed to simultaneously object and agree.

"I also propose an alternative to the multi-story building projects: the sustainable bungalow. Many people would rather live in detached spaces, in a park like setting, removed from the commotion of traffic, with services and work within walking distance, or within bicycle range. This of course entails the design of a new kind of city. And we will need a new kind of city for the future."

I continued my presentation following a more subjective approach.

"The city is a place where creative energies come together. An *Imaginopolis*: a confluence of creativity. We should structure or design a city so we can generate a more livable, and creative environment. Think of Florence in the Quattrocento, or Paris in the 1920s, London in the 1960s, a place where creativity and innovation can flourish. There is an optimal size where the outside inputs and the internal linkages are perfectly balanced. Unfortunately, today the creativity of cities is threatened by rampant housing costs and digital media. Digital media steals time from creativity, and even from... daydreaming."

I looked out beyond the audience to the late afternoon light coming in through the window.

"Daydreams are an important antidote to the increasingly structured and directed world of technology," I offered, "Imagine a city devoted to dreams, and even romance, even a city designed for love." A rustle of suppressed laughter moved through the audience.

"Can we take the time for love?" I was thinking about Paris, but then hadn't San Francisco once been a beacon for those who believed in love? Of course, that was in the '60s. Technology had replaced love in the new San Francisco. And wasn't love now considered a symptom or a clinical condition, something defined in the latest DSM? My train of thoughts unfolded and collapsed in an instant.

I resumed speaking, "It's important to recognize the impoverished ideas that lead us to a dysfunctional city, false ideas that are based on a misreading of the natural world. And here, I'm specifically referring to the philosophical foundation that supports the Neo-Liberal economic system, and all the attendant attitudes and practices, even the inordinate emphasis on marketing that dominates so much of our culture. These are faulty memes that encourage social pathologies and are used to perpetuate an immoral economic system."

"What about cities?" Someone in the audience remarked, sounding annoyed.

"We need to bring a more natural feeling into the city. There needs to be a diminishment of heavy automotive traffic, a mandatory reduction in size and weight of all vehicles traveling inside the city. This is perhaps my most radical recommendation for the American city. Following that crucial intervention, we can introduce green corridors winding through the city, green pathways leading out into the countryside. A city connected to the greater natural world, where we can place ourselves into the greater context of the planet, not just another generic urban matrix like a Dallas or a Kansas City. Here in San Francisco we still have glimpses of the bigger picture. When we look out on the bay we're reminded of where we are in the world. When we see the Golden Gate against the Marin Headlands, or the fog rolling over the hills, we sense the natural energy of the Pacific Ocean."

There was a rustling in the crowd.

"The technophilia we currently see in our culture is destructive to the planet, to humanity, and to cities. The technological system is inherently corporate, and exploitive, and aims to standardize and order all social life. Moreover, despite all the enthusiasm surrounding technology it remains incapable of addressing the global environmental crisis."

Now, a handful of people walked out.

"Cities have become increasingly corporatized, standardized. One example is what I'll call the Starbucks phenomena. Sure, people like consistency and reliability, but the proliferation of franchises drives out variety. It's all part of a deliberate corporate strategy to saturate the market and drive out small scale entrepreneurs, leading to a generic urban landscape. Also, part of this same shift, bookstores are rapidly disappearing from most American cities. This is part of a systematic marketing strategy launched by digital media companies. The result is not only the impoverishment of the American city but..."

"Everything is on the internet," the man in the front row interrupted me again.

"That's a myth. There are many things that are not on the internet," I countered.

"Go to the library," he retorted

"Yeah, but even the libraries are deaccessioning their collections to make room for more digital facilities. We're losing something in this transition."

There was some uneasy rustling in the crowd.

"This is all part of a greater change that's being foisted on the public. Digital media is sucking the oxygen out of the cultural sphere, debasing and degrading the level of discourse."

"Let's try to get back to the main topic," the curator remarked.

I continued.

"Because of these trends, we're seeing a degradation of the conditions necessary for creativity in cities. In all the historical cultural centers, Florence, Paris, London, or New York, we always see certain conditions that engender creativity. We see one to one interaction between artists, proximity to cultural institutions, free access to life in the city. Of course, that means affordable living and working space. As recently as the 1970's there was abundant cheap space in Manhattan. Berlin became an art center in large part due to the availability of affordable space. The systematic elimination of affordable housing is a factor that militates against the creative synergy of the city."

"New social models are changing the culture," one of the artists remarked.

"This enthusiasm for technology obscures the conditions that are necessary for creativity," I responded.

"It all depends on how you define creativity."

"Of course, but let's look at this from the historical perspective. We can chart several transformations in the 20th century leading up to our present situation. There are breaks or transition points in the historical continuum. First, World War I, then again after World War II; there is another break 1973-1980, and more recently 1999-2001. In each of these transitions something has been lost." More of the audience members filtered out.

"Let's try to wrap things up here," the curator admonished.

"Each of these breaks represents a retranslation point. Particularly after the 1970s, the Neo-Liberal economic system asserts an increasingly comprehensive control over the world. No section of the globe has been left untouched. The subsequent managed society presents the illusion of choice. With the digital media there is a flattening of relations. There is a move away from the embodied experience, to the digital sphere, a systematically controlled realm, a simulacrum. You've all read Baudrillard? Debord? All this is detrimental to the physical city."

"Ok. Thank you," the curator suddenly interjected, and then turned to the audience. "Unfortunately, we'll have to end the conversation on this note," she said. "We've run out of time. Let me thank all the artists, who kindly volunteered their time.

442

Thanks again for attending this provocative conversation with the artists of *Different Futures*."

Most of the audience quickly filtered out of the room.

I slowly stood up, feeling both relieved and frustrated. I walked over to the refreshment table and studied the offerings. It seemed that most of the other artists knew each other. I stood alone for a moment, sipping an orange juice, and looking around the room.

I was just getting ready to leave the room, when a man came up to me and introduced himself.

"I agree with everything you were saying," he remarked.

He was friendly, with a thoughtful expression, maybe in his late twenties.

"Particularly your global perspective, we can't talk merely about cities any longer," he explained.

"Exactly," I answered. "You know, I just don't think these people get it, really. The big picture is obscured by the hullabaloo surrounding technology," I said quietly, as we walked out of the conference room.

"This is San Francisco."

"Of course; it's the technological mindset."

"It's like a religion here," he replied.

"Right," I agreed. "The bulk of technological innovations have been gratuitous, only coincidentally addressing the real issues of life in the 21st century. The emphasis on social media seems totally out of place. It's just, I don't mean to pick on Facebook, but is Mark Zuckerberg providing toilets to third world countries, health care facilities to people in Africa, water purification?"

"I don't know."

"Anyway, the level of discourse on most of the digital platforms is banal, even infantile. How can we even talk about imagination or inspiration when everyone is glued to their devices? Cell phones enable the surveillance society. Silicon

Valley is the cockpit for the Orwellian future," I declared, as we walked out into the beautiful sunlit lobby of the museum.

He smiled and paused to pull something out of his backpack.

"Let me give you my card. We're having a meeting on Wednesday in Oakland. It would be great to have you join our group."

I looked at the card. It was all black, with a grainy textured surface. The word "*SynchroniCity*" was spelled out in florescent green letters.

"I'll think it over," I said studying the card.

"Great."

He shook my hand and walked away.

I stayed in the lobby for a while soaking up the pure white light that flooded into the space. The special San Francisco light, I reflected, a special light particular to this location on the coast. The entire lobby was suffused with the pure undiluted Pacific light.

It was then that I noticed a map hanging on the wall near the entrance to the exhibit. It was a daytime map of the world, showing the division between night and day, and the different times zones. The center of the map seemed to be the International Date Line in the middle of the Pacific Ocean.

I walked over closer to the map and studied its features. The terminator line curved across the center of Asia: sunrise in India. In the west, to my right the American continent was half dark, half-light: sunset in Kansas. There was a bar on top of the map indicating the time zones. There was a dark meridian line starting in the polar north going down through Ireland, Iberia, Morocco, and further south to the bottom of the map. The midnight line, I realized. Placed at the bottom of the map on either side of the Date Line in bold letters were, "SUNDAY" on the left, "SATURDAY" on the right.

To capture the true direction of the earth's movement, this map would have to gradually move underneath the illuminated day portion, the continents would have to move to the right, I thought. I remembered the globe on Splendent Cay, and how I had spent one afternoon lazily watching the progression of day across the Atlantic Ocean. There was also the strange dream I had, the vision of the earth moving through the time zones, passing beneath the meridian lines. It was really we who moved, not day or night. I had a sudden momentary glimpse of the movement of the whole world. An image, only, that seemed to transmit some higher reality into my mind.

I looked outside trying to connect this vision with the outside world. Facing south, staring up at the sky from this niche in the city, from this location on the edge of the American continent, we were always imperceptibly turning to the left, moving away from the light, and then after traveling through the night, we inevitably returned to the light.

Yes, soon the sun would slip below the horizon, and a golden orange band of light would rim this particular edge of the Pacific Ocean, and we would slip into night, into the starry realm.

Epilogue: A Year Later

The bus gradually ascended through the hills toward Siena. I was lulled to sleep by the sunlight and the motion of the bus. At some point halfway through the journey, I woke up, and swiveled my legs around to view the scenery on other side of the road.

It was then that I turned back to look at the man seated behind me. I hadn't noticed him before. His features were fairly innocuous, with short carefully trimmed hair, and wire frame glasses. He was looking down, immersed in his digital device. I glanced at the bag on his seat. The luggage tag read "Wright State University".

"You're from Ohio?" I remarked, remembering that Wright State was in Dayton.

The man laughed slightly,

"I live there, yes," he replied, looking up briefly from his device.

"I was born in Lakewood," I offered.

"Lakewood?"

"Near Cleveland."

"Oh, really."

He looked back down at his device.

Perhaps he wasn't familiar with the other parts of Ohio. I paused for a few moments looking again at the scenery on the opposite side of the bus.

"On vacation here?" I asked, turning back again.

"Not really, semester abroad. I'm leading a class on the geology of Tuscany." I now recognized something academic in his manner.

"And you?" He asked.

"I'm artist."

"An artist?" He looked down at his device.

"You're spending the day in Siena?" I continued.

"Not exactly," he said with a touch of weariness. "The class is visiting the cathedral with some of my colleagues."

"Perugino's frescos, what a treasure," I said almost to myself, remembering the spectacular interior of the cathedral from an earlier visit.

"I'm a scientist. Actually, those old paintings don't interest me."

"Really? Shouldn't science be tempered with feeling, intuition? Art in other words," I countered.

"Science is sufficient," he stated.

"You know, the origins of science are actually found in art. Right here in Tuscany," I explained.

"I'm not sure about that," he said with a touch of skepticism.

"Absolutely. Brunelleschi's invention of linear perspective set the stage for the whole scientific project. The discovery of perspective was a crucial development in Western history."

"Perhaps," he replied laconically.

"What about Leonardo da Vinci?" I continued.

"Leonardo?"

"Yeah. He didn't differentiate between art and science. It was all one field of inquiry for him. He discerned a divine hand in all the intricacies of nature."

He chuckled, and then added, "I'm an atheist."

I paused a moment, pondering his comments.

"What is God, anyway?"

"What?" he replied seemingly caught off guard.

"I mean, how do you define God?"

447

"What are you, a Philosopher?"

The tone of his comment seemed slightly insulting, as if being a philosopher wasn't serious. Still giving him the benefit of doubt, I persisted.

"I mean, unless we establish a definite sense of what we mean, a definition, we can't say something exists or doesn't exist. Right?"

He laughed a little bit, and then said, "Ok, a supreme being who controls the universe."

I continued. "But think back to the Enlightenment. Voltaire, even Jefferson and Franklin, they were all deists. They didn't think God was some bearded man standing on a mountain top. Didn't they?"

He was silent looking at the window.

I turned back around and peered through the window alone with my reflection for a while. However, I was unable to let the line of questioning die down, so I turned back around.

"What about Pico?" I asked looking back at him.

"Who?" He looked up from his device.

"Pico della Mirandola. I've been reading some of his work since I've been here in Italy. He was one of the first individuals to talk about human emancipation from the divine order, and with that, the whole notion of individual agency arises. We have the capacity to shape our own lives."

"Agency?" he snorted. "We're just wetware, a sack of bio-chemicals, programmed by our genetic code."

"What about free will?" I insisted.

"Doesn't exist, we're just products of our biological code."

"What about feeling? The subjective?"

"Researchers are able, or soon will be able to map the location of all those experiences with advanced techniques like positron emission tomography."

He seemed slightly irritated now.

"That's just an image. It doesn't explain what's going on. The map isn't the territory."

"Nevertheless, science will pinpoint the location of all those putative experiences, just like they're now mapping the source of prayer and religious faith to specific locations in our brains."

He almost seemed angry as he talked.

"But aren't different states of mind distributed throughout the brain, and even other parts of the body? Intelligence is distributed."

"No matter, it doesn't matter. Science will find the answers."

"...to the ineffable?"

I continued without waiting for his response, "Isn't science just a subset of the unknown, and the unknown, for many religious traditions is the same as God?"

"That's sounds like mysticism," he responded dismissively.

He fell silent, staring at the window. He had barely made eye contact with me during our exchange. There was something cold and distant in his demeanor. It seemed like he didn't take me seriously.

"Doesn't it seem that our conscious awareness sits on an interface between the outer physical world and our inner world of thoughts, feelings and bodily sensations? And it's in that interface or gap that we have the potential for agency, or freedom?"

He snorted.

I continued sketching out my idea.

"We aren't really aware of the bio-chemicals coursing through our bodies, our attention and awareness arises from some inner symbolic world poised between the outer world and the inner: the realm of the imagination."

"We're just bio-chemicals, nothing more, nothing less," he insisted, seeming fatigued.

Were we just biological robots? Automatons? I wondered. I looked over at the other passengers on the bus. For a few moments I felt some doubt. Maybe they were like automatons. Didn't I think that sometime? Maybe agency was merely a potential.

Stubbornly persisting with my line of thought I said, "There seems to be some sort of intelligence that informs all aspects of existence, something beyond the current scientific purview. Complexity researchers even say that the smallest molecular forms seem to orient themselves in an intentional manner and..."

"Are you're implying that inanimate matter is aware? Now, you're sounding like an animist."

It seemed to me that some of the people in the nearby seats were actually following our conversation, as if it was contest, not sure on which side of the conversation they would fall, waiting for a definitive conclusion to be reached.

"I'm just trying to indicate the limits of current scientific thinking. Science doesn't give us a coherent picture of the world, there is something it leaves out. Part of our being will always be beyond the purview of science."

He seemed to shuffle around as if he was ready to switch seats, and then responded under his breath, barely looking at me.

"I've had it with these Left Coast ramblings."

He looked out the window.

When we arrived in Siena, he silently disembarked staring down at his device as he walked down the aisle, ignoring me as if we had never conversed.

Later, I took another bus and traveled deeper into the countryside. The late summer light illuminated the resplendent landscape. Disembarking in a small village, I then set off by foot into the hills.

****

I closed my eyes and listened to the wind approaching from the distance. It swept through the hilltop, catching the upper lofts of the cedar trees, and filled the air all around me. I breathed in a pure dose of fresh air, then released it. I breathed in again, and then released the air.

The place holder of awareness had shifted again. Who was I now? Was I all myself? It seemed as if in each time zone, I had left something behind.

I must have lost consciousness for a few moments, for it seemed to come to me in an instant.

I saw a woman standing beneath an arc of branches and greenery. She was emerging from the leaves, or hiding partially behind them, or maybe she wore some garb woven from leaves, blending in with the background. Her eyes were a brilliant sapphire blue. Our gazes having met, she smiled softly, almost laughing with a slight exhalation. In her hands she held a woven basket filled with fruits or vegetables. As my eyes were drawn to the basket, she tilted it over, and the contents spilled out in an endless profusion of organic forms filling my entire field of vision. Such an abundance seemed impossible for a basket that size.

Made in the USA
Middletown, DE
06 November 2020